Remembering

Hope

By

PARASTOO REZAI

Paperback ISBN 978-1-7350782-0-5
Hardcover ISBN 978-1-7350782-3-6
E-book ISBN 978-1-7350782-2-9

This is a work of fiction. Unless otherwise indicated, all the names, characters, businesses, places, events, and incidents in this book are either the product of the author's imagination or used in a fictitious manner. Any resemblance to actual persons, living or dead, or actual events is purely coincidental.

Cover design by Infinite Signs

Edited by Killingitwrite.com

Formatted by SankalpArt (www.sankalpart.com)

With Gratitude

Writing a book is more difficult and emotionally harrowing than I could have ever imagined. Yet, it has been also one of the most rewarding experiences of my life, which would have not been possible without my primary cheerleader, my beloved Kamyar, who encouraged me during every struggle and celebrated all my successes.

I am also grateful to both of my children. Yasameen, my daughter, spent many hours patiently proofreading and sharing her wisdom and insights with me. Aideen, my son, continuously encouraged me to keep writing whenever he sensed any wavering in my conviction to finish this novel. I feel blessed to be the mother of such loving and compassionate human beings. I can't wait to see their positive contribution to society as they grow.

I appreciate the insightful encouragement from my editor, Gina Casto, and all my friends and family who spent countless hours reading drafts.

To Damione Macedon, a dear friend, I am grateful for his encouragement many years ago to pursue writing as a form of expression.

Dedication

To anyone striving to overcome insurmountable challenges, may hope and the will to persevere be forever paramount.

"You can cut all the flowers but you cannot keep Spring from coming."
~*Pablo Neruda*

Chapter 1

The only signs of life I could see in my beloved husband were the labored rise and fall of his chest and the fogging of the oxygen mask covering his handsome moon-shaped face. Sitting with him, I caught my body mirroring the movements of his chest with each breath.

The second tumor resection had gone without any complications. Still, two weeks after being discharged from the hospital, an unexpected fall while walking to the bathroom landed Omid back in the ICU.

As I sat next to Omid's bed in the hospital room waiting for him to wake up, time seemed to come to a complete standstill. I kissed his face and whispered into his ear, praying my voice would lead him out of the depths of his coma.

I rose from my chair and told his parents I needed to step out. They nodded, quietly reflecting their understanding of how I felt, watching as I stepped away from his bed, and absentmindedly slipped my feet into the barely worn black leather mules Omid had bought me for Mother's Day.

I quickly stepped out of the sterile gray private hospital room. I needed air. One more minute in that somber room, and I was certain I would come apart at the seams.

Every inch of my body, from the inside out, felt numb. The slightest movement, every word I uttered, contributed to my mental exhaustion. To accept my present circumstances was more than I could handle, and the very thought of going on without my soulmate, of living life alone, and managing everything by myself overwhelmed me. To say I was petrified would be an understatement.

A devoted, hardworking, unrelenting life partner, Omid meticulously harnessed our financial planning and work-related matters. Always the soft-spoken one in our relationship, Omid even kept his cool during occasional marital spats.

Whatever I wanted, I only had to hint at it, and he would know what to do. Either by tending to it, purchasing it, or finding a reasonable argument to talk me out of it. His larger-than-life smile and playful large almond-shaped eyes pierced through my soul every time he looked at me, providing constant reassurance that I was the center of his world. He lived his life making sure the kids and I were never disappointed. I lived every day feeling thankful for having made the right decision in becoming his wife.

Our love and the spark that ignited it was not considered commonplace in the Iranian culture. It had taken two trans-Atlantic flights and a leap of faith to initiate what would blossom into a twenty-year love story, rooted in Central London over a cup of tea and crumpets on a cool yet pleasant overcast summer afternoon at Café Durée.

I remember that fortuitous day twenty years ago as if it were yesterday. I had just arrived home from work and stumbled to close the car door with one foot while holding a pile of court documents under one arm and carrying a heavy purse on my shoulder. I heard the phone ring and hurried to open the door before the person hung up. I plopped the pile of papers on a step and searched for the house key inside the dark labyrinth of my purse. I finally got the door unlocked and ran inside, leaving the keys still jangling from the doorknob and forgetting the important papers sitting on the front steps.

Out of breath and sweaty, I managed to lift the receiver after the fifth ring. "Hello?" I asked, barely able to speak between heaving breaths.

"Hi, Bahar. It's me, Shirin. How are you?" my best friend asked in an excited tone.

"Oh, hi! Sorry, it took me so long to answer. I just got home from work. It's so nice to hear from you. How long has it been since we last talked?" I inquired with a slight teasing undertone.

Shirin, my childhood friend since we were five years old, had recently married Peter Stuart, a British man, and now lived in London. She moved there when she was just a teenager, and we tried to see each other at least once a year ever since, either in Iran or London. Although I was glad that she had settled down with the love of her life, I was also jealous we weren't talking as often.

"I'm sorry I haven't been in touch lately," Shirin replied. "Being married is more time consuming than I thought. I swear I've been meaning to call you, but something always comes up, and the time difference complicates things too. Anyways, how are you? How's work? How's life? How is the family?" Shirin threw out one question after another without giving me a chance to respond to any of them.

"Whoa! Take it easy. You're making me dizzy asking everything all at once. I am doing well. Just exhausted. I have a new boss who seems nice. And we just picked up a new client at the firm who wants to invest in a biotech company in Iran. It feels as if I'm at the office all the time. I barely get to see the family anymore. But things should wrap up in the next ten days or so, hopefully. I could use a break! How are things on your end?"

She paused a moment before answering. "You sound exhausted! I'm sorry they have you working such long hours. That sucks. Hey, you should come out and visit when you're finished with the contract. Peter and I would love to see you. You haven't visited since our wedding. Mom and I were just talking about you the other night. She misses you too!"

"I miss your mom too. Has she finally forgiven you for marrying a non-Iranian?" I asked, teasing Shirin.

"Yeah, she finally gave up. Thank God! I don't feel guilty anymore about not marrying one of the awful guys she tried to set me up with. You remember how horrid they were, don't you?!" Shirin added with a loud cackle. "Good riddance! Glad I don't have to deal with that crap anymore."

"Seriously! I'm glad you followed your heart. Our personalities aren't made for settling down with the male chauvinistic, domineering Iranian men our moms want us to marry. I'm still trying to keep my mom from marrying me off to some of them. I've found them all horrendous so far, and I'm getting tired of putting up with it. You're lucky you're done with it," I added with a loud sigh.

As I spoke, I thought about the horrible argument I had with my mom just the night before over a guy she wanted me to give a second chance to. He came from a wealthy well-respected family in the community. And to please my mom, I reluctantly agreed to meet him for dinner. Within the first hour of our first date, I decided I couldn't stand another minute in the company of the self-absorbed, boring, unattractive, mama's boy sitting across the table from me. I stood up and politely left before our meal arrived. I told him I had a stomach bug by gagging a couple of times to make the argument more convincing, then hailed a cab home without saying a proper goodbye. My mom was so infuriated with me that she insisted I call him to apologize for my behavior. I reluctantly obliged.

Shirin paused for a few seconds before resuming the conversation. "Well, besides calling to catch up, I do have an unusual proposition for you. And the timing couldn't be more perfect!"

"Okay. Let's hear it," curious to learn more.

"So, you know how I feel about this matchmaking business, but my mom said something interesting when we were talking about you the other day." Shirin paused before continuing. "Do you remember my cousin Omid who lives in the U.S.?"

"You mean the one in San Diego? Yeah, you mentioned he moved there when he was younger." *Shit, where is this going? Her too?* I thought, rolling my eyes.

"Yeah. That's the one," Shirin hesitantly began. "He's a doctor now and has a private medical practice. Anyway, my mom was talking to him over the phone a few months ago and asked if he was thinking about settling down anytime soon. He said he'd like to but hasn't found anyone that's caught his attention. So, my mom got to thinking it might be a good idea to introduce the two of you. She talked to me about it and asked for my opinion. I thought it was a pretty good idea too." Shirin paused to inhale.

A bit bewildered, I asked, "So, now you're trying to set me up too?"

"I know what you're thinking. But hear me out. Omid isn't like any of the Iranian men we've gone out with. I'm not just saying that because he's my cousin. Honestly, you've got to take my word for it. I'm surprised I didn't think about setting up you two before. He had to work and couldn't fly over for our wedding last year. Otherwise, you would've surely met already," she added without taking a breath.

"Aha," I interjected trying to figure out where she was going with this conversation.

"Anyways, he's a self-made, genuine, down-to-earth, hardworking, good-looking guy. Not to mention that he doesn't look like a werewolf with hair coming out of every orifice like that last Iranian guy you dated. And here's the biggest shocker," she added, "no receding hairline!" she said, bursting from laughter.

"Well, that's a relief!" I responded sarcastically.

"I'm telling you I think you'd like him, Bahar." Shirin paused, probably waiting to see if I would protest, and when I didn't respond, she continued. "Omid is coming to London in a couple of weeks. My mom asked him if he'd be willing to meet you if she made the arrangements. He was reluctant at first, but finally agreed. So, what do you think? The timing couldn't be better. Don't you think?"

It took me a moment to digest the information. Now I understood why she had called. I stood there, absentmindedly twirling the phone cord around my index finger until I felt a strong pang of pain from a lack of circulation. I winced and unwound the cord to relieve the pressure.

The truth was I was intrigued. In the fifteen years Shirin and I had been friends, she never tried to set me up with anyone. I vaguely recalled seeing a picture of Omid a few years back. His soft, inviting smile in the photo had etched a memorable impression in my brain. However, I had not thought about it since, until now.

"Now I see why you were so excited about my coming to see you after my project is over," I teased.

"Oh, come on! You know I'm dying to see you. And this would be fun! What's the harm in meeting him just once? It can't hurt, right?"

Shirin was very familiar with my likes and dislikes when it came to men. How could I refuse her?

As I contemplated my response, I started daydreaming. I had seen various pictures of San Diego with its vast blue ocean waters and high jagged cliffs overlooking the coast. I envisioned myself driving in a red convertible Mustang with the top down, listening to the radio while watching the beautiful sun disappear behind the precipice of the ocean during a glorious sunset. I could almost feel the humidity on my face and smell the salt-filled air.

"Hey, are you still there?" Shirin asked.

"Oh, yeah. Sorry. Just trying to process everything. Yeah, I guess I can give it a shot. Got nothing to lose, right?"

"Absolutely! And it'll be so nice to see you and catch up in person. And I swear there won't be any pressure. If you guys hit it off, great. If not, I swear I promise I won't pester you about it!" she said with excitement in her voice.

"Sounds like a plan. It can't get any worse than the guy I walked out on last week!"

"That's the right attitude! I don't think you'll regret this."

We spoke a bit longer and made the necessary arrangements. Once I hung up, I went to the front door to gather up the court papers that had blown away from the doorstep. I ran upstairs and yanked the key still in the lock and tossed it back into my messy purse. As I changed out of my wrinkled work clothes, I thought about the upcoming break and smiled. I couldn't wait.

I wore an oversized gray raincoat at the airport in Iran to cover my lacey white blouse and faded blue jeans underneath. But once the plane took off from Mehrabad Airport, I removed my baggy coat and the thick headscarf, brushed my hair out to revive its volume, and put on my gold dangling hoop earrings. During the flight, I carefully painted my fingers and toenails with cherry red nail polish and matched it with the lush red lipstick I had snuck in my purse. And last, just before we landed, I slipped on my open-toed high-heeled sandals. I felt free and feminine again, no longer subjected to the compulsory dress code for women by the Iranian government.

When the plane landed at London Heathrow Airport, the weather was cool and overcast. It was something I had come to expect from this city, regardless of the season.

As I looked out through the glass of the automatic sliding doors onto the street, becoming reacquainted with the organized chaos of the city and staring blindly at the row of black cabs queuing up to pick up airport passengers, I inhaled deeply. I had begged Shirin to let me hail a cab from the airport, but she wouldn't hear of it. I walked outside lugging my two oversized gray suitcases, regretting my refusal to accept assistance from the airport valet. I was planning to stay for two weeks but had packed enough clothes to last me for months.

Spotting Shirin's silver Range Rover headlights from a distance, I made my way to the curb, trying to avoid bumping into an elderly couple walking at a snail's pace in front of me.

Shirin skidded to an abrupt stop when she saw me and jumped out. "Bahar!" Shirin yelled as she gave me a warm hug. Turning to open her trunk, she asked, "Both of these suitcases are yours?! Probably filled with souvenirs for me," she teased and winked.

Together in the front seat, I looked over, smiled at my beautiful friend, and squeezed her arm. She appeared more mature than the last time we saw each other. There was a glow to her skin that made her face sparkle. Her eyes appeared serene; her demeanor playful.

"I'm so happy to see you! You should have let me take a cab. Traffic must have been awful," I reprimanded.

"Not a chance! I barely slept last night. I couldn't wait to pick you up! How was your flight?"

"It was great. I slept through most of it," I explained. "You should have seen my mom's face when I told her why I was coming out here," I added with a snicker. "She was speechless. Can you imagine my mom being speechless?" Shirin shook her head.

"That's too funny!" Shirin laughed heartily. "I'm glad you came. You and I have a lot of catching up to do."

"For sure! But first, tell me more about this secret cousin of yours. How come you never talked about him before and, more importantly, why is he still single?"

"I don't know. His name never came up before, I guess. Not sure why he's still single. But I know he works a lot. So, he might not have much time to go out and meet people," Shirin replied. "I know he's super smart. Graduating from Stanford and then going to Harvard Medical School is no small feat. He seems like a mellow guy overall though. I know he loves nature and loves to cook. My aunt and uncle moved out there five years ago from Iran. And my other cousin, Omid's older brother, lives in San Diego, too. The rest you're going to have to ask him yourself," Shirin instructed.

I nodded.

"Omid flew in a couple of nights ago. He's staying at a hotel in Central London. He thought you might enjoy going to afternoon tea, and I suggested you go to Café Durée. He made reservations for 3:00 p.m. tomorrow." Shirin's tone was more serious conveying the details of our date.

"Thanks for setting this all up," I said trying to sound grateful. *This is going to be interesting*, I thought.

Although Shirin and Peter lived only thirty miles away from the airport, it took us over an hour to arrive at their flat. I was grateful for our time catching up in the car, but also relieved to step out to stretch my legs after sitting through London's rush hour traffic.

Peter and Shirin lived in a two-story off-white brick building. Four steps were leading to a double door entrance, where a doorman stood waiting to greet us. "Good evening, Mrs. Stuart. Hello, Madame. Please let me help you with your luggage," he volunteered as soon as we stepped out of the car.

I greeted him with a smile and watched him flinch removing each heavy bag from the trunk and dragging them up the steps. There was a small lobby inside the building that had a musty smell reminding me of canned cat food.

We walked into her small flat, as Shirin placed a five-pound tip in the palm of the doorman's hand. He tipped his hat in gratitude and left. I looked around Shirin's flat as she led me to the guest bedroom. Being raised in a large five-bedroom, five thousand square foot villa in central Tehran, I always found the dollhouse-sized flats in London impossibly small and impractical. *I could never live in such small quarters.*

I changed into more comfortable clothes as Shirin put on some tea, and then we chatted for a while longer before my lids grew too heavy to keep open.

"You look like you're ready to pass out. You must be jet-lagged. Why don't you get some sleep?"

"I'm sorry. I was hoping to see Peter before going to bed, but I don't think I can keep my eyes open."

"Don't worry about it." Shirin nodded and stood. "Get some rest. You can see him tomorrow. He's having dinner with a client and it might be a while 'til he gets back." She handed me a glass of water and kissed me on the cheek.

With the glass in my hand, I wobbled toward the bedroom trying to not spill its contents. I felt inebriated from fatigue and fell asleep the moment my face hit the cool, inviting pillow welcoming me on the Victorian style bed.

Chapter 2

Nausea hit me as I left Omid's hospital room and headed toward the bathroom. I poured some cold water on my face and took some deep breaths. The fear of the unknown and the feeling of losing control made me dizzy. What would my life mean if Omid were no longer a part of it? *Stop thinking like that! He will beat this. You can't give up hope.* I scolded myself.

I pulled my curls back with a clip and stared at my reflection in the bathroom mirror. The last time I felt this jittery was on the morning of my blind date with Omid.

~~~~~~

I woke that morning, uncertain of where I was. It took me a minute to gather my thoughts and remember that I was in London, staying at Shirin's flat. I glanced over at the clock on the nightstand. It was half-past eleven in the morning. I had slept uninterrupted for over fifteen hours! The dark, cool room was the perfect setting for my prolonged rest.

As I emerged from the bedroom and entered the kitchen, I found a note on the table. Shirin and Peter had both left for work. "I hope you had a good night's rest," the note read. "Help yourself to anything in the fridge. Hope you have fun this afternoon. I can't wait to hear all about it! Love, Shirin."

She had left the flat key next to the note, and I saw the tea kettle was on, keeping the water warm. My sweet friend knew how I loved my morning tea.

I poured myself a cup and added some honey. As I sipped, I started thinking about my blind date with Omid. With every sip, the churning sounds in my belly grew louder, and I tasted the acid burning the back of my throat. I tried to distract myself by washing my teacup to avoid dry heaving from the intense anxiety.

I decided to take a hot relaxing shower to calm my nerves. When I came out of the steamy bathroom, I put on some Iranian music and sang freely. Feeling impatient about straightening my hair, I decided to wear it wet and naturally curly. Since it looked overcast outside, I tamed some of the curls with leave-in conditioner and prevented the frizz by working in large dollops of mousse inside my strands. The music and putting on make-up helped with my anxiety. *What's come over me? I have been on other blind dates before. Why am I so nervous about this one?*

I decided to wear my white ankle-high jeans along with a bright turquoise V-neck embroidered blouse. I put on my comfortable silver flats and headed out hoping to arrive early. I figured I would kill some time window shopping and look for souvenirs at Harrods.

The doorman opened the door for me as soon as he saw me coming down the stairs. "Good morning, Madame," he said with a nod.

"Good morning," I replied with a smile. "Thank you," I said, stepping outside and inhaling the foggy London air. I headed toward the street and flagged down the black cab driving towards me.

I got dropped off in front of Harrods shortly before 1:00 p.m. and spent the next couple of hours eyeing the purses and jewelry, and slowly making my way up to women's fashions on the third floor. I bought myself a couple of tops and a pair of gold earrings as a souvenir for my mom. Before long, the gurgling pangs of hunger in my stomach made me head over to the café.

I was thirty minutes early and found a seat with a direct view of the entrance. The anxious waiting re-ignited the acidic bile in the back of my throat and triggered nausea, not unlike what I had experienced earlier in the morning. As the queasiness resurfaced, I was grateful my stomach was empty, all while thinking: *Get a grip. You're being childish. Just breathe.*

I reminded myself that I was too practical to be nervous over a silly date. I didn't believe in fairy tale love stories and thought happy endings were only found in Disney cartoons.

I spotted Omid entering the café just a couple of minutes past three. Our eyes locked immediately, and I began realizing the futility of my earlier arguments about fairy tale love stories. I sheepishly smiled and raised my hand to wave him towards where I was sitting at the table.

His smile grew wider as he approached me. I was unable to unlock my gaze, even as he stopped to greet me in front of the table.

"Hi. You must be Bahar," he said, extending his hand. "I'm Omid." He had an athletic build and appeared to be at least six feet tall. I could make out the contour of his toned physique through the button-down shirt and slightly fitted blue jeans. He had a chiseled broad jawline and high cheekbones. The short, neatly trimmed goatee on his face was smartly groomed outlining his jawbone perfectly. His jet-black, wavy hair lay loosely on the corners of his face, as a stray strand teased the top of his forehead.

I felt a slight burn in my cheeks as I took in the scent of his spicy aromatic cologne. Trying to gather strength in my legs, I struggled to pull back my chair, so I could stand and shake his hand.

I held his grip for a few seconds before responding shyly, "Nice to meet you." When he gently released my hand, he took with it the wave of electricity that had sent pulses up and down my spine.

As he sat down, I continued to examine his face. He had full round lips and perfectly aligned white teeth that glistened when he smiled. I was grateful he was unaware of the spark he had ignited within me.

The butterflies in my belly continued to flutter as I retook my seat and tore my gaze away, looking down at the table. This person was nothing like the picture I had seen of him many years ago. Omid was leagues above any other man I had met. He could have easily been on the cover of GQ Magazine.

"I hope I'm not late," he said, looking at his watch and appearing flustered. "I thought we were meeting at three."

"Oh, no. You're on time. I was here earlier to do some shopping," I responded, glancing nervously at the multiple shopping bags next to my feet. "I guess I got a bit carried away."

"That's nice. Are you familiar with the city?" he asked, looking over at my bags. "I can't remember the last time I went shopping," he said with a slight chuckle.

"I've been to London a few times. It's one of my favorite cities," I replied.

"That's great. How was your flight? Did you just get in yesterday?" he asked with a voice that sounded as nervous as I felt.

"The flight was good. I got in a little after 5:00 p.m. yesterday. Shirin came to get me at the airport."

"She was telling me that you two are childhood friends who know each other from Iran. Is that right?"

"Yes. Shirin and I go way back. We used to be classmates in Iran," I replied.

"That's great."

There was a brief pause as I sat nervously fidgeting in my seat trying to find something to say. Omid also started looking around the café appearing uneasy. He finally started talking. "I haven't been back to Iran for fifteen years. I've lost touch with almost all my friends back home. I wish I'd been better about keeping in touch now that I think of it."

"Yeah. That's too bad," I said before catching myself. Realizing how rude I may have sounded, I followed up with a question trying to have Omid do more of the talking. "So how come you left?"

"I was fifteen and my brother was nineteen when we left. My mom and dad were afraid we would be drafted for the Iran-Iraq war. They paid a smuggler to take my brother and me to Germany. I didn't like it there and wanted to go to the U.S. My brother decided to stay in Germany until he finished his college degree, and I moved to the U.S. to live with a family friend until I graduated high school."

"Interesting. Is your brother still in Germany?"

"No. My family lives with me in San Diego. After I became a citizen, I brought my parents and brother to the U.S. They've been living there for about five years now," he explained.

Once he finished, another awkward silence settled around us. The waiter rescued us by walking to the table to take our order. I quickly picked up the menu and started skimming through the options. I didn't dare tell him I was dying of hunger.

While glancing at the menu he asked, "Have you been here before?"

I shook my head. "No, it's my first time. I can't decide. Everything looks good. Should we order the sweet and savory package for two?" I asked, taking control of the decision.

"Sure, that sounds good. I can go either way," Omid replied.

We ordered finger sandwiches and pastries to pair with the pot of Coconut Cacao, and Vanilla Earl Grey flavored teas. The ambiance of the café was wonderful, and my appetite was starting to return.

"So, how do you like living in Iran?" he asked, lifting an eyebrow and appearing interested.

I shrugged. "It has its pros and cons. I like my job and have gotten used to the way of life there. My younger sister left five years ago when she found a job in Rome. She keeps telling me I should go live with her."

"Have you ever thought of leaving?" Omid asked.

"I thought about it five years ago. But before I could leave, my mom got diagnosed with breast cancer. There was no way I was willing to leave."

"Sorry to hear that. Is she okay now?"

I nodded, grateful for his concern. "Yes. Thankfully they found the tumor in time. She had surgery and chemo. She's been cancer-free since she finished treatment," I said with a sigh of relief.

Teapots were placed on the table. While the steam from the pot of Earl Grey filled my nostrils with sweet scents of coconut, bergamot, and vanilla, Omid poured me a cup.

"I am glad she's better now," Omid said, picking up where we had left off. "You seem close to your family. What do you do in Iran?" he asked as he poured a cup of Coconut Cacao for himself.

I was starting to feel more relaxed and the conversation was beginning to flow more naturally. "I'm a lawyer. I work for an international law firm overseeing mergers and acquisitions of biotech companies."

"That sounds interesting. Is that a thriving industry in Iran?" Omid asked, sounding intrigued.

"Since the end of the war, Iran has been trying to re-connect with the international scientific community. The government has started giving out research grants to motivate discoveries."

The waiter returned to place a three-tier Country Rose designed porcelain tray in front of us with piping hot scones placed neatly on the bottom round receptacle, cucumber, deviled egg, and smoked salmon white toast finger sandwiches on the second tier, and glistening round clear gelatin covered fruit tarts on the top. My mouth started to water.

Omid smiled, watching me drool over the delicacies as he offered me the metal tongs. I laughed apologetically and took it from him. "Which one would you like?" I asked.

"Please go ahead," he replied watching me choose one item from each tier.

"Is it easy to practice law in Iran?" he continued.

"It has its challenges. I mean, the male chauvinism in our culture is hard to tolerate, especially in the legal and medical sectors. A lot of men seem to find it normal to "mansplain" things to women working in these fields. You know, to help a damsel in distress to understand the science or legal ramifications of multi-million-dollar transactions is a responsibility these men take seriously," I said sarcastically. "I should be fair, though. A few of them give me credit for my skillset. For those who don't, I have my way of letting them know their advice is not appreciated. But it gets exhausting."

"I can imagine," Omid said with empathy in his voice. "Can you practice law outside of Iran?"

I shrugged. "I don't think so. I am only licensed to practice law in Iran. If I go anywhere else, I'll probably need to pass an exam to practice there."

He raised an inquisitive eyebrow and continued. "Well, who knows where life will take you."

I tried to hide my smile, but he saw me and grinned.

"I don't think I've ever met an Iranian woman who is a lawyer. It's very refreshing. Your family must be proud of you."

I sighed. "I guess. But I know my mom thinks I intimidate men because of my headstrong personality and line of work. She's worried I'll never find someone to marry," I said visibly frustrated.

"With all due respect, I disagree with her. I find it refreshing to talk to someone with such strong convictions. If a man finds you intimidating, it's because he is insecure about himself. That's his problem, not yours."

I enjoyed speaking to Omid while thinking *Who is this guy? He seems too good to be true.* Not only was Omid extremely handsome, but he was also supportive of strong career-oriented women.

"Thank you for saying that," I said, feeling grateful.

"It's nothing but the truth." He raised his teacup as if making a toast and took a sip of his tea before gazing at me with a slight flutter in his right eyebrow that would be dubbed as Omid's trademark.

In our twenty years together, the flutter above Omid's eyebrow arch became his signature expression conveying love, fear, or joy. I recall the flutter on our wedding night, at my bedside during the birth of our children, and even on the ill-fated day he was diagnosed with glioblastoma, a brain tumor.

~ ~ ~ ~ ~ ~

That day, I arrived at the medical center and sat in the waiting room for a scheduled doctor's appointment. Wearing his medical scrubs, Omid arrived with beads of sweat dripping from the corners of his forehead.

My gaze followed him across the room as he signed in for his appointment before sitting next to me. "Are you alright?" I asked, taking his hand.

"Yes, fine. I had a last-minute patient. I had to run here after seeing him," he explained, taking deep breaths and wiping his forehead with a napkin.

I squeezed his hand. It was unusual for Omid to sweat or be out of breath. Watching him in that state worried me. We were seeing the doctor to discuss Omid's MRI results.

We walked into the doctor's private office as he stood up from behind his desk to greet us. We took a seat and waited for him to share the results. The doctor started speaking in a soft tone. "Unfortunately, I have some bad news. Based on the MRI, it appears that you have glioblastoma. I had a chance to speak with Dr. Stanley, who is the best neurosurgeon on-staff here. He agrees that the tumor is still relatively small and there is a good chance he will be able to remove it, but he won't know for sure until you have your surgery."

Not being familiar with the word glioblastoma, I turned to Omid and asked, "What's glioblastoma? What does he mean you have a tumor?"

Facing me calmly, Omid explained that he might have a brain tumor.

Still in shock, I turned to the doctor and pleaded, "This must be a mistake! Maybe you should repeat the test? Omid only complained of a few anxiety attacks and some dizziness. I think he is just tired and needs some rest."

Omid's beautiful dark almond-shaped eyes widened as he reached out for my hand. His eyebrow fluttered. How could my world shatter to pieces without any warning?

~~~~~~

Two years passed since we were told about the tumor, and despite receiving treatment, Omid was still fighting for his life. Keen on escaping my current surroundings, I sought refuge from the torment by reliving the dream-like era of my happy past. I pressed for the hospital elevator. *What I wouldn't give to turn back the clock and go back to share a cup of tea with Omid again.*

As the elevator door opened, I stepped inside and returned to the memories of our time at the Café Durée.

~~~~~~

Once we finished our afternoon tea, neither of us wanted the date to end.

"Do you feel like taking a stroll?" Omid offered.

"That sounds great. I can barely breathe. I can't believe how much I ate!" I replied, expanding my cheeks into two over-inflated balloons and crossing my eyes. We both laughed.

We decided to take a walk. Taking note of the heavy bags in my hand, Omid offered to carry them for me. He was such a gentleman to make the offer, and I knew I wouldn't last more than one block carrying them by myself.

We strolled through Knightsbridge, taking in the sights and sounds of the city. It was a lovely afternoon. We resumed our conversation from the café, sharing stories from our childhood and present lives, including our families and childhood friends. I found it so easy to talk to Omid and listen to him. He was a natural storyteller. Our conversations took us from the streets into Hyde Park, where we were greeted by luscious landscapes with picturesque rows of colorful tulips, fragrant jasmine shrubs, and luscious full-bloomed roses. The perfectly trimmed lawn in the park offered solace to tired bodies needing to relax. Mesmerized by the beautiful landscape, I stopped in front of fragrant rose bushes. The scent was intoxicating.

"You like roses?" Omid asked.

"I do," I replied. "They remind me of my grandmother. She loved roses."

"Were the two of you close?"

"Yes. I spent a lot of my childhood with her. When I was ten, she helped me plant my first rose garden in our yard. She passed away when I was thirteen," I went on with a sigh. "I keep a vase full of roses in my bedroom to always remember her." I started tearing up and turned to hide my face.

Omid gave me a minute to collect myself. He offered me a tissue. "I'm sorry," I said as I smiled and accepted the tissue. "I don't know why I got so emotional all of a sudden."

"Please don't apologize," he said as he placed his hand on my shoulder.

We continued our stroll through the park, so the conversation wouldn't end. As we walked toward a nearby underground station, I came to a stop just before the entrance.

"Thanks for walking me to the station. I hope I didn't stray you too far from where you're staying," I said.

"We passed my hotel a few blocks back," he said, waving his hand in the opposite direction.

"Oh, I didn't realize," I replied taken back.

"Yes. Well, I'm in no rush to get back. I've been enjoying our time chatting together," he replied, smiling sheepishly.

I blushed. "I think I'll take the tube to go back to Shirin's place."

"Do you mind if I come too? It's getting dark, and I want to make sure you get back okay." I nodded in agreement.

We took the Underground together to the St. John's Wood Station. After exiting the tube, I was still reluctant to say goodbye. But I knew it was late and Shirin would be worried that something had happened to me.

"I think I'll be fine walking a few blocks from here," I said reassuringly.

"Are you sure you don't want me to walk you to the house?" Omid asked sounding concerned.

"Yes, I'm sure," I replied. "Don't worry, I'll be fine."

Omid was smiling softly at me when I turned back to face him. The connection and chemistry between us felt surreal. It felt as though we were communicating through our eyes without uttering a single word. My cheeks started to turn red.

He slowly leaned in and planted a sweet kiss on my cheek in the gentlest manner. I inhaled as he stepped back. He paused for a moment and stared at me with his soft hypnotic eyes.

"Thank you," I whispered, smiling softly.

Omid smiled, turning red. "Thank *you*."

I giggled like a little girl.

"So, do you have any plans tomorrow?" he asked.

"No, I don't think so. Why?"

"I was thinking of taking you somewhere. But I want to keep it a surprise," he said with mischievous looking eyes.

"A surprise?" I smirked and raised an eyebrow.

Omid replied with a nod. "Wear something comfortable and bring a jacket."

"Fabulous!" I said with childish glee in my voice and clapped my hands together for added effect.

He laughed loudly appearing amused. At that moment, I knew I'd become addicted for the rest of my life to the sound of that beautiful laughter.

"Why don't I pick you up around ten tomorrow?"

"Sounds like a plan!" I replied.

I bid him goodbye and started walking towards Shirin's flat. Like a lovesick puppy, I couldn't wipe the smile off my face and kept biting my lips. My entire being had come alive.

Chapter 3

I stayed up most of the night, spending it with Shirin and Peter. We caught up over supper and a few glasses of wine. The more I drank, the more I confessed my positive impressions of Omid.

"I am so happy you guys hit it off!" Shirin said ecstatically.

Peter was amused by the conversation. Being a British bred gentleman, he mostly kept to himself and didn't say more than a few sentences during the entire evening. Although he had a sweet face and a kind smile, I couldn't see what attracted Shirin to settling for someone with his attributes. He seemed so bland compared to the men Shirin dated in the past. Regardless, my head was swirling with Omid, leaving no room for speculating about their love connection.

"Yeah, I know. He surprised me," I replied. "He is such a down-to-earth guy. I had a hard time saying goodbye even after hanging out for so long. We're getting together again tomorrow."

Shirin gasped in delight. She wanted to hear all the details. By the time I finished the step-by-step recount, my head was spinning from the effects of the wine. I excused myself from the table to use the bathroom, but instead of going back to the living room to rejoin the newlyweds, I turned off the bathroom light and wobbled over to my temporary bedroom. Fully clothed and still wearing the makeup from the day, I plopped on the bed and put my head on the inviting pillow where I fell asleep instantaneously.

The next morning Omid tried calling me at approximately 9:45 am. I had forgotten to set an alarm and my cell phone was still in my purse.

I fumbled through my purse to find the phone and answered it on the fifth ring. "Hello?" I asked sleepily rubbing my eyes.

"Good morning. It's Omid. Sorry, did I wake you?" Omid asked.

"Uh, that's okay. What time is it?"

"It's 9:45. I was getting ready to leave the house and wanted to make sure you were ready," he chuckled.

I brought my phone down to eye level to check the time. "Oh, shoot! I am so sorry. I can't believe I overslept," I said, leaving out the detail about the wine contributing to my prolonged hibernation. "Can you give me an extra half hour? I can quickly jump in the shower," I pleaded in an apologetic tone.

"Yes, take your time. I'll come by in about an hour then. I still need to pick up a few things from the store."

"That's perfect! Thanks. I'll see you soon," I said, hanging up in a hurry.

Shit. *This guy must think I'm such an airhead.* I sighed and jumped out of bed and headed straight for the shower. As I washed, I remembered I hadn't even checked to see if anyone was home. I hoped Shirin wasn't upset with me for disappearing on them.

Stepping out of the shower and with my wet hair tied up in a towel, I went to the window to check the weather. Pushing back the curtains, I was momentarily blinded by the bright rays of the sun piercing through the glass window. There wasn't a single cloud lingering in the beautiful London sky.

"Don't fret dear cloud, with the climate trend in London, tomorrow you'll be back to drown out the sun once again. But today, thanks to the sun, I get to wear my dress!" I said pumping my fist in triumph.

I matched my floral dress with a pair of comfortable white sandals and dabbed on a touch of makeup to give me a sun-kissed appearance. I opted for a more seductive look by applying lip gloss instead of lipstick. Using a curling iron, I tried to tame my curls as much as possible without much success. With the clock running, I eventually gave in to defeat and snatched my white purse and cardigan to head out of the room just as the doorbell rang.

I stood behind the front door in a trance-like state for a few seconds before turning the lock counterclockwise and twisting the knob.

Omid stood on the other side to greet me with his beautiful smile. "Good morning. I hope I gave you enough time. You look very nice and summery!" Omid said as he handed me a bouquet of yellow roses and placed a soft kiss on my cheek.

"Thank you. These are beautiful. You shouldn't have," I replied as I inhaled. After I placed the flowers in a vase, Omid extended his arm for me to hold as we left the flat.

"Good day, Sir. Madame," the doorman greeted us as he opened the door for us to exit the building.

"Thank you, Harry," Omid replied.

Puzzled, as we stepped to the curb, I asked, "How do you know his name?"

"Oh, we chatted earlier. I got here a little early, and Harry and I got a chance to talk a bit. He has worked here for the past fifteen years and was in the Royal Navy before retiring and getting this job."

I nodded. "Oh, I guess that explains why he is so courteous and proper. He probably learned it from years of training in the Navy," I said pensively.

He shrugged. "I guess. But I think most British people are very proper. It was nice chatting with him though. I like getting to know people and learning about their stories."

"Oh, yeah? Why is that?" I asked.

"I think it started a few years ago after I read *The Art of Happiness* by the Dalai Lama and Dr. Howard Cutler. Have you heard of it?"

"No," I replied.

We continued to chat as we walked towards the car. "Dr. Cutler interviewed the Dalai Lama to understand what makes humans truly happy. He sums it up by saying that human connection and empathy is all we need. I wanted to connect with the book's messages, so I challenged myself to meet one new person each day and learn as much as I can about him or her," he replied.

"Has your new approach made you a happier person?"

He paused for a moment before responding. "Honestly, it's hard to say. I *do* feel more connected to people since I started doing it. And listening to personal stories creates a special kind of bond. I guess to answer your question, I do feel happier," he said nodding his head appearing to reach that conclusion while speaking.

Omid guided me to a glistening silver convertible and opened my door. He turned on the ignition and put the car in reverse. A beautiful foreign song started playing on his CD player. Curious to learn the artist's name, I picked up the CD cover. It was *Andalusian Nights* by Johannes Linstead. The Spanish flamenco-style guitar fusion of Afro-Cuban, Middle Eastern, and Latin American melodies reminded me of our family vacation in Spain a few years ago. The melody was soothing and hypnotic. I smiled and relaxed further into my seat.

"Does this song remind you of someone or something?" Omid wondered.

"Yes. It reminds me of a trip my family and I took to Spain a few years ago. I love Spanish music. Are you a fan?"

"Absolutely! I love this style of music. Last time I was there I bought a bunch of CDs at a local store and listen to them everywhere I go. Where did you guys visit in Spain?"

"We were in the Southern region: Granada, Sevilla, Cordoba mostly. I loved it. Can't wait to go back soon," I replied wistfully.

Omid nodded in agreement. "It's truly a remarkable country. I've been to Spain twice. Once with my family when I was ten and the second time after graduating from college. The Moorish style of architecture is incredible. The people are so warm and friendly. They remind me of Iranians, so hospitable and inviting. Have you heard of a singer named Jose Merce?" he asked.

I shook my head to indicate I had not.

"A music store owner introduced me to Merce's music the last time I was in Spain. Let me play it and you tell me what you think," he said, changing out the CDs in the CD player.

I listened intently to the raw and raspy voice of the singer for a few minutes. It was a melancholic song.

"That's beautiful. I have to buy this CD before I go back to Iran."

"I have a better idea. Why don't you take this back with you?" he offered with a deep smile.

"Are you sure?"

"Yes. It's yours," he replied with a sweet-sounding voice. A warm sensation started to settle in the pit of my stomach as I observed his side profile while he drove.

"Thank you," I said timidly and continued to enjoy the music.

Chapter 4

As the elevator door opened, I stepped out, still unsure of where to go, so I scanned the glass-encased hospital directory. I wanted to find a place away from the hospital room, a place where I could be alone to collect my thoughts. Three possibilities caught my attention: the cafeteria to grab a sandwich, the chapel to pray, or the Meditation Garden. Eating was not an option with my anxiety-induced nausea. Praying for Omid's health seemed senseless because I prayed constantly, and God was not heeding my prayers. Meditating seemed to be a comforting reprieve to find solace.

Sitting on the round cushion of the ornate metal chair, I let my tears stream as freely and steadily as the flowing water fountain in the middle of the garden. Everything was happening so quickly. How could such a sweet fairy tale life turn so sour? We still had so much life to live. How did we get to this point? Did I contribute to this?

All these questions running through my mind were making me insane. The thought of breaking the news to the children made me agitated. The boys had never endured any economic, emotional, or other real hardships in their lives. We had always surrounded them with love and laughter as a family. Always celebrating holidays from all cultures, making a big fuss on birthdays, and never forgetting to recognize anniversaries. So much would be meaningless if Omid didn't recover. I couldn't bear the thought of his absence. I needed him to give me strength. But that would be impossible now.

I decided I would tell the kids about Omid's illness when we returned home. I wished Omid could comfort me by putting his hand on my shoulder like he always did for reassurance. My life was crumbling before my eyes, and the loneliness in my future becoming a reality.

I sat in the garden for nearly an hour, deep in thought, until a text drew me out of my trance.

I ignored the text and wiped the tears with the back of my hands, dabbing each cheek dry with my shirt sleeves. I was surrounded by a beautiful garden filled with roses. Forgetting for a second that I was still in the hospital, I inhaled the full-petaled sweet perfume of the fragrant roses. The scent took me back to memories of our courtship.

I reeled back to the picnic in Queen Mary's Rose Garden, in London, picking back up from the drive in Omid's car while listening to Spanish music.

~ ~ ~ ~ ~ ~

I still knew nothing about the surprise Omid had planned for me when he parked the car in front of Regents Park. I stepped out of the car as he opened the trunk. Within a few seconds, he held a large wooden picnic basket in one hand and a piece of white fabric in the other.

"Shall we?" gesturing towards the gated entrance.

We strolled into the park with the noontime sun as a perfect umbrella to the luscious green grass below our feet. We found a small area where Omid placed a white tablecloth and opened the picnic basket.

"Wow, this place is gorgeous," I whispered and then exclaimed, "Look at all those roses!"

Omid nodded with his eyes closing as he smiled. "You seemed to like nature during our walk yesterday. I figured you might like a picnic in this park. It has the most beautiful collection of roses in all of London."

I was speechless.

I watched as he opened his basket of treasures: a pair of porcelain teacups, saucers, and a teapot followed by the delicacies of finger sandwiches, freshly baked scones, strawberry marmalade, and biscuits.

"How many things did you manage to pack in that basket? You remind me of a male Mary Poppins," I teased.

He snickered sounding amused while taking out the thermos from the basket and pouring freshly brewed tea. He offered me tiny packets of sugar to sweeten my tea. All was perfect.

"I brewed regular Earl Grey tea instead of the vanilla one we had yesterday," Omid explained. "I like the color and flavor of this tea more. What about you?"

I took a sip trying to avoid burning my mouth and nodded. "I had never paid attention to the different types of Earl Grey. But I agree. This tastes better." I spread a rich, creamy layer of butter on my scone and sat back admiring the scenery. There were at least two dozen rose bushes in full bloom surrounding us with such strong perfumes, that I was fooled into tasting the flavor of the roses on my tongue. Looking around, I also spotted a weeping willow tree draped over a small white bridge near a glistening small lake in the park.

"These sandwiches are delicious. Did you make them yourself?" I asked between bites.

"Yes. This morning," grinning at my stunned expression.

"Are you serious? Even the scones?" I asked.

"Even the scones," he replied, looking amused.

"I'm glad it takes so little to impress you," he said looking flushed from embarrassment.

Our eyes locked for a few seconds before I stared down at my lap feeling the heat rise to my face. We grew silent for a few minutes.

Omid leaned in a little closer before he spoke. "You know I couldn't stop thinking of our date when I got back to the hotel last night. I enjoy spending time with you. I'm glad I let Aunt Maryam talk me into going on the blind date with you."

I nodded. "Yeah, I feel the same. To tell you the truth, I didn't know what to expect. But it's worked out great so far." As my arms and fingers spread over the blanket of food, I stared and said, "Thank you."

~~~~~~

My phone rang, jolting me back to the present. The roses in the Meditation Garden suddenly lost their color, and my world turned gray again. I wished I could go back to Regents Park and that spectacular day-the moment when my world started revolving around the man who had swept me off my feet with simple gestures and sweet sentiments. Glancing at the screen of my phone, I saw it was my mother-in-law trying to reach me again. Ten minutes had passed since her first text.

I grew worried. My heart started to race, and a surge of anxiety washed over me, causing my voice to quiver as I answered. "Hello?"

"Hi, Sweetie. How are you? Is everything okay?" Taraneh asked.

"Yes, I'm fine. I just came to get some air. Is everything okay with Omid?"

"He is still not awake," she replied.

She paused for a second. "You've been gone for a while. I got worried. Will you be back soon?" she asked sounding apologetic.

I knew she wanted to go home. Omid's father, Mansoor, had eye surgery last week and she was anxious to take him home and have him rest.

I sighed. Everyone had their hardships to deal with. "Yes, I'll be right back. I'm sorry. I lost track of time," I stammered.

I quickly stood up to leave, feeling guilty about having left them for so long. His parents were old and frail. It wasn't fair for me to leave them alone. Of course, they were worried about Omid's condition.

I glanced back at the mosaic water fountain before exiting the Meditation Garden. The design of the fountain reminded me of the one Omid and I discovered within a Moorish castle, during our honeymoon in Spain. Alhambra's large mosaic fountain featured four paths symbolizing the four rivers depicted in the Garden of Eden. Water, honey, milk, and wine symbolically converged into one body of liquid and flowed through the fountain's peak in one synchronous stream.

How I longed to go back to Granada and be newlyweds again. Even after twenty years, Omid and I were still in love. An invincible bond never wavering and remaining strong during the best and even toughest periods of our lives–a bond that risked being broken only by Omid's horrific diagnosis.

~~~~~~

The first signs of the cancer became evident a few weeks before Omid was diagnosed with glioblastoma. I remembered us quarreling in front of the kids driving back home after hiking in Torrey Pines Reserve Park. It was a beautiful sunny day, and we had ended the hike with a picnic along the beach.

"I wish we could do this every weekend. It sucks they make you take calls at the hospital every other weekend. I still don't see why you have to go in so often, while Jake goes to the hospital one weekend a month," I complained.

As soon as I uttered the words, Omid glared at me with an intensity in his eyes that I had never seen.

"Why is it that you can never be satisfied with anything I do? I work my ass off every single day trying to give you a comfortable life. To earn enough money so you can buy your designer clothes and go on expensive vacations. Instead of being grateful, you still find reasons to bitch about things! Unbelievable!" he yelled.

I sat stunned, not sure how to respond at first. My anger slowly started to creep in, and I started pushing back. "What the heck is wrong with you? Why are you being so rude? You have no right to speak to me like this! All I said was I wish we could spend more time together on the weekends. Get a hold of yourself and stop yelling."

He stopped the car abruptly and turned off the engine. The kids didn't make a peep but appeared worried watching us fight in front of them.

"I'm being aggressive?" Omid shouted. "You've got to be kidding me! I wish you could hear yourself talk sometimes. Nothing I do is good enough for you. And I'm getting damn tired of hearing you complain about it!" He opened the door stepping out of the car and slamming it shut behind him.

I sat in the car for a few minutes while he continued to yell with his arms flailing in different directions. I let him finish his rant and stayed quiet. Tears welled up in my eyes as I heard him continue to ramble.

"Why is Baba so mad?" my younger son, Koosha, asked with a quiver in his voice.

I reached out to clasp his small hand in the backseat. "It's alright, honey. He's just a little upset. He'll feel better in a minute. Don't be scared," I said reassuringly.

Kayvon remained quiet. I could see his nostrils flaring in anger as he glared at his father and continuously banged his fist into his upper thigh.

After a while, Omid calmed down and slid back into the car. No one spoke for the remainder of the drive home.

When we arrived home, the kids went to watch TV. I ran upstairs and locked myself in the bedroom. I cried for half an hour thinking about what had just transpired. For the first time in our marriage,

Omid expressed such anger toward me. I couldn't understand his verbal attacks. We had never raised our voices or cursed at each other during our marriage. Even during our disagreements, we had always been respectful of each other.

The outburst didn't make sense. After wiping my tears, I decided not to speak about it until Omid was calmer and I was able to figure out what was truly bothering him. Unfortunately, the opportunity never presented itself. Two weeks after the incident, Omid was diagnosed with glioblastoma. The doctor explained the tumor was likely the culprit for the outburst and responsible for some of his recent anxiety attacks.

~ ~ ~ ~ ~ ~

Before I walked back into Omid's hospital room, I rolled up a piece of tissue, licked it with the tip of my tongue, and tried to remove the black smudges of makeup, forming a horrid black halo under my eyes. I had to keep up the pretense.

Nobody needed to know the pain and burden I shouldered. Just as Omid never let me feel his fatigue, toiling away long hours and building a better life for our family. I had to keep my composure and not let fear or exhaustion from sleepless nights, endless doctor visits, surgeries, and treatments break my resolve to fight for my family. Nobody needed to know that inside I felt as if I were shattering into a million little pieces.

I quietly walked back into the hospital room to find Omid awake but unresponsive. He looked tired and defeated, with swollen cheeks and a moonlike face from the steroids he was taking. My once vibrant, energetic, handsome Omid looked dazed and confused.

I greeted his parents and saw Omid's face turn slowly in my direction. I detected a small twitch in his eyebrow as he stared at me. That familiar twitch that hinted he was worried about me. I cracked a half-smile with all the energy I could muster. Despite his pain and fear, I knew that Omid was still thinking of my welfare.

How could I ever compete with this man? I moved towards Omid, wanting to wrap my arms around him and let him know how much I adored him-to kiss him passionately, just like I had so many times over the years. He always brought me so much relief. To be in his arms for just a few seconds was all I needed. Impossible. He was attached to multiple monitors and had wires connected to devices on his chest, fingers, and nose. Instead of hugging him, I gave him a soft, lingering kiss on the forehead and sat on a chair adjacent to his bed. I took his free hand and stroked it before kissing it gently.

Even if he were unresponsive, seeing him awake was still a good sign. I held onto that positive thought for all it was worth.

Chapter 5

*T*he oncologist had told us it was normal for Omid's long-term memory to fade with this type of cancer, and depending on how far the cancer had metastasized, his motor skills could also diminish.

His hand lay limp in mine, silent, with loving brown eyes reaching into my heart. Deep down I felt the intensity of his love with images resonating from our life together.

~ ~ ~ ~ ~ ~

We walked past the tall steel gates of Buckingham Palace. "I can't believe how fast these past ten days have flown by. I'm not looking forward to going home," Omid said.

I twisted my lips into a frown. "I know. I was just thinking the same thing. I wish we had more time to spend together," I sighed.

He nodded with a smirk. "Yes, you seem to enjoy your tea, alright."

We stopped walking. Taking my hands gently into his, we moved closer with our eyes transfixed. "Bahar, you have been the best part of this entire trip."

We kissed for what seemed to be an eternity. With my eyes closed, I heard Omid's blissful words, "Has anyone told you how beautiful you are?"

My ears grew hot and my heart started racing.

I opened my eyes and smiled shyly. He lifted my hand and kissed it before placing it against his cheek. With my other hand, I started tracing the outline of his lips with my fingers.

As if being sucked in by a magnetic force, I leaned in again for a longer more passionate kiss. Every inch of my body started yearning for Omid. Trying to avoid losing control, I forced myself to unlock lips and catch my breath.

"I'm sorry if this is too much," Omid said apologetically.

"Don't apologize. Everything's perfect," staring and enjoying the reflection of my eyes in his.

"I agree," he whispered as he embraced me. "I've never connected with anyone like this. What are you doing to me, Miss Bahar? I shouldn't let you go back to Iran."

I giggled. "Well, maybe you'll just have to kidnap me and take me back to San Diego with you."

As he released me from his embrace, he drew my face closer with his hands and spoke in a gentle but serious voice. "I'm ready to kidnap you and never have you leave my sight. I know it hasn't been that long, but I can't imagine my life without you. You've put some sort of a spell on me," he confessed turning slightly red.

"I know exactly how you feel. I was worried I was the only one that felt that way. I've never felt more certain about wanting to be with someone either. Have we gone crazy?" I asked with a slight chortle. "People date for years before deciding they want to spend the rest of their lives together. How did we get to this point so quickly?"

"I don't know. All I know is I'm done searching. I've found who I want to be with. Bahar, I want to make you my wife. Would you consider being my wife?" Omid asked while getting down on one knee.

With my eyes welling with tears and hands trembling, I asked,

"Are you serious?"

"I'm dead serious. I want to spend the rest of my life with you, and I want that more than anything in the world," his eyes sparkling with happiness.

Standing outside of Buckingham Palace with the man who appeared to be my prince in shining armor seemed to be a fairy tale come true.

I tried to control my trembling voice while speaking. "Yes, Omid. I would be honored to be your wife!"

Before he could completely stand up, I leaped into his extended arms. Unable to steady himself, we toppled to the ground, one on top of the other, paying no attention to the onlooking passersby. Omid sprinkled my face with soft kisses. A magical moment.

We spent the next couple of days talking about logistics. "Since your whole family and all your friends live in Iran, don't you think it makes sense to have the wedding there?" Omid asked as we enjoyed an ice cream cone walking around Piccadilly Circus.

"Makes sense. But what about *your* friends and family? Don't you want to invite them to the wedding?" I asked.

"Almost all of my relatives still live in Iran. The only other family that needs to fly in for the wedding are my parents, my brother, Aunt Maryam, and Shirin, so that shouldn't be too hard. And we can have a small party when we are in San Diego so my friends and colleagues can meet my new wife." Omid grinned appearing to be daydreaming.

"I like the sound of 'wife'" as I brushed a gentle kiss on his soft lips with my chocolate ice-cream flavored mouth. "I have to warn you that my parents are going to want a big wedding. Knowing them, they will want to invite the whole city and make a big fuss over the details," I said frowning. "Are you sure you don't want to elope?" I pleaded.

"Oh, come on. It won't be that bad. It'll be fun to celebrate our special night surrounded by our loved ones. Let your parents plan a big shindig. We know they want to do it. They've probably been dreaming of the day ever since you were born. I'm sure they were not thinking that you'd marry and leave Iran."

"Yeah," I hesitantly agreed. "You're right. I'm sure they'll be devastated after I leave."

Sensing my mood shift thinking about leaving my parents, Omid changed the topic to our plans for the evening. It was our last night in London and Aunt Maryam had invited the four of us to dinner.

"Are you nervous about telling your family the news?" I asked Omid.

"I'm more excited than nervous. I kept my promise to you and waited for all of us to be together to share the news tonight. I can't wait to see the look of surprise on Shirin's face," he said with a devilish grin.

"I know! I was thinking the same thing," I laughingly admitted. "Every night, when she and I hang out, Shirin asks me endless questions, but I shrug and don't share too many details," I smiled and added, "It's going to be a fun night."

Omid shook his head while snickering. "She's going to be so pissed at us for keeping this from her."

Omid kissed my lips and held me tightly before stepping out of the cab, leaving me mesmerized for the duration of the car ride to Shirin's flat.

Chapter 6

*A*s we approached Aunt Maryam's house, I spotted Omid's car in the driveway. Earlier in the afternoon he called to tell me he needed to run an errand and would meet us at his aunt's house.

Peter parked next to Omid's car, and the three of us stepped out of the car and stretched our legs. I let Shirin and Peter lead the way as I inhaled the fresh scent of flowers in Maryam's front yard.

As we reached the door, I caught a glimpse through the front window of Omid and his aunt sitting on the living room couch. Shirin rang the doorbell and Aunt Maryam greeted us with a warm smile. We proceeded with our customary kiss on each cheek as I extended my arm with a bouquet of freshly cut wildflowers.

"Oh, these are lovely! Thank you, sweetheart," Aunt Maryam said, taking the bouquet and motioning for us to enter. "It's so lovely to see you! How have you been?"

The three of us stepped inside the circular rotunda as I spotted Omid standing behind Aunt Maryam waiting to greet us.

"Hi, Omid!" Shirin exclaimed, hugging him. "Bahar said you were coming later."

Omid stretched out his hand to greet Peter. "Yes, well I managed to find what I needed and got here earlier than I expected. Gave me a chance to catch up with Aunt Maryam," he replied.

Omid gave me a peck on the cheek and gently squeezed my hands.

Aunt Maryam led us to the living room for some drinks.

"So how have you been old chap?" Peter asked Omid. "We haven't seen much of you since you came to London. I guess we have Bahar to thank for keeping you from us during your visit. Well, come to think of it, we haven't seen much of Bahar either," Peter chortled as if amused by his snide remark.

My face turned crimson red. Shirin nudged Peter with her elbow. "Will you leave them alone? You should be grateful Omid and Bahar went sightseeing by themselves. It's not *their* fault we've been busy working."

Peter grew silent and shook his head sullenly. "You're right. It's our fault. I misspoke. My apologies."

As Maryam's help entered to announce dinner, Maryam declared, "Peter, I think you've been rescued just in the nick of time! Shall we go to the dining room?"

Peter stood up and offered his arm to Aunt Maryam. She wrapped her fingers around his elbow. "Something smells divine!" Peter exclaimed escorting her and leading us into the dining room.

Maryam was a widow of many years who was living alone since Shirin got married and moved out a year ago. Maryam and her husband had been married for fifteen years when they immigrated to England. The couple decided to migrate to escape the harsh restrictions the Islamic Republic of Iran had placed on women. Shirin's parents were professors at Tehran University at the time and didn't want her to grow up in a country where she was not given the same opportunities as those of men. With the new regime, women were mandated to wear headcovers and dress conservatively. The new laws also discriminated against females attending universities, having equal rights, and gaining employment with equitable pay.

Shirin was fourteen years old when she was uprooted from Iran and taken to England. She had a difficult time acclimating to her new environment at first. A year after migrating, Shirin's father passed away from a massive heart attack in his sleep.

With the unexpected loss of her husband, Maryam gave up her teaching aspirations and started a food catering business from home. She was able to be closer to her daughter, especially during the mercurial teenage years, while earning a decent income.

As with most new businesses, Maryam struggled at first, but eventually prevailed. Five years later, she was approached by a national food distributor to mass-produce her popular dishes and sell them to the public through a supermarket chain.

I had spent many days and nights at Shirin's house when her family still lived in Iran and subsequently during my visits to London. Shirin and I had enjoyed hanging out in the kitchen, while her mom prepared meals for us. Aunt Maryam always talked to us about the importance of being strong and independent women. She wanted us to grow up and serve as role models to younger generations.

Now in her sixties and a respected retired entrepreneur, Maryam is a role model for and a consultant to women who want to succeed in business. Maryam is soft-spoken and petite but draws respect every time she walks into a room. Being blessed with a beautiful complexion, she rarely wore any makeup aside from a subtle pink blush and clear lip gloss. When in public, strangers often confused Maryam as Shirin's sister, rather than her mother. Although Shirin adores her mom, she had once complained to me how much that confusion bothered her.

We gathered at the meticulously decorated dinner table. The relaxing ambiance of lighted candles created not only glistening silverware and wine glasses, but also a sparkle in our eyes that espoused an affirmation of a transcending moment in our lives.

We were gifted with Maryam's famous oval-shaped meat and potato cutlets decorated with fresh savory Iranian herbs and radishes. She remembered my favorite, Kashke Bademjan, an eggplant appetizer with traditional Kashk (dried sour yogurt topped with browned crispy fried onions), and Kookoo Sabzi, a vegetarian quiche. The colorful bowl of Salad Shirazi was filled with small cubed onions, tomatoes, Persian cucumbers, and freshly chopped mint, seasoned with fresh lemon juice. Ghormeh Sabzi prepared with herbs, stew meat, and kidney beans. Aromatic Basmati rice and crispy golden Tahdig. Maryam's final entrée: juicy chicken and beef shish kabobs skewered and interlaced with grilled onions, bell peppers, and tomatoes. A feast fit for royalty!

"Everything looks amazing!" Omid complimented Maryam while smacking his lips. "You must be exhausted from cooking all day. Thank you, Auntie."

Maryam beamed with pride. "My pleasure, Omid joon. I'm so happy we're together." Stroking Omid's arm and nodding at me, she lifted her hand to gesture for us to begin. "Please. Enjoy."

We savored every morsel as we talked and cajoled. After insisting we finish two servings of every dish and realizing we were on the verge of exploding, Maryam finally stopped heaping food on our plates. Having drunk two glasses of wine and devoured so much food, I was feeling drowsy.

"Maryam joon, this dinner was amazing. I can't remember the last time I ate so much. Thank you!" I said trying to catch my breath.

Maryam's smile widened. "I am glad you enjoyed it. We miss you, Bahar."

"I know," I replied, smiling over at her. "I'm glad it all worked out and I was able to fly out here."

Shirin nodded in agreement. "Well, *hopefully,* if all goes well, you will leave Iran for good," she smiled slyly, staring at Omid. I laughed, understanding what she was insinuating.

"I didn't know she was planning to leave Iran. How come you never tell me anything, Shirin?" Peter implored.

Shirin rolled her eyes. "Honestly Peter, sometimes I don't know what to do with you. She hasn't decided to leave. I'm just trying to see if Bahar and Omid plan to see each other after this trip."

Peter's eyes grew larger and more enthused. "Oh. I see, darling. Sorry, I wasn't following your meaning a minute ago," he said placing his napkin on the table and staring at Omid and me, as if waiting for an announcement. With my lips pursed, I avoided eye contact and fidgeted nervously in my seat.

Maryam finally spoke up. "Shall we go to the living room for dessert?"

"Mom, I'm about to explode! I can't eat another bite," Shirin protested.

Maryam chuckled. "I'm sure after you see what Omid brought for dessert, you'll find room."

I glanced at Omid feeling confused. "Is that the errand you had to run earlier?" I asked. Omid shrugged and smiled.

As we all rose to move to the formal sitting area, Maryam's help stepped out of the kitchen to clear the table. "Thank you, Angela. We'll have our tea and dessert in the living room."

"Yes, Madame," Angela responded with a tilt of her head as she returned to the kitchen.

A few minutes later, Angela offered us hot tea by going around the room with a tray in her hand. She then returned with a serving dish filled with puff pastries and placed it in front of me without offering it to anyone else. I was surprised by her action but remained silent.

Seeing my surprise, Omid stood up and picked up the dish. He brought it in front of me and said, "I know how much you like these. Why don't you take *this* one?"

Before I could respond, he smiled and placed the largest puff pastry on the plate in front of me. I was taken aback by the gesture and looked at him inquisitively trying to figure out why he appeared so amused. I waited until everyone got their dessert before taking a giant bite into mine.

"These look yummy. Did you get these from the Iranian pastry store nearby?" Peter asked, biting into the custard-filled pastry.

Before Omid could answer, I felt a tough metal object on my tongue and quickly spit it out into a napkin. Omid leaned closer observing my reaction.

"What the heck? What is *this*?!" I said in a bewildered voice while wiping the object with my napkin.

As I wiped the custard off, it quickly dawned on me that the object was a beautiful diamond cut engagement ring.

"Oh my gosh! You're unbelievable. How did you manage to do this? This is so amazing!" I gushed with tears stinging my eyes.

Omid pushed the table further out and kneeled in front of me, taking my hand. Shirin squealed with joy.

Omid started speaking softly, "I have spent every moment since we met dreaming of our lives together. Please accept this ring as a symbol of my committed devotion and make my dreams come true. Bahar, will you accept this ring and make me the happiest man alive?" Omid asked with a quivering voice.

I gasped as tears of joy started streaming down my cheeks. Nodding continuously, I brought my hand forward. Omid gently slipped the ring on my finger and leaned down to kiss my hand before sitting next to me on the couch. We kissed and started giggling as we listened to Shirin screaming and stomping her feet from excitement.

"Oh my God! I can't believe you guys are getting married. Peter, isn't this wonderful?" She asked, squeezing Peter's arm.

Peter nodded in agreement. "Yes, it is. It's fantastic news. Congratulations!"

Shirin ran over to give us a congratulatory hug. "I'm so happy for you two! Honestly, I'm in shock. I had no idea things were happening so quickly! How come you didn't say anything to me?" Shirin pouted.

I tried to reassure her. "I swear I wanted to tell you all of the details. But Omid and I were trying to get to know each other and sort out our feelings before announcing it to anyone. Everything happened so quickly. And you are the first to know about this. Our parents don't even know yet!" I paused to take a breath to assess her reaction.

Before Shirin could reply, Omid chimed in. "Bahar wanted to tell you, but I convinced her to wait until tonight to share the news."

Shirin stopped pouting and gave me a mischievous glance. "Oh my God. Your mom is going to *freak* out when she finds out you're engaged! She won't believe it when you tell her."

I laughed. "Yes, I'm sure she'll be shocked. But in a good way. Omid is the perfect package in every way," I replied pressing Omid's hand and smiling warmly at him.

"Well, I am thrilled for both of you!" Aunt Maryam finally interjected. "I couldn't think of a better match. I love you both dearly. I'm sure there will be a reason for celebration when the rest of the family hears the good news. When do you plan on telling your parents?" she wondered.

"We think it's best to tell them in person. It doesn't make sense to tell them on the phone since we're flying back so soon," Omid replied.

Maryam nodded in agreement. "Well, your secret is safe with us. You won't hear a peep from us until you share the big news with them," she said reassuringly. "Now, I think this news calls for a toast!"

We stayed and celebrated for a little while longer before leaving. Omid offered to drive me back to Shirin's place, so we could spend some time alone. I felt lighter, knowing I no longer had to keep the news a secret from my best friend. It had been a divine evening and we left his aunt's home feeling elated from sharing the good news with them. Everything was falling into place and I couldn't wait to make it official within a few months.

The next day we drove to the airport together and took a shuttle to the terminal. All morning, I was dreading our final farewell kiss at the airport. My flight to Tehran was departing a couple of hours earlier than his, and Omid had offered to accompany me to my gate before heading to the other terminal to catch his flight.

"Don't be sad," he whispered, tucking a loose lock of hair behind my ear. "It's only a few weeks of separation. I have already started looking for tickets to fly to Iran. I'll talk to my family when I get back and we'll buy the tickets right away. We'll use the time apart to make all the wedding arrangements. Remember what we talked about. I know you don't want a big wedding, but let your parents have some fun with the planning so they can feel they're a part of this too."

I nodded in agreement. He was right. Even though I didn't want a big wedding, I knew resisting my parents wouldn't be an option. I just couldn't help feeling like a hypocrite to my friends in Iran. Despite my best efforts to avoid the Iranian stereotypes, I joined the ranks of other Iranian women who had jumped at the opportunity to get hitched and move abroad–a typical fairy tale told by many Iranian women. Parents secretly wishing their daughter would find a nice suitable Iranian man offering her a better life and send her abroad after marriage. I had never planned for it to happen this way. But I struggled to find a way to explain how my circumstance was different from others.

The flight back home was uneventful, even the turbulence was tolerable. I spent most of the flight excited and anxious about the days ahead. Despite the challenges at work, I worried about starting a new career in San Diego and leaving my family and friends.

Ever since I was little, my parents always encouraged my sister and me to pursue advanced degrees. In Iranian culture, parents commonly encourage their children to pursue professions in the legal, medical, or technical fields. I had always had a knack for debating, so my parents weren't surprised when I pursued a legal path. Unfortunately, a few months after graduating from law school, my mom was diagnosed with breast cancer. I postponed looking for a job until her cancer was in remission and then accepted a position at a law firm specializing in corporate law.

I found my career choice and my employment at the firm enlightening, challenging, and thought-provoking. During my years as legal counsel, I learned about international mergers and acquisitions and met with clients expressing an interest in investing or acquiring businesses in Iran.

Despite being twenty-five years old, I still lived at home—not an anomaly in Iran. Unmarried children never moved out unless they were moving abroad or getting married. I lived a comfortable life and did not fret over any expenses while living with my parents.

Although I spent some of my free time with friends and work colleagues, I loved being in the company of my parents. We spent many hours in the evenings going on strolls and talking about work, gossip, politics, and current events. I cherished our time together and was keenly aware of my parents' mortality and fragility with age.

I closed my eyes to calm my thoughts and managed to fall asleep briefly in the uncomfortable airplane seat. I was startled awake by the overhead flight crew announcement informing us to fasten our seat belts to prepare for landing.

Peering through the window, I saw the runway and frantically searched in my purse for a tissue to remove my lipstick. I patted down my curly bed of hair and wrapped the gray roosari around my head to hide everything. The knot from the scarf against my throat always irritated my skin and made me feel claustrophobic.

It had only been six hours, but I already missed Omid. Six hours down and seven weeks, six days, and eighteen hours to go before I would see him again. It felt like an eternity, but I needed to use the time wisely to carefully uproot myself in Iran and prepare for a new adventure abroad with my soon-to-be husband by my side-a new and glorious chapter in my life.

Chapter 7

My dad jumped out of the car and grabbed my bags as soon as he saw me standing at the curb. "Welcome back!" he said as he kissed me on both cheeks.

"Hi, Baba. I didn't expect to see you. Aren't you supposed to be at work?" I was even more surprised by my mom waiting for me in the car.

I slid into the back seat and closed the door. My mom turned to greet me. "Hi, Sweetheart! How are you?"

"Hi, Maman," I leaned forward to kiss her on the cheek. "This is such a nice surprise. You both came to pick me up," I said warmly.

My mom shrugged. "Your dad took the day off, and we thought it'd be nice to come and pick you up together. We haven't had lunch. Are you hungry?"

I nodded. "I'm starving! I fell asleep when they served food on the plane. I haven't eaten anything but a bag of peanuts all day."

"Good. How about going to the restaurant you like?" Baba asked as he started the car. "I've been craving kabob, and I know you love their fava bean rice and lamb dish," he offered, seeking my approval through the rearview mirror.

"Sounds wonderful!" I exclaimed, licking my lips.

As we drove to the restaurant, we exchanged casual pleasantries. I sat poised waiting to be grilled with questions about Omid. But neither of them asked anything about him.

"So, how is everything here?" I asked in a nonchalant voice.

My dad stirred in his seat and loosened his grip on the steering wheel. He had always been a nervous driver. "Nothing new here. I've been busy working, and your mom's been busy with her things. How did your trip go?" he asked, focusing on the road.

I could feel my face grow hot and my ears started to burn. When I didn't answer right away, my mom turned in her seat and watched me as I fiddled with the air vent to get some air.

"Um, it was a good trip. I got a chance to hang out with Shirin, Peter, and Shirin's mom. I also met Shirin's cousin, Omid."

"Sounds great. What was her cousin like?" my mom asked, suddenly appearing intrigued.

"He's a gentleman. Very different for the other guys I've met," I stammered.

"I see. How so?" she continued to question while observing my body language.

I shrugged and stared out the window. "I don't know. He's just different. Just a very calm and courteous person. He's very smart, but not arrogant. Oh, and he's super fun. I guess he is what you call a good guy," flustered unable to find the right words to fully describe Omid.

"It seems as if you spent a lot of time together if you know so much about him," my dad observed.

"Yes, Shirin and Peter had to work almost every day, so Omid and I hung out and went sightseeing a lot." I turned and saw my mom smile sheepishly and gaze into my eyes. I felt my cheeks turn a deeper shade of red, knowing she could see right through me.

She reached back and squeezed my hand. "I've never seen you look so red, Bahar. It's cute."

I smiled sheepishly and held her hand, feeling comforted. We remained silent for the remainder of the trip.

Once we ordered our lunch at the restaurant, the conversation continued.

"So, are you two planning on getting to know each other more? Is he still in London or did he fly back?" my mom inquired.

"No, he flew back to San Diego this morning. But we do plan on spending more time together," I said, biting my lip shyly. Then I inhaled and decided to tell them the news. "I think Omid's the one. I can see myself with him for the rest of my life."

My parents put down their utensils and stared at me speechless.

"What do you *mean* he could be the one?" my mom asked, appearing flustered.

I took a long sip of my water and sat back, trying to appear confident as I replied. "Omid and I are officially engaged. He proposed to me before he left," I said, lifting my finger to display the shining engagement ring.

My dad stared at my finger and blinked a few times appearing confused.

"*What?*" my mom asked in a shrill voice. "What do you mean engaged? You mean to tell us that you just met this person two weeks ago and you now know him well enough to want to marry him?!" she continued with eyes wide open.

I nodded with conviction. "Yes! I know it sounds like a very short time, and I understand why you might be concerned, but I am one hundred percent sure about this. I know Omid is the person for me."

"I see." Baba sat back in his chair and turned to me with concern in his eyes. "I have to admit I'm speechless. This is not the Bahar I know. You are always so cautious with making decisions, especially when it comes to matters of the heart. I can still remember the ten-page pros and cons list you made about the boy you were dating a little over a year ago. After months of contemplation, you told me you two weren't a good match because he didn't floss one time after eating corn."

I started laughing out loud. "Yes, I remember that, Baba. There's nothing more annoying than a man who doesn't floss after eating corn."

My parents both started laughing and my dad shook his head, still appearing uncertain.

I leaned in and spoke softly. "Look, I get it. I know why you are both shocked. I know how this sounds. If it were my daughter giving me this news, I'd be worried too. But you need to trust me on this. I'm not a little girl anymore. I've spent a lot of time with Omid. Yes, I still need to learn more about him. We have a lot in common. I know his aunt and his cousin is my best friend. He's also told me a lot about his childhood and his parents and brother. He isn't rushing me into anything. Everything just clicked and we both felt it. We've dated enough people in our lives to know what we *don't* want. It makes the decision for what we *do* want so much simpler. You'll see what I mean when you meet him. You will fall in love with him as much I did. Please, just try and be happy for me."

My mom cleared her throat before speaking. "I know I've been urging you to find somebody suitable to marry. I guess I can't fault you for finally finding someone. But if you're this certain about your decision, then your father and I are very happy for you. We'll support you."

I leaped out of my chair and ran to embrace my parents. "Thank you! Thank you so much! It means so much to me that you are happy for me. You won't be disappointed. I love you so much!" With uncontrollable tears, I wrapped my arms around both my parents.

As we continued eating our lunch, I shared every detail of my trip. They smiled while listening to me talk about my admiration for Omid, but I detected a shrouded frown on their faces when listening to our plans to live abroad.

My mom's eyes widened when we started discussing details about the wedding. "If I'm not mistaken, you said Omid is planning to come here in less than three months. Do you realize that doesn't give us much time to plan a wedding? There is so much we need to do to prepare. We have to look for a large venue, call the caterer, look for a dress, and send out invitations," she paused to catch her breath. "My goodness, we are so behind!"

I laughed heartily, knowing she would never settle for a small celebration. "Relax, Mom. It'll be fine. We don't have to have a big party. If we just invite our close friends and family, we'll be good," I said, trying to dissuade her from a grand celebration.

My mom heard me speak but didn't appear to listen to a word I said. "Nonsense! Your dad and I will take care of everything. I have a perfect venue in mind. There is a beautiful villa outside of Tehran to have the wedding. Your father will call and check to see if they have any weekends available in August. It will be a beautiful outdoor summer wedding!" she said, clapping her hands.

My father smiled and nodded with a distant look in his eyes.

"Don't you worry. Just leave everything to us," she said with a twinkle in her eye.

"Okay, I trust you, but I want you to promise me that you will call Omid's mom and tell her about the wedding plans. Promise me we won't end up getting into a fight over the wedding plans like your friend Sheila and her daughter's in-laws. Five years have passed, and they still don't speak to each other because of a stupid quarrel over the color of the flower arrangements at the wedding! I don't want anything to ruin our special day," I said sternly.

My mom wafted her hand in the air as if swatting a fly. "Of course, I will involve his family. That fight is the most childish thing I've ever heard! We're all adults here. I will make sure to involve you, Omid, and his family in all the decisions. You just tell me what you want, and we will make all the arrangements," she said, appearing sincere.

She tugged at my dad's shirt while squealing, "I'm so excited our

Bahar is finally getting married!"

The next day my mom prepared a to-do list for the wedding and started contacting multiple vendors. After a few weeks, my parents were able to secure the venue, find a caterer, and finalize the contract with the wedding photographer. I was tasked with decorations, the band, and managing the RSVPs. We spoke to Omid and his family weekly to share information related to the wedding plans and often asked them for input.

The only decision I made without consulting anyone was my wedding gown. The seamstress was talented and managed to sew the dress of my dreams in just a few weeks. When I went to pick it up at the final fitting, I Pranced around the room wearing the wedding gown picturing myself floating down the aisle, with Omid's keen eyes canvassing me fervently. I couldn't wait for the special day when my Prince Charming would hold me in his arms and make my dreams come true.

Chapter 8

$\mathcal{I}$ caressed Omid's hand as he lay sleeping on the hospital bed, vividly recalling the time he had caressed mine during our vows.

~ ~ ~ ~ ~ ~

I took my seat next to Omid on the white upholstered bench, facing the ceremony table.

Omid leaned over and whispered, "Hello Beautiful."

I felt my cheeks become hot under the veil and whispered hello. He took my cold hand and placed it on his lap, squeezing it reassuringly. We exchanged our vows and declared our love for each other while watching our reflections on the gold etched mirror. The two lighted candles on the matching candelabras nestled adjacent to the mirror, on the traditional Sofreh Aghd table, cast a bright glow across our faces. Every item on the table was intentionally placed following thousand-year-old traditions, with the incense, decorative flatbread, colored eggs, coins, and sweets all symbolizing different wishes for our future.

Love and warmth emanated from family and friends as we exchanged our vows. Omid lifted my veil and his soft lips touched mine. My life had never been more blessed.

We sealed the union in the time-honored tradition of exchanging rings and by dipping our little finger in the jar of honey, symbolic of the sweet life, and feeding a small dollop of it to each other. The rest of the evening felt surreal. We danced, feasted, conversed, and laughed with our guests all night long. At the end of the night, after all the guests had left, Omid and I shared one last dance. We glided across the dance floor repeatedly confirming our love for each other at every turn. I didn't want the magical evening to end.

"You look stunning tonight," Omid murmured. "I can't seem to be able to take my eyes off you. I cherish you and promise never to take you for granted." I wiped a tear from his cheek. Leaning in to kiss him, my lips quivered with joy.

My parents arranged for a post-wedding gathering and invited Omid's family. It couldn't have gone any better. We enjoyed sharing embarrassing childhood stories, and of course, everyone teased Omid and me about our race to the alter.

At one point the conversation shifted to grandchildren. Omid's mom was the instigator of the topic and my mom quickly added her input. They tried to be subtle about their wishes, but that was not possible with these two mothers.

"We expect to see you and Reza visiting us soon in San Diego, especially when the grandkids come into the picture," she said, winking at my mom.

My mom snickered and her eyes glistened from joy. "You're right Taraneh joon! I better start looking for tickets soon. I don't want to miss out on squeezing those little cute cheeks soon!"

Omid and I watched the two mothers as they bantered about grandchildren. I sat on an upholstered chair with Omid perched on the armrest leaning on the back of the chair for support. He put his arm on my shoulder and grinned listening to the conversation. "For goodness sake! Do you ladies realize Bahar and I got married only two days ago? How about you give us some time together before bringing up the prospects of grandkids?"

Everyone laughed in unison, but we all knew whatever we said wouldn't change their minds. The hours flew by and before we knew it, it was 3 a.m.

Since it was so late, both sets of parents decided to sleep-in and forego sightseeing the next day. That left Golnaz and me to arrange an outing with Omid and his brother Navid.

The next morning, we started our day with breakfast at one of Golnaz's favorite restaurants in the city center. Even though I was the one who lived in the city, most of the sites were new to me. Golnaz was better versed to show us around.

"So much has changed since I was here as a teenager," Omid mused. "The street names and businesses have all changed, too. Many new shopping centers, looking so much like the malls in the U.S. More progressive than I pictured it to be."

"Yeah, everything was rebuilt after the Iran-Iraq war. So many people died in that stupid war. Don't let the façade fool you; people are still struggling," I said sullenly.

Omid furrowed his brows and frowned. Looking around he said, "You're right. With all the new developments, people walk around looking like zombies with sunken eyes and grim expressions."

"Do you see that alley there?" Golnaz asked tilting her head towards a dark alley sandwiched between two apartment buildings. "If you walk through there, you'll find nothing but addicts and needles on the street. Heroin and opium addiction are rampant, especially with the youth. So many young talented kids with their minds going to waste. It's awful!" Golnaz snapped.

Omid shook his head in disbelief. "That's a shame."

Golnaz nodded and continued, "It is. But let's talk about something more pleasant."

Golnaz looked at Omid and me affectionately holding hands. "I can't believe Bahar is married! I wish you guys could pay me a visit in Rome before heading to San Diego after your honeymoon."

"It would've been nice, but we only have a few days in Spain for our honeymoon before Omid has to be back at work," I replied. Wanting to pivot to a different topic, I said, "Speaking of Rome, I don't think Omid and Navid know how you ended up in Italy. Why don't you tell them?"

"Yes, I'm curious. Did you always want to live in Rome?" Omid asked.

Golnaz paused for a few seconds before shrugging her shoulders and responding to Omid's question. "Not really. After I graduated from college with a degree in public relations, I had a hard time finding a job here. Since I am fluent in English and Italian, I sent my resume to a few advertising companies abroad. I got lucky and landed an internship position in sales and marketing in Rome. After finishing my internship, I was offered full-time employment," Golnaz explained.

"That's awesome!" Omid replied. "Where did you learn to speak Italian?"

"We went to Italy for vacation when I was around ten years old. I just loved the sound of the beautiful language and fell in love with the country. We bought a few books during our visit, and I convinced my dad to find me an Italian teacher when we came back. I have been fluent in Italian since then," Golnaz said with her head held high appearing proud. "And of course, Bahar and I had a private English tutor who worked with us once a week since elementary school until we graduated high school."

Omid smiled. "Very impressive. I can only say a few words in Spanish, but they are mainly medically related words. And I still manage to mix that up when speaking to some of my patients."

"You got that right! Omid thinks buenos noches means good morning instead of good night!" Navid cackled.

Omid rolled his eyes at Navid and sneered, looking embarrassed. "That was only one time! Give me a break. Everyone can confuse those two phrases."

We all laughed at Omid's faux pas.

Shifting the topic of conversation, Navid asked, "How hard is it to become a lawyer in Iran?"

"Well, it's very competitive to get in. Very few people who go to law school actually graduate. Bahar graduated with honors in a class that only had two women enrolled in the program," Golnaz proclaimed with a boisterous voice, appearing proud of me.

Then Golnaz turned to Omid, "Your wife is unique, Omid. I'm not just saying that because she's my sister. She has been a real trailblazer advocating for women's rights in the workplace and challenging the chauvinistic system every single day."

My face flushed in embarrassment listening to her praise. "Please don't exaggerate, Golnaz."

Omid gave me a tight squeeze and kissed me on the neck. "Well, from what I've heard and known of Bahar, I'd say I'm one lucky guy."

"Have you given your work notice that you're leaving?" Navid asked.

Navid was Omid's older sibling by four years. He was a bachelor and worked as an engineer. He was a soft-spoken introverted person with similar physical features as Omid. Navid had more gray hair than Omid and wore it tied back in a ponytail. He also wore prescription glasses and loose-fitting clothes that made it difficult to delineate the contours of his physique. During my short time with Navid, I found him a bit intimidating and difficult to read.

"Yes, I gave them a month's notice. They were surprised by the news. My boss asked me to contact him after I pass the bar exam and get settled. He mentioned that he has some connections at firms that specialize in mergers and acquisitions in the U.S."

"It's nice of him to offer, but you have a long way to go before you can practice law in the U.S.," Navid interjected.

"What do you mean she has a long way to go?" Omid asked Navid, looking irritated. "What do you know about passing law exams? Last time I checked you studied engineering."

Navid didn't respond to Omid and continued to challenge me. "Do you know how many tests you have to take to practice law in California? Does the U.S. recognize foreign graduates?"

I shook my head unable to respond. Omid's nostrils flared in frustration listening to Navid's questions. I was starting to understand the dynamics between Omid and his older brother. The two didn't appear very close. "Why are you grilling Bahar about this stuff? How can she possibly know these answers right now?" Omid fumed. "Bahar will pass any exam they put in front of her, and I'm one hundred percent sure that my wife will be one of the best lawyers in the state. Any firm would be lucky to have her working for them!"

"Thank you for believing in me," I said with a deep appreciation for Omid's sentiments. "But Navid brings up good questions. I don't have the answers right now but will find out in due time. Right now, I just want to enjoy our time together," I said lovingly, squeezing Omid's hand.

Despite the occasional tension between Omid and his brother, it was nice having the four of us together sightseeing and exploring Tehran. I missed spending time with Golnaz and was happy Omid was also getting to know her.

It was so hard to balance the joy of starting my new adventure with Omid against the crushing sadness of leaving my past life.

The night before Omid and I were leaving on our honeymoon in Spain, I stayed up very late spending time alone with my parents. "Are you sure you and Baba are going to be okay by yourselves?" I asked my mom

"Oh, sweetheart, you worry too much. Of course, we'll be okay. You sometimes forget *we're* your parents and not the other way around," she teased. "You need to start focusing on building a new life with your husband and stop worrying about us."

"It's going to be difficult. I'm going to miss our afternoon walks and late-night chat sessions the most," I said, choking back the tears.

"Us too. But we will have them again when you visit. I know it's hard for you to start from scratch in a new place without having us around, but you have a wonderful husband who is going to love and support you. You're going to have a very happy life together. I just know it," my mom said reassuringly.

"Everything is going to feel so foreign to me," I replied. I lay on the bed, and she caressed my hair, grazing her fingers against my cheek like she used to do when I was young. Her caresses always relaxed me, and with every stroke, she brushed away another layer of apprehension.

"Once we're settled in San Diego, we'll make sure our paperwork is set, so you and Baba can come to visit us often."

"Absolutely! We would love to do that. Your father brought up the subject of retirement with me over dinner last night. Can you believe he mentioned he wants to retire in a few years?! He said it's high time he freed his days to spend with our future grandchildren," my mom gushed excitedly.

"Not that again!" I said with a smile.

"Oh, come on. If having children will convince your Baba to finally retire, let me have at least that to look forward to," she said teasingly.

"Well, I hate to break up the fun," my dad said with a scolding smile, "it's two in the morning and your flight leaves in five hours."

"Oh, Baba I don't want to sleep. I want to spend every second of my last night with you two," I said as I stood and gave him a tight embrace.

"I know, azizam." He stood back and gazed into my eyes. "I don't want you to leave my sight either. The house will feel so empty without you," he said with a sullen voice. When I started to tear up, he continued with a more cheerful voice. "Just think how great it will be not to worry about wearing a roosari or removing your make-up every time you want to leave the house. You're not going to deal with any of that nonsense anymore. You can dance if you want or sing as loud as you want, and nobody will ever bother you. I'm so excited for you!"

I nodded, too choked up to speak. "I know. I'm excited for me too."

That was the last night the three of us lived together in the same house for many years to come. Back then, I never envisioned a time I would live with my parents again.

Chapter 9

$\mathcal{I}$ sat in the dimly lit hospital room thinking about my first few years in the U.S. Initially, I was worried about how well I could adjust to the American way of life, but Omid made the transition easy for me. He helped me register for classes at a local community college to improve my English. I loved learning about American holidays, especially when Omid and I attended Christmas parties, Thanksgiving dinners, and Fourth of July picnics with his friends and colleagues.

It took me some time to learn how to navigate the arduous freeway system, but I eventually found my way around the city. To avoid daily trips to the grocery store, Omid told me about shopping in bulk from Costco. I remember the euphoria of walking down the aisles in the enormous warehouse and indiscriminately throwing everything into the shopping cart without a second thought. It was only after returning home with seven hundred dollars' worth of merchandise, that I decided to make a shopping list in advance.

"I see you're starting to adjust very well to the American way of life," Omid teased with a raised eyebrow, returning from his tenth trip to the car. After he placed the last box on the kitchen table, his hands reached for my waist, twirling me round and round until we embraced.

"I love watching the world through your eyes. You make

everything fresh and exciting," he said, nuzzling my neck and inhaling my scent.

I squealed and tried to pull free. "Stop, you're tickling me!"

Feeling playful, he continued to nibble on my ears and growled like a hungry lion.

I bellowed out with laughter and tried to reason with him. "Let me put away the ice cream before it melts."

He shook his head. "Not a chance. The only thing I'm craving right now is a taste of you," he said with a seductive voice leading me towards the bedroom.

I couldn't resist. Passionate lovemaking, whenever we were together, was also a new skill set I was beginning to master.

During our years together, Omid taught me how to enjoy life and not take myself too seriously. He also served as my source of strength, shielding me with his invisible cloak. He was always showering me with praise and celebrating my successes. Watching him now on the hospital bed attached to so many monitors, I felt a cold chill seeping in under Omid's protective cloak.

"Please don't leave me, Omid. Please don't give up. I need you here with me. I don't want to imagine a life without you," I said, sobbing into the sheets on his bed.

I placed his hand on my face and cried as he slept. I felt helpless but began thinking about the kids at home. I stood up and grabbed the phone out of my purse to check for any messages. Not finding any missed calls or texts, I called my nanny.

Sogol answered after the first ring. "Hello?"

"Hi, Sogol joon. How are you?"

"I'm good. How are you?" she asked softly.

"I'm worried about Omid. Sorry, I lost track of time. I should have called sooner. How are the boys doing?"

"They're okay. Both have eaten dinner, and I'm helping Koosha with his homework. Kayvon didn't have any schoolwork, so he decided to watch TV. I hope Mr. Omid will be home soon."

I smiled. She was always so formal when she referred to Omid. "He will not be discharged tonight, maybe tomorrow. When he occasionally wakes up, he doesn't talk. The doctor wants to run more tests."

"I see. I hope they find out what's wrong soon," she fretted.

I sighed and exhaled into the receiver. "Yes, me too." I continued the conversation, "I'm sorry for asking, but would it be okay if you spent the night with the boys? It's too late to ask my in-laws to come over. The boys love being with you."

Without hesitating, she responded, "Yes, of course! I already figured I would be staying since I hadn't heard from you. Don't worry about the boys. Kayvon doesn't need supervision; I will sleep in Koosha's room."

"Oh my God, you're such an angel. What would I ever do without you?" I'm so sorry to keep you away from your husband," I nervously whimpered.

"Please don't worry. Everything is under control here and Ali has no problem with me staying the night. Please get some rest and say hello to Mr. Omid for me."

"I will, thanks."

I heard Koosha's voice asking who she was speaking to. When she told him, he asked her about his dad.

Oh, my God, we need to stop lying to the boys about their father.

"Please tell Koosha Omid is doing better," I said before Sogol could ask.

As she tried to convey my message, Koosha panted, "Hi, Mommy. Where are you? When are you coming home?"

"Hi, my love. I'm at the hospital with Baba. He is doing better, but the doctor says they want him to stay here tonight. I think I need to stay with him to make sure he gets better quickly. Are you okay staying with Sogol and Kavyon tonight?"

He paused for a moment before responding. When he spoke, I could barely hear his voice. "I wish you guys could come home *now*. I'm sad you guys aren't here."

My heart broke hearing him speak. "I know Lovebug. I know it's hard for you. But I promise we'll have a lot of time to play together when I get back. I promise to bring you back a few Jell-O cups."

He didn't respond to my offer. Sogol took the phone. "I'm sorry Bahar joon. He just went to his room and handed me the phone. He'll be fine. I'll stay with him and read him a story until he falls asleep."

I thanked her and hung up the phone. Tears streaked my cheeks as I pictured the kids at home feeling sad and confused. I pushed the call button to summon the night-shift nurse.

Pacing the room to stretch my muscles, I eventually made my way to the semi-reclining chair in somewhat of a daze not having an update on Omid's condition. Absent during the doctor's rounds, I couldn't sleep until I talked with a nurse or the doctor.

While waiting for the nurse, I directed my attention to the sound of the beeping machines in the room. They reminded me of the fasten seat belt chime I was accustomed to hearing during take-off and landing. How I yearned to be on a plane with Omid heading anywhere but this cold, daunting room. I wanted to return to the day we landed in Spain for our honeymoon.

~ ~ ~ ~ ~ ~

We saw the light illuminated above our seat and heard the chime to fasten our seat belts, alerting us that the plane was preparing to land. I looked over at Omid and felt a flutter of excitement in my chest. I had opted for the window seat, so I could peek outside and marvel at the terrain below during the flight. As we descended under the fluffy clouds, a beautiful perspective of the country spun in full view.

I giggled like a little girl. "I can't wait to see the city again! I'm so glad we decided to come to Spain for our honeymoon."

Omid leaned over my shoulder and tried to catch a glimpse of the city through the square windowpane. "I know!" He kissed my cheek and interlace his fingers through mine.

Excited to be finally alone together, we spent our days exploring the wondrous Southern Region and devoted the evenings watching breathtaking flamenco shows. We had an insatiable appetite for the delectable feasts often followed by sensual lovemaking under the Andalusian skies.

Omid's charm and charisma were irresistible, his kisses and caressing enveloped my whole being. I yearned for more. I had never experienced this level of intimacy or intensity during sex.

With our blissful honeymoon coming to an end, we gifted ourselves with memories by buying CDs of newly discovered Spanish musicians. Now that Omid had a chance to connect with my life, I looked forward to knowing more about the place he called home.

As we made our descent, the downtown San Diego skyscape suddenly revealed itself. I pointed to the body of water below. "Where is that?" I asked.

He leaned in for a better look through the glass. "That's the San Diego Bay," he said, pointing to a glistening waterway filled with rows of docked sailboats. Those tall buildings you see to the south are part of the downtown and the commercial hub of the city. That's where you will find most hotels, the Convention Center, courthouses, and a lot of business offices." As Omid explained, the plane descended at low altitude over a large artery of freeways right before touching down on the tarmac.

I sighed in relief once I knew we were safely on the ground. "For a second there I thought we were going to land on the cars!" I said, unbuckling my seatbelt anxious to leave the hollow metal compartment hosting us for 13 long hours.

"That was the longest flight of my life. I'm so happy we're finally here!" I said, feeling grateful.

"I'm so glad I don't have to sit on another plane for a long time to come. You know I've been dreaming of this moment since I flew back from London. The last time I landed in San Diego, I kept imagining what it would be like sitting next to you after we got married." We kissed.

"Well, I hope it's as good as you imagined it to be," I teased, gently tapping him on the nose.

"Oh, it's so much better than I ever imagined," he grinned.

~ ~ ~ ~ ~ ~

There was a knock on the door before the nurse entered, interrupting my thoughts. "Can I help you with anything?" she asked. "I heard the buzzer for assistance."

I sat up and shook my head regaining my composure. "Yes. Hi. I'm sorry, I wasn't here when the doctor made his rounds. Do you know if my husband can eat anything?"

"Ah, yes. Dr. Stanley left instructions to hold solids until your husband's vitals are more stable. For now, the IV is giving him the nutrition he needs. Has he woken up since you've been in the room?" she asked.

"He briefly opened his eyes about two hours ago but didn't speak or respond to any of my questions," I replied.

She nodded. "Okay, well, we'll let him rest and see how he does in the morning. The doctor wants to see how he feels when the internal swelling in his brain subsides. He'll come by early in the morning to make rounds. We should know more then."

"Okay, thank you," I nodded distressingly.

She hesitated before continuing. "Will you be spending the night with him?" she asked.

"Yes. I want to be here in case he wakes up."

"Okay. I'll bring you a blanket." She paused and glanced at me, knowingly. "Don't worry. It'll be okay," she said comfortingly before leaving the room. I thanked her.

I sat there, clinging to her words while weeping. With the memories of our honeymoon, I sat in the cold dark room watching Omid fight for his life. The fear of losing him left me emotionally paralyzed.

Falling to my knees and raising my hands towards the paneled ceiling of the hospital room, I pleaded with God. "Please, don't let anything bad happen to Omid. I'm begging you to show mercy. If you want to take anyone, take me. He doesn't deserve to suffer like this!"

Chapter 10

$\mathcal{D}$r. Stanley gently tapped my shoulder as if he feared I would shatter into pieces with a harder touch. I opened my eyes and saw him hovering above my chair. At first, all I saw was the white coat, which suggested illness and sterility and a mental panic forever etched in my memory.

"Good morning, Mrs. Salehi," Dr. Stanley greeted.

I knew by his sullen gaze and empathetic smile that he had unpleasant news. I looked to my right and noticed Taraneh. I wasn't sure how long she had been in the room while I was sleeping.

I rubbed the sleep from my eyes and sat up. "Good morning, Doctor. How is Omid doing?"

"I had a chance to examine him. It looks as if the swelling has subsided." Turning towards the door, he asked, "May we chat in the hallway for a minute?"

Taraneh forlornly glanced at Dr. Stanley. She looked as if she were bracing for a hurricane. As I removed the blanket from my chest and stood up, I heard my close friend, Stella's voice for the first time.

"Good morning," she said, holding a cup of hot tea in her hand, smiling at me.

"Oh, hi! Sorry, I didn't see you before. How long have you been here?" I asked, feeling confused.

"Only five minutes, Sweetie," she said, kissing me on both cheeks. "I saw Taraneh in the parking lot, so we walked together. Dr. Stanley was examining Omid when we arrived."

I nodded feeling suddenly wide awake. "I'll be right back," I said following Dr. Stanley.

Before he exited the room, Stella asked if it would be alright if she accompanied us. She knew I was about to find out Omid's biopsy results.

Dr. Stanley nodded in agreement and walked into the hallway. He stood a few steps away from the door to avoid being within earshot of Omid and Taraneh. I reached out to hold Stella's hand feeling anxious about the dismal news.

"How are you holding up, Bahar?" he asked.

"I'm okay. Just not sure what to make of Omid's fainting spell. Do you think it has to do with the surgery?"

He looked down shaking his head. "I'm afraid not, Bahar. I just received the biopsy results this morning. It looks like we couldn't get the entire tumor out." He paused, looked up at me and said, "I'm sorry. There isn't anything more we can do."

Dr. Stanley paused as if waiting for me to react, but I was completely frozen. The walls started closing in around me, and my peripheral vision narrowed. My knees wobbled, and if it weren't for Stella wrapping her arms around me, I would have dropped to the floor.

"Bahar. Bahar honey, can you hear me? Are you okay?" Stella held my hand as I regained consciousness.

When I did, I found myself sitting on a chair with a nurse and Dr. Stanley standing over me, checking my vitals. I had blacked out.

I felt numb and dumbfounded. *Where am I? Did I just wake up from a nightmare? Why was Dr. Stanley here?*

Before I could make myself believe the bad news was nothing but a dream, Dr. Stanley explained I had just fainted after hearing about

Omid's biopsy results.

I started whimpering with my shoulders hunched over. Two years of doing everything imaginable to kill those cancer cells and they had no intention of dying. Omid had endured two life-threatening brain surgeries and two rounds of chemotherapy followed by radiation for nothing. No reward for being religious about daily exercise, healthy eating habits, and medication adherence either.

Stella gently rubbed my back and handed me a cup of water. "Please drink this. It'll make you feel better."

My hands trembled as I held onto the cup. I felt defeated after a long bloody war.

"I am sorry, Bahar. I know this is not the news you wanted. It's a very aggressive tumor that's not responding to anything we've thrown at it," Dr. Stanley expressed sympathetically. I shook my head as if shunning away the words from my ears. I didn't want to believe there were no options left.

"So, this is it? There must be something else you could try. Are there any clinical trials we can look into for new treatments?" I desperately asked.

"I've looked at the database to see if Omid would qualify for any studies. I haven't found any. I'll keep searching, but in the meantime, he can complete another ten-day regimen of radiation as a palliative measure."

"What does palliative mean?"

"Palliative means it helps slow the progress of the tumor but won't get rid of it. That will buy him more time," the doctor explained.

Closing my eyes, the tears dropped on the vinyl floor. "I see," I whispered. "Thank you, Doctor."

He nodded. "I'll check in on Omid in a few hours. The scan shows the brain swelling is improving, which is good."

After Dr. Stanley left us, Stella stooped down next to the chair, assessing me with a soft smile.

"I don't know how to do this anymore, Stella. I never thought he wouldn't beat this. You know what I mean?" I asked rhetorically.

"I know, honey. I am so sorry."

I puckered my face in frustration. "God, what am I going to tell the boys? The news will shatter their hearts into pieces. The rug is being pulled right out from under our feet. It's so damn unfair!"

Stella nodded and took a deep inhale. "I don't know what to say. I can't imagine how difficult this is for you, but I know how strong you are and know how resilient your boys are. I know you'll find a way to break the news to them. They'll be upset when they hear about their father. We will help you all get through this."

I shook my head, still in disbelief. "I can't bear the thought of losing someone I love so dearly. I've been watching his health deteriorate, and I still can't bring myself to accept this outcome. I don't think the boys will ever recover from this tragedy." My voice sounded more panicked with each passing moment. "I just want to run and hide where no one can find me."

"Let's not think about any of that just yet. Why don't we go outside and get some fresh air?" she suggested, helping me stand.

Following her absent-mindedly, I let her lead me downstairs and exit through the revolving doors of the hospital. I inhaled the fresh air and held it, trying to still my mind.

I started to think about Kayvon and how this news would affect him. Kayvon was going through puberty and enjoyed talking about his feelings with Omid. Kayvon and Omid had started a Sunday morning Son-Day-Fun-Day walk and talk ritual six months before Omid's diagnosis.

Even after Omid became ill, he continued the Sunday sessions. On days he was too weak to walk, they drove to a coffee shop and talked there instead. Over the past few months, Omid had been too tired to leave the house, and Kayvon started becoming angry with his father.

He thought Omid was making excuses not to spend time with him. Navid tried to fill in for Omid, but Kayvon refused to replace his father during these outings.

"Hey, will you please exhale before you pass out again?" Stella pleaded, bringing me out of my daydream.

I exhaled loudly. "Sorry, I was just thinking about the kids. They are so close to their dad and depend on him for so much. I don't know how I could ever find a way to fill the gap if he isn't around."

"I think we need to take a step back and not get ahead of ourselves. Nobody knows how much time he has left. He is alive now and the boys still have their father. Let's focus on the positive for now," she said, trying to calm my thoughts.

We ordered two cups of tea from the kiosk next to the hospital. The morning air felt cool against my skin, and the hot cup of tea soothed me.

When we walked back into Omid's room, I saw his eyes open staring at the wall in front of him. I ran over cheerfully and kissed him on the forehead. "Hi, baby!"

Omid didn't respond and just continued to look straight ahead.

"How long has he been awake?" I asked Taraneh, standing next to Omid whispering under her breath.

She stopped praying and looked over at me with a smile. "He opened his eyes a few minutes after you left. The nurse said the swelling is going down. They want to keep him under observation for another night. If he continues to improve, they will probably discharge him tomorrow."

"That's great!" I exclaimed, clasping my hands together.

"I told them my son is a fighter!" Taraneh said, giving Omid's hand a reassuring squeeze. Omid continued to stare at the wall without any response.

I turned to Stella and asked, "Would you mind staying here with Omid for a little bit?"

Stella nodded in agreement.

I reached and took Taraneh's hand. "Why don't we go get something to eat? It's almost lunchtime."

She hesitated at first, but then agreed to accompany me. We went to the cafeteria on the ground floor, where they were setting up for lunch. I didn't have much of an appetite and grabbed a banana while Taraneh got a sandwich and a cup of soup.

"Why aren't you eating anything, Bahar? You haven't eaten anything all morning. A banana isn't going to fill you up," Taraneh said, looking concerned.

"I'm not that hungry. I'll grab something else in a little bit."

We found an empty table and sat down.

"How is Mansoor joon? Is his vision getting better?"

"It's still not one hundred percent, but it's improving day by day. A body takes longer to heal when you're eighty years old," she said with a gloomy voice. "He wanted to come visit Omid today, but I told him to stay home and rest. I wanted to get here early in the morning, and if Mansoor had come, it would have taken him two hours just to get ready."

I nodded. She continued, "What did Dr. Stanley tell you this morning? Why did he ask you to step out of the room?" she asked, nervously fiddling with the spoon in her hand.

I looked down to avoid her gaze. "Oh, he wanted to share some test results." I paused for a moment. "It looks like some of the cancer cells are still there," I said through my cracking voice, trying to keep the tears at bay.

Her eyes widened. "So, what happens now? Are they going to do another surgery?"

I shook my head and looked up with tearful eyes. "Taraneh joon, there won't be any more surgeries. They've tried everything they could."

"What do you mean? There must be something else they can try.

They can't just give up like that," she grumbled. She pushed her tray forward and sat back folding her arms across her chest, looking defiant. "I think we should get a second opinion. I think he is getting better. Otherwise, he wouldn't be awake right now," she said.

I listened, not wanting to counter her. She was a mother in shock and feeling desperate. The sorrow in her eyes and the fear in her voice were unmistakable. My lips started quivering and I found it difficult to speak.

"I'm so sorry. I know this is awful news," I said.

She started sobbing openly. Slamming a fist on the table she declared, "This is *not* over! It can't be!"

I walked over to embrace her. "Shh, shh, it's okay. It's okay. We won't lose hope. I promise we'll keep looking for answers. Please keep your composure in front of Omid. He doesn't know about the test results yet." She sat frozen in place. "Are you listening to me Taraneh joon?"

She nodded, looking at me through hollow eyes. I dabbed her cheeks with a tissue and offered her a spoonful of soup. "Please eat your lunch before it gets cold," I pleaded.

Taraneh grew silent. After she absentmindedly finished her sandwich, I pulled a mirror out of my purse and offered it to her along with another tissue to wipe the smeared mascara under her eyes. We stood and headed back to Omid's room.

As we stepped into the room, I noticed Omid speaking to Stella in a very faint voice. I squealed from the excitement of seeing Omid lucid.

"Hi, there! I see you've come back to us," I chirped joyously.

"Stella, how did this happen? When did Omid start talking?" Taraneh asked, appearing shocked.

"I don't know! I was minding my own business, finishing my masters homework when Omid asked me for the TV remote."

I walked rapidly towards Omid. "I was so worried about you! How are you feeling?"

Omid smiled. "I'm fine. How long have I been in the hospital?"

"They admitted you yesterday. You've been in and out of consciousness since we got here. The doctor said you had some swelling in your brain from the surgery, but said the scans are showing less fluid than before," I replied.

Omid nodded and looked over at his mom. "Hi, Maman."

Taraneh walked over and kissed Omid on the cheek. "Hi, Sweetheart," she said, trying to choke back her tears. "It's nice to hear your voice."

"So, what were you and Stella talking about?" I asked jokingly with a raised eyebrow. "I hope Stella didn't tell on me for not getting an A on my last paper. You know how she's always on me about finishing my damn masters," I huffed and threw my hands in the air, as if surrendering.

"Well, you said getting your masters is the only way they'll let you take the bar exam; you've been procrastinating getting your degree for years. Someone needs to hold your feet to the fire. Am I right, Omid?" Stella looked at Omid seeking confirmation.

Omid's face turned serious. "Yes, Stella's right. You need to finish your masters," Omid replied.

"I know. You're both right. It's just been so hard to focus on studying with everything that's been going on lately. I promise I'll sign up for the next class." I sighed, unable to foresee when our lives would return to normal.

You just get better, and I'll do anything you say, I thought to myself.

Chapter 11

$\mathcal{I}$ stayed with Omid that night. Taraneh offered to cook dinner and insisted that she and Mansoor spend the night with the boys. I accepted because Sogol needed some reprieve.

I called home to tell the boys about the plans for the evening. Koosha answered the phone. "Hi, Mommy. How are you?"

Koosha was the younger and more sensitive one of our two sons.

"Hi, Sweetie. I'm doing good. How are you and Kayvon?"

"We're fine. When are you guys coming home?" he fretted.

"I'm sorry, Lovebug. But Baba and I are still at the hospital. The doctor says he needs to keep him one more night before he can get discharged. Don't worry, we'll be home tomorrow."

"But you said that last night," he protested.

"I promise: one more night. Guess what? Grandma is making your favorite spaghetti. Both she and grandpa will have dinner with you guys and spend the night. How does that sound?" I said, hoping to hear a joyful response. Not so.

"That's nice," he replied glumly. "Mommy, what's wrong with Baba?"

I swallowed hard before answering. "Nothing, Honey. The doctor just wants to run some tests to find out why Baba has been feeling so tired and sleepy all the time. Don't worry, he's feeling better and sleeping right now. I'll explain everything when we get home tomorrow. I know I said that yesterday too, but this time I pinky promise," I replied.

Trying to pivot to a different topic, I asked, "Are you and Kayvon finishing your homework on time and listening to Sogol joon?"

"Yes. We're both done with our homework. When are Tata and Grandpa Mansoor getting here?" Koosha asked.

"They should be there in a couple of hours. Can I speak with Sogol, please?"

"Yeah, sure. Bye Mommy," he said, and handed Sogol the phone before I could finish telling him I loved him.

From the moment Koosha was born, he was his daddy's sidekick. They always enjoyed spending time together in the basement, and on weekends I would often find them there, watching a sci-fi movie and snacking on Red Vine licorice sticks.

Koosha was excellent at imitating expressions and knew how to re-enact Omid's eyebrow twitches and facial expressions to a tee. I could always hear them laughing and making fun of each other in the kitchen on Sunday mornings while cooking breakfast for all of us. Kayvon and I always rated their culinary creations and made requests for our favorite breakfast dishes. I loved the apple and pecan waffles topped with chocolate sauce and whipped cream, while Kayvon preferred the eggs benedict with smoked salmon. It gave me joy watching Koosha and Omid spend quality time together and Koosha was becoming more confident in the kitchen.

Omid enjoyed cooking and experimented by making dishes from recipes around the world. Friends and family were often over on weekends tasting his creations and complimenting him on his culinary skills.

When we didn't have company, sitting around the dinner table as a foursome gave Omid and me the ability to bond more with the boys. Now thinking about our happy times and fond memories as a family was bittersweet.

During the past few months, Omid's illness prevented him from spending time in the kitchen with Koosha. Sensing his father's restriction, Koosha would prepare breakfast and serve it on a tray in the bedroom, where he lay next to Omid watching TV while his father ate.

When Omid was diagnosed with glioblastoma, we decided to keep the illness a secret from the boys. Kavyon had just become a teen, and Koosha was only seven years old. We were certain that Omid would make a full recovery and didn't want the kids to worry unnecessarily about possible negative outcomes. When Omid became tired and unable to spend as much time with them as he had, we explained that Omid's long work hours and sleepless nights were catching up with him. We told them that his doctors wanted him to rest more and not to overexert himself. It had been more challenging to explain why their father had bandages around his head after surgery or starting to lose his hair during chemo treatments, but the story about a skin tag removal on his head and the need to shave Omid's hair to gain access to the area, alleviated the boys' concerns. However, Dr. Stanley's recent discussion about Omid's biopsy results and the need for palliative radiation made it clear that it was time to share the news. The anticipation of that conversation made me nauseated and filled me with anxiety.

"How are the boys?" Omid asked, catching me off guard.

"Oh, I didn't realize you were awake," I replied, smiling.

"You don't have to pretend, Bahar. I know you're exhausted. Why aren't you going home? You need to rest," he replied.

"Don't worry azizam, I'm fine. The boys are doing well. I just got off the phone with Koosha and Sogol. I didn't get a chance to talk to Kayvon. Your parents are going to spend the night at our place. So, I'm going to stay right here with you whether you like it or not," I said, winking at him and glancing around the stale white room.

Omid shook his head in concern. "Thank you, but I need you to take care of yourself. You've done so much for me already. I hate putting everything on you," he declared.

I walked up to his bed and started stroking his cheek. "Will you please stop? You're not putting anything on me. I enjoy taking care of you. Stop saying silly stuff," I said, furrowing my brows.

He chuckled looking at my silly expression. "You're too cute to look mean," he said, grinning at me. "But seriously, it's supposed to be my job to take care of you, not the other way around. I'm tired of being damn sick and in bed all the time. It feels like crap. When will it all end?" he complained. "I promise never to take my health for granted again. I've planned so many trips in my head that I want us to take together."

"That sounds like a plan," I replied, trying to look hopeful. "Just be a little more patient. It'll all be better soon," I lied, especially with the news of the biopsy results weighing heavily on my mind.

Omid looked out the hospital room window. "It looks like such a beautiful sunset. I wish we could go hiking and have a picnic somewhere. It'd be cool to drive up to Santa Barbara for a few days even." I nodded holding onto his clammy hands. "I was thinking since the weather is getting warmer, it would be fun to take the boys boogie boarding after my scars heal. I think the sun and some fresh air would do all of us some good," he continued, with light returning to his eyes.

"Yeah, it's been a while since we went boogie boarding," I replied.

"I know San Diego's beaches are amazing, but if we want to take a family vacation, we can even start looking for flights to Europe and go to the south of Italy or France. I know how much you love Europe and miss your cappuccinos first thing every morning when we go there," he said, smiling at me.

I laughed at his reference to my love of European cappuccinos, which I drank like an addict every single day we were there.

"That sounds like a great idea! Now do me a favor and get better soon, so we can go," I pleaded.

He nodded and grew quiet. After a few minutes of looking out the window, Omid closed his eyes and fell asleep while holding my hand. I loved his energy and zest for life. He had such a positive outlook on everything and always saw the best in everyone. His rosy perspective always led to some heated arguments between us.

One argument I will never forget was when Omid discovered that his business partner secretly withdrew a large sum of money from their shared corporate bank account without telling him about it. I was furious when Omid told me what had happened, and I insisted that he confront Jake about it.

Despite my insistence, Omid refused to bring it up with his partner and even defended him. He explained that Jake was a newlywed with large expenses and was certain the debt would be repaid quickly. I vehemently disagreed with Omid's decision and advised him to treat the partnership as a business first, and then a friendship. Omid didn't listen and argued that Jake would make the same concessions for him if the tables were turned.

Now, many years since the withdrawal, Jake has still not repaid the money. Adding insult to injury, a few weeks ago I found out through the medical practice's accountant that Jake used that money to purchase a car for his wife on her milestone birthday. Given Omid's current condition, I decided not to share Jake's egregious and selfish action.

Once Omid was peacefully asleep, I released his hand and walked to the recliner. I elevated my legs on the footrest and shivered from the cold air streaming in through the ventilator above my head. I had grown accustomed to cold hospital rooms and carried a spare pair of socks with me in my purse. I put on the thick socks and tilted the recliner back, pulling the dreary gray thin blanket up to my chin. Although the lights were dimmed, I still found it impossible to relax. The relentless beeps coming from the nurses' station outside felt like constant hammering in my head. Had I been a nurse, I was certain I would have gone mad listening to those sounds for twelve hours straight.

Adding to the orchestra of sound, Omid's head had tilted to the side, causing him to snore loudly. I smiled, listening to the musical overture emanating from his nostrils. Oh, what memories it brought back. I had been kept awake many nights, listening to his snoring. Whenever I awoke at night, I gave Omid a little nudge to wake him just enough to tilt his body to the side, which helped stop the noise. Tonight, the sound gave me comfort. It confirmed he was still alive and peaceful. What I wouldn't give to keep him snoring next to me every single night for eternity.

I remember the first time I heard Omid snore during my second pregnancy. Our first son, Kayvon, was born five years after we were married, and Koosha came along six years later.

My pregnancy with Koosha had been uneventful until the third trimester. I remember one morning after dropping Kayvon off at kindergarten, I felt a sharp shooting pain and extreme pressure in my lower abdomen. Wobbling toward the women's restroom holding my belly, I squatted on the toilet and watched in horror as bright red blood oozed out of me, igniting a fear of a miscarriage.

I immediately called Omid and told him to meet me at the hospital, and he stayed with me on the phone while I drove myself to the ER just a few blocks away.

They put me into a wheelchair and rushed me into an exam room. Omid arrived shortly thereafter.

"Omid, I think I'm having a miscarriage!" I wailed.

"Don't worry, sweetheart. It's okay. Let the doctor examine you first." Omid did his best to reassure me as I lay in bed. I held his hand tightly and kissed his knuckles, wet from my tears. He stroked my hair to comfort me. My eyes glazed over, and I kept imagining the worst-case scenario.

The on-call doctor propped me up on the exam table and turned on the ultrasound device with a concerned expression on his face. The intake nurse asked me a series of questions, and I tried to answer them as best as I could while not taking my eyes off the monitor.

Omid and I both held our breaths as we waited to see some sign of life. A few moments passed before we heard Koosha's rapid heartbeat through the speaker and saw the fluttering of his beating heart on the monitor.

"Listen to that, Bahar. Do you hear the heartbeat? The baby is fine!" Omid exclaimed. He kissed my face over and over as we both cried from happiness.

The doctor announced with a stoic expression, "Well, Mrs. Salehi, you have a sub-chorionic hemorrhage. But the baby's just fine. I'd like to admit you and run some tests to make sure everything is okay. I'm not certain what caused the hemorrhage and would like to keep an eye on you for the next twenty-four hours before sending you home."

"Yes, that sounds good, Dr. Kizumi," Omid responded. "I'll stay with my wife and keep a close eye on her."

The doctor nodded and scanned Omid's hospital name badge and the scrubs he wore. "I see you're a physician as well," he said. He took out a pad of paper and scribbled on it. "Here is my cell number. Please call me if she experiences any cramping or abdominal discomfort. I advise you to limit any movement for the next twenty-four hours, Mrs. Salehi," Dr. Kizumi insisted.

I nodded. "Yes, doctor. So, there is no danger to the baby?"

"The baby is fine. The bleeding is around a membrane surrounding the embryo and the uterine wall. It happens in about three percent of pregnancies. I'm not very concerned about a miscarriage, but I still want to run some tests."

Omid stayed the night with me at the hospital. It was the first night I heard him snore while sleeping on the recliner under the neon lights in the hospital room. Even though I knew he was uncomfortable, he refused to go home. The onset of his snoring had been triggered by extreme fatigue and the extra weight he accumulated during my second pregnancy. The long work shifts, and our late-night snack binges were starting to catch up to him.

That night was the first of many I would listen to Omid snore in his sleep. He had rested on a reclining chair just like the one I was stretched on tonight and had watched over me just as I watched him this evening. Although I was concerned about a possible miscarriage back then, tonight a grim premonition haunted my thoughts.

I sat on the chair next to Omid's bed and watched the nurses come in and out of the room to check on him. Once the last nurse left the room, I took a medicine bottle out of my purse and fished out a tiny pink oval tablet of Xanax. The only way I would fall asleep and tune out the sounds was by taking the anxiolytic. I lay there for a few minutes after swallowing the tablet and waited for it to kick in. My eyelids slowly began to grow heavy and I fell into a relaxed trance before the small hand of the clock on the wall reached the nine o'clock hour.

Chapter 12

When we married; I was adamant about wanting to strike a balance in becoming a full-time mother as well as a full-time lawyer. I had hoped the California Bar Association would recognize my law degree from Iran and allow me to take the bar exam without requiring additional coursework. However, the U.S. recognizes only a few courses from international law schools, and I needed to get my master's degree in law before taking the bar.

I spoke English well enough for minimal daily conversation, but it took me some years to become fluent. After completing English language courses at the community college, I applied and got accepted for an online master's program. Omid was thrilled to see me pursue my law career and encouraged me to enroll as a full-time student. But I was apprehensive. The fear of letting Omid down by not passing weighed heavily on my mind and the reason I convinced him that I should extend my time in school.

The subject of my career was broached even during our most intimate moments. It was late Sunday morning and Omid and I had just made love. I didn't want to do anything other than snuggle with Omid all day. I put my head on his chest and started to speak softly. "What do you think if I take one class per semester so I can be sure I'm mastering the coursework?"

He wrapped his arms tightly around my body and kissed the top of my head. "But I thought you wanted to start working again. It took you two years to apply, and if you only take one class at a time you won't finish in two years," Omid said, gently tilting my neck up to look at my face.

I smiled shyly and avoided making eye contact. I was too embarrassed to tell him that I was afraid of failure. "You're right, it'll probably take longer to graduate, but I'd rather do it right than take too many classes at once and possibly fail. I'm not familiar with the school system here. I think doing it this way will ease me into it. I'll take more classes once I get the hang of it," I said reassuringly.

He stroked my shoulder with his fingers. "Okay, Sweetie. Whatever you think works best. I don't want you to feel as if I'm pressuring you. I'm just trying to be supportive. I know how much your career means to you."

I kissed his cheek. "It does, and being your wife and spending every minute I am awake with you means so much to me too." I picked up my head from his chest to face Omid. "Hey, I was thinking maybe we could use the time I'm still in school to go traveling more. I know we want to have kids in a few years. So why not use this time to explore places? What do you think?" I asked, wrapping the sheet around my naked body as I sat up excitedly.

He nodded, eyeing my movements. "I'm fine with whatever you decide. I just want you to be happy."

I jumped up on the bed and suddenly pounced on his body like a hungry tiger. Playfully growling, I nuzzled against his throat. "Grrrr. You're what makes me happy," I said, playfully nibbling on his ear.

Taking my playful cue, he growled ferociously and retaliated by flipping me over on my back and holding me down. His eyes glistened as he looked at me with a devilish grin. "So, you're in the mood for a fight, are you?" he asked nibbling on my naked skin and tickling me. I tried to push him away while shrieking and begging for mercy. His breath aroused and tickled me at the same time. It wasn't long before the curves of our bodies molded together as we made love again.

We spent the first five years of our marriage traveling. The plan was for me to graduate before trying to conceive. Instead of taking birth control pills or using condoms, I had convinced Omid to trust my fail proof method of keeping track of my menstrual cycles to avoid a pregnancy. Omid knew the risks with this method but didn't argue against it.

I found out I was pregnant with Kayvon a few weeks after a passion-filled weekend trip to Santa Barbara. It was apparent that I had failed to calculate the days I was ovulating that month. Although the news was unexpected, Omid and I were thrilled at the prospect of becoming new parents.

I managed to take one more class before giving birth to Kavyon. With two courses left to graduate, my commitment to motherhood quickly superseded my commitment to the legal profession, and I stopped taking classes. Omid never pressured me to continue studying after we had Kayvon. I had hoped to finish my masters once Kayvon was old enough to go to school, but plans changed again after I became pregnant with Koosha the year Kavyon was starting kindergarten.

Although I loved spending time with the kids, staying secluded at home with limited interaction with the outside world started to take a toll on my mental health. Seeing my social isolation, Omid encouraged me to take intermittent breaks and befriend other young mothers. Instead of socializing, I used my free time to run errands, do grocery shopping, or occasionally get my hair done. It wasn't until Omid signed us up at the local gym, that I met my close friend, Stella.

With me suffering anxiety and panic attacks and Omid unable to leave the office to help me, we hired a housekeeper. Eventually, I began yoga classes and met up with Stella for lunch and coffee. She was also a new mother and understood my struggles.

Even though my in-laws lived close by, I felt uneasy asking them for help. I thought if his family learned about my struggles, they would see my failure as a mother, and I was worried about being judged. In my culture, depression and anxiety are symptoms within one's control, and I didn't want them to think I was weak and unable to overcome my problems. Omid understood my concerns and never pressured me to ask them for help.

Unfortunately, the extra time off work and the expenses to hire help placed a great deal of financial burden on Omid, and it wasn't until many years later after he got sick that I became aware of the extreme debt we were under.

In retrospect, I wish he had shared more about his work, our finances, and our family. I selfishly thought that the world revolved around me: my stubbornness to ask his parents for help, to seek counseling, to take medication, and to get my law degree.

It was so heartbreaking to watch him suffer, especially when he had done so much to mitigate my suffering. I shook my head to stop the relentless thoughts coming at me like a lost ship in a stormy sea being beaten down by waves of memories from the past.

My phone rang, and I glanced at the screen and saw it was Stella calling.

"Hi Sweetie, how are you doing?" she asked.

"Hi. I'm fine, I guess. You know me. I'm an expert in making myself crazy with endless thoughts. How are you doing?" I replied, feeling frustrated at myself.

"I'm okay. Just calling to check in. What's going on? How's Omid? When is he getting discharged?"

"The doctor should be here any minute to check on him. We'll know more when he gets here."

"That's good." She paused before asking, "What's going on with you? What do you mean you're thinking crazy thoughts?"

I grunted. "I don't know. I keep playing things over and over in my mind wondering how I could've been so stupid. I was so damn blind all these years! To put so much pressure on Omid and not know *anything* about what was going on. If I had known, I would have done something. Maybe if I had, he wouldn't be sick right now!" I hissed angrily.

"What could you have done to keep him from getting cancer? We both know, nobody can *cause* someone to get cancer."

"I know, but I didn't help the situation either. All that backbreaking stress for so long," I said, shaking my head. "I can't bear to watch him suffer like this. It's so unfair. He's spent his life making sick people better. Why can't somebody make *him* better? Where is that good karma when you need it? Huh?"

"I know. I don't understand it either. I wish I had an answer for you," she whispered.

I rose from the chair I had imprinted onto my backside and began pacing the small area at the foot of Omid's bed. The Xanax was no longer in my system from the prior night, and the continuous stimulation to my brain was making my head feel hot and tingly all over.

"Just breathe, Bahar," I heard Omid say. I froze in place and looked up to see he was awake and watching me pace about the room. My eyes filled with tears.

"Stella, I'll call you back," I whispered and hung up the phone.

I walked over to his bed and kissed him. "Good morning. How are you feeling?"

Omid appeared stiff and tried to reposition his body. "I'm okay. Just a little sore from sleeping on this bed. From the sounds of it, I seem to be doing better than you," he said, smiling gently.

I looked away, trying to hide how nervous and upset I was. "What is this I heard about your blaming yourself for my cancer?" he asked in a serious voice.

I fidgeted nervously, biting my lip. "I'm sorry."

"Don't apologize. I get that you're worried, but don't you even think about blaming yourself for my cancer. If stress caused glioblastoma, then half of the world's population would be diagnosed with it right now. Nobody knows why people get cancer. If we did, we would avoid getting it. If you want to make me feel better, you need to stop this crazy talk. You hear me?" he asked with a furrowed brow.

"Yes, I hear you," I replied, nodding and squeezing his hand. "I just hate this so much!" I whined.

He smiled at me lovingly. "You look like you could use a hug," he said and pulled back the white sheet and lifted his arm so I could crawl into the bed with him. Wiping away a tear, I climbed on the bed and nestled my head on his chest. Breathing in his familiar scent, the tight muscles around my neck relaxed.

"I'm sorry if my crazy talk upset you. I just freak out sometimes. I promise to be stronger," I whispered.

His embrace gave me comfort. "You are one of the strongest people I know. Stop berating yourself. You're just tired and need to rest. Just close your eyes and everything will be alright," he said.

The moment I prayed for: to have Omid next to me protecting me for an eternity.

Chapter 13

"Good morning, Dr. Salehi, how are you feeling today?" the nurse asked with a smile as she watched me sit up on the recliner. She placed the breakfast tray on the table and rolled it toward Omid.

"Good morning. I'm fine, thank you," he replied timidly.

"Here is your breakfast," ripping the plastic wrapper covering the utensils. "Would you like me to help you?" she asked.

"No, I got it. Thank you."

Omid looked at the food but didn't make any effort to eat. Not wanting to offer more help, the nurse smiled as she walked toward the door.

With a grateful nod and smile, I whispered, "Thank you."

I moved the tray closer to him but knew better than to offer help. I knew he would scold me if I tried to feed him, so I sat down on the chair next to his bed to give him some space. I pretended to check e-mails on my phone, while secretly noticing his struggle with the spoon while trying to scoop food into his mouth. Omid was a proud man and would starve before asking for help.

Watching his face distorted in agony as he managed to cram the tiny morsels of food that remained on his spoon after the shaky journey from the plate to his mouth, made me want to scream. Instead, I sat and bit my lip. I hated watching him suffer. The man who had helped so many patients recover and regain full independence was now a helpless patient.

After struggling to eat two more small bites of scrambled eggs, he pushed the tray aside and looked up with a furrowed brow.

"Have you eaten anything?" he asked.

I shook my head. "Not yet. I'm not that hungry," I lied.

"Come, sit on the bed and have my breakfast. I'm not that hungry either."

I knew he was lying too. I got up and walked over to the bed. Picking up the tray and placing it on my lap, I placed a spoonful of yellow tasteless scrambled eggs in my mouth and then refilled the spoon to place in Omid's mouth. I was surprised he accepted my offer. We sat in silence for a while, consuming the rest of the meal together. We helped each other get through the meal, him supporting me emotionally and me supporting him physically. It was a silent unspoken compromise between the two of us. Once the tray was empty, I placed it on the table and pushed it aside to make extra room on the bed.

"The doctor will be here soon. I think he'll let you go home today," I said cheerfully.

He nodded but didn't respond. His eyes were empty and expressionless. They no longer had the softness and twinkle I had grown accustomed to. I couldn't read any emotion by staring into them. I wanted to tell him about the biopsy results but couldn't decide whether it was the right time. I couldn't gauge his emotional state and how the news would affect him. I needed to tell the kids about his cancer, and he needed to know why I decided to share the news with them.

I pursed my lips and asked, "How are you feeling?"

He paused a long moment before responding. "I'm okay. Feeling more alert than before."

Relieved to hear that and comforted by him being coherent, I took a deep breath and shared the news.

"Sweetheart, I talked to Dr. Stanley a couple of days ago. It looks like they couldn't get all the cancer with your second surgery. He said you might benefit from another round of radiation."

Omid nodded without any change to his expression. I wasn't sure if he understood the full extent of my words. I purposefully left out the information that the radiation would only be palliative therapy. But being a physician, he must have known what that meant.

After a moment of silence, he leaned forward slightly and asked, "How many more classes do you have to take to graduate?"

I was taken aback by the seemingly irrelevant question. "I think I have two more classes left. After that, I can register for the bar."

He sighed loudly. Watching his face grimace in frustration, I became concerned.

"What is it Omid? What's wrong?"

"Not sure how to say this, but I have to tell you something important. A few years ago we didn't have enough cash flow coming in to cover the mortgage, the office rent, and our monthly premiums for life insurance. I knew we couldn't default on the payment for the rent, so I prioritized and let the life insurance policy lapse. I was planning on reinstating it as soon as our finances got better, but I never got around to it. Then I got diagnosed with this stupid cancer and by then it was too late," he explained, looking down and avoiding my gaze.

I gasped. "Oh wow, I had no idea. I wish I would've known something sooner," I said, trying to hide the panic in my voice. "Why didn't you tell me we were having money problems?" I asked, trying to avoid sounding angry.

"I don't know," Omid said, shrugging his shoulders. "I guess I just didn't want to worry you or look like a failure to you. I thought I had it all under control. When the cash flow began to improve, I got sick. I'm sorry, I just never thought it would come to this."

I didn't know how to respond and started pacing the room in

silence.

Omid spoke again in a gentle voice. "You need to finish your masters so you can get your law license. I'm useless in my condition and God knows how long I have left. I need to make sure you have a source of income for you and the kids," his voice cracking. A trickle of tears streamed down the corners of his eyes as his lips quivered.

My body stiffened, and I felt the oxygen get sucked out of my lungs. I tried to keep my composure.

"Hey, come on now. I don't want to hear this nonsense about you not being here. You're going to be fine. Just focus on getting better, and I'll take care of everything else. You hear me?" I asked with a smile, gently wiping his tears with my thumbs and kissing his lips.

He nodded and looked at me with red tear-filled swollen eyes. It broke my heart to watch him cry. "I promise you I will take those two last classes and get it over with. No more excuses this time. Please don't make yourself upset over this. I got this!" I said, making a fist and aiming to punch the pillow next to his head. Omid tilted his head, appearing to taunt me with an exaggerated fearful expression on his face. Miscalculating my angle, my knuckles slammed the bed's backboard, creating a loud thump and making me wince from the pain. I cursed under my breath as I massaged my knuckles.

Omid took my bruised hand and started kissing my knuckles. He chortled and said, "Why don't you just focus on your studies for now and leave the boxing to the experts?"

I stuck out my tongue at him in reproach and we laughed heartily.

Truthfully, I didn't know the first thing about taking care of our finances. Since we arrived in the U.S., Omid managed everything and took care of our major household expenses. I didn't even know about the purchase and delinquency in payments on the life insurance policy until today.

Even though I had tried to console him, I was shivering with fear.

Chapter 14

$\mathcal{D}$r. Stanley told us Omid could be discharged from the hospital after he convinced him to do another round of radiation in two weeks.

We thanked the doctor and he shook our hands before leaving. Omid was silent. He slept during the car ride home while I drove rehearsing how to break the news to the kids. When we turned into the driveway, Koosha and Kayvon were standing by the door waiting for us.

Koosha ran quickly over to Omid's side and opened the door, startling him awake. "Hi, Baba! Welcome home!"

Omid appeared frazzled at first but smiled at Koosha. I walked over and hugged Kayvon. At fifteen years old, he was a carbon copy of his father in body stature and facial features. He was already half an inch taller than me, and the pediatrician was certain Kayvon would grow to be at least six feet tall by the time he finished puberty. Despite his age and height, he would always remain my baby. I dreaded the thought of breaking his heart with the news of his father's condition.

"Hi, Mom. How are you guys?" he asked as he stepped back to avoid my fussing over him.

"We're good, Sweetheart. I missed you guys so much!"

Seeing Omid still seated in the car, I made my way to lend him a hand to step out. Kayvon noticed and quickly walked over, offering his shoulder to his dad to lean on as they walked toward the house.

Koosha watched them walk past him and looked over at me with a puzzled expression. I ruffled his hair and squeezed his body against mine as we headed inside the house.

"What's wrong with Baba? Why is he walking funny?"

"Oh, he's tired and groggy from the medicine they gave him at the hospital. He just needs to rest a little, that's all," I reassured him.

He nodded, but his eyes were narrowed, and he looked unconvinced. I couldn't meet his gaze for fear of revealing the truth, so I focused on the ground as we continued inside.

"Do you want to rest in there?" Kayvon asked Omid, pointing to the living room.

Before Omid could answer, I interjected. "Why don't we have Baba relax in our bedroom. He's tired from the drive home and could use a nap."

Omid nodded, and Kayvon helped him to our bedroom. By the time he sat on the bed, Omid was breathing heavily from fatigue. I glanced at both boys staring at their father, with the same concerned expression on their faces.

Wanting to prevent them from further anxiety, I asked them to go to the kitchen. "Do you think you can make me some tea? Home-brewed, unlike the hospital's awful tea bags. I'll change and join you in the kitchen in a minute," I said, with a reassuring smile.

After a brief hesitation, Kayvon nodded and tapped Koosha on the arm, signaling him to accompany him to the kitchen. I helped Omid change into his sweats and fluffed the pillows as he lay back on the bed. Before I could step away, he tightened his grip on my arm and said, "I'm sorry you have to do this alone. I wish you didn't have to."

"Don't worry. Everything will be fine," I replied with tears filling my eyes. I took his hand and kissed it before releasing it.

I walked into our bathroom to freshen up. I looked horrendous with dark circles around my eyes and had tussled, frizzy hair that badly needed a wash. I ran my hand through my hair with some water and patted it down before wrapping the strands into a tight ponytail. Changing into my sweatpants, I opened my makeup drawer and applied some concealer and blush to my face. When I stepped out of the bathroom five minutes later, Omid was sound asleep.

I left the door open, just a sliver, and went to the kitchen where I found the kids sitting next to each other on the stools in front of the granite kitchen island. They were both looking at their phones and not speaking to each other. They usually had technology privileges on the weekends and got on their phones after breakfast. It was 10:00 a.m. on Saturday, and they were still wearing their pajamas.

"When did Tata and Grandpa Mansoor leave?" I asked as I walked in.

"A few minutes ago. Tata forgot Grandpa Mansoor's medicines at their house. She asked me to text her when you got here," Kayvon answered, while occupied on his phone. I hated it when they played on their phones while speaking to me but didn't scold them today.

"Did you text her?"

He nodded, still looking down on his gadget. "Yes, she knows you and Baba are back."

I opened the freezer door and pulled out two pints of ice cream. I didn't care if it was so early in the morning. Koosha loved Pralines and Cream, and Kayvon was a fan of Rocky Road. They looked surprised and gave each other a puzzled glance. I had never offered them ice cream this early in the morning.

Ignoring their reactions, I took out three small bowls from the cabinet, scooped out two large helpings of each flavor into each bowl, and slid the bowls toward them, then pulled out a chair and took a seat. I picked up my bowl and stuffed my mouth with a large scoop of the Rocky Road ice cream, the sudden brain freeze making me wince.

"Whoa, what's going on, Mom? I thought you wanted tea. Since when do you eat ice cream in the morning?" Kayvon asked, looking puzzled.

"Yeah, why are you acting so funny?" Koosha chimed in.

I waited for the brain freeze to resolve. I placed the spoon on the counter and took a deep breath before speaking. "Your Baba is sick. He's been sick for a while now, and the doctor isn't sure he'll get better." As I spoke, it felt like a clip from a silent movie showing a person mouthing words, and the subsequent expressions of the recipients transform from calm to dismay. Kayvon and Koosha stopped eating their ice cream and stared at me, blinking. I sat silently waiting for them to digest the news.

"What do you mean he's sick?" Kayvon finally asked. "What's wrong with him?"

"Well, he was diagnosed a couple of years ago with a brain tumor called glioblastoma. It's a rare, aggressive type of brain cancer. He's had two surgeries and other treatments to remove the tumor, but the doctors can't seem to get rid of it. We didn't want to tell you guys earlier, so you wouldn't worry, but he seems to be getting worse, and we thought it was time to tell you."

As I finished, I reached out to take hold of Koosha's hand, but he pulled away from me. "So, Baba is very sick?" he asked with tears in his eyes. "Is he going to die?"

I started to reply, but Kayvon interrupted. "Wait, you mean to tell me he's been sick for *two* years and you're telling us about this *now?* What the hell is wrong with you guys? Why would you keep this from us for so long?" he asked, glaring at me with rage in his eyes.

I squinted my nose trying to search for the right words to justify our decision. Failing to find a better explanation, I re-iterated, "Sweetie, we didn't want you guys to worry over nothing if he got better. We didn't mean to make you upset."

Kayvon's right hand made a tight fist, and the blood drained from his knuckles. He was looking down and breathing loudly. He appeared livid and shaking his head. "This is crap, Mom! All these months, you kept it from us. You knew I was mad at Baba because he wasn't spending time with me, and you didn't say anything. Why didn't you tell me he was sick?! Why couldn't you just be honest with me? I was so mean to him and he didn't deserve any of it!" he said, slamming his fist on the wooden table, causing the spoons in the bowls to jiggle.

"Please calm down, Kayvon. You're right. Maybe we *should* have told you guys sooner. I'm sorry. Please forgive me," I said, my voice shaking as I tried to control my dam of emotions from bursting. "I know you're shocked and angry. You have every right to be."

Kayvon sat back and folded his arm across his chest, his face twisted in anger. Koosha didn't speak but looked at me with a bewildered expression. After a while, Kayvon got up and dumped his bowl of untouched melted ice cream into the sink, making a loud clanking sound. "I'm going to my room. I want to be left alone!" he said, glaring at me and storming out of the kitchen.

I stood from my chair and approached Koosha. His lips were trembling while he tried to keep his composure. He pushed back his chair and threw himself into my arms, wailing uncontrollably.

I held Koosha tightly as I rocked him back and forth in rhythmic motion as I used to do when he was little. His body trembled in my arms as he cried, burying his face in my shirt. He stood there, crying for a long time before stopping to catch his breath.

"That's right, Lovebug. Let it all out. Mommy's here and I'm not going anywhere," I said, stroking his soft hair.

He continued whimpering like a wounded coyote. "I'm scared, Mommy. I don't want Baba to die. Why can't they just give him medicine like you give me when I'm sick and make him better?"

"It's not that simple, Sweetie. They've tried giving him every medicine they could think of, but they haven't worked. Nobody is giving up. We'll keep trying new things and keep praying for Baba to get better, okay?" I crouched down to his eye level and continued. "This cancer is stubborn and isn't going away without a fight, but Baba is fighting with all his strength. And we must do everything in our power to keep his spirits up. If I remember correctly, you have some funny jokes that would bring a smile to his face. What do you say we go keep him company and you can make him laugh? I bet he'd like that."

Koosha wiped his nose with the back of his hand and quietly nodded in agreement.

"Great. Why don't you go wash your face while I warm up some food for Baba? Then we'll go visit him," I offered, as Koosha hurriedly left the room.

Kayvon spent most of the day in his room and didn't come out despite my pleas to join us for lunch and dinner. Koosha's mood appeared to improve as he spent time with Omid, telling jokes, and watching his dad struggle to keep a straight face.

"I love you, Baba," Koosha remarked, snuggling against Omid's chest while smiling.

"I love you too, my little comedian," Omid said encouragingly.

We let Omid rest after dinner and put on a movie in the living room. Kayvon finally came out of his room a little after 9:00 p.m. He went to the kitchen and found the sandwich I had left for him on the kitchen counter, then casually walked over to the couch and plopped next to me without saying a word. The three of us stared at the television screen without talking. I could see Kayvon's red puffy red eyes, and it broke my heart to know he had been crying alone. Unlike Koosha, Kayvon never liked sharing his feelings, always exhibiting a tough exterior.

"I'm sorry," I whispered in his ear while he ate. His body stiffened for a moment before relaxing his shoulders. I stretched my arm across the top edge of the couch and drew his torso closer to me as he leaned back. He didn't resist my gesture.

Once the movie ended, I turned off the television and yawned. It was close to midnight, and it had been a long and emotional day for all of us. "Why don't we get some sleep?"

"Mommy, is it okay if I sleep with you guys tonight? I don't want to be alone," Koosha asked in a soft voice.

I thought about his suggestion for a few seconds before responding. "You know, that sounds like a good idea. If you and Kayvon want, we can pull out the sofa bed in our room, and you guys can sleep there with us. I am sure Baba will love having you in the room. It will be like a family slumber party," I said cheerfully.

Kayvon shrugged before answering. "Yeah, sure."

"Yay!" Koosha said, jumping off the couch to run to his room and grab his stuffed bear.

"Is Baba asleep?" Kayvon asked when we were alone.

"Yes, I gave him a sleeping pill a while ago to help him fall asleep. Koosha spent some time with him earlier. Maybe tomorrow you and Baba can have some alone time."

Kayvon turned to face me. "He can't go out, can he?"

"He can't drive. If you want, I can go pick up something from Starbucks, and you guys can hang out in the backyard."

"Yeah, okay," Kayvon replied nonchalantly.

"Great. Now come and help me pull out the sofa bed. Your old mom is gonna need to put your strong arms to work."

He nodded and stood. "Are you feeling better?" I asked, checking on him.

He shrugged. "I don't know. I just wish I knew sooner. It just doesn't feel fair."

I gazed into his eyes while speaking. "I'm sorry again for breaking the news to you this way. I know you're angry because we kept it from you. It was wrong of me to do that. Hopefully, you can forgive me one day."

Kayvon stayed silent for a few moments, looking away and

appearing deep in thought. "Yeah, alright," he finally said. Turning to walk toward the bedroom, he continued, "I looked up glioblastoma on the internet. There was a lot of information on it. Did Baba already have surgery and chemotherapy?"

I sighed. "Yes, they've tried it all. Remember when I told you Baba was having a mole removed and then had to have follow-up surgery to get the skin fixed?"

He nodded, recalling our conversation. "Well, those surgeries were to get rid of the tumor. He never had a mole. He lost his hair because of the chemo they gave him. He also had radiation. Now the doctor thinks he should have a second round of radiation."

"Oh, wow! And he's been sick for two years now?"

We reached the door to the bedroom, and I lowered my voice to avoid waking Omid. "Yes, it's been about two years. He's been using all his strength to beat this. Since you read up on glioblastoma, you know that most people don't get to live past a few months."

He nodded. "Right. That's a good sign, I guess. But the whole thing sucks."

We walked slowly and quietly into the bedroom. Kayvon helped me pull out the mattress inside the sofa bed. Then he walked over to where Omid was sleeping. Kayvon stared at his father, laying on the bed motionless and snoring. I could see the frown on Kayvon's face.

"Go ahead. Sit next to him for a few minutes. You won't wake him," I suggested prodding Kayvon to get closer.

He appeared reluctant and didn't move. Then he suddenly turned away and started walking toward the door. "No, that's okay. I think I want to sleep in my room tonight. Koosha can sleep here with you. Good night."

Before I could say anything, Kayvon had left the room and disappeared. He was trying to process so much all at once. I decided to give him some space.

Koosha came through the door a few minutes later with his pillow and stuffed bear in hand. He was wearing his favorite blue Superman pajamas. He rubbed his eyes and yawned as he walked through the door. "Hey, where is Kayvon? Why is he taking so long?"

I motioned for him to join me on the sofa bed. "He said he wanted to sleep in his bed tonight." Koosha started to frown. "But don't worry, you and I can sleep here together," I said, cuddling him. I started tickling his sides as soon as my arms were wrapped around him, and it set him squealing in laughter.

He squirmed around, trying to break free, and as soon as his little fingers found my body, he sent me shrieking and begging for mercy. We laughed until tears were rolling down our faces, and our heads flopped on the pillow, out of breath. Omid never even stirred from all the raucousness.

"I've missed you, Mommy."

"I've missed you too, Lovebug. I'm sorry I haven't been around much lately." I kissed his face and caressed his red cheeks. He had beads of sweat crystals on his temple. "Mommy loves you so much."

"I love you too," he said, with his head plopped on the cool pillow, smiling sweetly. "Can you tell me a bedtime story?"

With my head on the pillow next to his, I began with his favorite story about a boy detective and his loyal dog who were searching for clues to catch a thief. Already past midnight, Koosha's eyes shut before the story's end.

I slowly got out of bed and walked to Kayvon's bedroom to check on him. He was fast asleep. Tiptoeing into the room, I quietly draped the bedsheet on him and switched off the night light. Then I sat on his bed, just staring at his limp form and listening to his rhythmic breaths while he slept.

I grieved for my boy's broken heart. I was irate at God for inflicting so much pain and suffering on my family. Peering out the window, I cursed under my breath.

Chapter 15

Managing to sleep only a few hours, my eyes sprang wide open just before dawn. The house was eerily quiet, and Omid and Koosha were still fast asleep. I carefully got up and went into the kitchen, making sure not to wake anyone.

I had no desire to stay in solitude with my thoughts, for if I did, I would surely drown in them. Pouring some water into the kettle, I turned it on to brew tea, then opened the fridge. I found some bread, butter, and jam, and placed it all on the counter. Omid needed to eat something before taking his medicine.

I opened the containers and checked to make sure I was giving Omid the right number of pills from each one. He had prescriptions to help with his blood pressure, seizures, depression, and pain. I also included vitamins and supplements in hopes of subduing the tumor, based on an article I had read. Omid struggled to swallow his pills. Stella had scolded me about forcing him to take twenty pills a day; but I had not relented.

I poured a glass of orange juice, placed a piece of buttered toast on a small plate, grabbed the medicine bottles, and carried everything to the bedroom on a tray. The room was dark and musty when I entered. I walked over and pulled back the drapes to let some light in. I had delayed giving Omid his morning medicine to avoid waking Koosha, but it was getting late.

Omid flinched when the light hit his face. I sat next to him on the bed and placed the tray on my lap, waiting for him to open his eyes. "Good morning, Sleepyhead. How are you feeling?" I asked in a whisper.

He slowly opened one eye. "Hi. I'm doing okay," he replied, sounding raspy.

I placed the tray on the table and propped up the pillow to help him sit up. The speech therapist had instructed me to do this before giving him any food to avoid aspiration. "Are you hungry?"

He shook his head. "No, just a bit thirsty. Why are you whispering?"

I motioned in the direction of the sofa bed where Koosha was still sleeping. Omid turned his head and smiled.

He looked tired despite having slept over twelve hours. His face was puffy, and the dark circles under his eyes appeared to have found a permanent home. The thin bristles sprouting on his head appeared to be resurrecting themselves after the last failing battle with chemotherapy. He looked nothing like the Omid I knew before his diagnosis.

His lips parted slowly to accept the straw I offered him in the glass of orange juice. I retracted the straw as soon as I saw he had stopped swallowing. "You need to eat something before I give you your medicine. How about some toast?"

He shook his head. "I'm not hungry."

Despite his objection, I brought the toast to his lips, and he took a small bite without resisting. I watched him chew slowly and deliberately as though he was working through a difficult task. After reluctantly accepting a few more bites, I offered the orange juice along with each tablet I placed on his tongue. He made a concerted effort to swallow the tablets with each sip but had a difficult time with it. Small pools of orange juice started seeping from the corners of his mouth after each sip and swallow routine.

"These pills are so huge. I wouldn't even be able to swallow them," I said reassuringly, seeing the frown on his face as I dabbed his chin and mouth with a napkin. "I'll go to the pharmacy today and pick up the liquid formulations the doctor called in. I also found some liquid vitamins I'll pick up for you."

Omid didn't reply. Watching him gag and choke on the large vitamin pill a couple of times, I finally nabbed the large capsule from the back of his throat and tossed it in the trash can. He had suffered enough.

"Okay, you're done. Do you want to use the bathroom and wash up?"

"Yeah, sure. What time is it?"

"It's around ten. Let me help you clean up and get dressed. Then I'll wake up the boys."

He nodded, and we headed to the bathroom. I tried to help him brush his teeth and change out of his pajamas. He appeared tired and winded by the time we walked back to the bed, and the moment I had Omid settled, I heard Koosha rustling on the sofa bed. He sat up, rubbed his eyes, and stared at us as if trying to recall why he was there.

"Good morning, Lovebug!" I exclaimed cheerfully. "Did you sleep well?"

"Good morning," he replied, looking at me. Then he turned to Omid grinning, and said, "Hi, Baba!"

"Hi, my little man," Omid replied.

I tapped the bed motioning for him to come and join us. Omid sat up and I propped him up against the pillow so Koosha could snuggle against him. They looked so happy.

"Why don't you two relax here and watch TV while I go make breakfast for you and Kayvon?" I offered. Koosha took the remote and smiled.

"Can we watch the 'Wild Kratts' episode where they show those cool eagles? Please, Baba?" Koosha asked excitedly, batting his eyelashes.

Omid smiled and replied, "Sure, buddy. We can watch whatever you want."

"Just don't put the volume on very high, Koosha," I said and turned to Omid. "Do you need anything before I go?"

He smiled. "Just a kiss."

I felt my cheeks get red, and Koosha stopped fiddling with the remote to stare at us. I leaned in and softly kissed his lips.

"Thank you. For everything," he said after we kissed. I turned my face to avoid alerting him to the pool of tears welling up in my eyes. After picking up the breakfast tray, I pivoted and left the room.

I found Kayvon in the kitchen, still in his pajamas, scavenging for something to eat. Setting the tray on the counter, I quickly wiped away the tears with the back of my hand before he spotted me. "Good morning!"

"Hi, Mom," he replied sullenly.

"What do you feel like eating for breakfast?"

He shrugged. "Anything. I don't care."

How about I make some eggs for you guys? Koosha is in the room with Baba, watching TV. You want to peek in and say good morning to them while I make breakfast?"

Kayvon closed the cabinet door and turned. His eyes looked empty and sullen. "I'm gonna go brush my teeth first. I'll go see them after we eat."

He walked out of the kitchen and headed back to his room. I pulled out a pan and cracked a few eggs. It was Sunday morning, and I was doing my best to make things feel normal for the boys, but it was challenging with Kayvon.

Koosha walked into the kitchen as I was plating the eggs announcing that Omid had fallen asleep while watching TV.

"Let's let Baba rest while the three of us eat. We'll check on him later," I offered.

After we finished our breakfast, I asked, "So, what do you guys feel like doing today?" They both shrugged.

"Okay, since I hear no suggestions, how about this plan then? I was thinking maybe Kayvon can spend some time with Baba in the backyard while Koosha and I have some mommy and me time for a couple of hours." Speaking directly to Kayvon, I added, "I can go to Starbucks and get you guys something if you'd like."

Koosha's eyes lit up with excitement. "Sure, that sounds good, Mommy."

Kayvon sneered at Koosha. "You're too young to drink coffee, dork. Mom was talking about me and Baba." Then he turned to talk to me with a terse edge to his voice. "Can Baba even sit on the chair in the backyard? He had a hard time walking from the car to the house yesterday."

"He can't walk like he used to, but once you help him get to the backyard, he won't have any problem sitting on the chair for a while."

Kayvon didn't answer.

"Are you doing okay, Sweetheart? You know I don't want to force you to do anything you don't want," I said, attempting to get him to open up.

"Yeah. I just don't know how to take care of Baba. I mean what if something happens to him and he falls off the chair or something? I think I'm just gonna go and say hi to him in the room. We can do the backyard thing another day."

"Sure. Anything you like. Do you want to hang out with one of your friends later?"

"Yeah. I was thinking of hanging out with Jordan. He asked me to go swimming a few days ago, but Sogol wouldn't let me because you guys weren't home."

"Oh, okay. Is Jordan's little brother home too? Maybe Koosha could join you."

He shrugged. "I don't know. I'll have to check."

"Okay, why don't you go say hi to your dad, and we can figure it out after. Koosha, you want to go swimming with Michael? "

"Yes!" he said, excitedly.

"Alright then, that sounds like a plan. You run up to your room and change out of your pajamas, while Kayvon checks on Baba."

Koosha ran upstairs, squealing with joy. Kayvon hesitated a little before heading to the bedroom. "Would you like me to go with you?" I offered.

He nodded.

When we walked in, the television was still on, and Omid's eyes were closed. Kayvon approached Omid and slowly tapped him on the shoulder to wake him.

"Hi, Baba," Kayvon said and sat on the chair I had placed next to the bed. Omid opened his eyes and feigned a smile as soon as he saw Kayvon. He tried to lift his arm to touch Kayvon, but it plopped back on the bed before it was able to reach him. Kayvon flinched as he observed his dad's failed attempt.

"Good morning, Kayvon joon. So good to see you. How are you?"

Kayvon fidgeted a little before he answered. "I'm good. How are you?" he asked, with hesitation in his voice.

"I'm better now that you're here," Omid offered. "Your mom said you were pretty upset yesterday. I'm sorry I didn't tell you I was sick."

Kayvon stayed silent and sat there with pursed lips. I chimed in, "The boys just needed time to process the news, that's all. Kayvon is just worried about you. Isn't that right?" I asked Kayvon, trying to encourage him to speak.

Kayvon's eyes started to tear up. "Yeah, I'm sorry you're sick. Also, sorry for being such a jerk to you before," he said, choking back the tears and making a fist.

Omid looked at him with a puzzled expression. "What are you talking about? You just wanted to hang out with your old man. You were never a jerk."

"Yeah, well, I didn't know what was going on with you," he said, shrugging his shoulders.

"Sorry, buddy. We didn't mean to upset you," Omid responded apologetically. "But I'm happy you're here. I've missed you a lot."

Before Omid could finish his sentence, Kayvon threw himself on his father's chest and started weeping.

Omid stayed silent and let Kayvon shed his tears. I stood there watching the two of them with tears streaming down my face, unable to move. I hated seeing my family in pain. After a few minutes, Kayvon sat up and wiped his face with the back of his sleeve.

Once they started talking quietly, I left the room. I headed to the kitchen to find Koosha. He was still upstairs, and judging by how long he had been gone, I guessed he had gotten distracted playing with his Hot Wheels car collection. I didn't call him but sat down in the chair in front of the table filled with piles of unopened envelopes. I had so much to do and wasn't sure where to begin. My eyes were still tired from the lack of sleep.

I began opening one envelope after another, making separate piles in front of me. I then turned on the computer to check our bank balance and paid the utility and mortgage bills. Omid had simplified this process a couple of years ago and taught me to click on the tabs and type the amount due for each debt to avoid mailing in checks manually. Based on the balance in the account, it appeared as though this month's shareholder money from the medical practice had been remitted. I was uncertain how the money was being calculated or the terms behind that agreement, but grateful that it would be enough to cover our expenses this month.

After finishing with the payments, I logged on to my school site to check on my class requirements. I was grateful for the ability to enroll in the courses online. I wanted to finish this program and resume working.

I had just finished enrolling in my last two courses when the phone rang.

"Hello, may I speak to Mrs. Salehi, please?" the voice inquired.

"Yes, this is she."

"Hello, Mrs. Salehi, this is Candace from Dr. Lee's office. I've left several messages on your voicemail. I'm calling to confirm your mammogram appointment on Friday at 3:00 p.m."

"Oh, yes, I'm sorry. I haven't had time to listen to my messages. You said I have an appointment this Friday?" I asked, opening the calendar on my phone. I had completely forgotten about it. I was due for a mammogram six months ago. Missing my last appointment, I postponed it to this upcoming week.

I hesitated before asking, "Is there any way to reschedule the appointment?"

"Well, I can push your appointment back by two weeks, but Dr. Lee needs you to come in if you want to stay on her patient panel. Given your family history, she advises not to postpone this mammogram appointment," Candace replied.

"Yes, she's right. I'll be there. Thank you for calling." I put an alarm next to my new appointment, so I would receive a reminder the night before and hung up.

My calendar was filled with so many appointments for follow-ups related to Omid. This was the only appointment related to me.

Feeling overwhelmed, I picked up the phone and called my mom in Iran. She had been trying to reach me for the past few days, but I wanted to wait to speak with her after Omid was discharged. I had hoped to share some good news, but sadly, that would not be the case.

"Hi, Maman. It's me, Bahar," I said as soon as I heard her voice. She squealed on the other end, sounding excited that I called. I knew she had been worried about us and wanted to know how Omid was doing.

It took me a good thirty minutes to recount everything that had happened in the past few days. Between her words of encouragement and despair, I could tell she was just as scared as I was. I heard the quiver in her voice as she told me to be strong and that all would be okay. She was a strong woman. It had been some years since she battled with breast cancer and had beat it into remission. My mom's success at beating cancer was the reason I held out so much hope for Omid's prognosis, but the odds of beating glioblastoma are so rare that I was being naïve in thinking that all along.

"Mom, I told the kids about Omid last night. They were shocked at first and Kayvon became angry. They're doing better today. Omid needs radiation again, and I just signed up for my last two courses. Everything is just happening all at once!"

"I am sorry, Sweetheart. I can't even fathom how difficult this must be for you. Is Sogol still helping you?"

"Yes, Sogol has been great, but having her here is not the same as having family around. I know Omid's family is here, but they're also having a hard time dealing with all of this. Not to mention, Mansoor had eye surgery a few weeks ago. I just wish you guys could come and stay with us," I said with a soft childish sounding whimper.

She exhaled loudly. "My goodness, his poor parents. This must be so awful for them too," she said sullenly. "I'll give them a call and check on them afterward. In the meantime, I'll talk to your dad and see when we can visit. I think you can use our help."

"Oh God, that would be great! It would be such a relief to have you and Baba here," I said cheerfully.

"Now that your dad doesn't work, I'm sure we can arrange to come and stay for a while longer. I don't want you to worry. Everything will work out. You'll see," she said with confidence.

"I hope so, Maman. I feel so lost right now," I answered with a shaky voice.

I hung up before breaking down and sobbing uncontrollably. My body started shaking, and I dropped to the floor in a fetal position, hugging myself tightly. It was hard to catch my breath. I just wanted to curl up and disappear. I missed conversations with my parents about upbeat topics like weddings, birthdays, and new additions to the family. For the past two years, our exchanges only revolved around Omid's health.

When I heard Koosha coming down the staircase, I picked myself up off the kitchen floor and went to the sink to wash my face with cold water. Drying my face quickly with a dish towel, I reminded myself not to fall apart.

"Well, hello there, my little man. What took you so long?" I asked Koosha, attempting to sound chirpy.

He smiled and shrugged, holding a Hot Wheels car in his hand. "I'm hungry. Are we still going swimming?"

"Kayvon is still in the room with Baba, and I was taking care of some things while waiting for you to come down. Let's go in the room and see what they're up to."

We knocked before entering the room. Kayvon was sitting on the chair talking, and Omid's eyes were struggling to stay open. Kayvon smiled when he saw us approaching.

"Hey, guys. How's it going?" I asked with an upbeat voice.

Omid shifted his gaze and replied, "We are good! Kayvon has been updating me on what he's been up to."

I beamed at Kayvon. I was happy he spent some time alone with Omid. "Are you guys getting hungry? In the mood for some pizza?"

"Yes!" Koosha replied excitedly.

"Do you guys still want to go swimming?"

Kayvon shrugged. "I'm fine either way."

"How about I order pizza and we have lunch together? After that, you guys can go swimming for a couple of hours while Baba naps. We can all hang out again tonight after you get back."

"Sounds good," Kayvon replied, appearing content with the compromise. I detected a more upbeat mood in Kayvon compared to how he had sounded earlier in the day.

I ordered a large pizza, and we all ate it in the bedroom while sitting on the bed with paper plates in hand. I cuddled next to Omid and bit into the slice before offering him a bite to avoid making it look like he needed assistance. I could tell Omid was getting tired by the slur in his speech and his heavy lids. After lunch, the kids changed into their swimsuits and went swimming. I was grateful for my needed quiet time with Omid.

When I heard the door close, I climbed into the bed and snuggled next to him. "How are you doing, my love?" I asked, kissing him gently.

He nodded but didn't reply.

"It looked like you had a good time with Kayvon and Koosha today."

"Yes, it was nice," he replied as his eyes started to shut. Within seconds his breathing became heavy, and he started snoring. He had been awake for only five hours and already appeared exhausted. All thanks to that vile, vicious cancer eating away at his brain cells, every day expanding its stake and stealing more of Omid from us. I would give anything to duel with that pariah and prevent it from hurting Omid and the rest of my family.

Chapter 16

The kids spent the days going about their normal routines. Having them know about Omid's illness alleviated some of my stress, and I was happy there were no more secrets between us. Kayvon was still guarded with his feelings, and Koosha opted to sleep in our room every night, fearful of how much time he had left with his father. Both boys spent a few minutes with Omid in the morning before leaving for school, and I tried to schedule his naps in a way that allowed him to be awake when the boys returned home. Taraneh and Mansoor visited almost every day and devoted a lot of time engaging with Omid and the boys. Navid was also visiting more often on the weekends to take Kavyon and Koosha for ice cream or play basketball with them.

On Fridays, I usually met up with Stella at the gym in hopes of sweating out the anxiety from my body. I vehemently guarded these Friday morning workouts. The two hours of "me time" gave me the strength to continue my full-time responsibilities as a wife and nurse to Omid, mother to the boys, daughter to my parents, homemaker, keeper of finances, and silent partner of the medical practice.

One Friday after our workout, Stella and I decided to grab some coffee to chat. We picked up our drinks from the counter and found a place to sit. "You look exhausted, hon. Are you holding up okay?"

I sighed. "I'm doing my best to keep it together. It feels as if there's not enough time to get everything done, and I'm always behind."

"I can't even imagine. Is there anything I can do to help?"

I smiled warmly at her and shook my head. "No, you've done so much for me already. Just having these weekly workouts with you is great."

"They've been great for me too. Seriously, please promise me you'll ask if you need anything. I'm happy to help however I can," she said, leaning in to squeeze my hand lovingly.

I nodded. "I will. I promise. Love you, my friend."

"Love you too," she replied.

"By the way, what time is it?" I asked, suddenly looking around to find my phone.

Stella clicked on her phone to check the time. "It's almost noon."

"Shit, I almost forgot! I have my mammogram appointment in a couple of hours. I have to go home and get ready."

"Oh, that's right. It's today. Do you want me to go with you?"

"No, I'll be fine. Sorry, I gotta run. Can I call you a little later?" I asked as I stood to leave.

"Sure thing. Good luck. Let me know how it goes."

As I walked into the house, I heard the television in the living room and saw Omid sitting next to Taraneh watching *The Price is Right*. I was happy she had convinced him to get out of bed. Omid had been resisting my pleas to leave the bedroom for the past few days.

I kissed them both hello and kept them company for a bit. After a few minutes, I stood to leave, amused at Taraneh's enthusiasm in guessing the prices of the merchandise the contestants were bidding on.

I closed the bedroom door behind me, drowning out the excitement. The room had a semblance of normalcy without Omid lying on the bed half asleep in the middle of the day. I turned on the shower jets, and with my eyes closed, started humming a soft melody while visualizing the hot water rinsing away the sadness and ugliness of our lives down the drain.

After getting dressed quickly in hopes of being on time, I arrived at my appointment with five minutes to spare. The doctor's waiting room was full of patients. Seeing all the expectant mothers accompanied by their husbands made me smile. It hadn't been that long ago when Omid and I were expecting our first child. Although I loved my children, the pregnancies were unbearable. Nausea and sensitivity to smell had transformed me into a pressing wife. I remember asking Omid to sleep in another room because the natural scent of his skin would give me dry heaves. My relentless food cravings forced Omid to leave the house at all odd hours of the night to buy items to satisfy my whims. He never complained and was always ready to appease me even after coming home tired from a long work shift.

"Bahar Salehi?" the mammographer bellowed out. Her voice took me out of my trance.

"Yes, that's me," I replied as I stood.

Ever since my mom had been diagnosed with breast cancer, I had been getting a mammogram every year. This was the first time I had postponed it for six months.

I knew the routine by heart. I took off my top, wiped any deodorant residue off, and put on a crisp light blue paper gown with the front open. The mammographer knocked, and once I consented, she walked in and greeted me.

"Good afternoon, Mrs. Salehi. Nice to see you again." The mammographer and I got to know each other a bit more every time I came in for my annual mammograms. The last time we spoke, Omid was six months into his diagnosis and getting chemotherapy.

"How are you doing?" she asked.

"Hi Maribel," I replied with a sheepish smile. "I'm doing okay, I guess. But, I'm not gonna lie; it's been some tough few months lately."

She turned to look at me with raised eyebrows. "Oh no! Is everything alright?"

I shook my head. "Not really. My husband just got the results of his biopsy after his last surgery. It looks like the cancer cells are still there."

"Oh my gosh. I'm so sorry to hear that. That's awful news!" she replied, with her mouth wide open.

"Yeah, it's been tough for all of us. We finally told the boys about their dad."

"I see. How did they take the news?"

"They were shocked at first, of course, but they keep to themselves a lot. It's hard to know what's going on in their head."

"Poor things," she replied, shaking her head. "This must be so terrifying for them."

"Yeah, well it's been tough for everyone. I didn't want to burden you with my news," I said apologetically.

"No, of course. I'm just sorry to hear the news. I'll keep praying for your husband."

"Thank you. That's sweet of you," I said softly.

She walked over to help me position my body correctly for the scan. I inhaled and waited for the click before relaxing. After a few clicks from each side, she paused a few seconds to review the captured images. All normal routine until she hesitated longer than the previous scans.

"Is everything alright?" I asked, looking over at her scrutinizing the image on the computer screen.

"Um, yes. I just want to try another angle with the last image, if you don't mind," she said, repositioning my body for another scan of my right breast.

The machine beeped once more, and I exhaled. Maribel paused

another moment and asked, "You've been doing your mammograms with us for the past few years, right?"

"Yes, why?" I asked, feeling a bit more agitated.

"Oh, it's likely nothing. I just see a little area on the edge of your right breast near your armpit that is darker than it should be. I don't think there's anything to worry about. The doctor will look at the images and compare them with your previous scans. She'll call you with the results."

"When will she call?" I asked more concerned now than a few minutes earlier.

"You'll get a call within the next three days."

I thanked Maribel and left the doctor's office in deep thought. A few minutes later, my phone rang. It was our family friend, Payam. Being a lawyer, I had reached out to him a few months ago to get his advice on options for selling our share of the medical practice.

"Hi, Bahar, how are you?"

"Hi Payam, I'm fine. How are you doing?" I replied. "It's good to hear from you."

"Thanks. It's good to hear your voice too. How is Omid doing?"

"He's not doing so great. The doctor is starting to give up. He wants to try radiation again as a last-ditch effort."

"Oh, I'm sorry to hear that."

I was so tired of hearing that from everyone. "Thanks. We'll see how it goes." I paused for a few seconds. Then I continued, "So, any information on buying out our share?"

"Well, I'm afraid I don't have a clear-cut answer. I looked over the contract and have some questions for Dr. Skyler. I set up a meeting for next Tuesday to meet with him and his lawyer. Are you guys able to make it?"

"We should be able to," I replied. "You think Jake will give us a fair offer?"

"It's hard to say. We'll know more when we talk with him. I'll bring all the financial paperwork and the contracts. If you have anything else, please bring it with you."

I agreed, and after disconnecting, I sat silently in the car, thinking about the upcoming meeting with Omid's partner. I never got to know Jake Skyler as well as Omid did. Any positive impression I had of him quickly diminished after I learned about the fifty-thousand-dollar withdrawal for his wife's birthday gift and his lack of empathy for Omid's illness. Jake and Omid had been partners for over ten years. During this time, Omid had always made financial and personal sacrifices to help support their medical practice. However, after Omid had fallen ill, Jake never reciprocated these goodwill gestures with financial or emotional support. Jake had only contacted us in the first few months after Omid left the practice to discuss office-related matters, and then stopped calling or visiting altogether. The checks from the practice were still coming in, but I wasn't certain how long we could depend on them. I was anxious to learn about our fate.

I wanted to forget the events of the day and invited Stella and her husband, Shawn, for dinner that evening. Likely sensing my lack of appetite to discuss the doctor's appointment, Stella never brought up the subject.

Although Omid was not very coherent and appeared tired, we tried to spend the night with a sense of normalcy. Omid relaxed on the couch while the three of us drank wine and kept him company in the living room. Koosha, Kayvon, and Stella's sons ate dinner with us before going to the game room to hang out. Having friends over and exchanging stories about insignificant topics was exactly what I needed to distract me for the evening.

Chapter 17

The weekend was a blur. I filled Koosha's itinerary with playdates, while Kayvon hung out with his friends. In the evenings we ordered food and watched a few episodes of *Designated Survivor* together as a family. Koosha was now able to watch movies with some mature content without all of us needing to resort to cartoons or PG-rated films on movie nights. We spent most of the weekend relaxing and preparing for the busy week ahead.

Monday morning was Omid's first radiation session. He was scheduled to receive ten sessions, and I hated every minute of being back in that clinic. Everyone recognized us when we walked in. Patients rarely returned for a second cycle of radiation.

Omid walked painstakingly from the car to the radiation center. Since the second surgery, he had lost some of his peripheral vision and would veer to the right running into objects in front of him. I held him tightly and made it appear as if I was holding him out of affection, but in truth, I was keeping him from falling and injuring himself.

He had gained over twenty-five pounds in the last two years from being sedentary and the steroids, and his skin tone was now two shades darker. Even as I walked next to him and held his hand, I couldn't help but feel lonely.

We finished the radiation fifteen minutes later, and I helped him get dressed before heading to the car.

"How are you feeling?" I asked.

"I'm good," he replied, as I helped him climb into the car and buckle his seat belt. He leaned back and pressed his head into the headrest, with a sigh of relief. "I think we need to take you for a treat, young lady. You've been worrying way too much, and I need to see that frown turn upside down," Omid teased. Today he was more lucid, and he appeared to enjoy taunting me.

I laughed heartily. "Stop talking to me as if I'm five years old," I replied, pretending to pout.

"Maybe you should stop acting like one," he said with a smirk on his face. "Shall we get you some doughnuts to make you feel better?" he offered.

My eyes danced like a little girl's as I nodded. "Yes! Shall we go to our favorite doughnut store?" I smiled excitedly, putting the car into reverse and backing out of the parking spot.

Sidecar Doughnuts had been our favorite hangout for desserts, and we had been regular weekly customers for years until Omid became ill. Sitting across from each other, sharing a huckleberry-flavored glazed doughnut and a cup of coffee felt nostalgic.

"My God, we haven't been here in so long! This doughnut is the most delicious thing I've ever tasted!" I said, taking a big bite of the heavenly dessert and washing it down with a sip of freshly brewed coffee.

I brought the doughnut up to Omid's face to take a bite. He leaned in and carefully bit a small piece of it, taking care not to smear the icing all over his face.

I pretended not to notice him struggling to swallow and began to speak. "How do you like it?"

He nodded, looking pleased. "It's delicious! It hits the spot. We should come back again with the boys."

"We'll get a few for them before we leave. They have a lot of new flavors I want to try too," I said, looking greedily at the trays of freshly made gourmet doughnuts.

"So, you want to tell me what's on your mind? You've been quiet all day," Omid asked, looking into my eyes.

He could always read me like an open book. I shrugged. "It's nothing serious. I was just trying to figure out some things in my head. I'm just thinking about tomorrow's meeting with Jake," I began. "I don't trust him, and I'm worried he'll try to swindle us. How much do you think he'll offer to buy your share?"

Omid paused and made a concerted effort to swallow the small piece of doughnut still in his mouth before speaking. "I'm not sure. I think he'll make a fair offer. He's a good guy. I wouldn't worry so much if I were you," Omid replied, appearing confident.

"Really? I still don't see what's so good about him. I just hope he proves me wrong tomorrow. We'll go to your radiation in the morning and then drive to Payam's office. Navid will meet us there and the four of us can drive over together," I explained.

Omid stared out the window and grew quiet.

"Are you okay?" I asked.

He turned to look at me appearing glum. "I was just thinking about how things have turned out. I don't have much time left, and there's still so much I want to do."

I took his hand and caressed it. I tried to choke back the tears as I spoke. "Let's try not to think about sad thoughts. Let's just be in the moment and not get ahead of ourselves."

We sat there for a little while longer before heading home. Appearing exhausted, Omid didn't stay awake for dinner. He decided to go to bed early, complaining of a bad headache.

The next morning, I went for a short jog in the neighborhood to get rid of my jitters.

While jogging back home, I felt my phone vibrating in my pocket. I stopped to answer. "Hello?"

"Hi, is this Mrs. Salehi?"

"Yes, this is she. Who's this?" I inquired, as the caller ID had been blocked.

"Hi, Bahar, this is Dr. Lee. How are you?"

"Oh. Hi, Dr. Lee. I'm fine, thanks. How are you?"

"I'm doing well, thank you. Do you have a few minutes?"

"Yes, sure." I sat on the curb to catch my breath. My heart started racing. Dr. Lee had never called me before on the phone.

"I was reviewing your mammogram results. It seems as though one lymph node under your right armpit looks a little suspicious. I would like you to come in for a biopsy."

"Um, okay. What do you think it might be? Does it look like cancer?"

"I don't want you to be alarmed. Let's do a biopsy first and wait for the results. We'll know more then. Are you able to come in tomorrow?"

My hands started to shake, and my voice quivered. "Yes, that should work. Can I come in the afternoon?"

"Why don't I have you speak to Candace, and she can make the appointment for you. I'll see you tomorrow, Bahar," she responded before connecting me to her front desk.

After scheduling an appointment, I hung up the phone and stood to replay the conversation in my head. All I could hear ringing in my ear was the word *cancer*. I felt dizzy and leaned against the lamp post to avoid falling. *What if we both have cancer?* I wondered. I reminded myself to remain calm and focused on slowing down my breaths. *We will know more after the biopsy. No need to panic yet*, I kept reminding myself.

After that worrying phone call, I jogged back home to change quickly. I helped Omid get dressed and ready for our appointment, but something in his demeanor had changed, and he wasn't as responsive to the conversation cues as he had been the day before.

The four of us walked into the conference room. Jake was already sitting in the room with his attorney. He smiled awkwardly at Omid, watching him struggle to take his seat. We all greeted each other while seated around the conference table.

Jake's attorney spoke first. "Thank you all for coming today. I understand, Mr. Shahidy, that you're representing the Salehis. Is that correct?" he asked.

"Yes, that's correct," Payam replied.

"I also understand that you called this meeting to determine if Dr. Skyler is prepared to purchase Dr. Salehi's share of the medical practice?" he continued.

"Yes," Payam replied. "Given Dr. Salehi's medical condition, he is unable to continue working. In reviewing the contractual agreement of the partnership, when a situation like this occurs, the second party can offer to purchase his partner's share at an equitable, agreed-upon price."

"Yes, that is how we interpret the contract as well. Please keep in mind that since Dr. Salehi's diagnosis, the medical practice has been under a lot of financial pressure and struggling to meet demands to pay office debts and employee salaries. We have reviewed the financial statements from the past two years with our accountant and believe $275,000 is a fair value for the buy-out."

"What?!" I exclaimed, unable to contain my fury. I glanced over at Payam and Navid, stunned by what I just heard.

Payam looked over at me and blinked, sternly signaling me to stay silent. Then he turned to address Jake's attorney, "I see. As you can tell by Mrs. Salehi's reaction, the amount you are offering is significantly less than our estimates. Our value assessment of the practice places the partnership at close to one and a half million dollars. Based on that number, Dr. Salehi is seeking a payout of approximately $750,000. We arrived at this estimate based on ten years of corporate tax returns. With all due respect, what your client is offering to buy Dr. Salehi's share is significantly below that value!"

I was livid. I wanted to reach across the table and strangle Jake. I glared at him with contempt and cursed in Farsi under my breath in disgust. He avoided making any eye contact with us and sat silently with his head slightly bent, focusing his gaze on the table, without uttering a word.

How could this man be so vile and ruthless? To take advantage of a sick colleague and friend who had devoted his entire life to this medical practice was deplorable.

Omid sat next to me with listless eyes. He did not react to the dialogue. The doctor warned me about mental transitions from full coherence to sudden unresponsiveness. Given Omid's current state, I didn't volunteer him to speak. Navid continued tapping on the table, and I could see his nostrils flaring from anger.

"I am sorry you feel that way," Jake's attorney replied sternly. "As I said, the practice has taken a significant loss since Dr. Salehi left, and Dr. Skyler can offer $275,000 based on that value assessment," he concluded.

Payam abruptly rose from his chair and motioned for us to follow. "Well, then we won't need to waste time discussing this any further," he said. "We reject Dr. Skyler's offer. If you wish to reconsider, feel free to contact my office. In the meantime, I'll be counseling my clients to pursue legal channels to settle this matter." Payam then turned to leave the room, ushering the rest of us out before him.

Once we got into the car, I burst into a rage. "Can you believe that prick?! What a charlatan! After so many years of hard work and dedication to that practice, and this is how he wants to show his appreciation?! I was counting on that buy-out money to help with our living expenses. Oh God, what are we going to do now?" I sulked.

"I know it's not the news you were expecting to hear," Payam replied. "This guy is taking advantage of your circumstances and giving a low-ball offer. If you want to fight this, the only way to do it is to take him to court."

I glanced at Omid. He was silent. I wanted to yell but didn't know who to blame. After the anxiety-provoking call from my doctor and this afternoon's awful meeting, I felt depressed and helpless. Tears started to trickle down my cheeks. Navid caught a glimpse of my face from the rearview mirror and pulled the car over to the side of the road.

He twisted in his seat to face me. "Don't worry, Bahar. We'll get what that bastard owes you guys. I'll help Payam take this leech to court! I'll be damned if I let him take advantage of my brother like this," Navid hissed.

"Thank you," I whispered, nodding through the tears.

Navid then turned to Payam, who was sitting in the front passenger seat. "Please call me with anything you need. Don't worry about the costs. Just give me the details, and we'll figure it out. I want to teach this thief a lesson he never forgets!"

Payam nodded and spoke to all of us. "Will do. Just be ready for an uphill battle. We have a good case, but unless there is a settlement agreement, this could drag out for a couple of years. I want you to be ready for that."

Navid and I nodded. We had no other alternative but to accept.

Chapter 18

The next morning, I went with Stella to Dr. Lee's office for the biopsy. Stella was a nurse, and I trusted her to look after me if anything happened during the procedure. Fortunately, the procedure took less than half an hour, and I didn't have any complaints other than experiencing some soreness around the incision area.

Two days after the biopsy, I woke up to the sound of the phone ringing on my nightstand. I reached for it with my head still on the pillow, not ready to wake up. It was a few minutes past eight and I noticed the blocked caller ID on the incoming call.

"Hello?" I asked in a hoarse morning voice.

"Good morning, is this Bahar?"

"Yes, that's me."

"Hi Bahar, it's Dr. Lee."

I jolted awake and sat up on the bed as soon as I heard Dr. Lee's voice. "Oh. Hi, Dr. Lee. I'm sorry I didn't realize it's you. Is everything alright?" I asked, feeling my heart race in my throat.

"I'm sorry to be calling you this early. Your biopsy results just came in, and I wanted to call you as soon as possible."

"Yes, of course. That's no problem. What did the results say?" I asked reluctantly, wincing from fear.

"Well, I have good news and bad news. I'll start with the bad news first. Unfortunately, the results from the biopsy came back positive for cancer. The good news is that we are catching it early. I think it's important to quickly schedule you to see an oncologist."

I gasped for air and put the phone on my chest. I couldn't believe what I was hearing.

When I didn't speak, Dr. Lee asked, "Bahar, are you alright?"

"Um, yes. I'm just a bit confused, I guess. Are you sure I have cancer? I mean, when my mom got breast cancer, she did a whole series of genetic tests. All the results came back negative. I thought that meant I couldn't get breast cancer," I said, scared and confused.

"Well, those tests showed she didn't pass down certain known DNA mutations that would put you at higher risk of developing breast or ovarian cancer, but there could be other causes for developing breast cancer that are not related to those mutations. I'm sorry, this must come as a real shock to you. I don't usually call my patients to share the news over the phone, but Maribel mentioned your husband is dealing with glioblastoma, and I wasn't sure how quickly you would be able to come and see me."

"No, of course. Thank you for calling me. I appreciate it. I'm sorry, I think I'm just in shock," I replied, desperately trying to control myself.

This must be a mistake. That just doesn't make any sense.

"Yes, I completely understand. Do you have an oncologist in mind, or would you like me to refer you to one?"

"If you could refer one, that would be great. Is it possible for me to see the oncologist after my husband's done with his radiation? I'm his caregiver and drive him to his sessions."

There was a brief pause on the line. "As your doctor, I highly recommend you don't delay your care. It's hard to tell how quickly the tumor can metastasize, so earlier intervention can lead to a better long-term prognosis."

"I see. That makes sense. If I can get the number of the oncologist from you, I'll call today and make an appointment."

"That's great. I'll have my assistant help you with getting in contact with Dr. Lambert. I've worked with her before, and she's a great oncologist. I'll send your biopsy results to her as well. Did you have any other questions for me?"

"No, I can't think of any right now," I replied, still in a haze of confusion. I thanked her and hung up.

In disbelief, I looked over and found Omid still asleep. He slept through the entire conversation. I pulled off the covers and took refuge in the bathroom. Locking the door behind me, I kneeled in front of the toilet and started dry heaving. After a few minutes of hyperventilating while hugging the toilet, I stood and stared at my chalky complexion in the mirror. I was horrified at the woman staring back at me with deep listless tear-filled eyes and sunken cheeks. It bared no resemblance to the old Bahar who hummed while applying make-up to her high cheekbones and plump lips. There was no trace of that sexy and seductive woman who welcomed her husband's romantic kisses on the nape of her neck as she got ready for special occasions.

Stepping forward to take a closer look, I raised my arms and visually examined my breasts. Not noticing any differences, I pressed two fingers on my breast tissue and armpits, trying to feel for lumps. *If I can't feel the tumor, maybe the cancer is still in its early stages*, I told myself.

A knock on the door startled me. "Mommy, I need your help," Koosha announced. "There is a knot in my shoelace, and I can't untie it. I don't want to be late for school."

I pulled down my shirt. "Yes, give me a minute, Baby. I'll be right out." I quickly washed and dried my face and unlocked the door.

"Good morning, Handsome!"

He looked up at me, frowning. "Hi, can you fix this?" he said, holding a shoe in the air with laces tied together in a secure knot.

I took the shoe from him and smiled. "Of course, Lovebug. You pulled on the lace too hard and tightened it instead of loosening it."

I started playing with the lace, placing the shoe on the counter. It took me a few minutes, but after I managed to loosen the lace, I handed him the shoe. "Here you go. All done!" He smiled and put the shoe on. "Okay, now I need my thank you kiss," I said, pointing to my cheek and winking at him.

He gave me a quick peck on the cheek. I kissed him back and gave him a tight squeeze.

"Mommy, I'm gonna be late. I have to go," he whined, trying to break free.

"Alright, alright. Go. Have a good day," I released him before asking, "Did Kayvon leave already?"

"Yeah, he left a few minutes ago."

"Okay, see you later," I replied, disappointed in not seeing Kayvon before he left for school. I wondered if he was trying to avoid seeing us. It was apparent he was still having difficulty dealing with Omid's illness.

Once Koosha was gone, I called Stella. She was dismayed to hear the news of my diagnosis and offered to help with whatever she could.

"Thanks, Hon. I'll let you know once I make my appointment with the oncologist. I'm just processing everything right now."

"Of course, that makes sense. I'm sure you're still in shock," she replied.

"I have to also think of how I'm gonna tell the kids. I promised never to hide anything from them. I don't think Kayvon will ever forgive me if I keep this from him. He's already having trust issues from what happened with Omid. This whole thing sucks!"

"I know. But try not to get ahead of yourself. Let's wait and see what the oncologist says. We'll deal with one thing at a time. You want some company?" she offered.

"Not right this minute. Thank you though. I need to look for some paperwork related to the practice. Payam needs them by end of today for legal filings. Can we meet up later?"

"Sure thing," she agreed, and hung up.

I needed to speak to a family member and didn't want to alarm my parents before their flight. I dialed Golnaz's number. "Hey, Golzi," I said, trying to sound cheerful when she answered.

"Hey, you! How are you?" she replied excitedly.

My voice cracked as I began to speak. "I'm okay. It hasn't been such a great morning and I needed to hear your voice."

"Why? What's going on? Did something happen to Omid again?" Golnaz asked, sounding concerned.

My mom had already updated Golnaz regarding Omid's recent hospitalization and biopsy results. "Don't worry, Omid's fine. Nothing new has happened to him. He's still sleeping," I replied, trying to calm her.

"So, what's wrong then?" she continued, not sounding relieved.

"I'm sorry I never told you until now, but I had my mammogram a week ago and they found something. I had it biopsied and just got a phone call this morning from my doctor saying they think it might be cancer," I blurted out.

She gasped. "Oh my God! Are you serious?! What the hell? How is that possible?" She asked alarmingly.

"I know. I couldn't believe it either. I'm *still* having a hard time digesting it too. I'm supposed to go see the oncologist as soon as possible, and I guess I'll have more news to share after that," I replied.

She tried to sound calmer. "Hey, sorry if I flipped out. I just got caught off guard. I'm sure everything will be okay. I wish I could hug you. Do Mom and Dad know?"

I dabbed the tears on my cheeks trying to compose myself. "They only know about Omid. They're coming to stay with us for a few months. They fly in tomorrow. I didn't want to worry them until I saw the oncologist."

"That makes sense. Hey, I'm glad you called. I wish I could do something to help! I hate that you have to suffer like this," she lamented.

"Thanks. I wish you were here. I'll call you when Mom and Dad land tomorrow. They couldn't have come at a better time."

"Does Omid's family know? Are you going to have them help out too?"

I shook my head. "No. They're already so distraught about Omid's illness. Can't imagine adding a second layer to their worries. I'm going to wait a while before I let them know."

"It's so like you to put everyone else's needs above your own. You need to stop being so considerate and ask people for help. You hear me?" she asked emphatically.

"I know, you're right. It's just the way I'm built. It's hard for me to ask for help, but I'll think about it. I promise." I paused before continuing. "Thanks for the pep talk, Golzi. I feel much better after talking with you."

"Of course! I'm always here for you. I love you so much. Hang in there, Sis. Keep me posted on what the doctor says."

"I will. Love you. I'll talk to you later."

I hung up the phone and sat in solitude, reflecting on my mom's treatment journey when she got diagnosed. Her cancer was only in the breast tissue with no lymph node involvement. She had undergone a mastectomy and received six cycles of chemotherapy. I was certain the oncologist would recommend the same regimen at a minimum. Well, if the tumor had spread to my lymph node, then I would likely need additional treatments beyond what my mom had received.

I tried to stop thinking about my cancer and shifted my attention to what needed to be done today. I woke Omid and helped him get dressed for his radiation treatment. We were both silent in the car as we drove to his appointment.

Omid's speech was delayed today, unable to clearly enunciate. I wasn't sure if this was due to the side effects of the radiation or a sign that the cancer was progressing. I prayed it was the former.

The nurse was waiting in the lobby when we entered the clinic. "Good afternoon, Dr. Salehi. How are you today?" She offered her arm and escorted him to the back. Omid didn't respond and just stared at her. I nodded and smiled in gratitude.

The moment they were behind closed doors, I searched for my oncologist's number. Two years ago, I called an oncologist requesting a similar type of consult for Omid. It felt unreal that I was calling for myself this time.

My voice quivered as the receptionist answered. "Good morning. My name is Bahar Salehi. I'm a patient of Dr. Lee's. I need to make an appointment with Dr. Lambert, please."

"Good morning, Mrs. Salehi. Yes, I spoke to Dr. Lee's office about the referral. They've sent over your files. When would you like to come in?" the woman asked.

"Um, when is the doctor available?" I asked anxiously.

"Let's see. She seems pretty booked for the next month, but there was just a cancellation for next Friday at 11:00 a.m. Will that work for you?"

I opened the calendar on my phone and checked. Omid had his radiation then. "There isn't any availability after one o'clock by any chance?"

"No, I'm afraid not. This is the only open slot right now."

I sighed. "Okay, then. That should be fine," I replied, typing in the appointment into my phone calendar.

"Great. I'll email you some forms to fill out that you should bring with you to the appointment. Can I have your e-mail address, please?"

After providing her my contact information, I hung up and called Stella.

"Hi, Hon. How are you?" I asked.

"I'm fine. How are things with you?"

"Sorry to bother you again. I'm at the clinic with Omid for his radiation. The oncologist's office just called. They gave me an appointment for next Friday at 11:00 a.m., but Omid has his radiation then. I was calling to ask if you could take him to his appointment."

"Yes, I'd be happy to. Will you be okay with going to see the oncologist by yourself? Do you want me to see if Shawn could take Omid so I can come with you instead?"

I shook my head. "No, no, that's okay. I'll be fine. If you could just help with Omid, that would be great. I would've asked his parents or Navid, but his brother is working, and his dad still can't drive because of his eye surgery, and you know how Taraneh gets nervous when she drives on the freeways," I said, in desperation.

"Please, there is no need to explain. I'm happy to do it. By the way, speaking of parents, what time are yours landing tomorrow?"

"Oh, I think they land around eleven o'clock."

"Omid has radiation then, doesn't he? Do you want me to go pick them up? I'm off tomorrow," she offered.

"You're so sweet. Thanks for asking, but I already arranged for Navid to pick them up." I inhaled deeply, hearing cracking sounds from my torso. "I feel as if I'm always juggling ten things at once."

"I know, you poor thing. You have so much on your plate. It's enough to drive anybody crazy. I'm so glad your mom and dad are coming. It'll get much better once they get here," she reassured me.

"Thanks. I hope so. I keep worrying about how things will be with Omid and his treatment if I end up needing surgery soon."

"Didn't you say Omid only has a few more days of radiation left?"

"Yes, he'll finish next week."

"Okay, so that's only a few more days. He should be done by the time you have your surgery. So that shouldn't create an obstacle. If you're worried about this cancer, just remember, with all the advances in breast cancer, your chances of beating this are damn high! You can't compare what you have to Omid's cancer. The odds are stacked in your favor. If you don't believe me, just think about your mom's journey."

I smiled and nodded. Stella was right. I needed to stop panicking and be more pragmatic. "You're right. I just worry that things might be worse since the tumor has spread to my lymph nodes."

"Yes, that's true. But they can remove the lymph nodes that are involved and give you radiation after your surgery and chemo. Don't worry, you'll get through this. You just need to keep your body and mind stress-free. Speaking of which, when are we going to go work out?"

"Not sure yet. I'll give you a call in a couple of days to set it up."

"Sounds good. In the meantime, hang in there. Say hello to your parents. Love you!" she said and hung up.

My parents landed the next morning while I was at Omid's appointment. I felt more energetic from the deep sleep I had thanks to the Xanax. Unlike the day before, Omid appeared to be more lucid today.

My phone rang in the middle of his treatment, and I stepped out to answer the call. It was my mom calling.

"Hi, Sweetheart. How are you?" she asked.

"Hi, Maman! So good to hear your voice. How was your flight?"

"The flight couldn't end soon enough! After eighteen hours of turbulence, it feels good to be on solid ground!" she belted. "How are you? Navid said you're with Omid for his therapy. How's he doing?"

"Yes, he should be done soon. I made lunch for you and Baba and left it on the stove. Sogol will pick up the kids from school a little later. They were so excited when they left this morning knowing they would see you when they got home. You guys eat and get some rest. We should be home in a couple of hours."

"Okay, Sweetie. Kiss Omid for us. Baba says hello too. We'll see you guys soon. Love you."

I was ecstatic, hearing my mom's voice, knowing they would be at the house when we got there. I was grinning from ear to ear from excitement when Omid came out of the treatment room, assisted by his nurse. Stepping forward to offer my assistance, he shifted his weight to lean on me and latched onto my arm.

"He did great today!" the nurse proclaimed. "How are you feeling, Dr. Salehi?" she asked with a cheerful voice.

Omid paused a few moments catching his breath. "I'm fine. Thanks," he replied.

I kissed him on the cheek and thanked the nurse. "Guess what?! My parents just landed! Navid is taking them home from the airport," I squealed.

Omid smiled. "That's great."

I helped him to the car and buckled him in. Once behind the wheel, I put the car in reverse and started to pull out of the parking space. Glancing to my right, I noticed Omid staring at me intently.

"What is it? Are you alright?" I asked and stopped the car in mid–movement.

He smiled softly and didn't answer. I put the car in park and turned off the engine. "What is it, silly? What's that smile for?" I asked.

He continued to gaze at me, lovingly. Watching his expression made me teary-eyed, and I let the silence fill the air for a few moments.

He finally spoke. "I was just thinking about how wonderful you are. I appreciate you, that's all."

Tears started to well up in my eyes. Seeing Omid so alert and able to articulate his feelings, brought me so much joy. Hearing his words brought me comfort and made me hope that everything would work out in the end. Omid's parents had chosen the perfect name for him. Omid, which means hope in Farsi, is the perfect name for the inspiring, devoted, altruistic person that he is.

I kissed him passionately as the tears streamed down my face. Feeling out of breath, I sat back and replied, "I appreciate you, too. You have no idea how much." I pulled down the visor and looked at my face in the mirror. My mascara made black smudges under my eyes. "My goodness will you look at this face. I look like a damn raccoon!" I said, trying to clean the black smudge with a damp napkin. "I can't see my parents looking like this," I whined.

Omid tried to shush me. "You always look stunning! I wish you could only see yourself the way I see you. You're absolutely

breathtaking," he said, almost whispering.

Chapter 19

$\mathcal{I}$ sat waiting for the nurse to call me in to see Dr. Lambert, and as I looked around the room, I saw only one person who appeared to be my age sitting next to an elderly woman. Everyone else in the small crowded room appeared to be in their sixties and seventies.

I started fidgeting nervously in my chair, uncertain of how to pass the time. Flashbacks of Omid's appointments swirled in my head like a person with PTSD. Before I could escape the claustrophobic room, I heard the nurse call my name. I froze and didn't answer at first. When she called me again, I snapped out of my trance and replied.

"Yes, yes, that's me." *Keep it together, Bahar*, I scolded myself.

"Right this way, Mrs. Salehi." She pointed to the entrance, leading me down a small corridor and into a room. After checking my vitals, she handed me a gown and stepped out to provide me with privacy. I changed and sat on the exam table, waiting.

The clock overhead showed 11:30 a.m. Omid and Stella were likely just arriving for his appointment. He had two days of radiation left, and I was disappointed for not fulfilling my promise to be by his side for every treatment.

The oncologist knocked and stepped inside. My heart sank the moment she walked in. "Hello, Mrs. Salehi, I'm Dr. Lambert," she said, holding out her hand to shake mine.

She was a tall, slender, stunning woman who looked to be in her mid to late forties. She had a light complexion, high cheekbones, and long thick jet-black hair, that draped down her white coat, all the way down to her waist. Dr. Lambert's large dark eyes, long lashes, and lush, full lips were striking.

"Hello," I replied, shaking her hand.

She smiled. "How are you feeling today?"

I shrugged. "I'm a bit worried, but that's normal, I guess."

She nodded. "It would have been unusual if you weren't worried," she said, turning to the computer screen and typing in her password. "But I'm here to hopefully put your mind at ease and answer any of your questions."

"Thank you," I replied. Squinting to take a closer look at her profile, I asked, "Has anyone told you that you look like Salma Hayek?"

She shook her head and snickered. "No, nobody has ever told me that, but I'll take that as a compliment. Thank you," she replied, beaming. Then her smile faded, and her voice became more serious. "So, let's talk about what brought you here. I understand you have a positive biopsy result from a lymph node that was suspicious following a mammogram. Is that correct?"

I nodded. She continued, "It says here that you have a family history of breast cancer. Who was diagnosed with this?"

"Yes, that's right. My mom had breast cancer some years ago," I replied with my throat feeling dry.

Dr. Lambert started typing on the computer keyboard and nodded.

"I see. Any other family history of cancer?"

I shook my head. She continued to pepper me with further questions about my health and social habits. After documenting my responses, she washed her hands and walked over to examine me. She made circular motions around my breast tissue and pressed under my arms for some time.

"Well, I'm not able to feel anything. But the imaging and biopsy results confirm the presence of a malignancy," she began. I sat up once she completed her examination. "I want to order a body PET scan to see if we can locate the origin of the tumor. Right now, the mammogram only shows an anomaly visible in the right lymph node, which means the tumor must have originated from your right breast. Based on this information, I think the right course of action would be a right breast mastectomy along with the removal of the affected lymph nodes. After that, I recommend a six-cycle regimen of chemotherapy. Since the cancer has already spread to your lymph node, I think you need radiation as well. Did your mom have a similar regimen when she was diagnosed?"

I felt nauseated. "My mom received the same treatment except for radiation therapy. The tumor hadn't spread to her lymph node," I replied anxiously.

I was in disbelief. I was sitting on an exam table and talking about *my* cancer treatment with an oncologist. I recalled the fear I felt when Omid was first diagnosed. Never in a million years did I imagine experiencing the same trauma two short years later. I felt stuck in a perpetual nightmare.

"What are my chances of beating this cancer?" Before she had a chance to respond, I continued, "My husband has Glioblastoma. He was diagnosed with it two years ago and is losing the fight. The doctor says he doesn't have much time left. We have two young boys who are struggling to cope with the knowledge that their father is ill." My hands started to tremble, and I straightened my posture to avoid crying. "I just need to know my chances of surviving this cancer. I mean, do I need to prepare my kids for becoming orphans, or do I have a good chance of beating this?" I asked pointedly.

Dr. Lambert grew silent for a moment before speaking. She turned her chair and sat facing me, devoting all her attention to the conversation. "Listen, I'm sorry about what's happened with your husband. That's so unfortunate," she said, shaking her head in dismay. She then leaned forward and placed her hand on mine. "As your oncologist, I'm going to be straightforward and honest with you. Your treatment is going to be tough and you're going to have some rough months ahead, but I think with surgery, chemo, and radiation, you have a good chance of beating this. Do you have anyone to help you at home?"

I smiled as I replied. "Yes, I have my family and my husband's family to help us." I paused, trying to find the best way to phrase my next question. "It's just that I've taken care of my husband for the past two years, and I want to continue being there for him. Would it be a mistake to push back my surgery a few months?"

"If we want to increase your odds of beating this cancer, it's important not to delay. The quicker you have the surgery and start your chemotherapy, the better. The longer you wait, the more risk of further spread of the tumor. Does that help answer your question?"

During the drive home, I felt mentally and emotionally exhausted.

My parents were out visiting Omid's family, Omid was at his appointment, and the kids were at school. Presuming nobody was home, the sound of water from the guest room stopped me in my tracks. Not certain if my parents had returned earlier than I expected, I knocked on their door. Hearing no response, I opened the bedroom door and called out. "Maman? Baba? Are you guys home?"

The water turned off, and I heard someone rustling inside the bathroom. I tapped on the door, and when it opened, I came face to face with a wet hair dripping Golnaz covered in her robe, smiling back at me.

"Oh, my God! What are you doing here?" I squealed, unable to contain my excitement. I jumped into her arms for a warm embrace.

She finally released me and replied, "You didn't seriously think I would leave you all alone at a time like this, did you? There was no way in hell I was going to stay in Italy and let you deal with all this crap by yourself!"

"You have no idea how happy you made me, Golzi! I've missed

you so much! By the way, when did you get here? Did Mom and Dad let you in?"

"No, I didn't tell anyone I was coming. Other than you, only my boss and Giovanni know I'm here. I didn't want anyone to talk me out of coming. I found the spare key you guys hide under the plant in the front yard, and let myself in. I hope that's okay," she said with a twinkle of mischief in her eyes.

"But how the heck did you know?" I asked surprised. She grinned and didn't reply. "Well, I'm gonna have to change our hiding spot, now that you've figured it out missy!" I replied, laughing and pretending to disapprove.

She pouted playfully. Her stomach growled loudly. "Hey, do you have anything to eat? I am starving!"

"We don't have any leftovers, but I'll whip up something. I'm hungry too." I turned to walk out of the bedroom. "Get dressed and meet me in the kitchen. I have a lot to tell you," I instructed her with a warm smile on my face.

A few minutes later, Golnaz appeared in the kitchen. I handed her a bottle of Chianti to open, and she poured a generous serving for each of us. I dumped the small spiral-shaped pasta into the boiling pot of water and sat across from her on the kitchen counter.

The water was still dripping from her wet unbrushed hair, and her cheeks were bright pink from the hot shower. I looked into her large deep brown sparkling eyes that mesmerized so many of her suitors. Her natural beauty was breathtaking. She took a long sip of the wine and clanked the glass against the granite counter. Her playful personality and carefree spirit felt contagious, and her presence instantaneously lifted my spirits.

"So, what's going on with you? How were you able to get away so quickly?" I asked.

She replied while shrugging, "Oh, not much. After I hung up with you, I called my boss and told her the circumstances. She was very understanding and told me to take all the time I needed to take care of my family. So, I took her advice and booked the earliest ticket to come out."

I stood to drain the pasta, and the steam burned my eyes. "Ouch!" I yelped.

Golnaz laughed, looking amused. "I see you still haven't mastered the art of making a simple pasta after all these years."

"Oh, shut up," I replied, pretending to mimic her. "Just because you live in Italy, that doesn't make you an expert in cooking pasta," I shot back, jokingly. I pointed to the cabinets. "Just grab a couple of plates from there and utensils from the drawer and set the table, smart ass," I ordered.

She rolled her eyes, still smirking, and obeyed. We sat to eat as I ladled some Bolognese sauce on the piping hot pasta and topped it with grated parmesan cheese. The aroma of the food made my stomach gurgle loudly. It felt good to eat guilt-free and not be concerned about feeding Omid first.

"Yum, this looks so good!" Golnaz exclaimed, helping herself to a large serving. We ate silently for a few minutes.

"So, how are things going with you and Giovanni?" I asked.

Since the government didn't allow women to openly date in Iran, Golnaz had not been in a serious relationship until she moved to Italy. Over the years, she had fallen in and out of love with a few other men before finally meeting Giovanni. They have been dating a little over a year, and she appears to be smitten with him. Golnaz and Giovanni met at a party where he captured her attention by playing the guitar. Inquiring about the possibility of getting music lessons, a romance developed between them, and they have been inseparable ever since. Unbeknownst to my parents, Giovanni and Golnaz moved in together a few months ago.

"Things are going well. He said to say hello and sends his love."

"He's such a sweet guy. Thank him for me, will you?"

"Sure. Or you could just call him and thank him yourself later this afternoon," she teased.

Taking another sip of her wine, Golnaz gave me a sheepish smile.

"What's that smile for? What's lurking in there?" I asked, pointing to her head.

She blushed. "I don't know. I can't believe I'm saying this, but I think he might be the one."

"Are you serious? That's wonderful! Has he said anything?"

"Well, he hasn't proposed or anything, but let's just say the topic of marriage has come up once or twice," she replied, fiddling with her fork and appearing nervous.

"That's amazing, Golzi! I'm so happy things are working out for you," I said, feeling emotional.

"Yeah, well, we'll see how things go. But enough about me. What's going on with you? Did you get a chance to make an appointment with the oncologist?" she asked, her face turning serious.

I gazed at my plate without responding. I got up to clear the plates and placed them in the sink. Golnaz eyed my movements as she refilled our wine glasses. Having a full stomach and getting buzzed from the wine helped me to share the grim news about my appointment with the doctor earlier in the morning. After a detailed account of everything, I took a long pause to let it all sink in.

She put the wine glass on the table and walked over to give me a tight embrace while stroking my back. "You poor thing, I can't imagine how devastating this is for you." We stood silently as she tried to comfort me.

We walked over to the living room couch with our wine glasses in hand and resumed our conversation. "So, have you thought about what you're gonna do?" Golnaz asked with a concerned look.

"I told the doctor about my circumstances, but she recommended that I not delay the surgery. So, I'll call the surgeon tomorrow to make an appointment," I replied.

"I think you made the right decision. I mean, you of all people know that mom is alive today because she got treated as soon as she found out. You have to act quickly, too."

"You're right. I just wish I could wait a few more months. There's so much going on with Omid's health, my school, and the lawsuit for the office. I want things to get settled a little more before adding one more thing to my plate. You know what I mean?"

She nodded. "Yes, of course, but that's why we're here. Mom, dad, and I are gonna make sure everything gets looked after so you can focus on getting better. You can lean on us for anything. You know that, don't you?"

"Thank you. I'm such a lucky person," I replied.

"Well, don't thank me just yet. Let's see how thankful you are when you wake up every morning and hear the news on Iranian TV on high volume and the vacuum running at the same time! It seems like you've already forgotten our parents' routines," she said with laughter.

"Ah yes, Baba has already put in a satellite dish that picks up fifteen Iranian news channels and Maman bought a new Dyson vacuum the day after she arrived. She said the old one was not picking up the dust on the ground and was causing her allergies to act up," I said, laughing out loud.

Golnaz rolled her eyes comically and laughed along. "Maman and Baba will never change their ways," she concluded.

After a few moments, she stopped and gently brushed away a strand of my hair. "But seriously, Bahar. You know how much the three of us adore you, Omid, and the boys. There isn't anything we wouldn't do for any of you. Please take your cancer seriously and let us help. The sooner you start, the sooner it'll be over."

Suddenly the doorbell rang, ending our intimate chat. I opened the door and found Omid standing outside, leaning on Stella.

"Well, hello! Come on in, you two," I greeted them, stretching my arm for support as Omid stepped inside the house. "How was the appointment?" I asked Stella as I motioned for her to enter while I assisted Omid.

"It was fine," she replied. "Nothing much to report."

"That's good," I said, helping Omid walk to the living room. "Thank you again for taking him today." Turning to Omid, I said, "Hey, sweetheart. Guess who surprised us today?" He nodded but didn't respond. Instead, he continued walking down the hallway leaning on my arm.

When we reached the living room, I saw Golnaz scramble to her feet and turn in our direction to greet him. "Hi, Omid joon!" she bellowed, as soon as she saw him. He stopped walking for a second and looked up at her. His expression did not indicate any emotion, although I did detect a slight twitch in his eyebrows.

Golnaz's expression changed from joy to concern when he didn't respond. She walked over and kissed his cheek and took his other arm as we both accompanied him to the couch. Her lips started to quiver. His cancer had progressed significantly since the last time she saw him.

"Golnaz, you remember my good friend Stella, don't you?" I asked, trying to distract my sister.

"Yes, of course. Hi Stella. How are you?"

They greeted one another, then turning to me, Stella said, "I hope it was okay with you, but we took a small detour on our way back home."

"Oh, is that so? Where did you end up going?" I inquired.

"Well, since it's a sunny day, I thought it would do us good to go by the ocean for a bit. We drove to Torrey Pines Beach and looked at the ocean waves for a while. We didn't get out of the car but took in the view and inhaled the fresh breeze from our open windows."

"Wow, that sounds wonderful!" I exclaimed happily. "No wonder you both have color in your cheeks. Did you enjoy the detour, Omid?"

Omid remained silent and just stared ahead.

The last time we visited the beach, Omid and I spent the afternoon hiking the hills at Torrey Pines Reserve Park. The foamy waves against the orange-yellow backdrop of the sky were heart-stirring. After the sun set, we cooled our bare feet in the frigid ocean waves and ran around the beach playing tag. How I yearned to re-wind the clock.

Omid appeared exhausted, and Golnaz helped me take him to the bedroom to rest. Stella stayed to chat for a few minutes after we reconvened in the living room. I had arranged for Sogol to pick up Kayvon and Koosha from school, and they would be home soon.

I walked over to the stereo and turned on some music. Jose Merce's voice bellowed out of the speakers. I poured another glass of wine and resumed our sister time in a more somber mood.

"My God, I didn't expect to see Omid like that. My heart broke to pieces when I saw him walk in," Golnaz said after a long interval of silence.

"I know. There are times he's very lucid, and I forget he has cancer, but other days like today when he's completely unresponsive. The doctors can't predict when his brain switches between his two states. I never know if he'll have a good day or a bad day until he wakes up in the morning. Depending on how I find him, I'm either experiencing utter joy or intolerable grief."

Golnaz caressed my arm and nodded. "I'm sorry. I can only imagine how painful it is to watch him suffer."

I sighed and didn't reply. We sat for some time, quietly listening to music. Even though I didn't understand the words, the singer's voice scratched the surface of my tender heart, bursting the dam and flooding me with sorrow through each verse.

Chapter 20

My parents and Golnaz had prepared breakfast for the boys and sent them off to school long before I was awake. Omid was still asleep snoring next to me and had not budged the entire night. My head throbbed from all the wine I drank the night before.

Disheveled, as I entered the kitchen, Golnaz acknowledged my arrival. "Well, look who finally decided to wake up!" she bellowed. "Good morning, Sunshine!"

"I'd forgotten how loud your voice is," I hissed, pointing to my head and motioning for her to keep it down. The vibrations of her voice were like daggers in my skull.

"Oh, sorry. I guess it wasn't such a good idea for the two of us to finish a whole bottle of wine in one sitting," she jeered more quietly.

My mom frowned at Golnaz and shook her head with disapproval. "Oh, leave her alone, Golnaz." Then she motioned for me to join her. "Good morning, Sweetheart. Come sit down and have some breakfast. I squeezed you a glass of fresh orange juice. You can have that and some medicine to help with the headache," she said, handing me the glass.

I sat down and took the glass from her. "Thanks, Maman. At least I can count on *someone* to be considerate enough not to scream in my ear when I have a hangover," I said, glaring at Golnaz and playfully sticking out my tongue at her.

Golnaz huffed and crossed her arm across her chest pretending to be offended. "Have you guys eaten?" I asked.

My dad looked at the prepared breakfast table and said, "No. We've been waiting for you."

My mom had set the table filled with my favorite breakfast comfort food. I picked up a loaf of Iranian bread, Sangak, and spread a hearty layer of Bulgarian feta cheese and sour cherry preserves they brought from Iran. After I finished my bread and washed it down with hot tea, I ogled the plate containing sunny side up eggs garnished with small slivers of Persian cucumbers, fresh mint sprigs, chopped green onions, and tomato slices.

"Mom, this all tastes amazing!" I exclaimed, smacking my lips. "Thank you. You're seriously spoiling me. Sorry if I woke up so late. I didn't mean to make you all wait so long to eat."

"You needed the rest," my dad replied. "I'm glad you slept in. We drank some tea while we waited and got to spend some time with the boys. Kayvon and Koosha are two incredible boys. I couldn't be prouder of them," he added, appearing to beam with pride.

I nodded. "Thank you. I'm lucky to have them. I get my strength to fight every day because of them. Did they say anything about Omid? How did they appear to you?"

"Kayvon didn't mention anything about Omid. He only said he was happy we came and asked if we were planning to stay for a while. Koosha told us about Omid and explained what type of cancer his father has. He said he prays to God every night to make his dad strong enough to play with him again," he finished, choking back the tears.

"My sweet baby boy," I said, shaking my head and frowning. "This is so hard for them. I'm so relieved now that you guys are here. I can't thank you enough for coming. I know how hard it was to drop everything and come to my rescue."

"Don't be silly, my girl. You don't thank the family. We would never leave you alone at a time like this." I stood and embraced him.

Then I hugged my mom and Golnaz.

Once we finished breakfast, I made a tray for Omid. Before leaving, I turned to my parents. "I'll be back after giving Omid his meds. I need your advice and have to share some news when I come back."

They nodded and exchanged concerned glances. My mom knew how to read my mind, but I was certain she would never guess the news I wanted to share with them.

After I woke Omid and made certain he took his medicine, I asked if he wanted to join us in the kitchen. He shook his head and closed his eyes. I reluctantly let him go back to sleep and went back downstairs. Golnaz and my parents were waiting patiently for me in the kitchen.

"No luck getting Omid out of bed, huh?" Golnaz asked. I shook my head. "It's okay. His body needs rest. You need to stop worrying and focus on yourself more than ever. You have a long fight ahead, baby," she said, rubbing my back.

"What long fight? What are you two talking about?" My mom asked, sounding alarmed.

Golnaz and I stared at each other, unsure of how to share the news of my cancer. Golnaz initiated the conversation. "You know how Bahar and I are getting regular mammograms since you were diagnosed with breast cancer?" Mom nodded, and Golnaz continued. "Well, Bahar recently had a mammogram, and they found something suspicious. She went for a follow-up yesterday, and the surgeon wants her to have surgery and chemo like you did, Mom."

I watched my parents while Golnaz spoke. Mom stared at Golnaz, blinking rapidly and shaking her head in disbelief. Dad sat silently, looking down at his intertwined hands on the counter.

"What are you telling me, Golnaz? Are you telling me Bahar has *cancer*?" Mom shrieked.

I reached out to touch her and provide comfort. "Yes, Maman joon. I just found out. I didn't want to say anything until I spoke with the oncologist."

Neither of them met my gaze, and they were silent for a long time. It was hard to guess what was going through their minds. My dad finally broke the silence. "Okay, so now we need to focus on getting you better, Bahar. You need to save all your strength to get through the surgery and chemotherapy. Your mom, Golnaz, and I will coordinate everything and make sure you have help. When is your surgery scheduled?"

"Thank you, Baba. That means a lot. I was going to postpone my surgery until Omid improves. I made that promise to him and don't want to break my word. He still doesn't know about my cancer. Please don't say anything to him until I talk with him."

My dad shook his head vehemently as I spoke. He responded with a stern voice, "I want you to listen carefully, Bahar. For the past two years, your mother and I have watched you sacrifice your time and health to take care of your husband and the kids. You have been a doting wife, a loving mother, and an attentive caretaker. Now it's time to stop and pay attention to yourself. All this stress has hurt your body, and now that you're sick, I can't let you continue like this." I listened without speaking as he continued. "You know how much I love Omid. He is like a son to me, and I would give anything to make him better. Based on what you have told us his cancer has advanced, and there is nothing more that can be done. But your cancer is still in its early stages. Your mom is healthy today because she got treatment as soon as she found out she had breast cancer. I can't let you postpone your surgery until Omid gets better. You need to schedule your surgery right away."

The room was silent, and nobody spoke. I was surprised by my father's persistence and his tone when addressing me. I had never seen him so uncompromising about a decision.

His lips started quivering. "You're my daughter and I love you. I can't let anything hurt you. I beg you, please schedule your procedure now."

He choked up, unable to continue. My mom took over the conversation. "I know how hard it is to go through this treatment. You saw how emotionally and physically draining it was for me. It's going to be even harder for you because of Omid. The three of us are here to help, of course, but I think it's a good idea to also involve his family. What do you think?"

I shook my head, rejecting the suggestion. "Look, I appreciate your love and support. Listening to you now, I agree I shouldn't postpone my treatment, but I can't put Omid's care on his parents. His dad just had eye surgery, and his mom has severe arthritis. Neither of them can help Omid. Also, Navid is not an option because he works full-time. The most I can ask from his family is emotional support."

"Okay, I hear you. What if we get a nurse to help with Omid?" Golnaz offered.

"I thought about that, but I don't have the money to hire one right now. We're struggling as it is. There's just no way."

My mom stood up to get a glass of water while my dad took out a piece of paper and started dividing the sheet into two columns. "Okay. Let's start writing down what expenses we're talking about. I think once we see the numbers, we'll have a better idea of what you can afford."

After an hour of calculations, my dad dropped his pen and rubbed his temples profusely. "Well, at least we have a better idea of where things stand. To be honest, I didn't realize how much debt you were in. How long do you think the payments from the office will come in?"

"I don't know. We just filed a lawsuit against Omid's partner. I doubt if he's going to continue making deposits if we're taking him to court. Without that money, I can't pay the mortgage."

"I see. Have you considered selling the house to avoid foreclosure?"

"I'm not sure we can afford to rent a place with no fixed income right now. I've been going back and forth trying to find some way to make it work, but it's just impossible."

"You just worry about selling the house," Dad volunteered. "We need to find a place to rent once the house is sold. Your mom and I will take care of the rental payments until you finish your treatment and get a job. Now isn't the time for you to worry about money. You need to focus on your health." Before I could protest, he looked at Golnaz and said, "Why don't we look for a place with enough rooms that's comfortable for all of us?"

Golnaz raised her hand to shush me before I could open my mouth to protest. "I can start looking today. Since you guys are helping with the rent, I want to pay for a full-time nurse to look after Omid. If he has a nurse, Bahar, you can relax and focus on your treatment. Otherwise, you'll never stop worrying," Golnaz said decidedly.

"What are you all saying!? I can't let you guys pay for everything. It's just not possible," I said, shaking my head.

My mom raised her hand to silence me. "Now you listen to me. You might not remember everything you did for me when I was sick, but I sure do. I won't ever forget those nights you kept me company while your dad was stuck at work-not to mention the days you spent driving me to my chemotherapy sessions and doctor appointments. I recall those days vividly. You did more for me as my daughter than a mother would do for her child. You don't know how much that meant to me," she said, wiping the tears from her cheeks.

I hugged her. "I love you so much, Maman," I said, crying into her arms.

"I love you, too."

Golnaz startled us by suddenly clapping her hands and standing. "Then it's settled! You'll let Mom, Dad, and I help you with the finances. Now can we please talk about something else?!" A loud gurgling sound echoed from her belly at that moment, and we all burst out laughing.

After our conversation, I felt a surge of strength reverberate through me. I kissed Golnaz and thanked my dad. Just then, we heard a loud thud from upstairs. Frightened, I ran toward our bedroom. When I got there, I found Omid face down on the floor with a gash across his forehead. My dad and I helped him sit up while examining his face and body for any other signs of injury. Omid's face had turned white, and he looked startled and confused.

"What happened? How did you fall off the bed?" I asked, panic-stricken.

Omid looked around and then shook his head, unable to respond. Golnaz handed me a wipe to clean the blood from his forehead. He winced when the fabric touched his skin. It appeared he had slipped out of bed and hit his head against the sharp edge of the nightstand.

"It's okay, Sweetie. You're okay. I'm here. It's okay," I said, rocking him against my chest.

We helped Omid back to bed. Thankfully, the gash wasn't deep, and I covered it with a large strip of gauze. He sipped water through a straw and lay his head back down on the pillow. We moved the nightstand and placed large cushions in its place just in case he had an accident again.

"I'll buy a bed railing online today. We have to keep an eye on him for a concussion," I said.

"Can you move your legs, Omid?" Golnaz asked, leaning in to get Omid's attention.

He blinked several times and looked at his legs, trying to move them. There was no movement. After a few seconds, he whispered, "No."

Golnaz looked at me with a frazzled expression. Without speaking, she gestured with her eyes toward Omid's crotch. I looked down and saw his pants were wet. I quickly covered Omid with a blanket before my parents noticed. I didn't want Omid to feel embarrassed.

"Okay, well, I think Omid needs to rest. I'll stay with him and make sure he's okay. Why don't you guys get started on lunch and call me when it's ready," I suggested, leading the three of them toward the door. Golnaz nodded to indicate she understood.

Once alone, I went to the dresser and got Omid a fresh pair of trousers. I climbed on the bed next to him and helped ease him out of his pants and underwear as tactfully as possible. He was a proud man, and I knew he found this embarrassing. Thankfully the sheets were still dry.

I rose and quickly splashed cold water on my face to regain my composure. It was apparent the cancer was impacting his voluntary muscles, and his motor functions were starting to deteriorate. I started crying silent tears, washed my face, turned off the faucet, and headed back to check on Omid with a reassuring smile plastered on my face. I snuggled next to him, and we lay there with no soothing words being exchanged.

Chapter 21

Shortly after Omid's fall, Golnaz hired Danilo, a Filipino man in his late forties, as Omid's full-time nurse. Danilo had kind eyes and a soft smile. He was a tall, muscular nurse who transferred Omid from place to place when necessary, humming as he tended to his duties. I was thankful to have him.

Danilo spent his first few days learning about Omid's medication regimen and mobility needs. Since Omid was no longer speaking full sentences, I tried to explain Omid's likes and dislikes. The two men conversed with each other with Danilo asking questions and Omid responding with a nod or shake of his head.

I cleared a small space in the closet for Danilo's things, and he slept on the sofa bed in our bedroom. He watched over Omid at night, while I slept in the guest room with Golnaz. It was the first time in our marriage we were sleeping in separate beds, but there was no other choice. Hiring Danilo brought me peace of mind, and I was able to focus more attention on selling the house and scheduling my surgery. The results of my PET scan revealed a small-sized tumor in my right breast, which was likely the origin of cancer spreading to my lymph node.

I hoped to sell the house and find a new place to rent before scheduling my surgery. I discussed the plans with Navid, and he helped connect me with Jacob, a well-known realtor in the area who worked with international investors and knew people looking to purchase homes in our neighborhood. I wanted to sell the house and pay what we owed on it with some money left over for us to live on.

"There are four other homes in your neighborhood on the market," Jacob explained, "The prices are competitive. I have a client who's interested in one of them. If we reduce your asking price by $50,000, I'm confident the buyer will accept. He is also willing to pay cash."

"I was hoping to have some money left over after the purchase. I need to sell as quickly as possible, and I guess if the bank gets its money, and we cover all the closing costs without having to pay out of pocket, I'm fine with the plan," I replied, sounding desperate.

"I understand, Bahar. Navid explained everything to me. I am so sorry to hear about everything that's happening with you and your husband. I'll do what I can to help. Given your circumstances, I'll forego my commission this once. I'm looking to work with you in the future, and I'm sure when your finances improve, you can purchase your dream home with me," Jacob replied in an upbeat tone.

"Wow, thank you. I don't know what to say. Are you sure you're okay with doing that?" I asked with hesitation.

"Yes. Don't give it a second thought," he said and paused briefly before continuing. "I think once the purchase is complete, you might stand to walk away with $20,000. I know it isn't much, but that's my best-case estimate."

"Are you also calculating the $200,000 line of equity loan we have on the house?" I wondered.

"Yes, I'm calculating that loan plus any back taxes you owe on the house," Jacob replied.

"Bahar," Navid chimed in, "I know it's not much, but you'll be starting with a clean slate."

It broke my heart that all we stood to gain from our beautiful home was $20,000. We had hoped to get so much more from our long-term investment. I reluctantly conceded, and we reviewed some of the details before hanging up. Looking around the house, my heart felt heavy with the idea of leaving the only home Omid and I had bought together and the place we first brought Kayvon and Koosha to after they were born. I knew the children would be sad when they found out.

Just then, my parents and Golnaz walked in the front door with Kayvon and Koosha trailing behind them. They had spent the entire day at Balboa Park visiting the San Diego Air and Space Museum for Koosha and the San Diego Automotive Museum per Kayvon's request. My parents looked disheveled, and Golnaz's ponytail was hanging on by a loose rubber band ready to drop on the ground at a moment's notice.

"Hi, there!" I said cheerfully, seeing the kids enter with bright smiles and bags of caramel popcorn in their hands. "How was your day? Did you all have fun?"

Koosha ran forward and hugged me and then excitedly explained, "It was great! I got to sit in the cockpit of an airplane and got to be a pilot. It was so cool!" He then turned to glare at Kayvon. "If Kayvon hadn't whined about going to the car museum, we could have stayed longer and watched one of their pilot movies."

"You're such a whiner, Koosha," Kayvon protested. "We were in there for like ten hours before you finally let us go to the museum I wanted to see. We barely had an hour in there before they closed!"

"Come on now, boys," I scolded. "The important thing is you both got to go, and you spent time with Grandma and Grandpa, and Auntie Golnaz. The least you can do is thank them instead of bickering."

They stopped complaining and said, "Thank you," in unison. My parents smiled and nodded.

"Now, both of you go upstairs and jump in the shower," I commanded, pointing to the stairs. Then turning to my parents and Golnaz, I said, "You guys look beat. Why don't you go and freshen up while I prepare some tea?" They accepted the offer and headed to the room to change. I was heading to the kitchen when the doorbell rang. Not expecting anyone, I hesitated before turning the knob. Taraneh and Mansoor stood greeting me with a smile as soon as they saw me.

"Hi, Sweetheart!" Taraneh exclaimed. "We were just at the grocery store and bought some ripe mangoes. I wanted to drop them off for Omid since they're his favorite," she said with what appeared like an exaggerated smile.

"Oh, yes, of course. He loves mangoes. Thanks for bringing them. Would you like to come in?" I offered, obliged to invite them in despite my lack of enthusiasm to spend time with them in that moment.

Taraneh and I had exchanged heated words when we spoke on the phone two weeks earlier. I had called them to discuss our plans to hire a nurse for Omid and put the house up for sale. During our talk, I shared our financial difficulties, and before I could ask them for help, Taraneh started reprimanding us for not being more responsible with our money. Her tone and anger offended me so much that I ended our conversation before telling her about my cancer.

Inviting them into the living room, I left to turn on the tea kettle in the kitchen. The boiling water in the kettle felt very similar to the volcano ready to erupt inside me. I took a few deep breaths to calm myself before carrying a tray of hot tea and pastries back to the living room.

"Here are some fresh cream puffs my parents bought at the bakery yesterday. The boys hadn't found them yet," I said, setting down the tray and offering them a pastry and cup of tea.

"Oh, my favorite dessert!" Taraneh said cheerfully. "Mansoor and I will share one. The doctor doesn't want me to eat sweets because of my high blood sugar," she said, shaking her head. "But I can't resist these. You only live once."

"Thank you, Bahar," Mansoor said, wiping the whipped cream that landed on his chin. "How are your parents, by the way? We've been meaning to call them."

"They're fine and busy helping me with the boys. Today Golnaz and my parents took the boys to Balboa Park. Everyone's home now and getting showered and changed. They should be out shortly."

Taraneh pursed her lips and looked down. She took a sip of her tea and brushed off imaginary lint from her skirt. "That's nice. It would be nice if we spent some time with the boys too. Whenever you think it's a good day to take them out, let us know."

"I think that would be nice. You can ask them and see what day and time works."

"I'll ask when they come down. So, how is Omid?" Taraneh asked with a concerned voice.

The smile left my face as I sat on the couch. "I think he's doing worse. I'm not sure if the radiation helped him at all. Lately, he's been having more bad days than good days. It's been frustratingly unpredictable. Danilo has been a great help, looking after Omid while I take care of things."

Mansoor shifted on the couch. "Who is Danilo?"

"He is the full-time nurse Golnaz hired for Omid."

"That's wonderful," Taraneh replied. "I'm glad you got help."

"Yes, it is. I don't know what I would've done without my family's help," I said in an icy voice, feeling a resurgence of anger from within.

After a few seconds of silence, Mansoor finally spoke. "Listen, Sweetheart, I think we need to talk about the conversation you had with Taraneh a few days ago. I think there was a misunderstanding we need to clear up." I stayed quiet and let him continue. "Why didn't you or Omid share any of your financial problems with us before? We are Omid's parents. Why did he hide everything from us?"

I shrugged. "What can I say? Omid is a proud man. He didn't even tell me, and I'm his wife." My voice started quivering. "I feel awful about having to sell the house and making the kids leave their childhood home," I added, wiping a tear that escaped the corner of my eye.

"Yes, Sweetheart. I know you're hurting. I'm sorry if we upset you. We didn't mean to. We were just in shock. Please forgive us if we made you feel bad," Mansoor offered with his head bowed.

Taraneh nodded and leaned forward to embrace me. "Please don't be upset with us. We want to help however we can. I'm just sorry money is so tight for us; otherwise we would have given you what we had. But, you're all welcome to move in with us if you'd like."

My parents walked into the living room at just the right time. "There is no need for them to move to your place," my dad interjected. "Thank you for your generous offer, Taraneh. We've found a large condo close by, and it has enough rooms for everyone. We are going to stay with Bahar, Omid, and the kids until Bahar finishes her treatment. Then we can figure things out after that." I watched Taraneh and Mansoor's expressions change from relief to renewed concern.

"What treatment? What are you talking about?" Mansoor asked with eyes wide open, his gaze scanning the room for an answer from someone.

I took a breath and spoke up. "I've been wanting to tell you for a while now. I called to let you know about it when we spoke the last time, but after our scuffle, I didn't get a chance."

"You didn't get a chance to tell us what?" Taraneh asked. "What's going on? For the love of God, Bahar. Please tell me before I have a heart attack!"

"When I went to do my mammogram recently, the doctor found a lump under my arm. The biopsy showed I have breast cancer. They want me to have surgery and get chemotherapy," I said as calmly as I could.

It felt as if all the air was sucked out of the room. Mansoor's face turned white, and Taraneh smacked her palms together in disbelief. "How is that possible?!" Mansoor asked, breathing rapidly. "What do you mean you have cancer? How serious is it?"

"Please, I didn't mean to shock you. It's alright. I don't want you to worry. Everything has been sorted out. That's why Danilo is here to help with Omid, so I don't postpone my surgery. It's all very unexpected. I'm sorry I had to tell you this way."

"Oh, my God. Oh, my God," Mansoor kept repeating, rubbing his temples and rocking back and forth, clearly distraught.

My mom brought him a glass of water and sat down on the couch next to Taraneh and Mansoor. She spoke to them in a gentle voice. "Please, don't worry. The doctor says if she gets treated quickly, she will beat this. Plus, she has her sister and us here. Of course, you, Mansoor, and Navid have been a wonderful support all this time. It'll be fine. Yes, it will be fine," her voice trailed off, sounding like it was meant to comfort herself more than anyone else.

Mansoor shook his head. "What can we do? Does Omid know? What about the boys?"

"I haven't told Omid or the children yet. I'm not sure how to break the news without creating panic. I plan to talk to them soon. Maybe you guys can spend time with the boys and take them out to the movies or the park. Of course, visiting Omid would be lovely."

"Absolutely," Taraneh said, stroking my arm reassuringly. "I'm so sorry you're going through this, Sweetheart."

Mansoor spoke, clearly trying to choke back the tears. "The day you married Omid, I told you that God has given me the daughter I always prayed for. Please just focus on getting better, my strong girl. All the stress of life made you both sick. I *know* you and Omid will beat these cancers. You *have* to beat these damn cancers," he said before leaning into his palms to hide his face. His body shook as he cried.

I felt awful watching him. I walked over and kneeled in front of him. "Please don't cry. I'll be fine. Omid will be fine. Please don't do this to yourself," I begged him. Everyone in the room was now weeping openly.

"Listen, I need all of you to stay strong for us. I have no intention of losing my fight with this cancer. Please remember that we are still praying for Omid. The kids need you now more than ever. I don't want anyone crying anymore. The boys will be devastated if they come down and see you all crying," I scolded gently.

"Yes, Bahar is right," Golnaz replied as she walked into the room. "No more crying. Koosha and Kayvon will be down any minute."

"Hi, Golnaz joon. How are you?" Taraneh kissed Golnaz hello, then turned to Mansoor and handed him a tissue to wipe his face. "Why don't we go visit Omid? I don't want you driving after it gets dark."

"I'm sure Omid will be happy to see you both," I agreed. I also excused myself and went to the backyard to make a phone call. I felt lighter after my talk with Omid's parents but still anxious about talking to the boys and Omid. With that thought lingering, I called the surgeon's office.

I scheduled the surgery for mid-June, just one week after the boys finished school and two weeks after our move to the new place. I planned to send the kids to summer camp during the day to keep them distracted while I recovered at home.

Things were slowly starting to fall into place, and I was grateful to be surrounded by a strong support system. This was the first time I made so many difficult decisions without consulting Omid. His absence made all my recent efforts and decisions feel so much heavier.

Chapter 22

Moving day came quickly. Golnaz found us a four-bedroom spacious townhouse approximately ten miles away from our home, and we had to pack our belongings and move out within four days. The buyer offered cash to purchase the house with the price reduction, but wanted to close escrow as early as possible.

My heart sank when the doorbell rang. The movers stood on our doorstep with their dolly, ready to fill their truck with our belongings. The sea of boxes stacked in the hallway represented items we had accumulated over the years. What burdened my heart was the inability to pack the lifetime of memories, laughter, tears, and milestones we shared in this home.

The tears streamed down my face every time my eyes fell on a sentimental item Omid and I had bought during a trip or gifted to each other for special occasions. Over the years, it became a tradition to create photo albums from our numerous trips. Once each album was full, we would browse through the pages and reminisce about our adventure, while indulging in chocolates purchased from the countries we visited.

I filled two large moving boxes with approximately forty thick photo albums. The last album Omid made was from three years ago when we visited Prague. The album was filled with photos of the picturesque city famous for its orange shingled rooftops, ornate bridges, and gold-tipped towers. Omid loved exploring the city on foot and encouraged us to wear comfortable shoes to walk the cobblestone streets. During our three days in Prague, we took a breathtaking sunset cruise on the Danube River, visited glorious gardens filled with fully bloomed tulips and daffodils, strolled on the infamous Charles Bridge, explored the narrow laneways of Old Town, and dined in fine restaurants hidden within the spectacular squares of the city. The kids particularly enjoyed watching the fifteenth-century Astronomical Clock, where the twelve apostles and other figures paraded in procession across the clock face on the hour every hour. Omid had hand-selected every photo to include in our Prague album. Our smiles in every picture were a testament to our joyous time together.

It was hard for me to believe how much things had changed since then. I was losing count of how many tears I had shed mourning the loss of our former life. Feeling exhausted from the onslaught of constant turmoil, I prayed all would end on a happy note.

The kids dragged their fully dressed sluggish bodies down the staircase to allow the movers access to their rooms. Barely acknowledging me with a good morning, they headed to the kitchen and sat around the dining table. Their silence created a somber atmosphere that was in stark contrast to the animated morning breakfasts we used to enjoy together.

Kavyon and Koosha had matured a lot since they found out about Omid's illness. They each dealt dissimilarly with the news and expressed different emotions. Kayvon still exhibited a lingering animosity toward me, which I attributed to the fear of losing his father to cancer. Koosha was more fearful of being alone and cried over every small mishap. To avoid being alone he started speaking to an imaginary friend and insisted on bringing him everywhere. Uncertain of whether these responses were healthy, I consulted with the pediatrician to find a therapist. I wanted someone to help them navigate through their feelings and find healthy ways to cope with fear and pain. I scheduled their appointments in the coming weeks and planned to tell them about it after we spoke about the news of my cancer.

As the movers started hauling boxes to the truck, the house grew eerily quiet, with everyone looking as if they were ready to cry. Golnaz looked around and suddenly clapped her hands in excitement. "Well gentlemen, thanks for getting everything hauled away quickly. I'm going to head over to the new place and help unpack everything. Who wants to drive over with me?" she asked, glancing at Koosha and Kayvon. They didn't answer. "Come on, boys. You're not gonna make your poor aunt pick up those heavy boxes by herself, are you?" she asked, nudging Kayvon to respond.

"Fine, I'll come," Kayvon answered sheepishly.

"What about you, my little Superman? Whoever comes with me gets to go have burgers and shakes for lunch!"

Koosha perked up hearing about the reward. "Okay, Tommy and I will come and help," he said, pulling back the chair and pretending to grab hold of his imaginary friend. Golnaz gave me a concerned look, and I shook my head to prevent her from asking anything about Tommy. The three of them left the house together while the rest of us stayed behind to continue packing.

I decided to go to the bedroom and check on Omid. I walked in and found him eating breakfast. Danilo was feeding him bites and patiently waiting for Omid to chew and swallow before offering him another spoonful. There was a small trail of spit around Omid's mouth as he chewed with a listless expression.

Omid didn't react when I told him the movers had finished taking our things. For a mere second, I envied him for being disconnected from the immense burden of fear and sadness that kept swirling in my head. I took his hand and kissed it while I spoke to him, sobbing, "I'm sorry we're losing everything we built together. I'm sorry our happy memories have been boxed up." I thumped his hand on my chest. "Be strong, my love, and fight this! Please fight so we can rebuild again and create new memories together. Fight this monster and destroy its grip on your body and come back to me!"

Overcome with emotion, I crumbled to the ground and started pounding my fists angrily on the floor. My mom came rushing into the room and consoled me. She lifted my body and held me in her arms. "Let it out. Just let it all out. Don't let it simmer inside. I promise you things will get better. You and Omid are fighters. Think of today as a fresh start for all of you. A new chapter in a new book. A book with a happy ending when a year from now the four of you are on vacation having the time of your life. For now, try and channel all your energy and will to move past this temporary hardship."

It took me a few minutes to collect myself and stand. "You're right, Maman. If Omid could comfort me now, he would say, 'Sometimes, you must go through the storm to get to the rainbow.' He always reminded me of that during the difficult periods in our lives. He wants me to stay strong. Don't you, my love?" I asked, peering at Omid. He blinked, and a raspy sound emanated from the back of his throat. I nodded, understanding his intent, and leaned in to kiss his forehead. It was time to accept the circumstances and walk through the storm.

Chapter 23

We unpacked our belongings and slowly settled into the new apartment. The boys were not thrilled about sharing a room but didn't put up a big fight. They were spending more time together, and I heard Kayvon comforting Koosha from time to time when he was too scared and unable to sleep. My parents stayed in one room, while Golnaz and I became roommates in another. I gave the master bedroom to Omid and Danilo because it was the most spacious.

The Saturday morning before my surgery, I took the boys to the beach. We stopped and picked up a box of their favorite bagels, packets of cream cheese, and freshly squeezed orange juice on our way. We sat on one of the cliffs overlooking the ocean and nibbled on the bagels feeling nostalgic.

"Mom, I miss coming to the beach. We haven't been here for so long," Koosha reflected. "I wish Baba was here too."

"I know, Sweetheart. Me too," I said, hugging him tightly. Kayvon stayed silent and stared out at the surfers battling the rip current.

"Are you enjoying your bagel, Kayvon?" I asked, trying to get his attention.

He stopped staring at the surfers long enough to look at me and nod.

"So, I thought since it's just the three of us today, we could talk about how you guys are doing. Is there anything you want to ask me or feel like sharing?" I probed. Kayvon finished the last bite of his bagel and picked up his orange juice to take a long sip. Koosha sat up and wrapped his arms around his knees. "Kayvon, are you still feeling angry with Baba or me?"

"No, not anymore," he replied.

I looked at Koosha and stroked his hair. "What about you, darling? Is there anything you want to ask me?"

He shrugged his shoulders with a frown on his face. "I don't know. I just feel sad Baba can't be with us all the time. I miss hanging out with him."

"I know. I'm sure he misses hanging out with you too. I can't imagine how hard this is for you guys. So many things happening all at once. How do you both feel about the new place and your grandparents and Auntie Golnaz living with us? All the changes must be a little overwhelming."

"It's fine, Mom," Kayvon replied. "It's nice to have Auntie Golnaz around. She's fun to hang out with, and when everyone's around, I don't feel so lonely," he added with optimism. "Oh, by the way, Zaza just taught me how to play chess. He has some mad skills!"

Even though my dad's name was Reza, Kayvon called him Zaza ever since he learned to speak. I laughed. "Look out for Zaza! He loves to compete, and once he teaches you how to play well, he will try to beat you every time. He taught me how to play too. Let's play together some time, and I'll teach you how to outsmart Zaza."

"Yeah, sure. Sounds good."

"I like hanging out with Maman Pari. She makes the best desserts! She promised to teach me how to make a chocolate raspberry cake. She said it has a secret ingredient that she'll only share with me. I promised her I'll never tell anyone!"

"Yum! I can't wait to taste your cake!" I said, licking my lips. "I'm so happy to see you're bonding with my parents and Golnaz. They love you guys so much."

We finished our breakfast and decided to take a stroll on the beach. Koosha found some unique seashells to add to his collection, and Kayvon appeared more relaxed and even smiled on occasion as we talked. None of us brought our bathing suits to swim, but the water looked so inviting. Deciding to taunt them, I plunged both hands in the water and splashed the boys. They both stood stunned for a second before chasing me down the beach, seeking revenge. By the time they caught me, the three of us were dripping wet and laughing uncontrollably. I couldn't remember the last time I had laughed that much. I had originally planned to talk to the boys about my cancer, but decided to postpone our conversation until the next day.

After showering and changing, the boys asked for a family movie night at home. We ordered pizza and made popcorn to prepare for the evening. Golnaz decided to join us while my parents went to a friend's house. I surprised the boys by asking Danilo to bring Omid to the living room in his wheelchair. The boys were ecstatic to see Omid and ran to him the moment they saw him. Although he didn't say much, Omid smiled and nodded as he watched the boys laugh during the comical scenes of the movie. Seeing us all together felt like the perfect ending to an unforgettable day.

Unfortunately, the feeling of elation didn't last the entire weekend. As much as I wanted to delay speaking to the kids about my cancer, the conversation was inevitable. On Sunday I took the kids to the park after lunch and let them play soccer for some time before treating them to smoothies. They sipped on their drinks as I broached the topic.

"Boys, I have some news, but first, I want you to promise to listen closely and not get scared." Koosha froze with the straw in his mouth. The boys looked at each other, seemingly not sure how to respond. "Can you both promise me that?" They nodded and straightened in their chairs.

"Do you guys remember a while back when we talked about

Maman Pari and how she beat breast cancer?"

Koosha scratched his head, appearing confused. Kayvon spoke up. "Yes, I remember. Why?"

"Well, I wanted to know if you still remembered that story and how she beat her cancer. It's important because I want you to know that not every type of cancer is the same, and many people get cancer, and after treating it, go on to live very long and happy lives."

"Okay, so what does this have to do with your news?" Kayvon asked, sounding irritated.

"It's related because you guys know about Baba's cancer, and I've told you that his type of cancer is very rare and difficult to cure. While some cancers, like Maman Pari's breast cancer, are more common and much easier to cure. When she was told she had it, they had her get surgery and take medicine for a few months that made her weak and tired, but after she got done with her treatment, she wasn't sick anymore and has been healthy and strong now for a very long time." I paused to see if they were tracking along with me.

"Mom, I don't get why you're talking about Maman Pari. Is she sick again?" Kayvon mumbled the last question under his breath.

"No, not at all. You can see for yourself that she is healthy and there is nothing wrong with her. The reason I shared the story is so you know that breast cancer is very treatable," I said and paused. They were both looking at me with curious eyes as I continued. "Well, it seems that I might also have the same type of cancer that Maman Pari had, and the doctor wants me to have a small operation and take some meds to get better, just like her."

"Wait," Kayvon interjected, sounding alarmed. "*You* have breast cancer?"

"Yes, but it's nothing for you guys to worry about. I know you're both worried about Baba and think the same will happen to me. But like I said, brain cancer is not the same as breast cancer. The doctor wants me to have a small surgery tomorrow and then take some medicine to kill anything he can't get out during the operation. I didn't want to lie to you guys and promised I would tell you everything that was happening from now on. So, I'm keeping my word."

They remained silent at first while processing the information. Then Koosha's voice quivered as he spoke. "How do you know you'll get better? Didn't you think the same thing about Baba? What if you don't get better? What if both of you don't get better, and you both *die*?" he asked with alarm in his voice, visibly distraught.

Before I could answer, Kayvon scolded him harshly. "Stop it, Koosha! Mom just said she has the same cancer as Maman Pari. If Grandma got better, then so will Mom. Baba's cancer is different. You can't compare them."

"You're right, Kayvon. Please don't scold your brother. He is just worried, that's all." I turned to assure Koosha. "Kayvon is right, Sweetheart. There is no need for you to worry. I promise I'll get better."

Koosha stopped whimpering and climbed onto my lap to cuddle with me. "I'm sorry, Mommy. I didn't mean to say you were going to die," Koosha apologized.

"You don't need to apologize, Lovebug. I get it," I said, squeezing him tightly. "I'm going to have my operation while you two are at camp tomorrow. I'll stay at the hospital for a day or two and then come home to rest. I didn't ask Sogol to come since Grandma Pari and Grandpa Zaza are home with you. Auntie Golnaz will take me to the hospital and then come back home at night. Baba will also be home, of course, with Danilo."

"Why can't we go to the hospital? I don't want to go to camp tomorrow," Kayvon asked.

"The surgery will be very early in the morning, and it might take a long time. There is no point in your coming and sitting there. It'll be boring for you. Go to camp and have fun. You can call or text

Auntie Golnaz and ask about me. If you'd like, we can FaceTime too. The doctor said I only need to stay there for one night."

I gestured to Kayvon to move closer. He picked up his chair and placed it next to mine. I wrapped my free arm around Kayvon and kissed them both on the head.

"We'll be okay, my darlings. I promise," I reassured them, praying I would never have to break my promise to them.

When we got home, the kids went to their rooms to relax, and I headed to Omid's room. He was the last family member I needed to speak with about my cancer. I knocked before entering, and Danilo stood to greet me.

"Hi, Ma'am. How are you?" he asked.

"I'm well," I replied, glancing over at Omid and finding him awake.

"Hi, Sweetheart. What are you two up to?"

Omid swallowed and tried to speak. Struggling to hear him, I got closer to the recliner where he sat. "Exercising," he whispered.

I blinked in disbelief. Omid was speaking to me. "Wow! So happy to hear you've been busy." I glanced over at Danilo, grinning.

"Yes, the doctor has been doing well today, Ma'am. He was asking for you earlier," Danilo added shyly.

"Well, here I am," I said, reaching forward to hug him and kissed him on the lips.

I wasn't sure if I was thrilled about Omid being lucid today. I dreaded telling him my news; it would have been easier for me to know he wasn't able to comprehend the information enough to worry for me. "I'm so happy you're doing better, my love. I just got back with the boys and wanted to stop by and chat with you," I said to Omid, as Danilo excused himself from the room.

I thanked him and continued speaking with Omid. "I'm not sure how to say this," I stuttered. "But I'm having a mastectomy tomorrow because they found malignant cysts in my right breast and lymph node. I wanted to let you know so you don't wonder where I am the next few days. I don't want you to worry though. The surgeon and oncologist both assure me I have a good prognosis."

Omid closed his eyes for a moment. When he opened them, I saw a pool of tears about to overflow. His lips started quivering as he whispered, "No."

I wiped the tears from his cheek and started choking up myself. "You know I was with my mom when she went through her breast cancer treatment. It'll just take some time before I get rid of it, that's all. You just focus on getting better, because we have a lot of celebrating to do after *both* of us beat these cancers. You hear me?" I asked, no longer able to hold back my tears. I smiled while crying and put my head on his chest, holding him tightly. His chest comforted me and feeling his warm breath on my head gave me strength. "We will beat this. Both of us, together. You hear me?" I asked again more adamantly.

I waited for a response. I needed to know he hadn't given up and was continuing to fight. He finally replied with a gentle, "Yes." I closed my eyes and smiled.

Chapter 24

I awoke at 5:00 a.m. and took a shower. After getting dressed, I woke Golnaz and headed down to the kitchen to wait for her. I was told to fast before surgery and decided to take care of some paperwork before we left. The apartment was quiet, and everyone was fast asleep. I turned on my computer and quickly scheduled some online payments.

There wasn't much money left in our bank account. Omid's partner had started blocking direct deposits from the medical practice at the beginning of the month. That bastard made my blood boil. I was grateful Payam had agreed to represent us and couldn't wait for the judge to make Jake pay the money he was stealing from us. I prayed for karma to do its work and give him what he deserved sooner rather than later.

I signed some documents to finalize the escrow papers for our old house and felt relief from that financial burden being lifted from my shoulders. With approximately $20,000 left to us after selling the house, I had enough to pay for the lawsuit fees. I was grateful our other large expenses were being managed by my parents and Golnaz.

As I closed the lid to the laptop, I heard the shuffling of steps heading into the kitchen. "Good morning, Sweetheart," my mom said, coming in with her hair twisted in a messy bun peering at me through puffy eyes.

"Hi, Maman joon. Why are you awake? It's too early. Go back to bed," I scolded her.

Wearing her fuzzy terry cloth bathrobe snuggled around her body with a tight belt, she took a seat next to me and crossed her legs, at the same time, brushing my concern away with her hand. "Don't be silly. How can I sleep with you having surgery today? I wanted to see you off. How are you feeling? Is Golnaz awake yet?" she asked, looking concerned.

"She'll be down in a minute. I'm fine. I was just sorting through some paperwork. I left a note for the boys. I told them they could stay with you guys if they didn't feel like going to camp today. It took them a while to fall asleep last night. They were worried," I said, frowning.

"Don't worry about the kids. I'll talk to them and see what they want to do. Taraneh and Mansoor are coming by today. We'll all distract them. Everything will be fine," she said, kissing my face and caressing it for reassurance.

"Thanks. It still hasn't hit me that I'm having surgery. I haven't had a chance to even think about my cancer or feel afraid."

Golnaz walked into the kitchen at that moment dressed in jeans, a white T-shirt, and her favorite sneakers. She dug around for a coffee cup with a scowl on her face.

Mom rose to her feet. "Good morning. Did you not sleep well, either?" she asked Golnaz, heading to the coffee maker to brew her some coffee.

Golnaz shook her head and mumbled under her breath, "No. We were up until 2:00 a.m. talking."

"Go sit with, Bahar. I'll make you some coffee," Mom directed. Golnaz left the filter on the counter and complied. A few minutes later, Mom poured some coffee in a portable cup and handed her a small granola bar.

Golnaz and I stood to leave, and Mom smiled nervously at both of us. As we opened the door to step outside, she said a few prayers and passed the Quran over my head to bid me a safe outcome from the surgery.

She hugged me tightly before saying goodbye. "Golnaz, I need you to text me with any updates, you hear?" Golnaz nodded in agreement and kissed her on the cheek. As the car left the driveway, I could see my mom before she faded out of view with a silhouette of her in fluffy slippers waving at us.

We drove to the hospital in silence. Once we arrived and checked in, I was ushered to the pre-op area for an IV and placed on monitors. The realization that I was about to have surgery finally hit me. Not being able to fool Golnaz, she held my hand and didn't let go until they took me into the operating room.

"You are finally getting the boob job we talked about," she teased, trying to make me laugh. "Why can't you let me have something first for once? Seriously, next time you want a boob job, just say so. You don't have to make such a big production out of it," she said, squeezing my hand as I giggled.

"Yeah, I want to look sexier than you for once! So, suck it up and deal with it," I quipped.

We both got emotional as they wheeled me away. Golnaz blew me a kiss and waved as I turned my head to look for her before the doors closed behind me. I started shaking with fear and turned my thoughts to Omid for comfort. Positioned under multiple aluminum encased lights, I was startled when the anesthesiologist appeared next to me with a mask and full protective gear, reminding me of an astronaut dressed for a moon landing.

"Good morning, Mrs. Salehi, I am Dr. French, the anesthesiologist. I am going to inject a medicine that will make you sleepy. I want you to start counting backward from ten, please," she instructed.

I nodded and started to count out loud, imagining Omid next to me, holding my hand. Before I reached five, my eyes grew heavy, and my body went limp.

I woke to the sound of someone calling my name, feeling disoriented and everything appearing blurry. "Bahar, can you hear me? Bahar, I'm your nurse, Trish. You're in recovery right now. Your surgery is over. Can you hear me?" I turned to find a woman in scrubs, smiling down at me. I nodded and closed my eyes again. The next time I opened them, I saw Golnaz standing over me.

"Bahar joon, how are you?" I tried to reply but couldn't find my voice. My throat was dry, and it hurt to speak. Golnaz fed me some ice chips and dabbed my lips with a wet cloth. I wasn't in pain but felt an intense pressure on my chest. I noticed IVs and devices attached to my body and kept falling in and out of sleep.

The anesthesia finally wore off, and they transferred me to a private room. I was in pain and nauseated for most of the night. They started me on a morphine drip, which made me delirious. Golnaz later told me I spent the whole night talking with Omid. She said it broke her heart, listening to me talk with him about our vacation plans and ask for his input about birthday presents.

I was discharged two days after my surgery. The nurse reviewed instructions about how to drain and keep track of the fluid collected in a container next to the incision site and handed me a brown bag with supplies. The surgeon examined me and asked to see me back in ten days to remove the drain. I was anxious to be home with the boys and Omid.

Kayvon and Koosha were thrilled to see the car drive up and ran outside to greet me. They gave me gentle hugs taking care to avoid my right side. My parents set up a recliner bed in the living room so I could rest and be accessible to them. It felt good to leave the sterile environment of the hospital and be with my family again. My mom had made lunch, and the sweet aroma of my favorite Iranian dish, Ghormeh Sabzi, hit me. However, I still felt queasy, and only ate two spoons of the delicious vegetable stew. It made me happy to watch the kids eat their lunch with a hearty appetite. After the meal, Koosha kept me company, sitting at the foot of my bed, enjoying a bowl of chocolate ice cream. He had chocolate all over his chin and was completely unaware of the stains on his T-shirt.

I grinned, watching him eat. "You are the most handsome and messy nurse I have ever met, Koosha. Where did you hide *my* bowl of ice cream?" I pouted, pretending to look hurt.

He looked at me with wide eyes. "Oh. Sorry, I didn't know you wanted any. You want mine?" he asked innocently.

I shook my head and laughed. "It's okay, my love. Enjoy it. I'll eat some later," I reassured him.

Kayvon sat on the couch next to me, watching an episode of *Stranger Things*. He hadn't left my side since I arrived home, but he also hadn't spoken.

I tapped the bed with my left hand to motion for him to join me on the recliner. He paused the movie and walked toward me. He sat gently on its edge, appearing cautious.

"It's okay, my love. The surgery was on my right side. I can use my left arm, and you won't hurt me," I told him, reaching out to draw him closer.

"It's so good to see you both," I began. "You have no idea how much I missed you guys! I'm sorry we couldn't FaceTime in the hospital as I had promised."

"It's fine, Mom. Did the surgeon get the tumor out?" Kayvon asked intently.

I nodded. "Yes, he said he removed the tumor and all the tissue around it. He also got rid of some of the lymph nodes under my arm. He felt confident he took everything out."

Kayvon nodded and slowly looked up to meet my gaze.

Koosha put his bowl on the table and asked, "So are you all better now?"

"Well, now I have to wait a few weeks to heal. Then the doctor will give me some medicine every few weeks to make sure the cancer doesn't return. I won't lie, the medicine will make me feel weak, and I will lose my hair. But after it's all done, my hair will grow back in no time."

"Why do you lose your hair?" Koosha asked innocently.

"It's just a side effect of the medication. It won't hurt me, and it's only temporary."

They both sat in silence for a long minute, then Kayvon's eyes suddenly filled with a pool of tears, and his voice shook when he spoke. "Mom, is Baba going to die?"

"Oh, Sweetheart." I brought him closer. His dam burst while leaning on my shoulder, and he sobbed. Seeing his brother's reaction, Koosha started crying as well. I swallowed back my tears, trying to find the right words to console them. I had taken medications to numb the excruciating pain around the suture sites, but no dose of narcotics could numb the emotional pain of seeing my children so distraught.

"It's really hard to answer your question, Honey. God is the only one who can decide when he wants to take Baba up to Heaven. But even though Baba is getting worse and not spending time with you guys, he still loves you both very much. Did you hang out with him while I was at the hospital?"

"A little. But he was sleeping a lot," Koosha replied.

The boys eventually stopped crying and wiped their faces with a tissue. A shroud of peace surrounded the bed once the tears were dabbed dry. The tension was now replaced by a calm stillness in the room. I was happy the three of us had finally voiced our fears of the inevitable and put everything into words and tears. It felt like the deep cleanse we all needed.

Danilo knocked on the living room wall to ask permission to enter. Omid was sitting in the wheelchair wearing my favorite workout outfit with a freshly shaved face. "May we come in, Ma'am?" Danilo asked with a soft smile. "The doctor wants to drop by and welcome you back home." Omid had both hands on the armrests of the wheel-chair gazing in my direction with soft eyes and a twitch in his eyebrows.

"Omid! What a nice surprise," I screamed.

"Baba!" Koosha screamed and jumped off the bed to run toward him. He embraced Omid and kissed him on the cheek. Koosha beamed with joy seeing his dad out of the bedroom.

"Can I wheel Baba over there?" Koosha asked Danilo, pointing in my direction.

"Yes, of course. Be my guest," he replied, turning the handles over to Koosha and stepping aside.

Kayvon stood as Omid approached us. Awkwardly, he leaned forward and kissed his father on the cheek, then tapped him gently on the arm. "It's good to see you, Baba. You look great," Kayvon said.

"Hi there, handsome. I've missed you *so* much! How are you?" I asked ecstatically.

After several seconds, he whispered, "Good. I'm better now with you at home. You?"

"Much better after seeing you!" I said, beaming with happiness. The boys huddled around Omid and me for the remainder of the afternoon. Kayvon became more jovial and started giving us updates on the latest episodes of *Stranger Things*. Omid and I listened intently, and I mustered up as much oohs and aahs as I could, sharing my enthusiasm for a show I knew nothing about. Had it not been for the wheelchair and recliner, a passerby might have confused our cancer-stricken family with a picture-perfect foursome simply conversing and laughing together.

How I wish I could freeze this moment in time and never advance to the next scenes.

Chapter 25

The next few weeks were relatively uneventful. My parents and Golnaz tended to me around the clock. My mom busied herself, making nutritious and sometimes awful tasting concoctions, and forced them down my throat multiple times a day. She scolded me as I whined and explained that these mixtures helped her heal after her surgery. Although I missed my independence, it was nice to get pampered.

Every day the boys came home from camp, they visited their dad briefly before washing up for dinner. Judging by their sullen faces, I imagined they found the encounters emotionally draining. I also tried spending time with Omid. He was physically declining and no longer even able to sit up in the wheelchair. Danilo no longer brought Omid out of the bedroom, and it seemed that whenever I visited him, he was either asleep or unable to converse.

Witnessing Omid's rapid physical and cognitive decline made me anxious. To distract me from constant worry about his health, I decided to focus my attention on a fiftieth birthday celebration for him. To commemorate this big milestone, I planned a weekend getaway trip to Santa Barbara. Golnaz reserved a beachside apartment overlooking the ocean, and Navid hired a full catering company for the event. Despite the cost, everyone in the family was happy to contribute to make Omid's birthday a memorable one.

Omid, Danilo, the kids, and I made the four-hour drive in a rented handicap van to Santa Barbara the night before the party. Our parents, siblings, and some of Omid's closest friends arrived the next day for the celebration. Everyone appeared excited to celebrate the special occasion. We all knew our time with Omid was very limited, and it turned out to be an emotionally difficult weekend for everyone involved.

On the morning of Omid's birthday, the kids and I made our traditional pancakes for him. Since Kayvon was born, we celebrated every birthday morning with homemade pancakes and candles, while still in pajamas. The kids brought the pancakes in on a breakfast tray and laid it on Omid's thighs while he sat propped up in bed, leaning on Danilo. Koosha decorated the pancakes with slivered strawberries and bananas and topped them with freshly made whipped cream.

"Happy birthday, Baba!" Koosha exclaimed as he tried to feed Omid a sliver of the pancake with a fork. Omid slowly opened his mouth, and Koosha placed the piece on his tongue. Omid chewed slowly.

"This is..." Omid commented before pausing a moment, then he finally finished the sentence with "good."

Koosha beamed, and Kayvon smiled hearing Omid speak. It had been over a week since Omid had spoken a word.

"Happy fiftieth birthday, my Love!" I said, kissing him excitedly.

We all snuggled next to Omid as Danilo took a family photo. The window was wide open, and the ocean view from the bedroom was breathtaking. A cool breeze wafted through the window next to the bed, and we caught a glimpse of white seagulls flying over the majestic waves searching for their morning meal. The deep blue ocean water glistened under the sun's bright rays. A group of surfers paused to bask in the morning sun, straddling their surfboards. I saw a couple in the distance walking on the soft sand holding hands as the frothing waves touched their feet, bringing back memories of when Omid and I used to visit Santa Barbara on our romantic weekend getaways. I raised Omid's arm and slid my body under it. I loved feeling his warm pulsating body next to mine. I kissed him once again and rubbed his chest.

"I've loved every moment of building this life with you," I whispered into his ear.

Just then, the doorbell rang. The kids jumped off the bed and ran to open the door. "The guests are here!" Koosha shouted with glee.

I laughed, seeing their enthusiasm. "Everyone's here to celebrate you, Omid. It's time to make memories together," I said, caressing his cheek. "Let's get you dressed for the party!"

Danilo helped me get Omid ready. Once we were finished, I couldn't stop admiring how handsome he looked in his collared blue polo shirt and navy-blue jeans. How I wished I could hold his hand and walk out of the bedroom together to greet our guests. Despite being ill, he still had a way to bewitch me with his charm.

Danilo assisted Omid to his wheelchair. It was difficult to watch Omid struggle into it with limited control over his legs. It was unbelievable how frail and immobile he had become. It was only three years ago when Omid had planned a memorable surprise getaway for the four of us in Santa Barbara.

~ ~ ~ ~ ~ ~

Omid led us on a six-mile hike up a steep labyrinthine mountain for over four hours. Panting and tired from trekking, our physical exertion was handsomely rewarded with a jaw-dropping panoramic view of the vast Pacific Ocean. After commemorating our physical achievement with a family photo, we feasted on the mouthwatering picnic Omid had meticulously packed.

"Who's hungry?" Omid asked, pulling two large bags out of his backpack containing four turkey BLT sandwiches, veggie chips, chocolate chip cookies, and a thermos filled with hot tea. The boys smacked their lips and stared, waiting for Omid to finish setting the makeshift picnic table on top of the large oval-shaped rock. They grabbed their sandwiches and bit into them like two ravenous barbarians, while Omid and I sat shoulder to shoulder overlooking the mountain, sipping hot tea and nibbling on our cookies.

I inhaled the crisp, clean air and sighed contentedly. "This view is stunning. If I were to imagine what Heaven was like, I would imagine it would look something like this. Don't you think?"

He turned his head and gazed lovingly into my eyes. "I don't need to imagine what Heaven is like. Every day I wake up next to you is like Heaven for me."

~~~~~~

I could still feel the tingle from the chocolatey kiss on my lips on that mountain top. It pained me to see how much life and personality cancer had sucked out of my husband.

The volume of the voices from the living room continued to increase as more people arrived. The echo from the laughter reminded me of the parties in our old house. Gatherings where all guests understood that a party at the Salehi residence meant arriving ready to eat, drink, dance, and enjoy each other's company well past midnight.

I slowly wheeled Omid out of the bedroom and put on a brave smile to greet our friends. Everyone started to scurry around us to make space for Omid's wheelchair as we made our entrance into the living room. I paused in front of every guest to greet and thank them for coming. Everyone wished Omid a happy birthday as I wheeled him over to the gray couch underneath the windowsill. The windows were wide open, and the cool breeze was welcomed by my perspiring body. Navid knelt and lifted Omid out of his wheelchair and brought him to the couch. He placed Omid into a half-sitting position between the chaise and back of the couch with pillows tucked behind him for added comfort. Golnaz walked over and handed me a drink, while I mingled with the guests. Omid was quickly surrounded by family and friends, everyone showering him with attention.

"Happy birthday, Omid joon!" I heard a loud familiar voice exclaim. I turned my head and found Aunt Maryam leaning in to embrace Omid. Standing next to her was my friend Shirin and her husband, Peter.

I squealed from joy. "Shirin! Oh, my God. What a nice surprise! I had no idea you guys were coming today," I said, hugging her, Aunt Maryam, and Peter like an excited little schoolgirl.

"Surprise!" they all replied in unison.

"How did you guys manage to come?" I asked, confused.

"We flew in from London a couple of days ago," Shirin replied. "I was worried when you told me about your surgery and everything else that had happened. I wanted to see you in person and make sure you were doing okay. When we heard about Omid's party, Peter suggested we fly out and celebrate with all of you," she said, glancing at Peter lovingly, appearing grateful for the suggestion.

I hugged Shirin a second time and was overjoyed to see her. It had been many years since we had seen all of them. With everything that had been going on in our lives, I barely found time to speak to Shirin on the phone. Although we spent a great deal of time together at the party, Shirin and I were still greedy for more. They were staying with Peter's relatives in Los Angeles while visiting the U.S., so I made them promise to pay us a visit in San Diego before flying back to London.

Omid's fiftieth party turned out the way I had imagined. The atmosphere was warm, food and drinks were abundant, and the sound of laughter never left the room. Although Omid did not converse much, he appeared aware of his surroundings. It warmed my heart to see the soft smile on his face throughout the evening, and he didn't appear bothered by the numerous photos the guests took with him.

When it was time for the cake, Danilo helped move Omid to the center of the couch while Navid and I flanked him on both sides. Taraneh and Mansoor sat next to Navid, while my parents and Golnaz filled the rest of the couch, finding space next to me. The children kneeled in front of Omid, and we all sang "Happy Birthday" to him, admiring the extravagant double layer chocolate raspberry birthday cake. The sparkler candles produced a halo-like glow on Omid's face that choked me up. I closed my eyes to avoid crying and wished for Omid and me to be healed and celebrate his fifty-first birthday together next year.

"Happy birthday, Sweetheart," I whispered and kissed him as the candles fizzled out on their own. This moment was the last happy memory Omid and I shared as a couple.

Even though I wanted to freeze time and recycle the hours to keep the party from ending, the crowd started to thin around 11:00 p.m. Everyone except the four of us had a long drive ahead. The last guests to leave were our parents and siblings. Danilo wheeled Omid back to our bedroom after everyone bid him goodnight.

"Thanks for making the drive up. I could tell by watching Omid's face how happy he was to see you," I said, kissing Omid's family goodbye. I turned to my parents and Golnaz. "I can't thank you all enough for the endless love and support. Omid and I are cursed with an ugly disease, but we are also blessed with the strength you give us to fight our way back to recovery."

After closing the front door, I tended to the boys who had fallen asleep on the couch. I helped Koosha to the bedroom and got him changed.

"Did you have a nice time?" I asked Koosha, tucking him under the covers.

"Yes. It was a lot of fun. I can't wait to open the presents with

Baba tomorrow. I made him a Lego car set. I hope he likes it," Koosha said with bloodshot eyes.

I grinned. "That sounds wonderful. I'm sure Baba will love it. Good night," I said, kissing him on the forehead.

"Good night, Mommy," he replied with a smile.

Looking over at Kayvon's bed, I found him already asleep. I shut the bedroom door quietly and went back to the living room. The catering company had put the room back in order before leaving. The only sign left from the party was the fully wrapped boxes of presents on the coffee table. I slipped off my high heels and sat on the couch, reflecting on the day. For the first time in a long time, despite my fatigue, I felt peaceful and content. Replacing the relentless stream of negative thoughts and fears with the sounds of music and laughter revitalized me. After a few minutes, I turned off the lights and headed to the bedroom.

Danilo was sitting quietly on the recliner when I walked in. "I'm so sorry. I completely forgot you were waiting for me. You must be exhausted," I said apologetically.

He brushed his hand aside to alleviate my concern. "No worries, Ma'am. I'm fine." Before he turned to leave, he said, "I'll be on the couch if you need me."

I nodded and smiled back. Closing the door behind Danilo, I turned to lock it. I removed my makeup and changed into my pajamas. Although I was tired, I was feeling frisky. Sitting on the bed, I noticed Omid's eyes open, and he turned to face me.

"Hi, my love," I said, surprised to see Omid awake. "How are you feeling?" I asked, leaning against the backboard and caressing his arm.

I flung my slippers next to the bed and snuggled next to him. I missed his body next to mine and yearned for his touch. I couldn't even remember the last time we made love. I was longing for his soft fingers to explore my body and give me gentle kisses in intimate regions to arouse all my senses. His sensual lovemaking always left me breathless and yearning for more. Tonight, I craved that intimacy more than ever. My mastectomy had left me feeling less feminine. Although a full mesh was inserted under my skin to make it look like a breast, I still felt self-conscious. I was happy Omid was unable to rip off my clothes and nuzzle against my chest.

"Happy fiftieth birthday," I whispered, turning off the light and unbuttoning his nightshirt. I ran my fingers across his chest. He was propped against two pillows watching my movements closely. Kissing his neck, I leaned further in and dropped my hand lower on his body. Feeling the hardness against my fingers, I smiled mischievously and kissed him passionately.

"Bahar," he whispered with a quiver in his voice.

I slowly removed the pillows under his head and took off his clothes before throwing everything on the floor. I wanted to feel him inside me. Straddling my legs across his body, I felt his hardness against my inner thigh. The cool ocean breeze from the open window hit our bare bodies and sent a shiver down my spine.

I let out a soft moan as Omid penetrated me. Slowly rocking my body back and forth while sitting on top of him felt intoxicating. We gazed into each other's eyes while we made love. I felt his body tense up, and a trickle of sweat streamed down his temple with a final thrust. Arching my back, my body grew hot and began jerking with pleasure. The orgasm took my breath away and made me tremble over and over without letting up for some time. When I finally opened my eyes, Omid was out of breath, appearing to have also climaxed.

"That was incredible!" I said, gasping for breath. I lay my head on the pillow next to him and closed my eyes, slowly fading into a peaceful sleep. Neither one of us moved until the sun rose the next morning.

Chapter 26

Three days after Omid's birthday, I started my treatment. The doctor recommended six cycles of chemotherapy, with three weeks spacing in between each cycle. Stella explained the side effects and solutions on how to manage them. Unfortunately, there wasn't much I could do to avoid hair loss. Sensing I had lost my femininity with the removal of one breast, I felt as if losing my hair would be an additional blow to my self-confidence. Stella discovered a novel method that could reduce hair loss with the use of cold caps. However, the company claimed there was a thirty percent chance of hair loss despite the $3,000 cost. Given the exorbitant price tag, I decided against it.

Seeing my mom go through the treatment some years ago, I had a keen idea of what to expect for the next four and a half months. I knew the journey would leave me weak and vulnerable, but I was looking forward to getting it over with and moving on with my cancer-free life.

"You're ready to go in?" Stella asked, turning off the car. She was accompanying me to my first chemotherapy appointment.

I nodded. "I think so. The sooner I start, the sooner I'll finish, right?"

"Love your perspective," she said, smiling encouragingly. "Why don't you go in and register? I'll get your supplies and meet you inside," Stella said, opening the trunk.

She joined me in the waiting room with a portable cooler filled with ice packs. Last night she explained that placing ice packs on my hands and feet and chewing on ice chips could help prevent nerve damage and mouth sores. This type of prevention was not known during the time my mom received her chemotherapy. As a result, she suffered permanent nerve damage and took chronic medication daily to help with the pain in her fingers.

I was led to a reclining chair and Stella sat on a chair next to me.

The nurse introduced herself. "Good morning, Mrs. Salehi. My name is Leigh Ann. I will be the nurse giving you your first treatment today," she said, with a cordial voice.

After taking my vitals, she looked for a good vein and inserted the IV line in my left arm. "The entire treatment will take about one and a half hours," Leigh Ann explained. "I will give you some pre-medication first to help prevent any reaction from the infusion. Please, let me know if you don't feel well at any time. Okay?"

I nodded while holding my breath. Stella took hold of my hand and pressed it reassuringly. "I'm right here. I'll make sure everything goes well. You got this."

"Are you sisters?" Leigh Ann asked.

"Not by blood," I answered, "but I love her as if she were my sister."

"Aww. Love you too," Stella replied. "By the way, speaking of your sister, I need to text your parents and Golnaz to update them. I promised to keep them posted. Say cheese," Stella requested, raising her phone to snap a picture of me. She texted the picture along with a group message to my family.

"Golnaz will be pissed she isn't here," I teased. "But the policy says only one person is allowed with me, and I needed my nurse to hold my hand and calm me down," I said, taking her hand again.

Stella smiled. "Yes, she agreed to let me come for the first session.

After that, we'll take turns keeping you company."

"Sounds good," I said, yawning. Benadryl was making me groggy.

Stella had me put on gloves and socks before placing ice packs on my hands and feet. The chemotherapy and the ice made me shiver all over. Stella asked Leigh Ann to bring some warm blankets.

"There you go," Stella said, cocooning me inside the warm fuzzy covers.

"Why don't you close your eyes? Time will pass more quickly if you rest. Don't worry about me, I brought my computer to keep me busy."

I closed my eyes and didn't open them again until I heard Leigh Ann's voice. "Your infusion is almost over, Mrs. Salehi. How are you feeling?"

"Um, I'm okay. Sorry, I fell asleep. My throat feels kind of dry," I replied.

"You took a nice long nap. You can chew on the ice chips to help with your dry throat," she suggested, offering me a cup with a small plastic spoon in it. Stella took the cup and offered to feed them to me slowly.

A short while later, Leigh Ann returned to review some instructions for a device she placed on my belly. "The medicine that you are getting can lower your white blood cells and increase your risk of infection. I am placing this gadget on your belly. There is a drug that will be delivered under your skin via a cannula attached to this device in thirty-six hours. The drug will prevent your white blood cells from getting too low, but it can also make you feel tired, and you might have flu-like symptoms. You might also experience severe bone pain from it. I want you to take some pain medication starting tomorrow every four to six hours around the clock, so the pain doesn't get out of control. Do you have any questions?" she asked while placing a white pager-like object on my lower abdomen.

"I can't think of any," I replied. Once it was secured to my skin, a green light started blinking.

"After the medicine is injected, the light will stop blinking. That means you can remove the device and put it in this container," Leigh Ann explained, holding up a red biohazard receptacle. "If you have any questions, you can call the infusion center, and the on-call nurse will help you. Or you can call your doctor's office."

I nodded in agreement. After a few minutes, a machine started beeping, indicating the end of the chemotherapy infusion. Leigh Ann unhooked the needle from my arm, then placed a white gauze on my injection site and covered it with an adhesive. Stella and I slowly packed all my belongings and bid her farewell.

"How are you feeling? Are you hungry?" Stella asked, helping me to the car.

No nausea, but I had an appetite for something cool and refreshing. "Yes, let's eat something healthy. Maybe we can find somewhere with good salads and sandwiches."

We went to a buffet, and I filled my plate with lots of veggies and healthy options. It felt good to be out and enjoying a meal. A few hours after lunch, I started to feel bloated and had to take some medicine for heartburn. I didn't experience any other issues for a couple of days until the device finished delivering medicine via the cannula attached to my belly. The debilitating and excruciating pain was unlike anything I had ever experienced in my entire life. The pain felt as if someone were shattering my bones repeatedly with a steel hammer. It took about ten days and many doses of pain medication to recover from my symptoms. After two weeks, I was finally able to join my family at the dinner table without any major complaints.

My mom made it her routine to prepare home-made vitamin-rich foods and smoothies daily for me. I slept during the day and spent time with the boys and the family in the evenings. The boys didn't have a lot of energy when they returned from summer camp in the afternoons. They loved going on field trips to the beach, amusement parks, and the movie theater that was part of the expanded perks Taraneh and Mansoor had agreed to pay for. I was happy they were able to spend time with their friends and have fun instead of sitting at home worrying about us.

Two weeks after my first chemotherapy, I walked into the kitchen and found Golnaz and my parents huddled around the dining table, whispering.

Nobody noticed me until I was a few inches away from the table. I startled Golnaz so much that she practically jumped out of her chair. "For the love of God, Bahar. You almost gave me a heart attack!"

"Sorry, I didn't know you hadn't noticed me come in," I laughed, amused at her reaction.

None of them smiled or responded. My mom fidgeted with a wrinkled napkin, and my dad pretended to scrape something off the tabletop with his fingernail.

"What's going on? Why are you all whispering?" I asked, trying to read their expressions. My mom sniffled and tilted her face avoiding eye contact with me. When my dad looked up, his eyes had a pained expression. I prayed he was frowning because I looked so disheveled and still wearing my pajamas in the middle of the day.

"Hi, Sweetheart," my dad said, tapping the chair next to him, inviting me to sit down.

I sat down hesitantly, fearful of what I was about to hear. "Okay, now I'm sitting. Will someone please tell me what's going on!?"

He gently reached for my hand. "Omid can't swallow and hasn't been able to eat anything for the past twenty-four hours. The doctor has asked Danilo to keep a close eye on him, so Omid doesn't aspirate on his spit. He's not doing well, Sweetheart," my dad explained.

I blinked a few times, hearing a buzzing in my ear. I hadn't spent much time with Omid in the past ten days, due to my pain and fatigue. I suddenly felt dizzy, and my face became pale.

Golnaz stood up to grab me a glass of water. "Hey, drink this. You don't look so well," she said, sounding concerned.

I picked up the glass with shaking hands and took a small sip. "I'm not sure I understand. Are you telling me my Omid is *dying*?" I choked up, asking the question. My lips started to tremble, and tears started rolling down my eyes.

I leaned into my dad's open arms and sobbed in disbelief. My worst nightmare was coming true. Feeling a sense of urgency, I suddenly stood and raced to Omid's room. I walked into the room without knocking. The door banged against the wall with a loud thud upon my entry. Danilo looked up, appearing startled.

"Oh, I am sorry, Danilo," I apologized. "I came to see Omid. How is he?"

Danilo shook his head. "I'm afraid he's gotten worse, Ma'am."

Danilo stood and offered me his chair. Omid was lying on his back with two large pillows propped under his head. His eyes were closed. His hands lay beside him, palms facing up. His mouth was slightly open, and he lay there motionless. I heard him moan a few times, and then he was silent again.

"Why is he moaning? Is he in pain?"

"It's hard to tell," Danilo replied, "but moaning can be a sign of discomfort. He hasn't eaten anything for some time. I have been wiping the inside of his mouth with wet sponges to keep him hydrated. I've also been giving him pain medications."

I leaned forward and lifted Omid's hand to kiss it. He was suffering. I felt it. He never wanted to live in a vegetative state like this. Many years ago, when creating our Wills, he told me his wishes. He didn't want to suffer. When the time came, he wanted to end it as quickly as possible. He wanted to be cremated. Back then, I never imagined this scenario playing out before my eyes. We still had so many dreams to fulfill together. We had talked about dividing our time between living in the U.S. and Europe when we retired. We planned to buy a second home overseas one day. We also dreamt of becoming grandparents. There was still so much we wanted to do together!

"Why did it have to happen this way, Omid? Why do you have to leave me so soon?" I sobbed, hunched over, and held his hand against my face.

Danilo stood next to me in silence. Sensing I wanted privacy, he stepped out of the room and closed the door.

I put my head on Omid's shoulder. "I hope you're not suffering, my love. I know I sound selfish, but I don't want you to leave me. I don't want to go to sleep without your sweet arms holding me every night. You are the source of everything good in my life. How can I go on never hearing your soft voice, not inhaling your sweet scent, or not feeling your gentle kisses on my lips ever again? I can't imagine what life will be like without you. Everything will be meaningless if you leave me, Omid. God, please take me instead of him. I beg you to show mercy. Take me instead. *Please*, God. The pain is so unbearable." I melted into his chest, sobbing like a grief-stricken child.

Omid let out a soft moan but didn't move. I paused and drew in a breath. I felt selfish for unloading my fears and burdening him with my sorrows, so I slowly sat up and decided to provide Omid with some reassurance. I needed to give him peace of mind.

"Sweetie, rest assured the kids are my priority. They will hurt not having you here but will always remember what a wonderful father you are. Thank you for being the perfect man. You gave all you had to me, the boys, your family, your friends, and all your patients. You have brought color to this black and white life. Promise me you will watch over us from Heaven and guide me every day. You will always live in my heart. I love you so much." This time I tried to refrain from crying. I wanted Omid to feel strength through my words and actions.

I grabbed a tissue and wiped my face. I slowly stroked Omid's forehead and kissed his cheek. I ran my fingers through my hair to brush it aside. Feeling a fuzzy texture on my fingertips I glanced down to find a big clump of wavy hair in my palm. The side effect of my chemotherapy was starting to kick in.

Golnaz tapped gently on the door and walked in. "Are you alright, Bahar?"

I shook my head. "No, I'm not alright. I don't know what I am anymore, but I'm anything but alright. I can't believe I'm losing him. I should have visited him earlier. I neglected him. Now he has given up and is leaving me."

She walked over and embraced me. "No, Sweetie, you didn't neglect Omid. You've been sick. You can't blame yourself for any of this. Omid knows more than anybody else how much you love him."

I took a deep breath and lifted my hand to show Golnaz the clump of loose hair I was holding. She gasped.

"Oh, Sweetie, that's okay. You already knew your hair would fall out. Would you like me to shave it off? That way you don't have to watch it fall out little by little," she offered.

"Yeah, sure. I guess. It doesn't matter anymore. Nothing will ever matter anymore," I said grimly.

She put her arm behind my back and spoke to me in a gentle voice. "Why don't you go back to the room and lie down for a bit. Omid wouldn't want to see you suffering like this. Beating yourself up won't do either of you any good."

"I don't know how to leave him, Golnaz. How do you let the love of your life leave you just like that? How can I possibly let him go?!" I screamed. I banged my head with my fists and took a knee on the ground wailing hysterically. Golnaz followed me to the ground and tried to calm me to no avail. My parents and Danilo ran into the room to see what was happening.

My dad kneeled and swooped me up in his arms and carried me to my room. "Come on, Sweetie. You need to rest. I got you," he said, comforting me. My mom and Golnaz followed him out. My dad put my head on the pillow. Too weak to speak, the tears streamed down the sides of my face. An occasional wounded whimper was the only sound I could muster.

Golnaz sat next to me and handed me a glass of water along with a pill. I drank the water and swallowed the tablet without protesting. A few minutes later, my eyes shut, and I fell into a deep slumber.

I woke with my parents and Golnaz huddled over me. "Bahar joon. Bahar baby, can you hear me?" My mom asked with panic in her voice.

I blinked a couple of times and rubbed my eyes. "What time is it? How long was I asleep?"

"You've been asleep the entire night, and it's almost noon now. We were getting worried about you. How are you feeling?" Mom asked. "I brought you a tray of food and made you a smoothie. You need to eat something."

Golnaz helped me sit up. I took a sip of the cool fruit smoothie and felt the chill make its way down my throat. I felt reinvigorated. "Thanks, Mom. This is wonderful."

My mom smiled, looking pleased.

"How are the boys? How is Omid?" I asked, suddenly feeling alarmed.

"The boys are fine. They are at camp. I told them you had a headache last night and needed to rest. We sat and chatted with them about Omid. They visited him for a few minutes," Golnaz reported.

"Oh, my God. My poor babies. They must be devastated. I can't believe I slept so much. I needed to be there for them," I complained.

"Sweetie, what you need to do is to stop taking on so much. Don't forget your body is weak, and you're getting chemo. That's no joke. Let us take care of you," Mom pleaded. "The boys cried last night, but understand their father is dying. They want to say goodbye to him today. We'll be here to help them cope. Nobody says it's easy, but they're young and resilient. Trust me, they'll be okay."

"I hope you're right."

My dad joined the conversation. "I'm worried about *you*, Bahar. You're not paying any attention to yourself. There is going to be a lot more pressure on you in the next few weeks. Don't forget you have your next chemo coming up too. You need all the strength you can get."

"Okay," I sighed in agreement. "I understand your concern. I don't want to make you worry about me on top of everything else." I looked at the three of them, feeling grateful. "I don't know what I would've done without you here. Thank you," I whispered.

The children spent most of the night in Omid's room. I tried to rest as much as possible, but I couldn't leave my kids to mourn alone. I walked into Omid's room a little past 8:00 p.m. and found his parents, Navid, and my family in the bedroom. I saw Kayvon huddled in the corner with bloodshot eyes staring at his father and Koosha on the bed. Koosha clung to Omid's shirt, whimpering like a lost puppy.

Kayvon ran up to me and hugged me tightly. I caressed his hair. "It's alright, my love. I'm here. Everything's alright," I tried to console him. He started wailing, overcome with emotion. I held him tightly and tried to soothe him with my kisses. Koosha looked up from the bed and reached out his arms, longing for my embrace. Still holding onto Kayvon, we made our way to the bed.

Taraneh and Mansoor observed us through tear-filled eyes. My mom shook her head, looking grief-stricken, and hid her face in the palm of her hands, watching the three of us lay next to Omid.

Koosha hid his face in my chest, and Kayvon clung to my hand. "It's alright, boys. Baba is comfortable. Look, he is in a deep sleep." Koosha released me and turned to look at Omid. "The angels want him to go to Heaven with them. They want to take him there so he can watch over us and not suffer anymore," I said, choking back my tears.

"I don't want him to go, Mommy. I want Baba here with us,"

Koosha protested.

"I know, Sweetheart. I don't want him to leave us either. Even though you won't be able to see him, he will still be near us. You can still talk to him, and he can hear you."

"I hate God and all of his angels," Kayvon said angrily.

I rubbed his arms, nodding. "I know you're upset. Do you want to say anything to your Baba?" I asked Kayvon.

He nodded. "Do you want everyone to leave the room to give you privacy?"

He hesitated before answering. "Yes."

I got out of bed and motioned to everyone to leave the room. "We'll leave you alone, Sweetie. Come out when you feel like it.".

"No, I want you to stay, Mom," Kayvon said.

I nodded and told Golnaz to take Koosha. Once we were alone, Kayvon looked over at Omid and started speaking. "Baba, it's me, Kayvon. I don't know if you can hear me." He paused, and the only sound in the room was Omid's heavy breathing. Kayvon's voice cracked as he spoke. "I'm gonna miss you, Baba. Thanks for being such a good dad." He paused again, briefly, and inhaled. "Oh, and don't worry about Mom and Koosha. I'll be the man of the house like you would always ask me to be when you weren't home. I'll miss you, Baba," he said, starting to whimper. He looked over at me as if asking permission to hug his father. I nodded approvingly.

Kayvon's head fell on Omid's chest, as he sobbed. I put my hand on his shoulder and cried with him as he embraced his dad for the last time. I let him have a few more minutes before speaking. "Baba can hear you, Kayvon. He loves you very much. Do you have anything else you want to say?"

He shook his head. "Okay, Sweetheart. Why don't we ask Koosha to come in now and say *his* goodbyes?"

Kayvon nodded and headed for the door. He looked back one last time before exiting. Koosha walked into the room a few moments later. He ran to the bed and climbed into it where Omid was lying. I lay next to Koosha and kissed and caressed his arm. "Do you want to say anything to Baba?" I asked him.

"No. I just want to hug him."

We lay there for a long time in silence while Koosha clasped Omid's chest and watched him. After a while, his eyes started getting sleepy, and he fell asleep on Omid's chest. I waited until his sleep got heavier before asking Navid to take him to his room and lay him in bed. It was a few minutes past midnight. Golnaz told me Kayvon had gone to bed crying, and she stayed with him until he had fallen asleep. I nodded. My heart ached with indescribable pain. No child should ever have to go through this kind of agony. They didn't deserve this. None of us did. But I was grateful we at least had the chance to say goodbye.

Omid passed away at exactly 2:03 a.m. on Friday. I played his favorite playlist as we held a vigil for him until the very end. He left us peacefully, no longer moaning thanks to the morphine drops Danilo continuously applied under his tongue. I sat next to Omid's bed and held his hand as he took his last breath. My heart shattered to pieces as his body grew cold.

"He's gone," I said, sobbing and not speaking directly to anyone. Navid walked up behind me. He was hunched over and crying.

"Rest in peace, brother. I'll miss you," he said, staring at Omid's motionless body. "I promise you I'll look after Bahar and the boys. They'll never be alone," he said, placing a hand on my shoulder.

"Thank you, Navid," I whispered through the tears, reaching to touch his hand on my shoulder.

Hearing him speak with such conviction felt reassuring. Although I was grateful for everyone's support, I knew the support wasn't sustainable in the long term. I needed to get my masters in the next few months, even if it meant taking classes during my chemotherapy. It was important to pass the bar exam to practice law again. Omid was counting on me to take care of us. The kids were depending on me now.

Chapter 27

After Omid's death, days and nights started to blur. The kids and I spent the first few days crying and holding one another. The doorbell kept ringing, and someone was always answering the phone. The house soon resembled a flower shop with wreaths and arrangements. We started placing the arrangements in the backyard to help manage space and the boys' allergies.

"It's lovely to see how much people care. But I wish they wouldn't waste so much money sending flowers," my mother complained.

"The refrigerator is also packed with an insane amount of food," Golnaz chimed in. "I think we have enough food for the next three months!"

"I wish we could just go back to normal," I said sadly. "I just want Omid. I want our old home and my old life back. I don't want any of this food or flowers. I don't want to read the cards and be told to stay strong. I just want everything to go back to the way it was."

My father said, "Have you decided about whether or not you want to have a memorial service? Taraneh and Mansoor were asking if they can help you plan it. I'll leave it up to you, but I am not sure if it's a good idea to have you exposed to a lot of people with your high risk for infection during chemotherapy."

I sighed. "I know a lot of people want to come and pay their respects. I can't imagine not having a service for him, Baba. I owe him that farewell service. The kids need to see how much everyone loved their father."

"Okay, I respect your decision. Just tell us what you have in mind."

"My next chemotherapy is in a week. If we have the memorial service a few days after the painful belly injection to raise my white blood cells, my risk of infection will be lower. If it makes you feel better, I'll also wear a mask and not shake anyone's hand," I replied.

"That sounds fair," my dad replied, sounding more relaxed.

"Do you need us to talk with Taraneh and Mansoor and figure out the details?" Golnaz offered. "I don't want you to overexert yourself before the next chemotherapy."

"Thanks. That would be great. I know they're still upset with me about Omid's cremation. I am only honoring his wishes. They can't blame me for doing what he asked."

"Of course not, Sweetheart," my mom responded. "I'm sure they'll come around. They're just in shock. They were probably assuming you guys would follow the traditional Islamic burial method of washing the corpse and wrapping it in a white shroud for burial. Since neither of you is religious and you're honoring his wishes, they should come to terms with that."

"My heart breaks for them as well. I can't imagine how much they're suffering." I paused then added, "The weekend after the memorial, I want to hire a boat and go to Del Mar Beach with the family to spread Omid's ashes in the ocean."

"Okay, we'll help you arrange it," Golnaz replied. "Now get some rest, please. You look pale."

I closed my eyes and leaned back against the headboard. I was physically and emotionally exhausted. So much was going through my head at lightning speed.

"Bahar. Bahar. Wake up. I brought you some dinner," Golnaz announced. I awoke, startled by her voice. The light was on, and the curtains were drawn.

She placed the tray on my lap and waited for me to start eating. I sat up on the bed and picked up the utensils.

"How do you feel?" Golnaz asked as I ate with little appetite.

"I don't remember falling asleep," I replied, after swallowing a mouthful of rice and kabob.

"Yeah, you passed out while we were still talking. You've been napping now for over five hours. Mom didn't want you to sleep through the night without dinner."

"Thanks. I'm such a burden to all of you."

"Oh, please!" Golnaz exclaimed. "We're happy to help."

"I can't thank you enough for putting your life on hold for the boys and me. Speaking of your life, I've been meaning to ask you about Giovanni. How does he feel about your staying out here for so long? Is he coming to visit soon?"

"He is. He might even be coming to stay," she said, smiling widely. "He applied for an engineering position at Qualcomm when I first got here. He's already passed a couple of phone interviews. There is one last interview before they decide to offer him the job. I'm crossing my fingers it works out."

I swallowed my food. "That's great news!" I replied happily. "I can't wait to hear it's a sure thing."

After finishing my plate, Golnaz nodded approvingly. "Are you craving anything else? Shall I bring you some tea?"

I shook my head. "No, thanks. I'm full, but I do want to ask you for a favor."

"Sure, anything. What do you need?"

I ran my hand through my hair, and my palm filled with a clump of loose strands. "Will you help me shave off my hair?"

"Yes. Yes, of course," she said softly, sounding a little taken aback.

She pulled a chair in the front of the sink for me to sit down. I sat facing away from the mirror. She pulled my hair in a ponytail and took a pair of shears to cut it all off in one snip.

She handed me the ponytail, still tied with a rubber band. "What should I do with it?" I asked, holding the limp hair in my hand.

"Keep it for now. You'll figure it out later."

Golnaz turned on the electric clippers and shaved my hair row by row. When it was finished, I turned my head and looked in the mirror. I looked like a sickly woman with hollow eyes and sunken cheeks. I splashed some cold water on my face, secretly hoping to wash away the ugliness of the reflection in the mirror. I failed miserably. I opened the bathroom drawer and pulled out a blue floral cap I had purchased to lessen the discomfort of being bald. I felt awkward and apprehensive covering my head with it. It brought back the same level of anger and anxiety I felt when I was forced to wear the compulsory Roosari on my head to cover my hair in Iran. Although I was now bald, I still hated covering my head with any type of cloth.

Golnaz hugged me as I wept. "Please don't be sad. It's only for a few months until your hair grows back again. We'll find a nice wig for you if it'll make you more comfortable. You look beautiful, no matter what."

"Thanks. I'm tired. I think I'm going to lie down for a while." I released Golnaz and walked out of the bathroom.

"Sounds good," Golnaz replied, following me. "I'm going to check on the boys and take the tray back to the kitchen. I'll come to join you in a bit."

Trudging back to bed, I took note of the rows of pill bottles in varying sizes stacked in a row inside a small bin on the nightstand next to my bed. I now had a pill for every single symptom one could imagine. One for pain, nausea, itchiness, diarrhea, constipation, dizziness, anxiety, depression, and even sleep.

I grimaced, looking at the choices wondering which remedy would help glue my broken heart. Sitting on the bed with the shaded lamp shining on the bottles, I asked, "Which one of you can put me out of this misery? Which one is going to put me to sleep and prevent me from facing another day without Omid? Huh? What are any of you good for if you can't help me fix *that* problem?"

I snatched up the bottle of Xanax from the tray and shook it to figure out how many tablets were inside. Pouring the pink tablets onto my palm, I counted over twenty. They were such small tablets, but I knew taking one would put me in a deep sleep for at least the next eight hours. I had taken no more than ten tablets at most in my whole life.

Now my hands shook as I tightened my grip around the pills and thought about swallowing all twenty and washing them down with a glass of water. Raising my hand toward my mouth, I heard Koosha's voice outside the room.

"Is Mommy sleeping?" he asked Golnaz.

"Yes, Sweetie. She just ate dinner and is resting now. Why don't we go to the kitchen and have some ice cream together?"

"Okay," Koosha replied with excitement.

As the small patter of footsteps faded behind the closed door, I dropped my closed fist on my lap and yelled in frustration. "*God damn it!*" I couldn't do it. I couldn't be selfish and die. My kids needed me. It wouldn't be fair for them to go through the loss of yet another parent.

I forcefully opened the bottle and dropped the tablets back into it. Shoving the bottle into the nightstand drawer, I slammed it shut. Wiping away the burning tears of frustration, I stood and opened the bedroom door to join everyone in the kitchen. I needed to be with my kids. The last thing I needed was to be alone.

Chapter 28

Stella sat silently and watched as Leigh Ann started my IV infusion. "Okay, Bahar. You're all set. I'll be back in about an hour to check on you. Just let me know if you need anything."

"Thank you, Leigh Ann," I replied, nodding.

Once Leigh Ann was gone, Stella started to speak. "How are you and the kids holding up?"

"We're taking things day by day. Making the best of the situation, I guess."

"That's good to hear. I've been thinking about you a lot lately and trying to figure out what I can do to help."

"Oh, you and Shawn have already done *so* much for us. Honestly, I couldn't have asked for more. You're truly amazing friends."

"You would've done the same if the tables were turned. It's the least we can do at a time like this."

Stella covered my feet with a pair of thick socks. Then she held the ice packs on top of the socks before putting on another pair on my feet to hold them in place. She carried out the same routine for my hands before sitting back down and relaxing.

"You and Omid have always helped anyone in need. Everyone keeps asking us how they can help *you* now in exchange. Flowers and cards are nice gestures, but the money spent on those doesn't help you and the boys with anything."

I sighed. "I know. God knows we need the money more than flowers right now, but it's still a very sweet gesture. I'm grateful for the outpouring of love."

Stella nodded. "Have you thought of alternative sources of income?"

I sat thinking for a minute. "Well, I have a lot of designer things gathering dust in the closet. I'm sure they're worth some money." I shook my head sadly. "I can't believe how much money I spent on those frivolous things. If I could go back, I would trade every single designer purse and dress I own to have one more hour with Omid."

"Don't be so hard on yourself. All of us like nice things. You had a good job before and bought what your heart desired. After getting married, Omid continued the trend because he saw how happy it made you. There's nothing wrong with that. Liking designer things and buying them doesn't make you a bad person. I'm sure you would've done things differently if you had known how much debt you guys were in."

I thought about it for a few minutes. She was right. Omid had never shared our financial troubles. I blamed myself for having blinders on as well.

"I never thought I would see this day. The Bahar, with designer clothes and purses, eating at the finest restaurants, and traveling around the world, is selling everything she owns to avoid bankruptcy."

"I know, Sweetie, but remember, this is temporary. Before you know it, you will finish your studies and have an amazing job."

I felt ashamed. "The truth is, I don't care about any of that stuff anymore. I just want us to be happy again. I miss the simple things in life. I miss laughing, family breakfasts on Sunday mornings, or just sitting together and watching TV on a Friday night. Nothing is more precious than health and peace of mind. Everything else you can go without."

"I completely agree."

"I would love it if you can help me go through my closet and find things I can put up for sale. I've seen people selling items online. Have you used any of those websites before?"

She nodded. "Yes, I've sold some of my things online. I think it's a great idea. I'm happy to stop by and help out."

"Thanks. Let's plan on it after the memorial service and the private ceremony on the boat. My classes are also scheduled to start soon. I'm anxious to get everything done quickly."

"That's a great idea," she replied, sounding pleased.

"I'm not sure how much information I can retain. I can barely recite the alphabet, but I've got no choice other than to get it done."

"I'm sure you'll do great."

As we pulled into my driveway later that morning, I turned to Stella and said, "Thanks again for taking me. Golnaz has had her hands full getting things set up for the memorial service."

"Please don't mention it. It's a pleasure. I enjoy having you all to myself for a few hours," Stella replied, leaning in to hug me. "I'll stop by a little later to pick up your boys for the sleepover at our place."

"Yes. They are so excited to spend the night with your boys. They've been talking about it all week. It's the first time I've let them spend the night at anyone's house, but you're not just anyone. I think it'll do them good to have a change of atmosphere."

"We're thrilled to have them. My boys have been excited thinking about it too."

I kissed her goodbye and walked into the house. I wanted nothing more than to find my bed and take a long restful nap.

Chapter 29

$\mathcal{I}$ spent the next couple of days taking numerous painkillers and other mind-numbing cocktails of medicine. I knew I was breathing and eating, but there was no other sensation of feeling alive. On the day of the memorial, I got out of bed and dressed without much thought. The drugs had numbed my pain. I felt like a mobile mannequin programmed with basic movements. I methodically put on my black dress and situated a short pixie cut wig. I had never worn it until today. It felt odd to see myself in the mirror with another person's hair on my head. The wig represented yet another new adjustment.

Stella brought me a few pairs of gloves and a face mask. My immune system was weak. The smallest exposure to any infection would surely land me in the hospital. The oncologist was adamant about minimizing my contact with others. However, in all her years of practice, she hadn't imagined a scenario where her cancer patient would be mourning the death of her spouse, who had died from cancer as well. She reluctantly gave her consent to letting me be present at the memorial service, but advised me to take the necessary precautions.

The hotel conference room had a capacity of five hundred people. Looking behind me, I saw that every single seat was taken with mourners wanting to pay their respects. Row after row of people sat donning black mourning attire while listening to stories and memories shared on stage by Omid's friends and family. Sounds laughter and tears filled the room throughout the two-hour service.

Koosha, Kayvon, and I sat in the front row and listened to the eulogies. We shed our tears in silence. Not having the strength or courage to stand and deliver my remarks, I asked Golnaz to share them with everyone on my behalf. She read my words in Farsi and then in English, paying homage to the man I loved so dearly and thanked everyone for their love and support through Omid's illness.

When she finished the eulogy and stepped off the stage, I felt a dam of emotions burst within me. I started wailing uncontrollably and uttering incoherent sentences. "Omid! Omid, Sweetheart, where are you? Everyone's here to see you. We're all waiting for you. Look, Kayvon and Koosha are here too. Omid, my love. Why aren't you here?" I wailed hysterically.

"Mommy, please stop! You're scaring me," Koosha pleaded, looking frightened.

My mom and dad tried to console Koosha as Stella and Golnaz picked me up gently from the ground and quickly escorted me out of the hall. I continued to scream Omid's name ripping off my wig and throwing it on the ground.

The rest of the service continued without me as I rested on a cot crying silently in the adjacent room. After the last mourner left the hall, Stella returned and helped me to the car. Koosha and Kayvon were already seated in the back seat. I stepped in quietly and turned my head to see how they were doing.

"I'm so sorry, babies. I don't know what happened. I'm not feeling like myself lately with the medication. Are you both okay?" I asked, reaching to touch them in comfort.

They both nodded and avoided my gaze. They were treating me like a fragile porcelain doll. I sensed they feared I'd shatter.

Turning my body to face the front, I closed my eyes and rested during the fifteen-minute drive home. Once we arrived, Stella led me to the room and helped me undress. She handed me a glass of water and a Xanax. "There you go. You'll feel better soon." She kissed my forehead.

I shook my head. "Nothing will ever be okay, Stella. Nothing will ever be okay again," I protested.

"Come now. Just close your eyes and try not to think. I'll be outside helping Golnaz bring things in. Call me if you need anything. I'll leave the door open, okay?"

I lay there for a few moments until my eyes grew heavy. As I fell into a deep slumber, I dreamt of Omid. We were sailing, the gentle breeze brushing against our faces. My hair flung wildly as the boat cut through the choppy waves. I sat with my back against Omid's chest as we headed toward the horizon. He embraced me while holding the blanket on my lap to keep the wind from blowing it into the waves. We watched the beautiful sunset as his cheek nuzzled against my ear. His warm breath caressed my skin. I was smiling, but had tears flowing in the wind. He tightened his grip, the smile never waning from his face. He still had hair, and I could not see any traces of his illness. The soft glow from the sun's rays illuminated his face and made his brown eyes sparkle.

He looked happy and peaceful. Whispering into my ear, he said, "I will always love you, Bahar," and kissed me on the neck.

I felt him pulling away, but I resisted. I held onto his arms. "No, you can't leave! I won't let you go." His body started to suddenly dissipate before my eyes until he vanished.

"No!" I screamed and startled myself and Golnaz awake. The room was pitch dark. Despite the beads of sweat trickling down my temples, my body shivered.

"What's wrong? What happened?" she asked, sounding concerned.

"Sorry, I'm fine. I just had a nightmare," I said reassuringly. "Go back to sleep," I continued.

I flipped my pillow over and removed my pajama bottoms. I was experiencing a hot flash from the low estrogen levels. The damn drugs were putting my body through a roller coaster ride. After cooling off a bit, I took a sip of water and closed my eyes again.

This time when I fell asleep, I saw nothing but darkness. I preferred that over bittersweet nightmares that ended with me losing Omid. Having endured his loss while awake, I dreaded the idea of losing him in my dreams as well.

On Saturday, we rented a small boat, and twenty of us set sail to release Omid's ashes in the ocean. It was a small family affair. Kayvon played a mix of songs from Omid's playlist as Koosha held onto the urn that contained his father's ashes. We set sail a little after 4:00 p.m. and walked to the bow just before sunset to release his ashes into the water. Seal's song "Love's Divine" played in the background. The scenery was a replica of my dream. As we released the ashes, a warm breeze spiraled around me, giving me the sense of Omid's presence engulfing me. Wrapping my arms around myself, I closed my eyes and hummed to the song.

Once we released the ashes, I embraced the boys. I tried to comfort them as best as I could. Kayvon was visibly crying, his tears turning into sobs.

"It's okay. It's okay, baby" I said, relieved to see Kayvon release some of the pent-up emotions.

"I miss him, Mom," Kayvon said between sobs. "I wish he was still here. I want to talk to him again," he said, continuing to sob.

"I know. I miss him too," I responded, stroking his hair. He was starting to look as handsome as his father.

As we got closer to the dock, Koosha pointed to the sky and shouted, "Mom, look! There's a bird right up there!" I looked up and gasped. A huge bird with drawn-out wings circled high above us. It dove down momentarily, flying right above our heads. I gasped when

I realized it was an eagle. Eagles were Omid's favorite bird. He kept a collection of eagle statues and a large hardcover picture book of them in his waiting room at work. When Kayvon and Koosha were younger, Omid and the kids would binge-watch several *National Geographic* documentaries about them. Seeing one fly over us now was a sure sign to the three of us that Omid was still with us. We all stood on the dock watching the majestic eagle make multiple circles above us before flying out toward the horizon.

As we walked back to the car, an air of calm overcame everyone. We drove home in silence with the kids looking out the window in search of that glorious eagle. It warmed my heart to watch their wide-eye expressions in hopes of catching a glimpse of their father once again.

Chapter 30

During the next few months, I completed four more cycles of chemotherapy. The side effects were debilitating. Every time I reached the third week after chemo and felt my energy return, the next cycle would land me back in bed. When I wasn't sleeping or receiving visitors, I studied for my classes.

The kids were seeing a therapist to help them through the grieving process. Golnaz and Navid were also making sure the boys were keeping up with their schoolwork and monitoring whom they befriended at school. My parents took care of managing the household and making sure we had everything we needed to live comfortably. Despite Omid's absence, our new lives began to develop a daily routine.

We celebrated with a hot fudge sundae after dinner in the evenings following my chemotherapy infusions. Koosha had the honor of checking off a box on the paper he had created. He displayed the sheet on the fridge to remind us how many more cycles were left.

Kayvon and I were bonding much more. With the help of the therapist, he was regularly speaking to me about his father. We would spend time talking about Omid and our memories together. Although it broke my heart, I knew it was part of the healing process for him to grieve openly.

I also started seeing a therapist to help me cope with my grief. The talk sessions helped me recognize that I wasn't to blame for causing

Omid's cancer by putting extra financial burden on him. She made me realize that I was not culpable for his cancer, just as no one could be blamed for mine. We occasionally spoke about the conflicting feelings of relief and sadness that loomed within me. The relief of knowing Omid no longer required round-the-clock care and was free from any discomfort. Countered by the heavy fog of melancholy that shrouded my heart from the immense loss.

A month after my chemotherapy ended, the oncologist recommended six weeks of radiation. I continued my studies while receiving chemotherapy and radiation and received my masters degree a week after my cancer treatments ended. With the completion of my degree, I felt a tinge of happiness return to my life.

"I'm so happy for you. You did it!" Stella exclaimed, hugging me as she entered the kitchen. She had come over after hearing the news.

"I can't believe it's finally done," I replied, hugging her ecstatically.

"You are my hero. Grieving, receiving cancer treatment, and finishing your masters all at once is no small feat. What you've accomplished is unheard of!"

The kids entered the room with a large chocolate raspberry cake with shaved chocolate bits sprinkled on top. There was a large inscription on the cake in red coloring that read, "Congratulations!" To my surprise, my family, Omid's family, Stella's husband, their boys, and even Sogol streamed in behind them.

"Oh, my goodness! What's all this!?" I exclaimed, clasping my face in shock.

"You didn't think we wouldn't recognize such a great accomplishment without a celebration, did you?" Golnaz asked. She gathered everyone behind me for a photograph.

As I smiled for the picture, surrounded by the people nearest and dearest to my life, I let the warmth of their love energize and give me hope for the future. I didn't care if I was bald, thin, and with burn marks on my body from the radiation treatments. I didn't think about the pending lawsuit for the medical practice or our financial hardship. I envisioned Omid staring back at me as I blew out my candles. I saw his face beaming with pride. For once, I didn't feel guilty about being alive.

We spent the evening laughing, eating, drinking, and sharing funny stories. I laughed out loud for the first time in months. It felt glorious. Although Omid's parents were present, they were quiet for most of the evening. Being ill and preoccupied with studying in the past few months, I hadn't spent too much time with them. I was happy to see them tonight.

"How are you, Taraneh joon?" I asked. I handed her a hot cup of tea and sat next to her on the couch, far away from the crowd. While sipping from my cup, I waited for her to respond.

"I'm doing okay, I guess," she began. "I picture Omid everywhere I look. I just can't stop thinking about how much I miss him every day. Every place I go or every special event we attend rips at my core when I think how much he deserves to be here."

"I know what you mean. I often feel guilty for outliving him."

She nodded. "Just imagine how much guiltier a mother feels outliving her son. That goes against everything Mother Nature intended." She sighed.

With a more cheerful tone, she added, "So, you finally finished your masters! Omid would have been so proud of you. I know the past few months have been hard for all of us, but what you did is so admirable. Bravo."

I smiled. "I wish he were here to celebrate with us. The next task is to prepare for the bar exam. That's going to be difficult to pass."

"I'm sure you'll do fine. I see that little sparkle in your eyes again. You had lost it for a while. When do you plan on taking the test?"

"I'm planning on taking it in February. I should get the results before Memorial Day weekend. Hopefully, if all goes well, I can start looking for a job at the beginning of summer," I said, thinking about the long journey still ahead.

"Well, I think you deserve a break after the exam is done. A small getaway to recuperate and renew. Maybe you can go somewhere for a few days with your friends," she suggested. I smiled without replying. I wasn't sure I had the means to treat myself with our current financial situation.

After everyone went home and Golnaz and I started cleaning up, I recapped my discussion with Taraneh with her. Golnaz listened intently.

Her face perked up, and she clapped her hands together when she heard about Taraneh's suggestion to take a trip. "Yes! That sounds like an amazing idea. I think we should do it! It'll be so much fun to go on a girl's trip and get away for a little while."

I hesitated. "I don't know. I haven't traveled without Omid for as long as I can remember. Plus, I feel guilty leaving the kids. Don't you think it's selfish?"

"Are you kidding me?! You are the least selfish human being I have ever known. Your body and mind have just survived a category four hurricane. Nobody deserves to get away for a few days more than you. Come on," she coaxed, "We could go somewhere for a few days. Plus, the boys couldn't come even if you wanted to bring them. They have soccer practices, remember?"

"That's right, I forgot about that. But I can't *afford* to go anywhere! I don't have a job yet."

"All you have to do is to buy a ticket using your airline miles. If we ask a couple more people to join us, we can split the other expenses, so it won't cost a lot."

I thought about what she said. I had to wait a few weeks for my test results after taking the bar. Until I had the results, I wouldn't be able to get a job. "Who were you thinking of asking to join us?"

"That's the right attitude!" she cheered. "Well, I think we should ask Stella. We can also ask Shirin to meet us wherever we end up." Golnaz said, sitting on the couch and tossing her feet up. "Oh, this is going to be so much fun!" She grabbed her phone and started searching.

Amused, I laughed. "Whoa, take it easy there. You aren't going to start planning for it this late at night, are you?"

"No, but now that you've agreed, I want to at least pin down the place we want to visit. Where do you feel like going?"

I couldn't think straight at first. Golnaz caught me off-guard with her inquiry. I had memories everywhere with Omid. We both loved Europe so much that we visited almost every big city there. "Um, I guess one of the places we always planned to visit but never had the chance is Portugal."

"Perfect! I haven't been to Portugal either. Your test is in February. So, we can't go then. And we need to be here with family for the Iranian New Year on March 20th. So, I'll look for some deals in late March or early April."

I nodded in agreement.

"Yay! Before I look for flights, I'll text Shirin and Stella and let them know," she replied, typing. "Once we figure out the exact date, I'll request time off from work."

"Sounds good. Now let's go to bed. I'm exhausted," I said, yawning. The idea of traveling made me happy. It felt good to look forward to a new adventure. It also gave me more motivation to get through my studies and focus on the road ahead.

Golnaz didn't look up from her phone as she said, "You go ahead. I'll be right there." Then she suddenly looked up and grinned. "This is going to be just what you need! You won't regret it."

Chapter 31

$\mathcal{I}$ spent most of December studying diligently. I was more energetic, but my ability to retain information was proving to be challenging. I continued to stay focused and looked forward to putting this exam behind me once and for all. I had a new sense of purpose and wanted to prove that I still had fight left in me. Plus, I wanted to earn my vacation to Portugal by working hard. The idea of traveling and getting away from everything gave me the motivation I needed.

As Christmas got closer, the dread of the family holiday started to creep in. Every Christmas, we planned a family getaway. Omid would take time off from December twenty-fourth until January second. This year I had to maximize my time studying and couldn't spare the time to take the kids anywhere.

My parents were returning to Iran for a few weeks, while Omid's parents had plans to go to Arizona to visit their friends. Golnaz was flying to Italy and spending Christmas and New Year's with Giovanni's family, and Navid planned to travel to Mexico with some of his co-workers.

When I told Stella about my plans to stay in San Diego and study through the holidays, she asked if the boys wanted to join them on their ski trip to Lake Tahoe. I hesitated at first but seeing how excited the boys were to be with their friends, I finally relented.

"Are you sure you'll be okay by yourself, Mommy?" Koosha asked before leaving on the trip.

"We don't have to go if you don't want us to," Kayvon chimed in.

"Don't be silly, guys. I appreciate your concern, but I have lots to do here. I need to focus on studying. I don't want to retake this exam. I promise, next Christmas we'll go somewhere nice, just the three of us. Is that a deal?" I asked, smiling encouragingly.

The kids nodded in agreement. Stella would arrive soon to pick them up. They were getting an early morning start and driving to Lake Tahoe.

"Now remember, I don't want you to argue with each other. They're being sweet to invite you. I don't want either of you misbehaving. And please be careful skiing. We don't want to see any broken bones. Come back with only good memories. Got it?"

"Yes, Maman," Koosha bellowed back.

"Yeah, got it," Kayvon replied, throwing his heavy bag over one shoulder.

Shawn and Stella pulled into the driveway. They popped the trunk, and Shawn stepped out to help with the bags. Their sons were sitting in the backseat waiting for Koosha and Kayvon.

"Good morning. How are you?" Stella asked, stepping out of the car.

"I'm good. How are you guys? Ready for the long road trip?" I asked.

"Yeah, I think so. It's good to get an early start," Stella said, watching the boys jump into the car. "By the way, did you check to see the sales on the website recently? I think you'll be pleasantly surprised," she said, smirking.

"No, I haven't. The last time I checked, I think one small item was sold, but that was around two months ago." I studied her face. "Now, I'm curious. I'll check today."

"Please do." She hesitated before saying goodbye. "You sure

you're going to be okay by yourself?"

"Oh yeah, I'll be fine," I said, swatting her concern away with my hand. "Go and have fun. Feel free to scold the kids if they misbehave."

She kissed me goodbye and returned to the car, leaving me waving to them as they sped away. Closing the door behind me, I picked up my phone and logged onto the website to check the total sales of the merchandise Stella and I had put online. I shifted the phone back and forth to make sure the number I read was correct. Everything in my account had been sold, and the total amount was tallied to $90,000. I couldn't believe my eyes!

My hands shook while texting Stella. "This is unbelievable! How did you manage to sell all my stuff? I'm speechless."

She texted back with a smiling emoji. "I thought you'd be happy. You had a lot of hidden treasures in that closet of yours. Those things were worth a pretty penny."

"I don't know what to say. You're the best friend a girl could ever ask for!"

I wondered how many of my things she had bought herself or talked friends into buying. I was thankful to her and felt a sense of relief to have some money on hand.

I spent most of the following days in pajamas studying, other than the times I took intermittent breaks walking around the neighborhood or working out in the gym. I enjoyed being accountable only to myself. I ate breakfast food for dinner and indulged in chocolate cake and ice cream whenever I had a craving. Dark thoughts occasionally crept in, robbing me of my inner peace. That's when a long drive and meditation helped me to get centered again and focus on the present.

The kids called me every night to tell me about their day. I could tell from the excitement in their voice that they were having fun. After our evening chats, I allotted some free time to watch *Game of*

Thrones. I got lost in the dark series revolving around power, lust, death, and destruction. It was a nice distraction from the sappy love stories I used to watch. Realizing happy endings are seldom found in real life, I preferred watching storylines with sick twisted plots that closely mirrored my own life.

I spent Christmas morning on video calls with the kids as well as Golnaz and Giovanni in Italy. Putting on a red dress and painting my lips a shade of tomato red, provided a festive flair to ward off any anxieties they felt about me spending the holidays by myself.

"You look beautiful, Bahar," Golnaz said when she saw me on the video screen. "Where are you headed?"

I lied and told her I was invited to attend church with our neighbor friends. "They insisted I have Christmas dinner with them."

"That's wonderful! I'm glad you're socializing again. I miss you. Can't wait to see you," she said, blowing me a kiss with her hand.

"I miss you too. Now go spend some time with Giovanni and his folks. Say hi to everyone. Tell Giovanni I can't wait for him to visit," I replied, blowing her a kiss in return.

I hung up and sat in silence. The apartment was bare–no decorated Christmas tree, wrapped gifts, or the sound of Koosha and Kayvon giggling. It lacked all the sights and sounds from our past Christmas mornings. Although I was born into a Muslim family, we always enjoyed celebrating all holidays regardless of religious or cultural denomination. Omid and I especially loved celebrating Christmas and Iranian New Year.

The kids always received gifts from Santa in late December, and the Iranian Santa, Amoo Norooz, would also surprise them with presents on the first day of Spring. We wanted the boys to assimilate with the U.S. culture while cultivating their Iranian heritage by recognizing Iranian traditions.

Omid would always initiate the winter holiday season by bringing home a fresh Christmas tree the day after Thanksgiving. Christmas lights were installed around the exterior of the house by a professional hired hand. None of those elements were present this year. My heart and the apartment both felt cold and empty.

Video chats completed, I looked forward to quickly ending the day. I silenced my phone, wiped off my makeup, put on pajamas, and slipped under the comforter. Washing down a Xanax tablet with a sip of water, I drew the curtains and stared at the empty pillow next to me.

The tears started to fall. "Merry Christmas, Omid," I whispered, stroking the empty pillow. "I miss you so much it hurts. I miss everything about you. Our late-night chats in bed. Our little tiffs and the intense lovemaking after we made up. I wish I could touch you right now. I wish I could see your sweet, handsome face and hear your gentle voice. If I could wish for a miracle, it would be the miracle of having you here again."

My tears soaked the pillow. Eventually, my eyes grew heavy until I fell into a long and deep sleep.

I spent the remainder of the holidays falling into a routine of intense studying and exercising to let off some steam. I spent New Year's Eve alone watching the final episodes of *Game of Thrones* and falling asleep before midnight.

The kids returned on New Year's Day. "Hi, guys. Welcome back!" I exclaimed as I flung the door open and hugged them one by one. Stella had escorted them to the door.

Koosha jumped excitedly into my arms. "Hi, Mommy! Happy New Year!" he said, tightly embracing me.

"Happy New Year!" Stella said, greeting me with a kiss on each cheek.

"Hi, Mom. How are you?" Kayvon asked, also appearing happy to be home.

The boys went up to their rooms to unpack their stuff, while Stella stayed for a few minutes to chat before heading home to tend to her family.

"So, how was it?" I asked when Koosha and Kayvon joined me in the living room. The fresh air had brought color back to their cheeks, and they looked healthy and refreshed.

Kayvon's lips appeared chapped. He put some Chapstick on them before answering. "It was fun. We went skiing every day. I even tried snowboarding one time."

"Wow, that sounds fun. Did you try snowboarding too?" I asked, turning my gaze to Koosha.

"No, all you do is fall on your butt when you snowboard. I like skiing better," he proclaimed. "We stayed in a cabin with two rooms. Ben and Alex shared a room with us. There were two bunk beds. Kayvon even let me sleep on the top bunk a couple of times!"

"It seems like you both had a great time," I replied, happy to see my boys again.

The day later my parents flew back from Iran, and Golnaz returned from Italy a week after that. The house was full again, and the boys returned to school. I continued to study for the bar. Mom resettled into her routine of manning the kitchen and reconnecting with friends, while Dad busied himself reading and watching television during the day and taking long walks in the evenings for exercise.

Although we were all busy with our itineraries during the day, we made a point to spend every evening having dinner together. It was nice to have everyone back in one place. Although I had enjoyed my days of solitude during the break, being surrounded by family pushed me to focus on the future instead of the past.

Chapter 32

Exam day arrived. Golnaz drove me to the test site at the Anaheim Convention Center. Leaving me at the curb, she said, "You're gonna do great." Then she referenced a quote from *The Marvelous Mrs. Maisel* TV series where Midge, the protagonist, was encouraged by her manager Susie before getting on stage. "Tits up, Midge!" Golnaz cheered.

I laughed and straightened my posture as I pushed out my chest before stepping out of the car. I waved at Golnaz as she sped away. My stomach was empty, and the unrelenting anxiety of failure made me nauseated. The sour taste in the back of my throat made me gag. I closed my eyes and slowed my breathing. The fear of failing the bar and not being able to retake it for another few months terrified me. I had spent more than half of the money I received from selling my things to pay for additional legal fees for the lawsuit. With less than $40,000 to my name, this test was my only shot to pull us out of the abyss of financial uncertainty.

The large convention room was filled with rows of tables separated by six feet to mitigate the risk of cheating. Each table had a single chair with a number taped behind the seat. There were two number 2 pencils on top of an otherwise bare tabletop. I checked in by presenting my ID and was directed to my seat. I estimated there were at least five hundred people in the room. Almost everyone fidgeted in their chairs while waiting for the test booklets to be distributed. I took my seat, and the proctor started speaking at 8:30 a.m.

"Please do not open the packets that are being distributed until all instructions have been given. You will be told when to begin," she announced. "You will have exactly three hours to complete the morning portion of the exam. You must raise your hand when you're ready to turn in the packet to the test monitors who will be walking around the room. There will be a one-hour lunch break. You need to be back in your seats by 1:00 p.m. For the afternoon portion of the exam, you will have two essay questions and a ninety-minute Performance Test. Once you are finished and turn in your test booklet, you are excused for the day. Please write legibly and refrain from talking. No electronics or other papers will be allowed for the duration of the exam. Are there any questions?" she asked and paused.

The only noise during the entire exam was the whooshing sound from the vents that blew cold air into the room. My feet started tapping nervously under the table as I began counting in my head to distract myself.

I was grateful once we were told to open our booklets. I was so immersed in the exam that I didn't realize how much time had passed before the proctor announced that only thirty minutes remained. Most of the essay questions appeared rather straightforward, but I kept second-guessing my responses until the very last minute.

"Time's up!" the proctor announced over the microphone. I placed my pencil on the table and closed my booklet.

For the one-hour lunch break, I chose the closest deli within walking distance of the convention center. By the time I ordered and received my food, I had to race back to avoid being locked out of the room. The afternoon session was less complicated than the morning one. I raised my hand to turn in my exam packet after completing the Performance Test with fifteen minutes to spare. My stomach was growling, and my head throbbing as I exited through the double glass doors. Spotting Golnaz's car from afar, I waved her over and jumped into the car the moment she drew close to the curb.

"Thank God you're here early. I just couldn't sit in that room any longer! I'm starving and need an Advil," I said, laying my head back against the headrest and closing my eyes.

Golnaz frowned. "Sorry to hear that. My head would throb too if I had to take an exam that lasted for eight hours!" She reached into her purse and took out a small travel size bottle of Advil. I took the bottle and washed down two capsules with a large gulp of water.

"Finish the whole water bottle," Golnaz suggested. "You're probably dehydrated. I don't understand why they don't let you guys take any water or snacks in with you. How can anyone cheat with a water bottle?" she asked, shaking her head.

"Who the hell knows! I'm just happy today is over. Do you mind if we go to the hotel and order room service? I want to take a shower, change into my pajamas, and relax. I need to get to sleep early tonight. One more day of exams, then I'm done."

"Of course. But don't you dare tell me you're tired tomorrow. After this test is done, we're going out to celebrate!"

Once at the hotel, Golnaz ordered dinner while I showered. We ate and relaxed while watching television before falling asleep at 9:00 p.m. I started my morning with a full continental breakfast before Golnaz dropped me off for the final day of testing. The questions turned out to be multiple-choice, and I felt more comfortable with my knowledge about that portion of the exam. When I turned in my test packet and walked out of the hall, the muscles in my neck relaxed, and a sense of relief came over me. I exhaled for what felt like the first time in months.

Golnaz greeted me with a large bouquet of pink roses and a

beautiful card. "You're the best sister anyone could ever ask for!" I said, hugging her tightly.

"You've worked so hard. I'm so proud of you. Now it's time to go celebrate!"

We drove to a quaint restaurant nearby. Famished, I ordered the steamed mussels and clams while Golnaz chose the braised short ribs. After devouring the last morsel of my custard-filled puff pastry, I sat back and sipped on my wine, enjoying our lighthearted conversation.

"My goodness, that was delicious," I said, embracing the dance of flavors on my palette and feeling lightheaded from the alcohol.

Golnaz laughed. "I've missed seeing your beautiful smile."

"It's been a long time since I felt relaxed. For the past few months, all my thoughts have been about the funeral, my treatments, the bar, and the lawsuit. Today was a big day for me. I feel like I finally fulfilled a dream I'd put off for so long. Pass or fail, I did the best I could."

Golnaz raised her glass. "Well, cheers to you. For finally fulfilling your dream."

We clinked our wine glasses and sat drinking and chatting for a long while. Once back at the hotel, I went to bed and slept soundly and peacefully.

Chapter 33

*T*he Vernal Equinox falls on March twentieth almost every year. That means all around the world, the Iranian New Year, or Norooz, is celebrated at the same time. This year we celebrated the New Year without Omid. I forced myself to continue the traditions to keep Omid's memory alive. He always wanted us to gather around the traditional Haft-Seen to ring in the New Year regardless of the hour of the day. Every year, the boys enjoyed getting new clothes and shoes for the event. They also looked forward to finding hidden presents right after we rang in the New Year.

I remember one particular year Omid woke the boys at 5:30 in the morning since the Equinox fell at 5:40 a.m. and thirty-two seconds. The year before that, it fell on a more reasonable time of 6:02 p.m. and forty-seven seconds. The boys and Omid had been able to go to work and school, and return in time for the festivities.

Every year Iranians complete a thorough Spring cleaning of the house. We also set a Haft-Seen table that contains seven items starting with the letter S. Another vital item on the Haft-Seen is a small goldfish to symbolize life. Each year we named the small goldfish that we adopted. The boys enjoyed taking turns and looking after their new pet.

I would always task Kayvon to grow the sprouts from wheat or lentils. The sprouts, called Sabzeh, were symbolic of nature and an essential item for the Haft-Seen. Through the years, Kayvon had become an expert in this task. He knew exactly when to soak and drain the plate of seeds to have the sprouts grow to a perfect length right before the New Year.

The kids enjoyed coloring hard-boiled eggs and decorating them with their unique decorative flair. With the eggs representing fertility and the other seven edible items representing different aspects of life and virtues, we would complete our Haft-Seen by placing brand new bills inside the Quran. The crisp new money was a gift to visitors who came to see us during Norooz.

This year I mustered up all the courage and excitement I could to keep the traditions and make it special for the kids. I woke the boys at 7:00 a.m. and placed their new clothes on their beds. Deep down, I didn't want to celebrate. This was a holiday centered around family, renewal, and traditions. Without Omid, I couldn't bring myself to continue some of the traditions we had developed over the years. For example, every year after the Equinox, Omid would go out and pretend to be the messenger of love and health. He would ring the doorbell, and we would open the front door with a smile as he presented us with a bouquet saying the famous verse, "I bring you happiness, health, love, and the gift of togetherness. Will you permit me to enter your home and stay for the year?"

This year, my dad filled in for Omid. None of us greeted him with the same enthusiasm as when Omid rang the doorbell. My parents and Golnaz bought gifts and found good hiding places. I watched Kayvon and Koosha run around the house and the backyard searching for their presents. It made me miss Omid even more, but I was thankful that the traditions he had begun continued to be enjoyed by the boys.

Despite my grief, I was grateful to start the New Year under one roof with my parents, Golnaz, and the kids. I reminded myself that most of our hardships were behind us. Sitting around the Haft-Seen and praying, I asked God for health, happiness, and a brighter future.

"Why are you not looking for your present, Bahar?" Golnaz asked playfully.

"What do you mean? The gifts are supposed to be only for the kids," I said, raising my eyebrows curiously. Golnaz smiled and motioned for me to search the room.

"But that's not right," I whined. "Now, I feel bad. I didn't buy you guys anything. I thought we had agreed on this."

"It's alright. We didn't expect any gifts from you," Mom chimed in. "This year has been a challenging year for all of us, but particularly for you. We just wanted to get you a little something. That's all."

The kids helped me search for my gift. After a few minutes, my eyes fell on a Tumi luggage set hidden deep inside my closet. I squealed in excitement and ran out, rolling the luggage set behind me like a family of ducklings.

"Thank you so much! This is lovely," I said, hugging my mom, dad, and Golnaz in gratitude. I loved their gesture of kindness. Although I was grateful for such a nice luggage set, I was also concerned about the cost of such an expensive gift. I was beginning to tally costs more carefully and discouraged large price tag purchases in our home.

"I'm so glad you like it," Dad commented. "You deserve this plus so much more. We wanted to get you something you could use for your upcoming trip."

After breakfast, we called relatives overseas and in San Diego to wish them a Happy New Year. My last call was to Aunt Maryam and Shirin.

After three rings, Shirin picked up the phone at her mom's house.

"Hi, is that you, Shirin?" I asked when she said hello.

"Yes, of course it's me, silly," she said, laughing into the receiver. "Who else does she have as a daughter?"

I laughed too. "Happy Norooz. How are you?"

"Happy Norooz to you guys too. We're doing well. I've been counting down the days until I see you in Portugal," she replied. "Peter's been teasing me about not having too much fun on our all-girls trip. Of course, I told him we plan to do nothing *but* have fun!"

We chatted for a few minutes before Shirin passed the phone to her mom.

"Hi, Bahar joon," Maryam said, answering the phone.

"Hi, Aunt Maryam. Happy Norooz!" I replied happily.

I loved Aunt Maryam like I loved my mother. Especially after our dinner in her home with Omid over twenty years ago, I had found a much deeper respect and appreciation for her as a single mother and businesswoman. I wished she lived closer to us. It would have been wonderful to spend time with her and learn from her experiences of losing her husband many years ago.

"Happy Norooz to you too, darling. How are you doing?" she asked with a kind voice.

"I'm doing okay. We're taking things day by day. It's especially hard during the holidays. I miss Omid a lot."

"I know, Honey. We all miss him. I know how you feel. It took me years after Shirin's dad died before I felt whole again. Life had less meaning for me without him. I want to give you some advice. Something I wish someone had given me when I was a young widow. Don't continue living in the past. Move forward and keep yourself open to new things. I know you can't imagine the idea of anyone replacing Omid ever again, but a time will come when someone will enter your life. Don't make the same mistake I made and push him away out of fear or guilt. I want you to stay true to your heart but also keep an open mind. Do you know what I mean?"

I was surprised by her advice and grew pensive. I hadn't expected her to be so frank in her discussion. She was a woman who had rejected so many suitors after her husband's death. I never knew she had any regrets about her decisions. Deciding to leave the details for another day, I promised to keep an open mind and bid her goodbye.

"What's the matter, Bahar?" my mom asked as I hung up.

I was quiet for a moment pondering Maryam's words. I looked at my mom and shook my head. "Oh, nothing. Shirin and Aunt Maryam asked me to say hello to all of you and wished everyone a Happy Norooz. Aunt Maryam will call you later to talk. They were invited for dinner at a friend's house."

I cleared my throat and added, "Speaking of which, Omid's parents are waiting. Is it okay if you and Baba drive the boys over? Golnaz and I need to make a pit stop somewhere."

My parents agreed, and the four of them left together. Golnaz and I headed to Del Mar Beach. I was missing Omid and needed to visit him. I had wanted to for the past few months but had not found the courage. Speaking to Maryam gave me the push I needed to visit Omid and have a heart to heart with him. I wanted to update him on the events from the past few months and ask him to forgive me for not coming sooner. I was slowly starting to accept his premature departure from this world.

We went to a beautiful spot overlooking the Pacific Ocean. The San Diego mist covered the landscape. I brought a bag full of fragrant rose petals, and holding the bag in my lap, we drove along the road leading to the ocean.

The closer we got, the more emotional I became. Golnaz finally parked the car and turned off the engine. Leaning over, she placed her head against mine. "I know it's hard. He's been waiting for you. Go talk to Omid and tell him how much you miss him. I'll be here in the car if you need me."

I nodded, unable to speak while choking back my tears.

I opened the car door and held the handle for a few seconds before inhaling deeply and stepping out. Like a scene from a nightmare that was never supposed to happen—I was visiting my sweetheart as a widow. The man I was supposed to grow old together with was nowhere in sight. The man I was supposed to have my happily ever after with was no longer by my side. I felt a pang of anger hidden in my deep sorrow. This was our fate. I couldn't continue to question why it had to end this way.

I walked toward the cliff overlooking the ocean. My footsteps were slow and hesitant. I kneeled and started sobbing. I couldn't stop the tears as I spoke to Omid. "I'm sorry it's taken me so long to visit. Sometimes the pain of missing you makes it impossible to breathe!"

I wailed while hunched over, until my body felt limp and listless. Eventually, I felt a small tug at my back. I took Golnaz's hand and stood. I gave her a small reassuring smile to let her know she needn't worry about me. She handed me some tissues and rubbed my back, then picked up the bag of flower petals that now lay in the dirt and handed them to me.

I started conversing with Omid again. "I brought your favorite flowers today. The petals of fragrant roses like we first smelled at Regents Park. We celebrated Norooz this year without you, but I felt you there. The kids did too. Every time I look at Kayvon, I see your face. Every time Koosha smiles, it reminds me of your smile. They want to come to visit you."

It took me a minute to gather my emotions enough to continue. "They still cry every night, remembering you, wanting you to tuck them in. I comfort them with stories of you and the things we did as a family. I'm doing the best I can for them. I finished my treatment. I kept my promise to you and took the bar. I'm not sure how I did, but I did my best."

That familiar sense of loss welled up inside me, but I quickly battled it back. "I'm trying to build a life for our kids as we talked about so many times. It's so hard, Omid. Oh, I wish I could still see you and talk to you, to hold your hand and hug you. I still can't seem to make sense of it all. You left too early!"

"The family wants me to take a break and get away. I resisted at first, but I finally agreed. I'm going to Portugal for a few days. The travel bug we both shared is still alive in me. I wish we could go together. I'm going to the country we always wanted to visit. I promise to buy a little figurine for you as a souvenir. I'll visit a sweet shop to bring back some sweets to nibble on while looking at the album from the trip. But it won't be the same without you. Nothing will ever be the same without you." I put my face in my hands.

Golnaz leaned her head toward me. "Bahar joon, Omid is with you in spirit. He sees everything through your eyes."

When I said nothing, she added, "Why don't we spread these beautiful petals over the ocean waves and let him smell their perfume?" she suggested, handing me the bag of petals.

I scattered the petals into the ocean. The blue water cradled the red petals, rocking them gently in a hypnotic rhythm. We stood silently a few minutes overlooking the cliff before Golnaz gently took my hand, and we returned to the car. I looked back and whispered, "I love you" before we drove away. I had only stood on the cliff for a short while, but my body felt emotionally depleted.

We arrived at Taraneh and Mansoor's home an hour later than we intended. I could tell from the looks on their faces they were concerned about my swollen eyes and smeared makeup. They were all waiting for our arrival before eating the traditional herb-infused basmati rice with the side of white fish. I excused myself to freshen up in the bathroom. The boys were in the bedroom, playing video games. Golnaz stayed in the living room to explain where we had been. Once I composed myself, I plastered on a smile and called the boys to join us for our Norooz meal. Nobody mentioned the detour in front of the boys.

Sitting around the dinner table, Navid raised his wine glass for a toast. We all followed his lead. Even Koosha and Kayvon had wine glasses filled with sparkling apple cider and seemed happy to be a part of the festivities. "I want to raise a toast to my brother Omid. He will live forever in our hearts. We will always remember him during these gatherings. I also want to toast my amazing sister-in-law, Bahar. I love and admire you so much. The day Omid made you his wife, our family expanded. I got a new sister and my parents, a new daughter. We are so happy to celebrate Norooz with all of you. Happy Norooz, everyone!"

"Cheers!" we all said in unison and clinked our wine glasses. After eating, we played cards and board games together. Returning home later that evening, our stomachs were stuffed, and our thoughts filled with new memories of our first Norooz without Omid. The first of many new memories we had to create in his absence. It had been a bittersweet day.

Chapter 34

$\mathcal{I}$ packed relatively light for the ten-day trip. I was happy to leave home but didn't feel energetic due to the lack of sleep during the past couple of nights. What energy and enthusiasm I lacked, Golnaz and Stella made up for? We all met at our place, and Stella volunteered to drive over to LAX with her car. They blasted music during the whole car ride. The two-hour trip was smooth. By the time we arrived at the overnight parking area to drop off the car, my mood had changed for the better.

Even though we were all similar in age, our personalities were quite different. Stella was prim, proper, and soft-spoken in public. In uncomfortable situations, she would turn bright red in embarrassment and remain quiet. Golnaz was the naughty playful one and always spoke loudly and directly without caring about whom she offended. She meant no harm by her snide remarks. Being too sensitive would lead to a break in friendship with her. Golnaz was loyal and would sacrifice anything for her friends and family. She spoke four languages and had experienced life more outside of the U.S. than inside it. She also had a lust for life that was contagious. We leaned on her to plan the logistics for our trip. Shirin planned to meet up with us a few hours after we arrived in Porto. She was a gentle and considerate friend. She didn't like surprises and always planned for the unexpected. For example, when traveling, she would pack two of everything in case one got lost.

As soon as our flight took off, I fell asleep. I always enjoyed watching movies or playing games on long flights with the boys, but this time I felt I only had enough energy for sleep. Thankfully, there was minimal turbulence. I felt safe and secure enough to stretch my legs and rest. After waking, I found a bunch of wide mouth drooling pictures on my cell phone. The girls had kept themselves entertained during the flight taking pictures of me and had even asked the flight attendant to take part in their shenanigans.

"You girls are mean!" I said, playfully jabbing Golnaz in the ribs and sticking my tongue out to Stella.

Golnaz laughed. "You're lucky we didn't put a side-by-side of you and your bald head drooling against the yellow bald drooling emoji and upload it on Instagram."

We landed in Lisbon first before taking a connecting flight to Porto. Upon arriving, we immersed ourselves in the warm and inviting Portuguese culture. Golnaz had reserved a hotel overlooking the Douro River, and we arrived just in time to catch a glimpse of the mesmerizing sunset. I poured the three of us a glass of wine, and we slowly sipped it as we bid the sun a final farewell for the evening. Shirin arrived a few hours later. We decided to try seafood for our first outing, and reunited, the four of us headed to the restaurant for dinner.

We feasted on freshly caught fish and other seafood. The waiter paired every recommended dish with a unique wine from the collection inside the restaurant's wine cellar, and we finished our meal with the most scrumptious Portuguese custard-filled dessert pastries called Pastéis de Nata.

"Oh, my God! This dessert is out of this world!" Golnaz exclaimed, biting into her second Pastéis of the night.

"God, I wish Omid could have tasted this," I said in a soft voice. "I have never tasted anything like it."

Shirin smiled at me and refilled my glass with some Port wine. "My cousin always had great taste in food. His place is empty here," she said, giving me a gentle side hug.

I raised my glass. "I'd like to make a toast to my sister and two of my closest friends. Thank you for making this trip a reality. I wish Omid could've been here with us. In his absence, I couldn't imagine being in any other company, but with the three of you. I love you."

I was a little intoxicated as we walked back to our hotel along the Douro River sidewalk. Golnaz started to explain some facts she had learned about the tile work displayed along the exterior walls of various residential and government buildings.

"I read that every tiling work you see tells a story about something that happened in Portuguese history," she explained as we passed by the entryway to the Porto Train Station.

"What's the history behind this tile work?" Shirin asked, eyeing the painting displayed on the white tiles taking up the entire twenty-foot-wide wall of the train station.

Golnaz started reading from her phone. "It says this is a painting of a royal wedding back in the day."

Before she could continue, we were interrupted by a couple of young Portuguese men who also appeared intoxicated.

"Are you ladies, English?" the first man asked with a broken English accent.

"No, actually," Golnaz replied assertively. "We're from a country called None of Your Business! Come on ladies, let's go," she said, locking arms with Shirin and me, and walking rapidly.

We arrived at our hotel, breathless and sweating. "Why did you have to be so short with him? Poor guy was only making conversation," I said.

"I didn't like the way they were staring at us. I didn't want to risk it in case they had bad intentions," she replied.

The moment we walked into our room, we launched our shoes in the air, and the four of us plopped on two separate beds exhausted. Shirin and Stella fell asleep almost immediately while Golnaz and I chatted a little before following them.

"Thanks for looking out for us tonight," I said, kissing Golnaz on the cheek.

She gave me a soft look. "I promised Omid I would take care of you. I told him that he could count on me. I have to make sure I keep my promise," she said with tears in her eyes.

"Oh, Sweetie, I can take care of myself. Don't forget, the hardest part is over. This whole experience with Omid and my cancer has made me a stronger person. Nothing can break me anymore. I need you to start thinking about your life now. You've done more than enough for me and the boys."

She nodded and turned off the light. I held her hand to give her reassurance until we both fell asleep.

After spending a few days in Porto, we decided to take the train down to Lisbon. The ride was about three and a half hours, and I spent it reading a book, chatting with the girls, and fiddling with mind-numbing arcade games on my phone. I missed the kids dearly, but the trip was infusing some life back into my veins. I was starting to find my cheerful, playful side again. I was hungry for joy and happiness, and the sound of laughter with my travel companions was nourishment for my soul.

We didn't find Lisbon as visually stimulating as the lush landscapes of the Porto region. The city was structured into different quadrants of cobblestone-laden pavements with uphill and downhill streets throughout the city. The windy steep streets and trolleys in Lisbon reminded me of San Francisco. There was also an ever-present breeze in the city that prevented ventures outdoors without a thick jacket during the day and evenings. Just like Porto, we spoiled our palates with delicious fresh seafood and lots of good wine every night. We took late-night strolls in the city, watching street performers and musicians catering to the tourist crowds.

On our last day in Lisbon, a driver picked us up from the hotel and drove us to the south in the Algarve region. The trip took about five hours but felt a lot shorter as we listened to music, and our driver shared tidbits about Portuguese history and culture. He was a handsome, engaging young Brazilian man who was easy going and enjoyed sharing stories about his private life. He played Portuguese and Brazilian music for us, and we played some Iranian music for him.

"So, what brings you ladies to Portugal?" the driver asked. The car fell silent for a moment before I replied.

"We're here to celebrate life and friendship. I think it's the start of a new tradition for us–to explore the world together at least once a year. What do you ladies think?" I asked eagerly.

"That sounds lovely!" Stella said ecstatically.

"Let's do it!" Shirin exclaimed.

"I'm in!" Golnaz said, smiling at me.

We arrived in Carvoeiro just before sunset. The vast cliffs and expansive blue ocean that surrounded the coastline looked like postcards from Heaven. Our hotel was a resort with a swimming pool overlooking cliffs facing the ocean. The beauty of the region was indescribable. We booked a two–hour boat excursion to explore all the unique caves along the coast only accessible by ocean vessel, and I took copious pictures to freeze moments in time from every spot. Even though three of us were traveling from beautiful San Diego, known for its majestic coastline and views, the Portuguese Southern Coastal Region did not fail to impress us.

By the end of our fourth night in the region, I felt fully charged and unable to contain my newfound zest for adventure. I started asking strangers to teach me Portuguese and engaged with some of the locals. The people in the region were genuinely friendly and welcomed us with open hearts. When the day finally came for our departure, I found it hard to board the plane home.

"I wish we could stay here forever," I said as we drove to the airport.

"I know. I can't get enough of this place," Shirin replied. "I'm so glad you included me in this trip. It's so good to see you happy and healthy again. I can't wait for our next adventure."

"Oh, I wish you could come back with us," I said, hugging her. "I promise I'll try and come to visit you soon."

"Please do. Mom and I would love to see you," Shirin said. She handed me a large bag. I opened it and found small boxes of my new favorite custard-filled dessert, Pastéis de Nata, as souvenirs to take home. "I got these for you and the boys. I figured you could tell them about our trip while having dessert together."

I started to tear up. "You're always so thoughtful. Thank you," I said, embracing her tightly.

Shirin held me with tears rolling down her face. "We live on different continents, but I'm always here for you. Only one phone call away."

"Okay, ladies. Can we please stop the waterworks?" Golnaz scolded while drying her tears with her shirt sleeve.

Shirin headed to her gate, and we eventually headed to ours. At the check-in counter, I asked the attendant to check the airline miles Omid had earned flying on their airline. "My husband passed away this past year, and this is my first time traveling without him," I explained. The attendant asked for some information and asked me to wait until he returned.

"What's going on?" Golnaz asked curiously.

"I'm waiting to find out how many miles Omid had on his account. The attendant is checking."

He returned after a few minutes. "I'm very sorry for your loss Mrs. Salehi. Unfortunately, our company doesn't offer mileage transfer of deceased people to their next of kin. I explained your circumstances to my manager, and he would like to offer you an upgrade to first class for the remainder of your travels."

"Oh, that's very nice of you. I'm traveling with two others, though. I don't want to leave them, but thank you for the gesture," I said gratefully.

Golnaz walked up next to me. "I'm sorry, Sir. My sister here isn't thinking clearly. She will take the upgrade." She turned to me in a scolding voice. "Why are you refusing the offer?"

"I didn't want to leave you girls. Are you sure you're okay if we don't sit together?"

Stella laughed. "Um, yeah, I think we can find other drooling passengers to take pictures of, Bahar."

"Absolutely," Golnaz replied. "I just hope they offer bibs in first-class for drooling passengers." We all laughed.

I got to board the plane first. I found my seat in the third row. It was a window seat. After getting situated and buckling in, the flight attendant came by to offer me a glass of water. The plane looked full after several passengers boarded. The seat next to mine remained empty. I prayed it would stay that way for extra space, but then a moment later, I saw a tall, lean middle-aged man step onto the plane before the doors were shut. He appeared out of breath.

He was smartly dressed in a striped blue collared shirt and dark blue Docker pants. He carried a black leather bag across his right shoulder. The flight attendant welcomed him aboard. Holding his raincoat in one hand, he started toward the empty seat next to me. I moved my purse closer to provide him more space and faked a soft smile to appear welcoming.

I was annoyed with the prospect of spending the next eleven hours of the flight sitting next to a sweaty stranger. He quickly stuffed his bag under the seat and glanced over to greet me.

"Hello," he said with a smile as he buckled his seatbelt.

I nodded in return and smiled. He had a kind face with a small mole in the lower corner of his left cheek. His skin was tanned, and he sported a sleek hairstyle with subtly graying hair near his temples. He was quite handsome. My gaze briefly caught his glance. He had soft hazel eyes with a twinkle of excitement emanating from them. Guessing from the small creases on his forehead and between his brows, he looked to be in his late forties. Even though he was sweating, I only detected a pleasant waft of his cologne. The fragrance was a combination of citrus, pinecones, and sandalwood.

"I almost missed the flight," he began. "There was a bad accident on the road. If they hadn't let me skip the line at security, I never would have made it," he explained, still trying to catch his breath.

I continued to smile but said nothing. As the plane took off, the flight attendant came down the aisle and offered us drinks. He took two glasses of cold water and drank them both with one breath. After a few minutes, he turned to me again and offered greetings properly.

"Sorry, I kept rambling earlier without properly introducing myself. My name is Dara," he said, extending his hand to me.

I shook his hand, and an odd sense of shyness came over me. "My name is Bahar. Dara sounds like an Iranian name. Are you Iranian as well?" I asked, with surprise.

"Yes, I'm half Iranian." He flashed me a smile, then continued. "My father is British, and my mother, Iranian."

"I see." Not sure what else to say, I turned my gaze to the window. I started fidgeting with my sleeve feeling self-conscious. The captain then spoke over the loudspeaker. He alerted us to some rough air he expected during the flight from a cold jet stream heading toward Europe. He recommended we stay seated as much as possible with our seat belts buckled when not using the lavatories.

Every muscle in my body tensed with the news of turbulence. "Great," I said, mumbling more to myself than anyone else. "I guess I won't be doing much sleeping on this flight."

"Are you afraid of flying?" Dara asked.

Embarrassed that he'd heard me, I replied, "I just don't like turbulence. It makes me feel out of control, and I prefer having control over things."

He laughed. "Wow, I wasn't expecting such an honest reply. People usually don't express their fears that readily," he said. "Since we're confessing, I'm not a big fan of turbulence either. I usually take a pill and try to sleep on international flights. Maybe we can distract each other by talking."

I nodded in agreement, uncertain of what to say next. "Do you live in Portugal?" I finally asked.

He paused for a moment before answering. "No, I was in Portugal on a business trip. How about you?"

"I live in San Diego. I was here with my sister and some friends on a girls' trip, celebrating," I added, regretting the last part of my explanation.

"I see. What are you celebrating?"

Hesitating, I evaded his question and asked him instead, "Were you born in Iran?"

Dara seemed to pick up on my reluctance to respond to his inquiry and accepted it. "I was born in Iran," he replied with his British accent, "and my family immigrated to England when I was eleven years old. That was after the revolution and during the Iran–Iraq War. My parents were both professors at a university in Iran in the engineering department. My father was in Iran on a sabbatical when my parents met. They married shortly afterward and had me a year later. My sister was born three years after that."

His voice grew softer as he continued. "My parents passed away about ten years ago in a car accident, but we still have our family home in London. My sister lives in the city as well, so I spend half the year there and the other half in San Diego. What about you? Were you born in Iran?"

"I'm sorry about your parents. That must have been awful. Yes, I was born in Iran." With hesitance, I added, "I moved to the U.S. when I got married twenty years ago."

"I see. Does your husband work in San Diego?" he asked innocently.

I froze for a second unable to breathe. Then my eyes filled with tears as I looked away toward the window to avoid discovery.

"I'm sorry. Did I upset you?" he asked, seeming to be flustered by my reaction.

I shook my head. I fanned my face to stop myself from crying. "Please don't apologize," I finally got out. "It's not your fault. I just... Your question just caught me off-guard, that's all," I added.

I continued explaining. "My husband passed away last summer from a brain tumor. I'm still a bit in shock over all of it. This is my first trip to Europe without him. My sister and friends wanted to take me away to celebrate my health after getting treated for breast cancer and taking my bar exam."

"Oh, wow!" He blinked, appearing unsure of what to say next. After a moment, he said, "I am so sorry for your loss and hardship. I can't imagine what you've endured."

"Thank you. Losing a loved one is very hard, as you know."

The attendant brought our dinners just then, breaking the awkward silence lurking between us after that exchange of information. After we ate, I resumed our conversation and focused it back on him.

"What line of work are you in?" I asked nonchalantly.

"I work for a company called Globios. It's a global pharmaceutical company based in the UK. I'm the Chief Scientific Officer for the company and travel often in search of mergers and acquisitions in the research arena. My permanent residence is in London, but I recently bought a place in San Diego since I spend half my time at our new R&D facility there."

"That sounds fun. When I was in Iran, I represented a

pharmaceutical company and helped them with legal advice for international mergers and acquisitions. It was stressful, but a very fulfilling job."

"No kidding!" Dara appeared surprised and pleased by that bit of news at the same time. "That sounds wonderful. Are you still practicing law?"

I shook my head, and before I could reply further, we hit a rough patch of air. I froze out of fear.

"It's okay," he said in a soothing voice. "Just keep talking. It'll be over soon."

I nodded and began to speak. "Foreign lawyers can't practice law in the U.S. until they finish a one-year masters program and take the state bar. I didn't finish the masters program until this past year. I took the bar in February and should find out the results in the next few weeks."

"That's awesome! I'm sure you'll pass with flying colors," he said, appearing to study me closely in between sips of wine.

I was nearing the bottom of my wine glass and starting to feel less tense from the turbulence. Dara was also a great distraction.

"Do you have any children?" I asked, taking care not to prod too deep but hoping to uncover his marital status.

"I was married once, but we divorced after two years. I don't have any children. My wife suffered a couple of miscarriages during our marriage. She had a difficult time with it, and we never really recovered after her second miscarriage. But I do have a niece and nephew that I adore. My sister is married to a French businessman, and they're planning to move to Paris in a couple of months. I'm happy for them, but sad that my niece and nephew are moving so far away from me. Although my sister is younger than I am, it feels as though she is more like a mother than a sister at times," he said, chuckling.

"It's always nice to have family who looks out for you."

"Yes, very much. I can't imagine what it'll be like without them in London," he said pensively. "But now I can spend more time in San Diego. Fortunately, my job allows me to work remotely. I only make occasional trips to London for mandatory meetings."

We spoke a bit more during our meal and drank a few glasses of wine to soothe our nerves during the few hours of turbulence we experienced flying over the Atlantic. I gradually started to feel sleepy. Once he opened his laptop to work, I put in my earphones to watch a movie and relax. One hour into my movie, I started to doze off. I was startled awake when I saw Golnaz standing in the aisle, speaking to Dara. She saw my eyes open.

"Hey Sleepyhead," she said, holding back a grin. "I see you're nice and comfortable here while the rest of us are stuck in the sardine can section in the back."

I took off my earphones and shot her a surprised glance. I didn't want her to embarrass me in front of Dara. I started mumbling, a bit uncertain of how to respond. Then I finally said, "Golnaz, this is Dara. Dara, this is Golnaz, my sister," I uttered, eyeing her carefully, hoping she would behave.

"Oh, hello, Dara. Nice to meet you," she said, stretching her hand to shake his.

"Nice to meet you as well," he said with a warm smile. "If you would like to spend time with your sister, I'm happy to swap seats with you."

"Oh, no, thank you. I appreciate the offer," Golnaz replied, "but my friend is back there. She would never forgive me if I left her alone and came up here to fly in luxury. I was just checking on Bahar to make sure she was staying out of trouble. I'll leave her to your capable hands to keep her out of mischief. This one can be a handful sometimes," she added with a devilish grin.

I knew my cheeks had to be bright red. "I'm sorry, my sister likes to joke around. She and I always banter back and forth. She finds every opportunity to tease me. I hope you weren't offended."

He grinned and nodded his head to assure me. "Of course not, siblings live to tease each other. My sister's the same way," he added with a laugh.

I watched the rest of my movie and ate one more meal before dozing off once more. I woke just as we approached San Diego.

"Good morning," Dara said, smiling over at me. "We are almost here."

"Good morning." I sat up and touched my face to make sure I hadn't drooled in my sleep. Thankfully I hadn't.

"Well, it was nice getting to know you," he said as our plane landed. "Thank you for sharing your story with me." He then reached into his pocket, pulled out his wallet, and removed a business card which he handed to me. "Please call me once you get your exam results. With your background in international law, our company could use someone like you."

I was so stunned I hesitated to accept the card. "You think I would qualify? I haven't worked since we moved to the U.S."

"Let's wait and get those test results, and then we can speak after that. Don't sell yourself short. You have traits that one doesn't learn on the job. Companies look for grit, character, and people passionate about their work. I think those traits supersede any work experience for a hiring manager," he assured me with a stern tone.

I felt a flush of heat move over my cheeks as I took the card. "Thank you so much," I replied, my voice so soft it surprised even me. "That means a lot."

A sense of dread struck me having to say goodbye. There was something about Dara, something comforting and familiar. It had been so long since I was in the company of a man so lively, good-natured, handsome, and genuine. I also experienced a pang of guilt for being attracted to him.

Once the plane arrived at the gate, we said our goodbyes. He deplaned before me. I waited for the girls to come up to the front of the plane to join me. Golnaz had a silly grin on her face. I glared back to keep her from teasing me. I didn't succeed.

"Where did Romeo run off to? Did he make a run for it before I could jump him?" Golnaz asked, laughing loudly.

I pinched her side, causing her to squeal in pain as I pushed her toward the exit. "Shut up and get your ass moving," I responded.

Stella stuck out her bottom lip in a pout as though she were offended. "What? You mean you had us sitting there, uncomfortable in economy class while you were having bubbly with your new *business class* suitor?" she teased.

"Oh no, not you too!" I rolled my eyes. "He was a nice guy who got me through the turbulence by chatting. That's all."

"Oh please! You're so full of it," Golnaz shot back. "Your face tells a different story, my sweet Bahar," she said, still teasing me.

I knew they were right, but I had no confidence in thinking Dara would ever take an interest in someone like me. I had too much baggage. We exited the plane as my brain tried to erase the memory of him, while my heart was busy concocting a plan of its own.

Chapter 35

A week after returning from my trip, I underwent breast reconstruction surgery. After my recovery and physical therapy, I started to feel more feminine again and no longer avoided looking at myself in the mirror. The doctors removed the liquid–filled mesh and replaced it with a silicone implant that felt softer and more natural to the touch. My hair was finally growing back, and I was starting to enjoy wearing makeup and dressing in more feminine outfits again. Overall, I had developed a more positive outlook on my physical and emotional being.

My extra energy allowed me to spend more time with my kids. I was able to drive them to their weekly swimming and soccer practices. They also continued with their piano and Farsi classes. Koosha and I signed up for a weekly baking class as a special activity for us to do together. Kayvon opted to go biking with me once a week along the coast as our bonding ritual. We also made a point to plan at least one fun activity for the three of us to do on the weekends. Seeing my progress, my parents decided to return to Iran for a few months to sort out their affairs. Golnaz also resumed her work with a new clientele pool. The role allowed her to live in San Diego, but required her to travel often to various states. Since Giovanni was moving to the U.S., they were looking for a place to move to once he started his job at Qualcomm.

As the weeks passed, I found a new rhythm with friends and family without Omid's presence. I tried to resume my social life and went to parties on occasion, but the pain and emptiness in my heart never left me. I now mourned Omid's loss discreetly and reserved my tears for late nights while everyone slept. I didn't want the boys to see my suffering. I strutted in front of the kids every day with a smile on my face and positive words to give them the strength to persevere beyond their grief. As Memorial Day approached, my anxiety increased. I had to quell my panic with multiple deep breaths thinking about the email I would receive with the test results.

Friday night before Memorial Day weekend, I sat behind my computer and waited anxiously for 6:00 p.m. to come around. I logged into my account at the top of the hour and clicked on my inbox to find an email from the State Bar Association. Holding my breath, I clicked on it and read under my breath. I froze when I came across the word "...congratulations." I passed the bar. A sense of relief washed over me. Overjoyed by the news, I screamed and banged my fists on the table, saying, "Yes, yes, yes!" repeatedly. Hearing the commotion, the boys came into the room to see what was happening.

"What's going on?" Kayvon asked, looking confused.

"Come here, my love," I said, motioning to him to read the computer screen. He paused and read for a few minutes. "No Way! You passed it!" Kayvon said happily.

Koosha stood by his brother, wearing a huge grin on his face. "That's so awesome, Mommy!"

I hugged them tightly with tears of joy streaming down my cheeks. "I can't believe I passed. This is incredible news, boys!"

After a few moments of kissing and hugging each other, the boys decided we should celebrate the occasion. We decided to go out to buy a cake and some balloons. I sent them to their rooms to change while I called some people to share the news.

I screamed into the phone as soon as Golnaz picked up her cell phone. "I passed the bar, Golnaz! Can you believe it?!"

She squealed with joy. "What? That's incredible! Congratulations! I'm *so* happy for you!"

"Thanks. I still can't believe it! Feels like I'm dreaming or something."

"Well, I believe it! You worked so hard. I'm so proud of you!" she replied. "Have you told the boys yet?"

"Yes, they heard me screaming and came to check on me. We're going out to get some cake to celebrate. I wish you were here."

"I know. I'm bummed. But you guys enjoy the festivities. We can celebrate again in a couple of days when I get back."

After I hung up with Golnaz, I called my parents in Iran. In my excitement, I forgot they were twelve hours ahead of us. I only realized I woke them when my mom answered with a sleepy voice. "Hi, Maman. Guess what? I passed the test!" I bellowed out.

It took her a few seconds to reply, but as soon as the news registered, she congratulated me through the sound of her sniffles.

"Thank God! I've been praying for good news to make you happy, Sweetheart. I'm so happy my prayers were answered." She then handed the phone to my father, who also congratulated me.

The boys waited for me patiently as I spent the next hour calling Stella, Shirin, Navid, and Omid's parents. I was so overjoyed I couldn't sit still. Once I hung up, the three of us went to the bakery and bought a decadent black forest chocolate cake that made our mouths water. They also insisted that we pick up some mylar balloons. When we got home, we placed the cake on a stand and arranged the balloons behind the dinner table. Koosha placed a candle on the cake and asked me to make a wish before blowing it out.

I looked at the boys with misty eyes. "I'm not sure what to wish for. I have the most amazing boys in the world. You two have been so wonderful this whole time. I can't thank you both enough for being so patient, loving, and understanding. You have handled it all like true warriors. I'm so proud of you both!" I leaned forward to hug them.

Koosha stopped me before I could blow out the candles and ran upstairs. Kayvon and I stared at each other with a puzzled expression. Less than a minute later, he returned with a framed picture of his dad hugged tightly against his chest. Seeing the framed picture of Omid broke my heart.

"We have to celebrate this with Baba," Koosha proclaimed, placing the picture frame on the table next to the cake.

"Yes, you're right, my sweet boy." I stroked his hair and planted a kiss on his cheek. We all got misty eyed.

After I blew out the candle, Koosha asked in a hoarse voice, "Can we eat the cake now?"

I couldn't hold back my laughter as his simple question withdrew the heaviness that hung over the room. "Yes, Sweetheart. We sure can!" I said with a snicker.

I cut a large slice of the cake and watched them devour their share while chugging a cold glass of milk. Sipping on a hot cup of tea and forking the cake on my plate, I closed my eyes and leaned against the chair, grateful for this moment.

Things were finally starting to fall into place. I savored the victory from this battle and looked ahead to winning future ones.

Chapter 36

The last piece of the puzzle in need of sorting was the lawsuit around the medical practice. The papers had been served, and the lawyers were now speaking about going to mediation. I had a great lawyer on the case and felt confident in his expertise. Jake Skyler's lawyer was a bully who was quickly learning his threats and letters to intimidate us were failing. We knew we had the right to claim Omid's share of the practice. My lawyer's advice was to avoid negotiating and not accept any offer less than what was owed. I left the legal battle up to him and hoped for a quick resolution. I needed to focus my full attention on finding a job.

"Kayvon, I need your help. I need to make a LinkedIn profile. Auntie Golnaz said I need to have a profile so recruiters can search for me, and possibly offer work opportunities. Can you please help me?"

"Yeah, sure, Mom. It's not that complicated. I'll do it after school today. I just need a good picture of you and your resume," he said, as he kissed me on the cheek before heading out the door.

"Thanks, baby. Have a great day at school. Love you!" I hollered back before the door shut.

Koosha had already left with the carpool mom who picked him up fifteen minutes ago. After breakfast, I hovered over my computer, trying to work on my resume. Frustrated that I had no information to fill in the work experience space, I started cursing myself for not having a single job or internship to write down during the entire time I had been in the United States. Omid had been right about me working all those years. From the day we arrived in the U.S., Omid asked me to study and take the required courses to get my license and practice law again. We had gotten into some heated arguments over the topic. When I complained about language barriers, he had hired a tutor to help me become fluent in English. When I complained about the boys, he hired a nanny to free up my time. Despite his encouragement, my fear of failure prevented me from taking the bar. I still feel guilty recalling the arguments we had on the subject–not to mention the regret I feel about adding more stress on Omid.

I shifted away from the negative thoughts and refocused on my resume. Fluffing the content highlighting my work representing the multi-million-dollar company and serving as legal counsel during global mergers and acquisitions took up half the page. I filled the rest with information about my academic career, as well as competencies and other skillsets. After lunch, I made the final edits and found a digital photo of myself taken a few years ago. I wanted to show the side of me that I remembered before my body started to break down.

That evening I watched Kayvon create my professional digital fingerprint on LinkedIn. He showed me how to navigate the software and how to find other professionals with a similar line of work. Not being able to sleep that evening, I went back to the site and started to navigate through various profile suggestions under my network. After scrolling and pressing on a few to connect, I came across Dara Mesri's profile under the suggestion tab. My heart skipped a beat.

I had completely forgotten about Dara. I was unable to recall where I had put the business card he had given me. I saw a picture of Dara on his profile. He was classified as the Chief Scientific Officer for Globios Pharmaceutical Company as he had told me during the flight. I pressed the Connect button on his profile page with some reluctance. Feeling silly for being nervous about clicking a button, I shook my head. I felt as if I were asking him out on a date!

Not being familiar with the LinkedIn platform, I went under his profile to snoop around. There were some interesting postings related to Globios R&D and other company-related press releases. Jumping back to his profile page, I continued to stare at his demure smile, observing him dressed in a navy-blue professional suit and red tie.

Emotions I didn't want to feel began to swirl inside me. I quickly closed the laptop and turned off the light to go to sleep. That night I dreamt about Dara. We were seated at a restaurant having a candle-light dinner and drinking wine. At one point, he reached across the table to take hold of my hand. I was reluctant at first and feeling a bit shy. After a few minutes, I slipped my hand into his palm. We both sat silently for some time. A bit later, the waiter headed over to our table. "Would you like more wine, Madame?"

Stunned by the familiar voice, I looked up and saw Omid as the waiter. He held a bottle of wine in his hand, and white cloth draped over his shoulder. Flustered, I released Dara's hand and stood.

"What's the matter, Bahar? Are you okay?" Dara asked, frowning. He stood as well and followed me as I sped toward the exit without responding. Dara suddenly turned and looked at Omid, unsure of what had transpired.

Omid smiled at Dara and said, "Don't worry, she'll be back. She just needs more time." Then Omid walked away.

I suddenly woke and sat up. It took me a while to get the perplexing dream out of my head. Guilt for what I had dreamt haunted me. I felt as if I had betrayed Omid. At the same time, recalling Omid's face and his consent helped calm me.

I reminded myself that it was just a dream. Unable to fall back asleep, I retrieved my laptop from the floor and began checking my emails. I found two email notifications telling me people were looking at my profile. My heart stood still when I realized Dara would also know I had been viewing his profile.

"Oh, crap," I mumbled, panic sinking in. *Why didn't Kayvon tell me LinkedIn alerts the site owners when someone views their profile?* I thought LinkedIn was similar to Facebook, where nobody knew who was looking at your page.

I opened the LinkedIn page and found a message from Dara in my Inbox. I inhaled and held my breath while reading it.

"Hi, Bahar. Nice connecting with you again! How are things? Looking at your profile, I think congratulations are in order! I see you are open to recruitment. We have an opening at Globios for a legal counsel position if you are interested. I'm in London and can share more information if you'd like. Feel free to text or call me on my cell and let me know. Congrats again!"

His note caught me off guard. He remembered our conversation on the plane. I knew I was under-qualified to work for a company such as Globios, but maybe he could help guide me to apply anyway. I decided to email him on LinkedIn instead of texting or calling.

I wrote back, "Dear Dara, so nice to hear from you. Thanks for your kind words. I'm thrilled about passing the bar. Thanks for telling me about the position. I would love to apply, but I'm not sure I have the qualifications. If you recall, I don't have any work experience here in the U.S. I would welcome your advice. Best, Bahar." I added my telephone number before reading the note a couple of times and pressing the Send button. I finally closed my laptop and went back to bed.

I woke early the next morning, from the sound of the door slamming shut as the boys left for school. I looked at my phone screen to check the time and came across a text notification from an unfamiliar number. Unlocking my phone, I read the message. "Hi, Bahar. It's Dara. I just saw your reply email on LinkedIn. It's 8:00 a.m. in London, and I'm heading to the office. I have a meeting today with some of the members of the C-suite and our legal team to discuss an acquisition we have been working on. I'll do some research on the open position and the qualifications needed. I'll let you know what I find out. Is the resume uploaded on LinkedIn your most recent one? Please let me know. Have a great day! Best, Dara."

I sat for a few minutes, holding my phone with a myriad of thoughts racing in my head. *Should I reply right away? How long ago was the text sent?* I raised the phone again and noticed it was sent some time ago. Quickly calculating the eight-hour time difference, I realized it was now 4:00 p.m. his time.

Without waiting too long to analyze my reply, I wrote back, "Good morning. I just saw your text. Sorry I didn't respond earlier. The resume on LinkedIn is my most recent one. I appreciate your looking into it. Thank you again. Best, Bahar."

I pressed Send and got out of bed. Ten minutes later, my phone chimed again with a text notification. My stomach dropped.

"Hi, Bahar. I am headed home from work. Our meeting got postponed until tomorrow. I'll download your resume and take it in with me tomorrow. Can I call you later to discuss?"

My pulse raced as I read the note. The thought of speaking to him made me nervous. It would be easier to text. I scolded myself for being childish and replied, "Yes, of course. I have a few errands this morning, but I'll be free in the evening if it works for you. I think 11:00 p.m. my time is around 7:00 a.m. London time."

"Yes, that's correct. That works out great. I'll call you then. Have a great day!" he texted back.

I plopped my head back into the pillow with heat emanating out of every pore. *Get a hold of yourself, Bahar! He's just an acquaintance helping you with a job.* There was no reason to suspect more than that. I threw the phone on the comforter and headed to the shower to cool off.

The rest of the day, I spent on the computer emailing my former colleagues in Iran to get information on legal updates and reading up on the evolving world of global mergers and acquisitions. I enjoyed having my old passion to focus on. It was also a welcome distraction from my financial concerns.

After dinner, the boys and I watched an episode of *The Great British Baking Show.* They headed off to bed around 9:00 p.m., and I retreated to my bedroom after tidying the kitchen. After completing my bedtime routine, I sat leaning against the headboard of the bed, propped up against my pillow. A text notification from Dara flashed on my phone screen at exactly 11:00 p.m. I had remembered to save his number on my phone and smiled when I saw it.

"Good morning. Hope I am not texting too late," he wrote.

"Not at all. I was just up watching TV," I lied. I didn't want him to think I had stayed up waiting for him to contact me. Even though I had been.

"Great. I'm headed to work. Would you rather chat live or talk via text?"

I thought about it for a minute. I was too flustered to talk on the phone. I lied and told him it's better to text since so I don't want to wake the boys.

"I understand. How was your day?" he texted back.

"It was productive. I took care of some errands in the morning, then I reached out to some old colleagues in Iran. I also brushed up on the new laws and regulations around global mergers and acquisitions."

"Good for you! I like your tenacity."

"Thanks. How is your morning going so far?" I asked.

"It's a rather dreary morning. It's overcast and looks like it might rain. But hearing from you and your progress makes it all less gloomy ☺."

"Well, I'm glad I could help ☺. The weather is always gloomy in London, but I have plenty of good memories from my time there.

There is a nice coffee shop near Harrods called Café Durée. You should go there for afternoon tea sometime. They have the best selection of scones and savory sandwiches. Enjoy one for me," I wrote back with a smile on my face.

There was a moment of pause before he replied. "I will. It's busy at work this week. Hopefully, we can go there when you're in London one day."

I didn't respond, and Dara quickly changed the text subject. "I printed your resume last night. I'll run it by the team during our meeting today. It seems you've had a long day. Call or text me after you wake up, and I'll give you an update."

Like a teenager, I felt my heart pounding in my chest. I reminded myself to stay professional and calm down.

"Sounds good," I responded quickly. "I'll text you when I wake up. Have a good day!"

I forced myself to sleep and woke up at 9:00 a.m. feeling fully rested. Thankfully, I didn't have any nightmares, hot flashes, or the need to use the bathroom in the middle of the night. I grabbed my cell and found two new texts from Dara.

"Good morning. Hope you slept well. I presented your resume to the team and gave them some background information about you. They were impressed. They want to set up a video chat with you."

I read the second text right after. "Just between us, Globios is bidding for a biotech company in Iran that is developing a treatment for Alzheimer's disease. They are looking for someone who can speak Farsi and understands commercial law in Iran. I think this couldn't happen at a better time for you."

This was such amazing news. I felt like pinching myself to make sure I wasn't dreaming. I wrote back quickly. "Good morning. That's such wonderful news. I don't know what to say. I'm speechless. Thank you!"

"My pleasure. By the way, look where I am?"

He uploaded a selfie picture of a three-tier cake stand filled with a variety of tea sandwiches and pastries. He sat with an amused expression holding a teacup filled with hot tea.

I laughed out loud. "Oh, wow! That looks delicious. Enjoy!"

"Next time, you'll have to join me. You were right, the pastries are incredible!"

The undertone in his text sounded so sweet. I couldn't help but grin as I studied a closeup of the comical expression on his face. I wished I were there having tea with him at that moment. A part of me was intrigued by Dara, while another part of me was overcome with guilt. It had been less than a year since Omid had passed. *Shame on me for even allowing these exchanges to take place*, I scolded myself and didn't respond to his last comment.

I spent the night angry at myself for going against my promise to never allow any other man to enter my thoughts. I took out our family photo album and tried to erase Dara from my mind. I looked at travel photos with Omid and me posing together. We appeared so happy and in love.

The next morning when I woke, I wrote Dara a simple text and only addressed the interview discussion from the prior day. "Good morning. Thank you again for yesterday. I welcome the opportunity to speak with the team on a video call. I'm available and can schedule a call at their convenience. Have a wonderful day. Bahar."

I tossed the phone on the bed and headed to the kitchen to have breakfast with the kids. Not only would I not permit myself to stray and indulge in romantic thoughts, but I also knew the boys would never forgive me if I betrayed their father by becoming close with another man so soon after his death.

As I walked in, I caught them both hunched over their cereal bowls, each engrossed in their iPhones. "Good morning, guys."

"Oh, hi, Mom," Kayvon replied without looking up.

"Good morning, Mom," Koosha chimed in.

"Whatever happened to no technology during meals?" I asked, turning on the tea kettle.

They both locked their phones and straightened, appearing annoyed about the interruption.

"I'm sorry, but rules are rules. I've unlocked your phones, trusting that you will show good judgment, but I can go back to monitoring your use and lock them back up again."

"Okay, okay," Kayvon quickly replied. "Relax, Mom. We turned the phones off."

"Why were you smiling before?" Koosha asked, clearly trying to shift the focus back to me. "Did something happen?"

"I'm glad you *saw* that," I said sarcastically. "As it happens, something good *did* happen. I sent my resume to a pharmaceutical company looking to hire. The company is based in London. They also have an office in San Diego. They want to interview me!" I said cheerfully.

"Oh, wow, Mom!" Kayvon exclaimed, smiling at me.

Koosha grinned. "So, you're going to get a job in London? Do we have to move there if you do?"

"No, Darling. I'll only accept the job if we can stay here. They're a global pharmaceutical company that buys other companies around the world. I may need to travel a few times to London for work. I'll know more after the interview. Let's keep our fingers crossed and our toes for good measure," I teased, laughing to lighten the mood.

"When is your interview?" Kayvon asked as he emptied his bowl in the sink.

"I'm working on getting it scheduled. I'll know more today or tomorrow," I replied as I slid into a chair at the table with my hot tea and toast.

He leaned in and kissed me on the cheek. "Good luck. You'll do great!" he said before jetting out the door.

Koosha jumped out of his chair next to me when he heard the car honking outside. "Oh! My carpool's here. Love you, Mom. Have a good day!" A moment later, he slid out of the door.

They were growing up too fast and slowly becoming independent adults. I sat there at the table alone, wishing Omid were here to see them. To see how wonderful they were turning out, and to celebrate their milestones with me.

After breakfast, I took a long hot shower with all kinds of thoughts circling in my head. I questioned my qualifications for this position. The thoughts continued as I got dressed and sat behind my computer to read emails from my former work colleague in Iran. He had written a thorough breakdown of new legislation impacting commerce and acquisitions by foreign companies interested in investing in Iran. Learning new information brought me some peace of mind.

I received a phone call from Globios Human Resources sometime around 11:00 p.m. The HR person asked me for my email address and other contact information. Shortly after, I received an email link to apply for the Global Counsel position online. With trembling hands, I started filling out my information. It took me over two hours to fill out the application and upload my resume.

Things were moving rapidly now, and the stakes were high. I needed to learn the do's and don'ts and didn't have a minute to waste. I reached out to Golnaz asking her to help me prepare. I needed her advice on how to succeed in my interview and what questions to expect.

My life was beginning to present me with new opportunities, and I was beyond excited to seize them with humility and gratitude.

Chapter 37

$\mathcal{J}$ received a request for a video conference call a week after I submitted my application.

I called Golnaz right away, telling her the news. She was thrilled about my new job prospect and teased about Dara and me becoming more than work colleagues.

"Will you stop bugging me about this?" I begged her. "We reconnected via LinkedIn. He's just a friend trying to help me get a job at his company. There is nothing else going on."

She pretended to be offended. "Oh, fine! Don't be such a stick in the mud. I know when a man is interested in someone. The spark in his eyes on the plane was unquestionable. He thinks you have the right qualifications for the job, but I don't think there's anything wrong with thinking of him as more than a friend."

I sighed and rolled my eyes. "I give up! Yes, he is a handsome and sweet guy. But I'm not interested in exploring anything romantically. That would be wrong. It would be a betrayal to Omid."

Golnaz paused briefly. "I'm sorry. I didn't mean to upset you. I'm just having fun. You're still so young, smart, and beautiful. You have so much life left in you. Don't get me wrong, you and Omid were truly a match made in Heaven. You had the love story we all wish for, but the Omid I knew would want you to be happy and live your life to the fullest. Just as you would have wished for him under a similar circumstance."

I had to swallow the lump in my throat before I could reply. "I know you're looking out for me, and I love you for it. If the tables were turned, I *would* want Omid to find love and be happy again. I guess I just need time to feel comfortable with the idea."

"Okay, that's fair. I promise I won't tease you anymore!"

We hung up after a few minutes. It felt strange no longer having Golnaz as a roommate. She and Giovanni found an apartment nearby and were now engaged to be married. She surprised us all by accepting his proposal. I was thrilled to see them entering a new chapter in their lives. My parents were still in Iran with plans to visit us in two weeks. I called them and told them about the new job prospects. I anticipated a face-to-face interview in London if I passed the first phase of the virtual interview. My parents offered to fly out and stay with us for a month in case I needed them to watch the boys.

My late-evening routines were starting to gradually change. Dara and I were conversing almost nightly between 10:00 p.m. to midnight via text. He woke up early every morning at 6:00 a.m. London time to text me while getting ready and commuting to work. We had numerous exchanges concerning the position and the company's vision. He prepared me for my video screening interview and explained the detailed process if I advanced to a face-to-face assessment.

On the evening of my first interview, I sat in front of the computer, sweating as I answered one question after another. There were four people seated around a table, and each took turns asking questions about my academic and work history. They also asked me to give examples of how I overcame challenges in my life. I gave them a brief synopsis of my recent hardships and how I persevered.

Although it was hard to see their faces close-up and guess what they were thinking, I was pretty sure I connected with them on an emotional level when I saw one of the interviewers dab her eyes after I explained the circumstances around Omid's cancer and my subsequent diagnosis. The middle-aged woman had a kind face and nodded often during the interview. Before I hung up, she offered her condolences about my loss and thanked me for being so open with them about my hardships.

Once we disconnected, I inhaled deeply and let my shoulders fall. I didn't realize how tense I had been until the interview ended. It was already past midnight for me, so I stripped off my clothes and tossed them on the bathroom floor, then turned on the hot water and took a nice long shower.

I felt good about my interview. I had answered their questions candidly and honestly. If they considered me for a follow-up interview, I would be thrilled. Even if they didn't, I was still pleased with myself for working so hard to get this far.

I was happy Dara wasn't there for the session. I wanted to be certain that if I got this position, I had achieved this based on merit alone.

The next morning, he sent me a text at 8:00 a.m. and asked if he could call me. I sat up on the bed with my stomach in knots. I waited for the phone to ring. Although we had chatted via text on so many evenings, I had not heard his voice since our plane ride several months ago.

I answered with some hesitance. "Hello?"

"Good morning, Bahar. How are you?" he asked, his tone upbeat.

"I am doing well, thanks. How are *you*?"

"Well, from the sounds of it, the interview went very well. The panel loved you! After your interview, the lead counsel practically knocked my door down and barged in to thank me for introducing you to the team. She was also very touched by your personal story. They want you to come out and meet them in person for a follow-up interview in two weeks."

"Wow! Really? That's... That's *wonderful* news. I didn't expect they would answer so quickly. Thanks for calling and letting me know."

"Of course. My pleasure," Dara replied. I could hear the smile in his voice.

We exchanged a few more pleasantries before hanging up. I arranged to fly out to London in two weeks. They wanted me to learn about the organization and meet with the CEO and lead counsel of the company.

In addition to educating myself about the new role, I felt it was also necessary to brush up on my professional look and attire. I asked Stella to accompany me to the hairstylist to get a professional cut and style. My hair was now just above my shoulders in length and had gotten curlier after chemotherapy.

We also spent a full day shopping for business suits. My body was now shapelier, and with the new breast reconstruction surgery, I felt more confident about how I looked in the tight-fitting attire. Golnaz scheduled a session with a makeup artist to teach me how to apply eyeshadow and eyeliner to portray a modern businesswoman look.

The night before my flight, I happily packed my suitcase with the new attire and makeup I purchased for the short trip. The boys were happy with my new bob and told me I finally looked *cool* to them.

My parents were back from Iran, and I was overjoyed to have them visit us. It was comforting to have them here to watch over the boys while I was gone. Although I was nervous about the interview, I was more anxious about seeing Dara again.

It was one thing to text someone every night, but to see him in person required a different set of social skills. One I hadn't practiced using in such a long time. I feared he would be disappointed after seeing me again, and I was unsure of what to make of our relationship. Seeds of a love interest had inadvertently sprung within me. The longer we stayed in touch, the less I could resist it.

The company bought me business class tickets direct from San

Diego to London Heathrow. A driver holding my name on a sign met me at the exit and drove me to the hotel in Central London.

As I sat in the backseat en route to the hotel, memories of the sights and sounds of the city came flooding back. We drove by familiar places Omid and I had visited so many times during our trips to London. I recalled our love story and how I felt the first time I arrived here, anticipating my blind date with Omid.

The weather was unusually warm for this season, so I opened the window, allowing the soft breeze to caress my face.

My phone rang, and the moment I saw it was Dara, an overwhelming sense of shyness came over me. "Hello?"

"Welcome to London!" Dara bellowed on the other end.

I let out a slight chortle. "Why, thank you."

"How was your flight? Was there a lot of turbulence?"

"It was pretty uneventful. I slept like a baby."

"Happy to hear it. I was worried you would be tired. Are you open to having a quick dinner?"

I hesitated at first. My interview was scheduled for early the next morning. But I didn't want to disappoint him. "Sure, that sounds lovely."

"Excellent! Do you have any food restrictions or preferences?"

"No, I'm okay with anything. You can choose."

"Great! I know of an excellent Italian place close to your hotel. I will pick you up around 7:00 p.m. No need to dress up."

I thanked him and hung up. I was a bit jet-lagged, but also incredibly excited to be in London again. There was something about this city that ignited my soul and invigorated me. The liveliness of this European city and watching people hustling about was an absolute delight. I excitedly looked on as we drove by stores and coffee shops filled with people. I couldn't wait to immerse myself in the crowd as soon as I had the chance.

Before departing, I called Shirin to tell her about my short visit.

We made plans to meet up as soon as I knew more about my schedule. She was thrilled to hear about my interview and wished me luck.

Arriving at the hotel, I checked in and had my luggage taken up to my room. I took a long shower, then put on a dark blue dress with a sash that wrapped around my waist and tied on the side. The dress highlighted my body's curves more than some of my other outfits, while still feeling comfortable.

Just a few minutes before 7:00 p.m., I got a text from Dara informing me he was waiting in the lobby. Stepping out of the elevator, I worried I had forgotten what he looked like. He saw me as soon as I walked out and approached with a wide grin on his face.

He wore a nice casual blazer with a light blue dress shirt underneath and had paired it with dark blue slacks. His hair was a bit grayer than the last time I saw him but was styled like Richard Gere in the movie *Pretty Woman*. Our gazes locked for an instant. Releasing a nervous laugh, I smiled back at him. I wasn't sure how we should greet one another. It seemed Dara was experiencing the same uncertainty. After a moment of hesitation, I extended my hand as he leaned in to kiss me on the cheek in the Iranian tradition.

After our awkward greeting, he initiated the conversation. "It's so nice to see you again. You look lovely."

"Hello," I said, turning red and feeling self-conscious. "It's nice to see you again too."

"It's much better to be face to face instead of texting each other for a change, don't you think?"

I nodded and smiled. "Yes, it is."

"You must be starving," he said and gestured toward the hotel door to allow me to exit first. The valet had brought his car around and was holding the car door open for me.

At first, I gasped at the sight of his silver Audi. It was so much like the car Omid had driven on our first outing to Regents Park. Sliding into the passenger seat, I said nothing. We drove through the narrow streets of London while making small talk. Dara had made reservations for two at a very quaint and posh Italian restaurant. They seated us in a semi-private area with only three other tables set for diners.

"So...are you nervous about tomorrow?" Dara asked toward the end of the evening as I shamelessly devoured another mouthful of the creamy and rich homemade cannoli. I was already bursting at the seams from eating the scrumptious lasagna covered with a rich layer of bechamel sauce.

I shrugged. "I don't know. I guess I should be nervous," I replied. "But when I reason in my head, I can't imagine anything being more nerve-wracking than what I've gone through these past couple of years. I've done all I can to prepare. I listened to your advice and looked up everything you mentioned. If it doesn't work out, I can't say I didn't prepare enough."

"That's a fair assessment. I'm confident things will go well tomorrow. It would be a loss to Globios if they didn't hire you. You have every trait that suits this position. You're passionate, smart, driven, and highly motivated in your area of expertise. On a personal note, you are strong, independent, and humble. You're honestly the perfect package all around," he said, blushing slightly at the utterance of his last phrase. My cheeks started to burn too.

"You're too kind. I think you're giving me much more credit than I deserve. I appreciate the boost in confidence the night before my interview." I stared into his eyes a little longer than I intended to. The waiter came up and forced us to break our gaze.

"Would you like to order anything else?" the waiter asked.

"I think we're set," I replied quickly and placed my napkin on the table to hint at wanting to leave. I was starting to feel the effects of the wine, and worried about losing my inhibitions in the company of such a charming man like Dara.

Sitting in the car in front of the hotel, Dara said, "If your interview hadn't been in the morning, I would have offered to go for a stroll. We'll plan for another time. I think we need you rested and at your best tomorrow."

I nodded in agreement and reached for the door handle to step out. Leaning over, I placed a kiss on Dara's cheek and thanked him for dinner.

Just before I turned to slide out of the car, he unbuckled his seatbelt and turned to face me. I twisted my head around, surprised by his action. He put his finger under my chin and tilted my face toward his.

"Bahar, I meant it when I told you before that I admire your strength. You are such an incredible woman. I hope it works out and you are offered the position." He paused briefly before adding, "But even if it doesn't, if it's alright with you, I want to get to know you better. You have an aura about you that's hard to resist."

Caught off-guard by his words, I became flustered. I wasn't expecting this to happen so quickly. Not knowing how to respond, I hopped out of the car and inadvertently slammed the car door behind me. I practically ran up the stairs toward the revolving door of the hotel without looking back.

My head was spinning, and my heart was beating so fast I felt it was about to jump out of my chest. I nodded at the doorman and jammed my finger on the call button of the elevator. Once on my floor, I walked rapidly toward my room. Fumbling with the key card, I opened the door and shut it behind me once safely inside, then crumbled to the ground on my knees in the entryway and began to sob.

My emotions covered every spectrum from elated, petrified, angry, to guilty. I knew I had developed feelings for Dara, but I wasn't sure how I would come to terms with them. I couldn't possibly have feelings for another man so soon. What about Omid? How could I be such a heartless person to feel this way for another man so soon? I felt weak and unfaithful to my promises.

I fumbled with the wedding ring still on my finger and stared back at my mascara-stained face in the room's hallway mirror. I pitied the woman looking back at me. She looked like a fragile, confused person trying to understand how to proceed. I searched for the right answer in my reflection, and as I sat there, my phone vibrated in my purse. Still seated on the floor, I opened my purse and retrieved it.

Dara had texted me. "Hey, are you okay?" I didn't reply after reading it.

He sent another text a few minutes after. "I hope I didn't upset you. I'm so sorry if I've offended you."

I stared at the screen, not knowing how to answer. I was grateful I didn't have to respond to him in person.

Finally, I wrote back. "It's fine. I was just caught off-guard. No other man has spoken to me that way since Omid. It was a bit unexpected."

"I understand. I'm sorry. I didn't mean to upset you. Let's talk after the interview or when you're ready. In the meantime, just ignore what I said. Please forgive me."

There was nothing to forgive. I hated making him feel bad about being true to his heart. None of this was his fault. I was just damaged goods, and it wasn't fair to put him through this turmoil.

"It's fine. Thanks for dinner. Have a good night," I replied and pulled myself up from the floor. I washed my face and put on my nightdress. It was already close to midnight, and as the effects of the wine started to wear off, my head began to throb. I took two painkillers and washed them down with a full bottle of water. I had too much riding on tomorrow's interview. I needed to sleep. My romantic whims wouldn't put a roof over our heads, and I was too old to be playing these teenage games. I set my alarm for 6:00 a.m. and turned off the lights.

The next morning, I took a cab to Globios Headquarters. Dara had texted and offered me a ride to the office, but I respectfully declined. I needed to stay focused and being around Dara made me nervous. I hadn't slept well and had tossed and turned all night.

When I arrived, the team greeted me warmly. I was led to a large conference room where the CEO, Ronald Turner, and the Lead Counsel, Georgina Winston, stood up to greet me. The Human Resources representative was also present during the interview. We spent a little under two hours, covering various topics about the roles and responsibilities of the position. I learned more about the company' culture and aspirations. When the interview ended, I walked away from it feeling good about the four-way dialogue.

While waiting in the atrium of the lobby for my driver to take me to the hotel, I received another text from Dara asking how it went. "It went well," I wrote back. "I liked the CEO very much. Georgina Winston was so kind and professional. Everyone in this company here has been so pleasant."

"Well, everyone, except for me ☹," he texted back.

I didn't respond.

"Are you feeling up for afternoon tea?" he wrote.

I wasn't ready to face him just yet, and I had hoped to meet up with Shirin later today. I wrote back, "Do you mind if I take a rain check? Maybe tomorrow? I have plans to meet up with one of my best friends this afternoon."

"Yes, of course."

Feeling guilty and sensing that I had disappointed Dara, I sent him another text when I arrived at my hotel. "How about we meet on Saturday for afternoon tea? I want to properly thank you for all you've done."

"No thank you is necessary, but I'll gladly accept your offer," he wrote back.

My flight wasn't until Sunday, and I thought meeting up in person before I left was the polite thing to do. At least that's how I reasoned my need to see Dara again. I spent the rest of the day relaxing. I got dressed and met Shirin in the lobby around 4:00 p.m.

"Hi, you!" Shirin screamed as soon as she saw me step out of the elevator. "I can't believe you're actually in London!" We embraced and exchanged pleasantries.

"So, where do you feel like going?" she asked as we walked arm in arm. "You know mom was upset when she heard you were in town and weren't going to visit her. I told her about your hectic schedule. She wishes you the best of luck."

"Thanks. I'll call her before I leave. Do you want to go to Regents Park? I've been wanting to go there, but didn't have the heart to go alone."

Shirin gave my arm a reassuring squeeze. "Sure, I'd love to."

She knew what Regents Park and the Rose Garden meant to me and remembered my detailed accounts of the romantic picnic Omid had planned for the two of us. We called a cab to take us to the park.

As we sat in the car, Shirin asked me about my interview. After telling her all about it, I also shared with her a bit about how I was introduced to the company via Dara. She listened intently and offered little opinion.

"You know," I began as we got out of the car, "in my wildest dreams I never imagined coming back to London and returning to Regents Park without Omid at my side. I had always imagined we would reenact that picnic one day with the kids joining us. I wanted to build a whole new set of memories here with the four of us. God had other plans for us, I guess."

"I know, it's so heart-wrenching to think about. You two had the most beautiful love story. It breaks my heart just thinking about it."

I tried desperately to shake off the sadness. It was an overcast day and windier than I would have liked. We stopped in front of the Rose Garden.

"Are you ready?" Shirin asked, taking my hand.

I nodded and resumed walking. The park and the garden had not changed since the day of our picnic. The roses were in full bloom. Strolling past the iron gates, every step reminded me of the path Omid and I had taken that first day. In my head, I heard Omid's voice telling me to close my eyes as he led me down the gravel road to the Rose Garden. The memory triggered a trickle of tears down my cheeks.

"It's alright. Lean on me if you like," Shirin offered in a comforting voice.

We found a bench near the lake and took a seat so I could steady myself. The ducks sensed our arrival and waddled toward us in search of food. I smiled, watching them. "You know, if Omid were here, he would have gone to buy them food. He cared so much about everyone and everything in life. He was such a gentle soul. He always said we should value every moment and not overthink things. It's as if he knew he wouldn't be here for very long."

"My cousin was a very wise man," Shirin replied. "I agree with him one hundred percent."

"I just wish I knew what it means to be happy. Everything feels meaningless. He was my compass. With him gone, I don't know which way to turn," I whimpered.

"After twenty years of being with him, you must have a good idea of what makes you happy. You know Omid would scold you if he saw you sitting here wallowing in self-pity. You were hit with a tsunami that turned your life upside down. It's time to rebuild again. You need to try and move forward. I know Omid would have wanted that."

I nodded. "I know. It's just so hard. I'm learning how to be strong again. I wish he were here and could talk some sense into me." Just then, as if the heavens were sending me a signal, large raindrops started falling on my eyelids.

The rain started falling more rapidly almost instantly, and we both got drenched. It felt cleansing and cathartic. As if the rain was washing away the past in the place where it had all begun. Everyone in the park rushed away with umbrellas in hand, trying to escape the rain. Neither of us budged. I soaked it all in, and soon, the sad tears transformed into happy ones. Shirin and I sat on the bench like two little kids laughing hysterically, staring at each other's soaked faces.

It wasn't until lightning struck that we decided to head back. Once at the hotel, I invited Shirin up to my room. We took turns taking hot showers and getting into dry clothes and bathrobes. We spent the rest of the evening sipping hot tea and devouring finger sandwiches I ordered from room service.

Our excursion and Shirin's presence lifted my spirits. The burden on my chest felt lighter. Her accompanying me to the park and being a part of the first and last chapter of Omid and my love story felt therapeutic. Maybe that was how it was meant to happen.

Shirin spent the night and comforted me as she had done when we were younger. I told her about Dara and all that had transpired between us. She listened intently and advised me to listen to my heart and leave the guilt behind. Later in the evening, we watched a movie until our eyelids were too heavy to keep open. We both dozed off with the television blaring, and the lights still on. It was a great ending to an eventful day.

Chapter 38

*D*ara picked me up around 4:00 p.m. Saturday. He looked very handsome, wearing a loose collared shirt and jeans. He greeted me with a soft smile and gently kissed me on the cheek. I got the impression he was trying to maintain his distance for fear of offending me.

"Are you ready for our afternoon treat at Café Durée?" he asked, pulling the car out of the hotel driveway.

"Yes. I haven't been there in so long," I said excitedly.

We chatted a bit about the weather in London and made some other small talk about how the city had changed while he drove. Neither one of us brought up the uncomfortable conversation from the first evening.

The hostess seated us in the outdoor open area as soon as we arrived.

"This is so lovely," I observed. "They've expanded and remodeled. I love how we can sit outside now." After placing our orders, we handed the menus to the waiter and sat silently for a moment.

I was caught up reliving the blind date with Omid in my head when Dara interrupted my daydreaming. "Are you alright? Is something the matter?"

"Oh, I'm sorry. This place just brings back a lot of memories. This is where I met my husband, Omid, for the first time. I was just thinking about how uncertain and interesting life can be."

"That's true," he said with empathy in his eyes. "From the way you describe Omid, I can see he meant a great deal to you."

I nodded. "Yes, he did. I mean, he still does. You know, I used to think we can control everything that happens in our life. But as I get older, I realize how wrong I was to think that."

"If being here upsets you, we can go somewhere else," he offered.

I shook my head and leaned forward in my seat to touch his hand. "No, this is perfect," I said, reassuring him and gazing into his eyes.

Just then, our three-tier tray of scones and sandwiches arrived. The aroma of the Jasmine and Darjeeling Tea seeped out of the porcelain teapots left on the table to brew. I removed my hand from his and welcomed the pause.

"Would you like me to pour the tea for you, Madame?" the waiter asked.

"Yes, please," I replied. It all felt a bit like a déjà vu moment from my dream a few nights ago with my sitting across from Dara and the waiter offering me wine instead of tea. The exception, of course, was that the waiter was not Omid and I was not panicking. After the waiter poured the teas and left us, Dara placed a cucumber triangle sandwich on both of our plates with the silver prongs and prodded me to continue speaking.

I took a sip of my tea and breathed in the aroma from the cup as if inhaling a fine mist of expensive perfume. After placing the teacup back on the table, I resumed the conversation. "Dara, I feel as if I owe you an apology. My behavior the other night must have surprised you. You have been nothing but kind and supportive ever since the day I met you. I want you to know how grateful I am to have you in my life."

"I feel as if you are going to insert a 'but' after saying that, and let me down gently," Dara replied, raising an eyebrow, his mouth twisting into a smirk.

"No, it's not that at all," I immediately replied. "I just need to clear things up a bit. I seem to teeter between emotions when I'm around you."

Dara nodded and remained silent, allowing me to speak my mind. "For the past two and a half years, my life has been a mess. You know a lot about the things I've been through. Floating on minimal life support and constantly living in fear of how to survive the monsoon, I never expected the storm to end. Now that the waters have calmed, I'm starting to swim ashore. My heart, body, mind, and soul are slowly starting to heal. Everything is starting to reboot, and I guess I'm just pacing myself."

I shifted in the chair and watched him, as he listened intently, his gaze completely focused on mine. "You represent a wonderful phase of my life," I went on. "I feel things for you that I never expected to feel. I enjoy being with you, talking to you, and sharing my thoughts freely. I'm learning how to welcome that without feeling panic or guilt. I want to honor Omid and what he meant to me all these years, but I also realize that I owe it to myself to allow new feelings in my heart, to make room for others who make me happy." I choked back the tears and looked down, trying to avoid eye contact.

Dara put down his cup and leaned forward, his brows pinched with an expression of concern. "Hey, come now. There's no need to pressure yourself like this. You don't owe me an explanation. Things are just fine between us."

I laughed and swiped at the tears. "You see? This is the reason it's so hard to stay away from you. You always say the right things and are so understanding."

He laughed, looking amused, then clasped his hand with mine and gently pressed it. "Listen, I *understand* your pain, Bahar. It was very difficult for me when my parents died unexpectedly. My world spiraled out of control for the first couple of years. I felt guilty and scolded myself whenever I was happy *or* sad. I didn't know how I was *supposed* to feel. But I promise you, it will slowly get better. Time will help heal your broken heart," he said reassuringly.

"I hope so."

"I *know* so. Trust me. I know losing your soulmate is different from losing your parents. The sadness lingers and eats away at you no matter who you've lost," he paused. "Don't be so hard on yourself. We both feel something for each other, and it'll take time to sort it all out. But there is no rush to have all the answers. Neither of us is going anywhere. Let's just enjoy each other's company and not overthink things. I think teatime is a great place to start. Don't you?"

I smiled and nodded. "Yes, I would love to drink tea with you anytime. That sounds wonderful."

We spent the remainder of the afternoon talking over sandwiches and lathering our scones with Devon cream and lemon curd. Dara shared a few stories from his childhood, and I told him a bit more about my family. The tense afternoon slowly transformed into a calm and pleasant one. I was sad to see it end as he dropped me back at the hotel.

When Dara leaned in to kiss me on the cheek, I met him halfway and embraced him tightly. He held me in return. We sat there for a short while, getting accustomed to the new normal.

He finally released me and sat back in his seat. "I hope you have a good flight tomorrow. The driver will come to pick you up at 6:00 a.m. to give you enough time to check-in and grab a cup of tea before your flight. I know Human Resources will be in touch with you soon. I hope it'll be the offer you are hoping for."

I opened my mouth to speak, but Dara continued. "We can talk more after you get back home. By the way, I bought my ticket and will be to San Diego in a couple of weeks. Maybe we can meet up when I'm there and find a place for afternoon tea," he said, removing a strand of hair next to my eyes and winking at me.

I smiled. "That sounds lovely. I'm looking forward to the call from Globios, and most importantly, I'm looking forward to hearing from you soon," I replied and winked back at him as I stepped out of the car.

Chapter 39

I texted Dara and Shirin separately the next day while I waited to board the plane. I thanked both for taking the time to hang out and told them how much I appreciated having them in my life. Before turning my phone on airplane mode, it started to ring.

"Hi, Bahar, how are you? It's Payam. Is this a good time to chat?"

I was caught off-guard by his call and quickly muttered, "Yes, hi. How are you? Is everything alright?"

"Yes, everything is fine. I just wanted to give you an update on the lawsuit and my discussions with Jake's lawyer. Are you back from London yet?"

"Um, no. I'm about to board the plane. But I still have a few minutes. Can we speak on the phone, or do we need to meet in person?"

"Yes, I can share what I have quickly. After bringing in a forensic accountant and offering them our findings, I think his lawyer realized that we have a very strong case. He was likely worried you would win the case in court, and they would end up paying what you are owed, plus all the legal fees. They just emailed me a settlement offer letter. They're offering to pay $300,000 to you upfront and another $300,000 to be paid in $5,000 monthly increments until the balance is paid in full. They argue that during the last two years of Omid's life, he was unable to see patients, and didn't generate any revenue for the practice. Also, they deducted the payments that were paid during those two years from the final offer. In short, you will not be getting the full $750,000. I think it's still a good offer, and you should consider accepting it."

"I see. The amount and the payment scheme are just different from what I expected. You don't think we could try to negotiate and get $700,000 from him as a lump sum?" I asked.

"We've been in negotiations for a few days now. I've done all I can to have him pay a larger sum upfront. The lawyer says Jake doesn't have the money to pay more and doesn't have the collateral to get a loan. We either accept his offer now or risk taking him to court. Keep in mind if he loses the case in court, he can file for bankruptcy. In that case, you may never see any money. With this offer, you are somewhat assured of a payout."

With a sigh, I sat back, giving myself a moment to run it all through my mind. "I was hoping to get the full amount and not let him negotiate for a lower one," I continued, thinking out loud. "But the $300,000 would be a good down payment for a new house. The monthly payouts will also help with mortgage payments. I'm also looking forward to not dealing with that low-life slime ever again. I think given those advantages, we should accept the offer, Payam."

"Alright, that sounds great! I know this whole process has been difficult, but I think this is a fair offer. I'll go ahead and draw up the paperwork and email it to you so you can sign and return the papers after you land. Does that sound good?"

"Yes, that sounds great. Thank you again, Payam. Thank you for fighting on our behalf and for representing us. You're genuinely an amazing human being. My family and I will always be indebted to you."

"My pleasure. I'm happy it all worked out. Have a safe flight, and I'll talk to you soon," he said and hung up.

I sat there, smiling to myself, a huge sense of relief filling me from the turn of events. The tempest was truly starting to subside, and the sun was finally beginning to shine again.

Golnaz and the kids picked me up from the airport. I had missed them immensely and had so much news to share. We headed straight to lunch after I picked up my luggage. I shared the good news about my interview and the settlement while eating our meal.

The kids and Golnaz were thrilled about the news and prospects of us moving back into a house. The possibility of a fresh start was exciting for all of us.

"When do you hear about the job?" Golnaz asked after we left the restaurant.

"They said it should be in the next few days. I hope it works out. I like the company and its culture. It's exactly what I had hoped for as a starting point in my career. I take that back," I quickly amended. "I never expected to even be *considered* for such a position with my lack of work experience, but they were interested in the work I had done when I was practicing law in Iran. I also felt a personal connection to the people with whom I interviewed."

"That's so wonderful to hear. I'm keeping my fingers crossed," Golnaz replied with a smile.

When we got home, my parents were there to greet me. I spent some time catching them up on the news as well. Grinning and appearing elated on my behalf, my mother said, "I am so happy for you! I pray for good news!" My father nodded in agreement.

"I hope so," I replied. "I should find out soon enough. I can't wait for the 2.0 version of my life to start."

"I think it already has, Sweetheart," my father said happily, and I couldn't help but smile, hearing him say that.

I retired to my room a few hours later and texted Dara to let him know I had arrived safely. I also shared the news about the settlement with the medical practice, leaving out the monetary details.

"That's fantastic news!" he texted in response. "I'm so glad it ended in your favor!"

"Thanks. Me too," I replied, my eyes burning from fatigue. Then with a deep exhale, I laid back on the bed and closed my eyes.

I fell asleep with the phone still in my hand, and the light still on. When I woke, the sun was glaring into my eyes from the windowpane. I glanced at the clock to see it was already 8:30 a.m. Trying to recall where I was, I slowly remembered the series of events from the prior night and realized I was now back in San Diego and in my bed.

The jet lag and the mental fatigue had claimed me. I stretched my arms over my head and lay there on the bed, staring at the ceiling with no urge to move.

After a while, I picked up my phone and opened my Facebook app to catch up on friends and scroll through the feeds. I decided to change my profile picture with a new one to represent the 2.0 version of myself. I couldn't remember the last time I had felt so relaxed. After about thirty minutes, I opened my inbox to check emails. I had over fifty-four emails waiting for me, a daunting reality, but I didn't let it get me down. I simply began working through them by deleting all the spam emails that were cluttering my inbox. After removing miscellaneous emails, I saw two that were of importance. One was the email from Payam forwarding me the settlement letter for Omid's practice, and the other was from HR at Globios.

Clicking on the email from Globios, I found an offer letter to hire me as the company's Global Counsel Deputy Advisor. The letter went on to provide details with a six-figure salary, 401K benefits, health and life insurance, as well as three weeks of vacation per year. I couldn't believe my eyes. I had to read the letter twice just to digest it all.

During my interview, I was told to expect a response within a week. I wasn't expecting them to decide so quickly. I also couldn't believe they were offering me the job!

I took a few minutes to catch my breath before calling Dara on the phone. He answered on the second ring.

"I take it you received the offer letter?" he said, as soon as he picked up the phone.

"Yes! Wait, you knew about this?"

He laughed. "Yes. They told me the news yesterday, but I didn't want to ruin the surprise for you until you read your email."

"Oh, my God. It all feels so surreal! It feels like I'm dreaming. How can I ever thank you?"

"Oh, I had nothing to do with it. You earned this position based on merits alone. I told you that Globios would be lucky to have you. I assume you'll accept the offer?" he asked in a teasing tone.

"Yes, of course! How could I not? You have no idea what this means to me. What it means to the boys. It's just so wonderful!"

"I am happy to hear it. You truly deserve all the happiness in the world."

"Thank you. I can't wait to share the news with my family!"

"Well, I better let you go, so you can do just that. There's a lot of paperwork that needs to be processed. Don't procrastinate in replying to the email. I also need you to do something else for me," he added after a slight pause.

"Of course. What can I do?"

"I want you to pencil in a time for us to go for afternoon tea when I fly back to San Diego. I need to congratulate you in person."

"Absolutely! Consider it done! I know a very nice place near Old Town. The owner is British and puts together the best afternoon tea ensemble."

"Sounds great! Enjoy your day and congrats again!"

Drunk with happiness, I hung up the phone and immediately jumped up on the bed, bouncing like a little girl and squealing. I snatched up the picture frame of Omid as I landed on the floor with both feet and kissed his face in the photo of us standing next to each other and smiling.

With tears of joy streaming down my face, I whispered, "I did it, baby! I'm finally a career woman again like you encouraged me to be so many years ago. It took a while, but your vision for me is finally realized. Thank you for believing in me and for the nudges. I know you're watching, and I hope I made you proud."

My life up to this point had always been centered on planning and certainty. I had explicit expectations of life based on what I had brought to it. A happy ending with the man I had chosen to marry and grow old with. Bringing two beautiful kids into this world. Watching them grow and figure out their path in life. We played by all the rules and abided by all the norms, finding a balance between our cultures and our lives in the US. In the end, God had other plans for us. For reasons I may never understand, we were not meant to fit into the mold I had envisioned for our lives.

Who knows where the path will lead to with Dara? As Omid told me on numerous occasions, love is from the heart, not from the brain. What challenges and experiences does life still have in store for me? Would my cancer ever come back? Will I be successful in my new job? Will the boys be okay? I now see that there is beauty in the uncertainty of life. Life revolves around experiences and how we choose to react, the people we choose to surround ourselves with, and the examples we set for others. I have come to realize, the more I try to control my future, the less I will feel in control.

Tightening my grip on the frame, I promised myself to let go and stop resisting. I am nothing but a small fish in the vast ocean of life, and if I just keep swimming, the waves breaking over me will never hold me down.

$\mathcal{D}$ear Reader,

I hope you enjoyed reading this book and will consider leaving me an honest review. You may interact with me on social media: https://linktr.ee/p2rezaibooks

With deepest gratitude,

Parastoo Rezai

About the Author

*P*arastoo **Rezai** lives in San Diego, California, with her devoted husband, two heart-warming children, and one rambunctious puppy who follows her around like a shadow wherever she may go. Parastoo received her bachelor's degree in Biochemistry from UCSD, a Doctor of Pharmacy degree from the University of Southern California, and a masters degree in Pharmacoeconomics from the University of Florida. For much of her career, Parastoo has worked as a Clinical Pharmacist, serving various disciplines within the profession. When not working, she devotes much of her time to pursue other passions such as reading, writing, traveling, and spending time with family and friends.

Her inspiration for this novel comes from deep empathy for individuals coping with hardships and how triumphing after each struggle is possible if hope continues to reside in our hearts.